THE GOLDEN BALANCE

The Golden Balance

by

ARTHUR D. HALL

CROWN PUBLISHERS, INC.
New York

For **Yvonne** *and* **Mac**

At eight, Senmut, the Egyptian, went from nakedness to manhood, putting on an apron like his father's. Chance and his intelligence drew him rapidly up the scale of leadership in Egypt's Eighteenth Dynasty.

The old Pharaoh was training his own child for the royal succession, the Princess Hat-shep-sut. When she took the throne, first as Royal Wife of the new Pharaoh, then as regent for his warlike son, and, finally, by a stratagem, as queen, she joined Senmut with her destiny. A love story blazed up to defy the tide of history itself.

Today little is left of those splendors. But here is a story built with marvelous accuracy from the true events of the Golden Age: The sudden flashing of palace and army feuds, the expedition to the land of Punt (Africa), the building miracle of the great Temple of Thebes—such episodes as these give a rare background to this great love story from the past.

Pronouncing Glossary of Characters

Aahmes Pen-Nekheb	AH-mes-pen-NEK-heb	General of the armies.
Amen-hotep	AH-men-HO-tep	Pharaoh, father of Thothmes I.
Amen-hotep	AH-men-HO-tep	Son of Senmut.
Antef	AHN-tef	Steward of Senmut.
Aset	AH-set	Concubine, mother of Thothmes III
Ateferu-Re	ah-TEF-ru-RAY	Father of Paheri.
Hapu-seneb	HAH-poo-SEN-eb	Chief Priest of Amon.
Harmose	HAR-mose	Blind harper.
Hat-nefer	haht-NEF-er	Mother of Senmut.
Hat-shep-sut	haht-SHEP-sut	Daughter of Thothmes I.
Imhetep	im-HET-ep	Father of Puy-em-Re.
Ineni	in-EN-ee	Senmut's master, Steward of Amon.
Khufu	KOOF-you	Early Pharaoh.
Ma-herpa	mah-HER-pa	Steward of Hat-shep-sut.
Ma-ka-Re	MAH-KAH-RAY	Hat-shep-sut's throne name.
Men-kheper-Re	MEN-keper-RAY	Thothmes III throne name.
Menti	MEN-tee	Became General of the army.
Mentu-hotep	MEN-too-HO-tep	Early Pharaoh.
Meryt	MER-it	Younger daughter of Hat-shep-sut.
Min-Hor	min-HOR	Senmut's wife.
Nebiri	neb-ER-ee	Foreman under Senmut.
Neb-taui	neb-TAO-ee	Priest.
Nefer-peret	NEF-er-PER-et	Royal Treasurer.
Neferu-Re	NEF-er-oo-RAY	Elder daughter of Hat-shep-sut.
Nehessi	ne-HES-ee	Captain of the King's Ships.
Paheri	pa-HERE-ee	Prince; friend of Senmut.
Parihu	PAH-ree-hoo	Chief of Punt.
Penati	pen-AH-tee	Architect.
Pharaoh	FAY-ro	Title of Egyptian kings.
Puy-em-Re	PWEE-em-RAY	Pupil of Senmut's.
Ramose	RAH-mose	Senmut's father.
Senmut	SEN-moot	Steward of Amon.
Sen-usert	SEN-usert	XIIth dynasty Pharaoh.
Sit-Re	sit-RAY	Nurse to Hat-shep-sut.
Tet	TET	Overseer of Temple Shops.
Thothmes I	THOTH-mes	Father of Thothmes II and Hat-shep-sut.
Thothmes II	THOTH-mes	Father of Thothmes III.
Thothmes III	THOTH-mes	Son of Thothmes II and Aset.
Thuti	THOO-tee	Royal Treasurer.
Tura	TOO-rah	Viceroy of Kush.

Foreword

Action in *The Golden Balance* starts in 1590 B.C. and ends in 1465 B.C.—two hundred and thirty years (according to some historians) before Moses was to lead the Children of Israel out of Egypt.

In those early years of what we now call the XVIIIth Dynasty, Egypt was approaching its golden age when, under the leadership of six successive Pharaohs, it would dominate the known world. And this particular period (one of vision and growth, of experiment, of hesitation and boldness) has been the focus of the author's enthusiastic study for thirty years—mainly, he admits, to indulge an incurable Yankee inquisitiveness as to the affairs of neighbors three thousand years and six thousand miles removed. He is no bearded savant (being practically hairless and able to squeeze his brains into a size 6⅞ fedora), so it will be safe, he thinks, to call this his interpretation of an era.

The following notes may be of help to those not overfamiliar with the ancient Egyptian scene:

The Egyptians, throughout their dynastic history, referred to their country as "The Two Lands, Upper and Lower Egypt": *Lower Egypt* the northern portion from the Mediterranean to a little south of Memphis, *Upper Egypt* from south of Memphis to the First Cataract.

For the ancient Egyptians, the Mediterranean was *The Great Green,* and the islands (Crete, Cyprus, etc.) *The Isles in the Great Green.*

Naharin and *Two River Land* were their names for the great Euphrates basin, and the Euphrates River was *The-River-that-Flows-Backward.*

Khatti was their name for the Hittites; *Nubia* and *Kush,* the region adjoining Egypt south of the Cataracts; the *Rutenu,* the people of northern Syria; *Libyans,* a pastoral people living west of Egypt on the Mediterranean coast; and *Tehenu,* the name given their country.

vii

The ancient Egypt heaven was variously called *Underworld, Fields of Aahlu,* and *Islands of the Blessed.*

Where feasible, the author has used the ancient Egyptian names (rather than Greek or Arabic) for cities mentioned: *Abdu* for Abydos, *Hatnub* for Tell el-Amarna, *Menefe* for Memphis, *Nekheb* for El Kab, *Yebu* for Assuan, etc.

Finally, it is manifestly impossible for him to acknowledge adequately his debt to the writings of scores of authorities on Egyptology which it has been his rewarding pleasure to consult through the years. Special mention, however, should be made of outstanding work in the field by the Metropolitan Museum of Art, and appreciation expressed for their permission to use unpublished material.

ARTHUR D. HALL

Monterey, California
June 11, 1955

CHAPTER I

Year 16 of the Reign of Thothmes I

He was eight years old. When he remembered his apron, he walked stiffly beside his mother, avoiding her hand and striding to match the long step of his father, fitting his feet into the splayed prints that marched before him in the dust of the high road. It was a sobering promotion from nakedness to the dignity of clothing, and since he was old enough to wear an apron like his father's and to go with his parents to market, he had passed childishness and was a man.

To others in Egypt it was like any other day. Re crossed the heavens in his flaming sun-boat, and the morning wind blew coolly from the north. Pharaoh, in his palace, interrupted the Royal Treasurer to explain to the child, his beloved daughter Princess Hat-shep-sut, an obscurity in the tax laws. Priests, ending the early temple service, ate from the choicest of the offerings and gossiped in the leisurely manner of men whose work is light and assured. Carpenters pounded, slaves sweated, women gathered at the watering-places and screamed at errant children, and scribes in all corners of the kingdom mended their reed pens and headed clean strips of papyrus: "Year 16, third month of the Inundation season, day 4." For these it was just another day.

But for Senmut it was a day big with promise and wonder, and while he remembered the new apron, he must scowl as his father scowled, and clear his throat roughly and spit, and take long steps, and ignore his mother.

This lasted through a dozen breaths, and then the questions that filled his throat would not be denied, and he darted ahead to where his father plodded in blind mentation, knotting his fingers, mumbling.

"Will we see the mayor's house, Father?" asked Senmut. "Will

1

we see the mayor, and the scribe who writes the mayor's thoughts?"

Ramose neither heard nor saw; he had his private worries. He was a simple man, a man of the soil—but today he must speak before the mayor. "It is this way, Your Excellency. . . . This is how it is, Excellency. . . ." Hands, and not a tongue, were a farmer's tools; and if he knew which seeds to save for planting, what crops to rotate, if he knew to a drop the moisture required to bring a vegetable to marketing perfection, was that not enough? Perhaps there were men in Egypt who liked to talk in the presence of officials, but Ramose was not among them. He rubbed his skull in desperation and wet his lips: "This is the way it is, Your Excellency. . . ."

Senmut danced back to his mother who, with the gentleness especially reserved for him, answered his flood of questions as she could. Tu-shennet was not a city, she said, just a clustering of houses on the Nile's edge and a marketplace where farmers of the neighborhood met to barter. She had never seen the Great City where the king lived, nor had Ramose; it was six days', eight days' walking to the south, and the mayor said it was filled with palaces and gardens and temples, with men who drove the broad avenues in chariots, and women who rode in golden chairs carried on the shoulders of slaves. The mayor had seen the Great City of Thebes, but . . . well, the mayor was a great man and honest, Senmut would understand, but his tales were memorable for color rather than accuracy. For example, he told how on a feast day the streets of Thebes were swarmed as far as the eye could reach, and this must be absurd exaggeration, for how, even if Thebes were as big as six farms, could such a throng live and get their bread there?

Hat-nefer shifted the basket, with its load of onions and roll of coarse linen and its pairs of new straw sandals, to her other arm and took Senmut's hand. Later in the farming year beans would be added to her burden, and lettuce and corn, to be traded for honey and fish and oil and cheap incense; she was a large woman (in weight worth three husbands like Ramose) and proud of the strength that allowed her to labor in the fields beside her man, to cook and mend and nurse and carry for him.

Yes, she continued, today Senmut would stand beside the Nile, mighty and slow-moving, though today there would be no ships

2

passing, for today was the 4th Athir and a man who sailed the river this day would return to find his house in ruins. This was an old legend and no one remembered its beginning, but he would see: on the 4th Athir no ship sailed the Nile.

When, in the distance across the level checkerboard farms and ditches and canals, they saw the houses of Tu-shennet huddled in the shade of sycamores, and the Nile shining like a silver thread in the sun, Senmut pointed and tugged at his mother's hand to hurry; but once near the village, he did his sight-seeing from the protection of her bulk. Muddy alleys, filth and squalor, rubbish and smells and dogs and pestilent flies—this was his first village. He had not known such conditions. Their house was of mud and of two rooms for the family living and eating and sleeping, but it was swept daily and it was clean, and in the space before it the jars and pots and bits of rope and hoes and spades and plows, all the articles that make up the wealth of the poor, were placed neatly.

And so many people—more in one place than he had seen in all his life. Ramose, immersed in his thinking, ignored them, but the mother called a bit of gossip here and there. To one acquaintance, a young woman carrying an infant astride her hip, she presented Senmut. "*My* baby," she said with pride, brushing the hair from his eyes, "though he thinks he is a man, now, with a new apron. Yes, our neighbor has complained again and my man is speaking to the mayor today."

"You haven't heard?" said the woman. "There are rich men, two lords, with the mayor, and he is out of his mind with importance."

"Rich men—lords—in Tu-shennet?"

The woman's expression showed that she was thinking: You poor creature, to live on a farm where nothing happens. She shifted the child and pointed. "There, through the trees," she said, "there is their ship."

Hat-nefer sucked in her breath. "Husband, Senmut—look!"

A magnificent galley swung in the restless current of the Nile, loosely anchored, by poles thrust into the mud, a few yards from shore. Now, ships at a distance were no novelty for Senmut. Daily from the farm he watched their passage, sail bellied when headed south, bare-masted and the rowers toiling when going north—the junky rafts of fishermen, lumbering freighters, sleek

3

barques of officials and princes. In imagination he had sailed them all—always as captain—but even his dreams had not pictured splendor such as this.

It was long and slim and ablaze with color, gold and red and blue. Behind the tall mast was a house with curtains for walls, and a shining chariot was atop the house, and tied to the mast was a strange animal—"a horse," the woman called it. There was a cage in the fore part and one at the rear; in one, his mother said, stood the lookout who watched for hidden shallows and signaled directions to the steersman whose place was in the rear cage. Men were lounging now about the deck, rowers and sailors —twelve, said his mother, adding them nimbly on her fingers.

"The ship came in the dark of the night," the woman said, eager to retell her tale to new ears, "last night, and I heard their calling and my man ran to the mayor's house. The old lord is a great prince—from his cursing—and he is furious that they cannot sail the river today, but this is the fourth Athir, of course."

"Why did they stop here, then," asked Hat-nefer, "if there is such haste?"

The woman explained with a patient smile: "A boat, a fine ship like this, cannot travel the Nile in darkness. In the night the lookout cannot see the channels, you understand, or the mud bars, so it must tie to the bank."

This was interesting but tiresome, and Senmut tugged impatiently at his mother's shift. "Where are they now, the two lords?"

The woman answered him. "There's little business will be done in Tu-shennet this day. They are at the marketplace, and everyone stands gaping and staring and forgetting trade. The old lord has a collar of gold and shining gems that—come, see for yourselves. And hear him swear; the thin lord speaks softly, but the voice of the old one is the Nile in flood."

The marketplace, beyond the houses and the muddy pond where cattle drank, was circled by farmers and their women and children, all gazing in quiet and respectful awe. Ramose shouldered a way to the front.

"There," said the woman. "And see the mayor, how he struts and puffs."

One of the lords was thin and one was old, to Senmut seeming like ordinary men except for dress. The thin one wore a long

4

white gown that reached his ankles, and laughter-wrinkles played about his eyes, and he sat his stool and talked quietly with the mayor who bobbed and fussed and sweated in an agony of bliss.

The other lord was squat and fierce and there were scars on his head, more scars than hairs. His dress was a pleated kilt of linen with shining threads worked into a border, and there was gold on his hands and arms, and a broad collar of jewels set in gold covered his massive chest.

The woman nudged Senmut's mother. "The thin one is a priest and is called My Lord Ineni. My man told me. And the other is the Lord Aahmes; he must be one of Pharaoh's warriors, from his scars and his leg."

Senmut saw then the giant scar that pinched one leg to half the thickness of the other, and he saw how the great man, frowning and muttering his discontent, rubbed the shriveled leg absently, nursing and favoring it.

The mayor, with bows and apologies to his guests, explained so all could hear that this was the day of his court, the day set aside each month for hearing of complaints and settlements of disputes; it was a bore and a bother, but the poor of the district depended on him—he spread his hands helplessly. His august friends would understand? The Lord Ineni smiled and the Lord Aahmes growled, so the mayor slapped his hands and his scribe came running, to squat meekly beside the great man his master and write the wisdom that issued from his mouth.

Senmut, with so much that was new and amazing to watch, danced with excitement. Could the mayor hear all these complaints in a single day? . . . And were the people come to lay their troubles before the mayor, or to see the lords? . . . Did the gold and jewels signify that the one lord was greater than the other? . . . How did the old lord get his scars and his shriveled leg? . . . Could just anyone talk with the lords, as did the mayor? Could his father Ramose? . . . How could the marks made by the scribe in writing be like the sounds spoken by the mayor? A thousand tormenting questions, and no one with the interest or knowledge to answer them.

For a while his attention focused on the scribe, noting how that worthy, conscious of his importance in the scheme, folded his legs just so and smoothed his apron to make of it a writing

5

desk. On this he spread his strip of papyrus, set gourd of water and palette beside him, selected a pen and scrubbed its moistened tip on a bit of charcoal, and was ready. He attended alertly to a farmer's stammered plea and to the mayor's smooth-tongued answer, and then drew with care on his papyrus; and if the mayor asked, the scribe read to him what was written there. This to Senmut seemed greater magic than that tall green stalks of corn sprang from small seeds hidden in the earth, or that the sun, dying each day in the west, yet was born again each morning in the east.

Also, Senmut watched the two lords, how the one sighed and fretted and nursed his withered leg, and voiced a stream of grumbling protests against his boredom, while the other, the thin priest, listened with genuine interest to interchange between peasant and official. He had nice eyes, this one, and his glance was like the rays of the new sun touching, warming the body. He might be a lord, but he was no one to fear.

When it came the turn of Ramose to speak, he caught Senmut's hand in desperation and drew his son with him before the three stools. There he hitched his apron and scowled and dug with a toe in the dust, but the words so carefully rehearsed were gone from his head. He said, "Your Excellency—Excellencies," and his tongue stuck in his teeth. Then he signed to Hat-nefer and she smoothed the shift over her ample hips and spoke for her husband.

"It is this way, Excellencies . . ." she began.

"A moment," said the mayor fussily. "The woman does not live who can voice a man's thoughts exactly. Am I right, My Lord Ineni, My Lord Aahmes?"

These nodded gravely and the mayor bowed thanks for their agreement and dismissed Hat-nefer with a graceful flourish. "It is this way," said Ramose finally. "I am Ramose the farmer. Hat-nefer is my wife, and this is our son. Senmut is eight and he is not strong; thin he is like a reed, as you see. And we have other sons and these work on the farm, so he—Senmut, that is—Senmut being not strong, he watches the goat."

The eyes of the two lords and the mayor were watching Senmut rather than Ramose; in apparent embarrassment over this attention, the boy squatted and, between sly sidelong glances, began to smooth the dust at his father's feet.

"That is all he must do," Ramose continued, "watch the goat that it does not stray. Now, Excellencies, what does he do? He forgets the goat. He plays with stones that he digs from the waste land, and the goat feeds on our neighbor's vegetables.

"Now, how can I pay our neighbor for his loss? When the crops are in and the taxes paid, there is barely enough to keep us till the next harvest. This is my trouble, Excellencies—how can I repay my neighbor?"

The silence that followed Ramose's voice, while he furtively wiped sweat from his head, was broken by a rumbling curse.

"Bones and blood of the Holy Osiris!" exclaimed the Lord Aahmes, pointing to where Senmut squatted in the dust. "Ineni—do you see?"

The Lord Ineni nodded.

"But—look, Ineni, one who can neither read nor write. The son of a farmer. Writing the name of the god!"

His smothered roaring carried to all ears and there were nudgings and whisperings among the villagers.

"Is it magic?" Aahmes insisted.

"No magic," said Ineni, and beckoned to Senmut.

The boy, unabashed, stood close beside him, returning smile for friendly smile.

" 'Senmut,' " said Ineni, "it means 'brother of truth'; it is a good name. Tell me, Senmut," he continued gently, "there were marks on the stones that you dug from the earth?"

The boy nodded. "I could lay the whole of my finger in some of the cuttings. I copied them, over and over in the dust."

Ineni smiled and drew the child within the circle of his arm. "Tell me something more, Senmut; if you had one wish, what would that wish be?"

"To read," said Senmut promptly, "and to write. Unless that is two wishes."

Some of the villagers tittered and Ramose grumbled to his wife, "Reading! Of what good is reading to a farmer? Another goat, now . . ."

The old soldier touched Lord Ineni on the shoulder. "Like Pharaoh's daughter, perhaps? You yourself have said that Amon favors her. Now this farmer's boy—the same alert, inquiring mind. You see? Amon working in him, also?"

"Perhaps," said Ineni, and turned to Ramose. "It is a sign,"

7

said Ineni. "I am a priest and know something of the ways of the gods. Senmut is no farmer and fails in the simplest task; yet, with Holy Amon's help, he teaches himself to write. Now, there is a school in Amon's temple at Thebes, the College of Priests, where boys learn to become scribes. Senmut belongs there; he will learn reading and writing and sums. . . ."

"But the cost!" Ramose was stunned by the picture that was offered. "When the taxes are paid . . ."

"Senmut will bring honor to Tu-shennet, so the village should share in his training. Come to His Excellency the Mayor on the first day of each new season and choose from the town's store of grain and oil and linen, and he will send it to me in Thebes. This will pay the cost of the boy's learning."

Senmut saw the stricken look in his mother's face. She was thinking, My Senmut—my baby. He heard the exciting buzzing of the villagers: one of Tu-shennet's boys to be a priest! He heard Aahmes' angry growl: "Better bowman than priest material in those shoulders. . . . Well, I'll give him strong legs; I'll give him the best legs in the priesthood."

Then his father spoke. Briefly, for Ramose was no talker. "Well," said Ramose, "if there is no cost, now . . ." and nodded his consent.

CHAPTER II

Year 22 in the Reign of Thothmes I

It was the kind of show the less privileged members of Egyptian society loved.

Pharaoh, returning from a tour of the northern provinces, had granted audience to friends and well-wishers, and the boulevards leading to the Royal Palace were thronged with the merchants and laborers of Thebes, to watch the pageant of arriving chariots and splendid carrying-chairs.

The noisy crowd cheered its favorites and applauded with good-humored roars the chanting of the runners who sought passage for their masters.

"Way for Lord Tura, Viceroy of Kush, Prince of the South!" shouted servants of the House of Nekheb.

"Way for Lord Nefer-peret, Overseer of the House of Gold and the House of Silver!"

"Way for the Lady Tui!"

"Way for Lord Aahmes Pen-Nekheb, General of the King's Armies!"

From his position near the end of the procession, young Hapu-seneb heard the shouts, and drew his round and boyish features into what he hoped was an effect of dignity. Several things, he feared, conspired against realization of this goal. For example, at thirteen and a half years, he was bigger than his father, and—he mentioned this aloud—the father's chariot was ridiculously small for two riders; he must maintain a precarious balance on the small space left him behind his father. Then, too, his apron, while of fair quality, was not of royal linen, and his stick had a glazed instead of a golden knob. Now Thuti— his friend Thuti had a chariot of his own, a splendid affair of gilt and painted leather.

His father was unmoved by the son's eloquence. He was not a prince, he replied, as was Thuti's father; neither could he dip his hand at will into the Royal Treasury as could Thuti's uncle.

Hapu-seneb countered, reasonably, that the chariot did not have to be gilt; an ordinary affair—serviceable, like the one they were in—would suffice. And he was old enough to be trusted, surely; Thuti, now, was only a year older. . . .

"No," said the father.

"Why not?" said the son. And continued, "Look, you are Governor of the Fish Province. At home, the people of the district honor and respect you. But what will they think when it is told that we rode to Pharaoh's palace crowded like farmers going to market? It is a matter of dignity, of pride."

His cause was not helped by the fact that his voice was changing; the mellow and deep-toned utterance, so carefully practiced, ended without warning in a squeaking falsetto.

Hapu, Governor of the Fish Province, smiled comfortably. "When you grow up," he said, "we will talk further on the subject."

The ride ended in silence.

Hapu-seneb's pique disappeared as soon as he lost his father in the luxurious rooms of the palace. It was his first visit, and the impulse was to gape; he restricted expression, however, to an owlish solemnity, and eased, with murmured apology, between groups of noble ladies and their escorts—and became hopelessly lost in the maze of chambers.

Then he spied his friend Thuti, who, impeccably dressed and mannered, was whispering into the ear of the ravishing young wife of an official of the court. The lady fled, and Thuti, sighing, took Hapu-seneb's arm and led him to the populated areas.

Hapu-seneb found Thuti worthy of every admiration. Men of discrimination listened to the young prince's words; ladies smiled at him. He possessed an ease of manner, a smile that charmed, an air that bespoke experience and knowledge beyond his years—accomplishments which welcomed him to every circle. Hapu-seneb watched him and copied his expressions, his infrequent gestures, modulations of speech.

Everyone worth knowing was in the palace this day. Hapu-seneb saw the priest Neb-taui, one of their instructors in the College of Priests, and steered his companion from the neighborhood. They bowed to Lord Ineni, Steward of Amon and King's Architect, and Hapu-seneb said, "Senmut must be back."

"Has he been away?" said Thuti carelessly.

"He sailed north with Lord Ineni. Remember? Something to do with repairs to Ptah's temple in Menefe."

"Ah?" said Thuti, and stopped a group of passing slaves who bore trays of small cakes and jars of wine.

"Try one of these pastries; you will find them delicious. And here—a cup of this wine, a foreign vintage and quite unlike our domestic varieties."

Hapu-seneb nibbled and sipped, and ventured praise of the refinements of his friend's taste. When Thuti nodded gracious acceptance of the compliment, the boy dared an original opinion; squinting at the painting of a flock of ducks soaring across the high ceiling, he murmured, "Excellent, isn't it? I have seen flights of birds like that over my father's estates in the north."

"Good enough," said Thuti, "if you like ducks. I prefer— here, in the next room, is some really fine drawing. Come."

He led the way to another antechamber, the walls of which were decorated with spirited pictures of the dance, portrayals of maidens performing the difficult and spectacular cartwheel.

The boy was dubious. He wanted to please Thuti, to win his smile of approval. But, after all, one could see ritualistic dances any day in the temple, while birds in the marshes associated in the mind with gentle north winds and happiness and holidays. Or perhaps Thuti was interested not in the subject, but in excellence of presentation. Hapu-seneb studied the drawings.

Thuti indicated the line of a well developed thigh. "A sure brush. See—with a single stroke. One of Ineni's best artists, of course; a man who knows his craft, and"—Thuti smiled—"his model."

"You know everything, Thuti," Hapu-seneb sighed.

"A matter of observation." Thuti laughed lightly. "Watch the details, my boy, the little things, and you can't avoid success. Tell a woman the exact coloring of her eyes; identify the scent she adopts."

"Aren't you afraid of corrupting a simple nature, Prince?" said a voice behind them.

Thuti's quick frown dissolved into a smile when he saw Paheri—Paheri with his easy manner and his new priest's dress,

11

Paheri who one day, when grandfather and father were dead, would be Prince of Esneh and the South.

"What a thought, Excellency!" said Thuti. "You would not thrust our young friend into this naughty world with only the biased preparations our schools offer? All sums and holy precepts?"

A fourth boy, following Paheri, joined in the laughter. He was dark and thin and muscular, and wore the distinctive cut of apron peculiar to students at the College of Priests.

"You are a qualified instructor, Thuti," he said, "if gossip can be trusted."

Thuti bowed and accepted a cup from a near-by slave girl and toasted the newcomer: "To your large ears, Senmut." He turned to Paheri. "The priest's dress becomes you, my friend. Egypt has gained a servant whose name will bring her honor."

Before Paheri could reply, Senmut interrupted. "Wait until you hear his very first appointment! May I tell, Paheri?"

"If you think its importance rates boasting."

"Of course it is important," said Senmut eagerly. "Before the initiating ceremonies were ended, even. He walked into the temple a novitiate priest—as each of us will when we finish the studies—and he walked out with the title 'Draughtsman of Amon'!"

" 'Draughtsman of Amon'!" Hapu-seneb was awed.

"Congratulations," said Thuti.

"I know artists who have aspired all their lives to that honor," said Senmut, "and it is Paheri's, at sixteen, and without asking."

Thuti waved toward the painted figures on the wall. "Perhaps Pharaoh will decorate other rooms of his palace, and you, Paheri, will be commissioned to make the drawings from which the artists copy. May I come and watch—if the girls are like these?"

"You are appointed now to select and pose the models, My Lord." In a serious tone Paheri added: "The gods favored me, but—thanks. Senmut, however, is the one with a real story to tell. Have you heard what..."

At this moment the sound of a single trumpet echoed through the chambers.

"Pharaoh!" Senmut cried.

The four youths hurried to the audience hall where, as students, their place was toward the rear. This was to their advantage, for they could see without being conspicuous, could whisper among themselves, and could exercise some control over Hapu-seneb's excited twitchings.

The hall was vast, its ceiling supported by a double row of columns—not unlike the great hall in Amon's temple, Hapu-seneb thought. The lamps, set at intervals in the walls, seemed outshone by the flashing brilliance of gems and gold worn by the throng that awaited Pharaoh's entrance—representatives from every province from the Cataracts to the Great Green. Princes, priests, officials of government, and their women. The ladies made an elaborate display with their enormous wigs, their necklaces, armlets, bracelets, rings, nodding to friends, gesturing. There was a restless movement and the hum of conversation throughout the hall.

Then a door opened and a hush fell over the assemblage; every back bent as Pharaoh, Lord of Upper and Lower Egypt, Aa-kheper-ka-Re Thothmes, entered with officers and suite.

A stranger to Egypt, seeing this little man alone, would have ignored him. Short in stature, with an oversized nose and corded shanks, he might have passed anywhere for a master-baker. It would require a perceptive glance to note the refinement of features, the strength and firmness of character, the kindliness of the eyes.

Ahead of Pharaoh marched picked men from his armies; surrounding him were the Royal Fan-bearer, Royal Butler, Royal Herald, and servants and officials of the household. Then came the Hereditary Princess, the King's Daughter, Hat-shep-sut, with her attendants. A stifled buzz of comment echoed Hapu-seneb's whisper: "Where is young Thothmes? Where is Pharaoh's son?"

"Sulking again, perhaps," someone answered.

And Senmut said softly, "Who cares about the boy when his sister is in the room? Have you ever seen such dignity, such grace?"

"Thuti thinks she is skinny, and her lips too thin," said Hapu-seneb.

"She's the loveliest woman in this room!" Senmut protested.

"Woman! She is fourteen—just your age."

"She is still more beautiful than anyone—than anything."

13

"Sh-h-h!" said Thuti. "Must you quarrel like peasants?"

Senmut drew aside, and Hapu-seneb whispered to Thuti, "You don't like him, do you?"

"Senmut?" Thuti shrugged. "I neither like nor dislike commoners. I ignore them."

"You know his family, then?"

"Do you? Does anyone? I judge by actions. Quiet now, youngster, and watch the ceremony."

Pharaoh was on his throne, his daughter seated beside him. On the king's right were grouped his closest friends and officials; on Hat-shep-sut's left, her ladies. As the elite of Egyptian society advanced, in order of rank and court preference, the name was called aloud by the Royal Herald; obeisance was made while Pharaoh spoke a few words and named each to the princess. A simple ceremony, indeed, but one which could have lifelong influence on a man's career and fortune.

The line seemed endless, but the ordeal was made easy by moments of interest. The young prince of a northern province, for example, who, in his nervousness, tripped over his staff and knocked a dowager's wig askew. And the pompous official who saw the chance to get his personal petition directly into Pharaoh's ear and had to be led from the dais. When one of Hat-shep-sut's attendants, the Lady Sit-Re, leaned forward in sight of all and adjusted a displaced curl on the princess' wig, Thuti swore under his breath. "Another commoner," he snapped.

Pharaoh interrupted the ceremony here, beckoned to Lord Ineni, and conversed with him. When Ineni nodded, Pharaoh spoke a command to the Royal Herald, who bowed, and with staff held straight before him, marched down the aisle. A shiver of anticipation ran through the audience and heads turned to watch his progress.

Hapu-seneb picked at Thuti's arm. "What does that mean?"

"A public honor, apparently, for someone not included in the original listing."

"Who?"

"You, perhaps. Pull in your stomach and try to look intelligent."

The Herald stopped before the young men and touched Senmut's shoulder with his staff. The boy's face went white; he stared in unbelief at his friends, and stumblingly obeyed the royal command. Hapu-seneb danced with excitement. He thought from Thuti's expression that the latter was ill.

"What?" Hapu-seneb demanded. "Why is Senmut summoned? What has he done? Is it for punishment, perhaps?"

"I think I know," said Paheri.

"What? What?"

"Senmut saved the king's charioteer from an accident while hunting in Menefe."

"Senmut? Hunting with Pharaoh? I don't believe it," Thuti said flatly.

The Herald's announcement was heard by all. "The student-scribe Senmut, son of Hat-nefer," and Senmut made a low obeisance.

Pharaoh spoke to the boy softly, words for his ear alone, then nodded to his daughter. Princess Hat-shep-sut's greeting, Hapu-seneb thought, was even more gracious than her father's. She smiled, too; he was sure that he saw her smile. Then at the king's sign, the Royal Butler brought forward a gleaming bow and laid it in Senmut's hand, and a murmur of delighted surprise arose from the audience.

"You were right, Paheri." Hapu-seneb laughed. "I envy him!"

Thuti's eyes blazed. "Quiet, you fat fool!"

Yet when Senmut returned to his friends, Thuti's voice was warm in congratulation.

Hapu-seneb demanded, "What happened, Senmut? What did His Majesty say? What did Princess Hat-shep-sut say?"

Senmut shook his head slowly, and in his eyes . . .

Paheri said later, "It was as if he saw the stars in heaven for the first time; as if he had heard the sweet voice of Holy Hathor."

Hapu-seneb had been thinking. This was an effort and required certain preparations and adjustments. He sat alone in a corner so distractions of a foreign nature could not intrude. He twisted his forehead into furious knots, shut his eyes, and waited. The theories which he wished to examine were elusive, but he was patient; one by one they would peer from their hiding and venture into the open.

These theories concerned Senmut. Was he, or was he not, of noble parentage? Thuti said "No" and brought strong evidence

15

to support his guess. Paheri smiled noncommittally; he listed Lord Ineni's and Lord Aahmes' support as proof that the boy was of no ordinary stature. He cited Pharaoh's gift and Princess Hat-shep-sut's unusual (for her) interest; and he hinted at the possibility that there might be, at some future date, an alliance by marriage with the House of Nekheb. Senmut himself said nothing.

To date, Paheri's "evidence" overbalanced Thuti's. Hapu-seneb pondered the possibility of supplying, through his own ingeniousness, a few facts rather than so much conjecture. The germ of a neat idea lay just beyond his grasp.

When his father wrote that the family barque would be at his son's disposal to bring him home for the holidays, Hapu-seneb's idea quickly matured.

First, the boy learned that Senmut, too, planned to spend the vacation at his own home in the north. Next, that Lord Ineni had arranged for his free transportation on a stone barge going to Menefe. And lastly, that Senmut's holiday would be delayed a week awaiting the barge's departure.

There were inferences to be drawn from these findings, and Hapu-seneb decided that they all supported Thuti's contention; also, that Senmut's family was of so little account that it did not own a boat, and that Senmut found no humiliation in the prospect of journeying on a stone barge. Of course, there was the chance that his family's barque was in use elsewhere; this had happened to Hapu-seneb once and he still reminded his father of the outrage.

He put his idea into motion by bewailing to Senmut the monotony of solitary travel. "Two days," he wept, "with nothing to do, no one to talk with. Don't you find it depressing?"

"It has never bothered me," said Senmut dryly.

"Your family is coming for you?"

"No, Ineni has arranged passage for me on a stone barge. The captain is good company; he tells me the river gossip, and I relate the newest court scandals. And there will be plenty of beer on board."

Hapu-seneb scratched his head to indicate that he was stimulating memory. "Tu-shennet—that is the name of your town? How far north is Tu-shennet?"

"Three days by stone barge; a short day with good rowers."

16

"Well, then. Come with me, Senmut. As my guest. You have seen my father's boat; it is comfortable."

"You are too kind," said Senmut, and his glance seemed to the guilty Hapu-seneb a little sharp.

"No. I am being selfish. I want company. And we can start tomorrow, if you wish. As a favor."

"Well..." said Senmut.

They pulled away from the Theban quay at daybreak, Hapu-seneb being fussily hospitable and apologizing because his father had sent "this old raft" with only six oars, and shouting at the men to row harder, as his guest was in a hurry.

Senmut brought two small bundles aboard, and he handed one to his host. "Figs and a small melon. We can enjoy them later."

Hapu-seneb could hardly hide his indignation; did the fellow think that he could not feed a guest? He set the parcel aside without comment and pointed to the other bundle.

"Gifts for the household? I sent mine ahead; a writing palette for my father, of polished wood and with his name inscribed in gold; and for my mother a dozen fragile stone cups. Little things, of no great account, but people living in the country enjoy small refinements. Now—are you comfortable? Are you thirsty? Wine, or beer? I have both in the jars yonder. This is better than the stone barge. Wait—you forgot your new bow—unless it is in this bundle..."

"I did not bring it," said Senmut hastily. "My father would not be interested."

Not interested—in Pharaoh's gift? Hapu-seneb filed the remark for further study, but made no comment. He pointed astern. "See, we are making good time; Thebes is disappearing around the bend of the river. Now this is comfortable, isn't it? Ah-h-h..." He stretched full length on the mat beneath the straw shelter set on poles, and they lay silent for a while, relaxing, enjoying the motion of the boat and the freedom from scholastic discipline.

"How did you happen to go with Pharaoh on the hunt, Senmut?" Hapu-seneb asked presently. "I never heard the whole story."

"Pharaoh asked Lord Aahmes and Lord Ineni, and Ineni requested permission to bring me." He smiled. "Ineni is a friend as well as master. We had been working hard at the temple, supervising the reconstruction. He supervised, that is. All I did was scribe's work, keeping record of the blocks of stone delivered at the quay, checking their numbers against the master-plan—you know the work."

"Pharaoh was not hunting, you said."

"No, he rode out with us and then watched from a pavilion with his officers about him. We were out of his sight most of the time, though, in draws, or behind outcroppings. I think His Majesty feels his age. Like Lord Aahmes, people and crowds worry and old wounds bother him. He said once that he needs the desert—its quiet and its long views and the wind in his face. The hunt was merely an excuse."

"Tell about the lion again. Please, Senmut. It's exciting."

"Well, Ineni got an antelope, and Lord Aahmes an ibex and a wild bull—a huge one. And I wounded a hyena, but lost it in some brush. While I was driving back and forth trying to start it, I heard a shout—and there was Lord Aahmes running beside his horses with the broken chariot dragging behind. It had hit a hole and thrown him, but he still held the lines. You know how he can swear; they could have heard him back in Menefe.

"Pharaoh saw the trouble and sent another chariot to replace the broken one, and then it happened. The driver was rounding a tumble of rocks when the lion leaped. He looked as big as this ship. I yelled and loosed; he was a long bowshot away, but the god Amon must have guided my arrow to catch him in the flank, and slow him enough so Aahmes' arrow could finish him as he fell, right across the chariot."

"That was good shooting."

"It was a lucky shot; I had no time to aim. I told them that, but Pharaoh insisted it was my arrow that slowed him."

Hapu-seneb looked at him with envy. "This won't hurt you, you know. Thuti says that if Pharaoh didn't know you before, he does now. What did he say at the audience?"

"Nothing in particular." To Hapu-seneb's surprise, his companion's face reddened. "That is . . ." Senmut made a vague gesture. "I don't remember. I heard him, I guess, but . . ."

"Do you remember what Princess Hat-shep-sut said?" Hapu-seneb asked slyly.

The flush deepened on Senmut's cheek and neck. "Yes," he answered. "I shall never forget that."

He turned to watch the distant shore. "She's lovely, of course," he said, "but it's more than that; it's a . . . well, a quiet beauty, a beauty of spirit as well as of face. It was trying to say something—the spirit, I mean. To me. A message of some kind . . . But why to me?"

Hapu-seneb felt for the bundle of good-luck charms that hung from his girdle. He was not sure that he liked this business of spirits giving obscure messages. If the gods were supposed to be hidden, let them remain hidden. He was prepared to offer them every respect, and to make propitiatory offerings; all he expected in return was that they give thought to his needs and desires. Relationship between gods and men could be as simple as that, and there was no need for such complications as direct interference, in either direction.

This was a new side to Senmut that Hapu-seneb neither recognized nor liked. In the class rooms, Senmut had the ready answer, the neat copy; he was alert and aggressive in games, a leader in any mischief in the school. He carried himself with a certain airy confidence; none of the precise elegance of Thuti, of course—but then, Hapu-seneb thought, who could outshine Prince Thuti?

It was time for a change of subject. "I am thirsty," he said. "Some wine, perhaps?" It was thin, cheap stuff, and Hapu-seneb made a mental note to tell his father that someone important in Pharaoh's court had been insulted by such peculiar hospitality. He smacked his lips, however, and poured a second cup and stood with Senmut beside the lookout in the bow of the ship.

"Koptos," he said. "We're making good time, aren't we? Has Tu-shennet a good quay?"

"There is no quay. It is a village; a few huts, a marketplace, the mayor's house—that is Tu-shennet."

"Your father's estates are behind it? Bordering the cultivated land? That is wise planning; many princes build near the river for convenience, thus using acres that could produce corn or flax."

"My father is not a prince," said Senmut, "nor . . ."

"Oh, well"—Hapu-seneb nodded agreeably—"neither is mine. Governor of the Fish Province, you know. The old man

19

takes care of himself, though; I know titled estates that would like his income. Well, are you hungry? I have cold goose and some fine cakes...."

The rest of the trip passed quickly; Re, in his sun-boat, had lost none of the strength of manhood when Senmut pointed. "Under those sycamores; that is Tu-shennet."

"Not impressive, is it?" said Hapu-seneb, and gave a signal to the captain to steer for the shore. "Let me carry your bundle."

"It's not necessary for you to get wet."

"What? Leave a guest in the middle of the river? Is this as close as you can go, Captain? It's not deep, Senmut—see, to your knees only."

On the bank Hapu-seneb shifted the bundle to the side away from Senmut. "Which way? I'll walk a little with you."

"Come, Hapu-seneb, you've done enough. Accept my thanks for a pleasant journey, and ..."

"Nonsense. I want to get the cramp out of my legs from all this sitting. Which way, Senmut?"

He saw from his companion's frown and the steady glance that his little trick was in danger of exposure, so he stamped his foot and rubbed his knee and grimaced horribly. "You lead, Senmut; it will be all right—it does this sometimes."

For a while he remembered to limp, following the tracks made by Senmut in the dust of the narrow embankment between fields. But Senmut set a stiff pace, and the wind had died, and the sun lay hot on the land, and he sweated and puffed and swore breathlessly, and switched the bundle to the other arm. He thought that he felt sandals in the package. Senmut strode ahead without speaking or looking back, so Hapu-seneb felt again, under the covering. Straw—cheap straw sandals—and a length of coarse linen! These ... gifts for the household?

Was Senmut playing one of his senseless jokes? Hapu-seneb stopped and searched the horizon; there was nothing in sight, nothing but endless fields, and, above the cultivated land, a few dismal mud hovels that pigs would be ashamed to call "home."

Senmut disappeared behind one of them. Hapu-seneb hurried so he would not be left behind, and almost collided with a fat woman in an ill-fitting shift who, her hands on Senmut's shoulders, was beaming up into his face. Senmut took her hands in his.

20

"Hapu-seneb," he said, "this is my mother. This is 'Lady' Hat-nefer. And here"—he indicated a stooped gnome whose face was stained with sweat and the dirt of the fields—"here is 'Lord' Ramose, my father."

Presently Hapu-seneb remembered to close his mouth. He tried to speak; instead, meeting Senmut's burning eyes, he thrust the bundle into the other's hand and fled. And he did not stop his running until he was safe aboard his father's ship.

CHAPTER III

Year 24 in the Reign of Thothmes I

The king, a shriveled little man with a fighter's chin and weary eyes, sat in the midst of pomp and glitter and moodily damned the cheating gods.

In his youth—a hundred years ago, it seemed—he had made a pact with Amon. "Give me a son," he had prayed, "and I will make you king of all the gods of Egypt, and the glory of your house and city shall be as the sun's glory, passing belief. Give me a son worthy of the title 'Pharaoh,' and I will leave him the world for a kingdom." Then he had made great sacrifice of oxen and fruits and wine and costly incense, had instructed his ministers and gathered his generals, and kept his vow.

Today, Amon was acknowledged King of the Gods of Egypt, with priests and slaves and estates and farms and cities, with wealth that rivaled the king's. The Temple of Amon was the mightiest house in Egypt, towering, sprawling, with secret chambers and vast halls, with statues and obelisks and massive gateways, and shops and libraries and dormitories. And Thebes —"Heaven on earth," it was called, and "heart of the empire." Heart and head, rather, to which was drawn the wealth of all nations and from which radiated laws for the conduct of all men. Pharaoh had kept his share of the agreement, a fact which the treasure piled before him now in the temple courtyard confirmed. Tribute from the rulers of the known world—weapons, chariots, skins, blocks of lapis lazuli, jars of scent, jewels, bolts of fine cloth. Ivory from the deserts south of the Cataracts, heavy rings of gold from the forests and plains of Two River Land. Men everywhere shuddered when his name was spoken and divided their hoardings with Pharaoh.

For love of Amon he had done all this—and because it was

good business to deal squarely with the gods. He had been lucky, yes, but mainly in his choice of ministers and advisors—Aahmes for fighting, Nefer-peret for finance, Ineni for building, to name three. And he had paid them (if loyalty can be bought), and their names were big in the land.

All right, he had fulfilled his part of the bargain; how had Amon kept his? Amon had given him a son and a daughter by the Great Royal Wife, and another son by a concubine. The first son was a likely lad, the second a weakling; the first had beauty and bearing and promise, the second not even good sense. Perhaps Amon thought that, in giving two sons where one was requested, his obligation was ended; but the early death of the first, even before he could be declared heir to the throne, neutralized the situation, and now Pharaoh was ending his years and passing his life's work to—a girl and a moron!

He glanced at the youth beside him on the great double throne, and groaned. The gods really had made a mess of the poor boy. Pimples are expected in adolescence, perhaps; but he doubted if any other youth of fifteen in the whole of Egypt was so heavily afflicted. And clumsy, and dull-eyed—and the length of his memory was already a scandal; the kher-heb must prompt his every response in the temple services. This was a sad start for governing an empire—Pharaoh knew so well. For he, too, had been mothered by a concubine; he, too, reigned only because married to a queen of solar blood, and had lived his life under correction and surveillance and criticism. It had taken determination and resourcefulness to bring Egypt to mastery of the world—and how could the child beside him, unaided, hold it there?

Pharaoh shrugged the unpleasant subject aside and turned his attention to the ceremony. It was one of the few festivals of the year that still gave him solid satisfaction, this of "Receiving the Tribute"; the quality and value of gifts sent him by foreign kings told, better than spies, of continued recognition of his authority. He felt no animosity, no rancor against the groveling envoys, men whose fathers and grandfathers he had slaughtered or enslaved. It had been a pitting of wills and skills, and while they and their masters remembered that the loser pays, he was disposed toward a benevolent overlordship.

Representatives of most of the courts of the civilized world crawled here in the dust before him, and he amused himself by an exercise of memory, identifying the country of each by some racial characteristic, some detail of adornment; heavy-bearded Babylonians, blue-eyed Libyans, black Kushites, Semites in parti-colored robes—this chap with the curled pigtail who pressed his nose to the pavement and strained gutturals through his beard was from far Khatti-land. He'd be sweating in that padded robe, for the mountain-men could not take this Egyptian heat. Stubborn fighters, though, these men of Khatti-land.

The elaborate ritual of the service, developed by his priests to impress barbarians with the Pharaoh's wealth and majestic divinity, was a full-dress affair requiring the participation of priests and princes, even of Amon himself. The god rode in his splendid barque carried on the shoulders of thirty priests, hearing the thunderous praise of the temple singers, watching the gyrations of the temple dancers, sniffing the reek of costly incense, while his son, the Pharaoh, received for him the tribute.

Set in the courtyard of the temple before the throne was the balance used in weighing the tribute. A giant, shining affair, the machine was copied from ancient pictures of that golden balance by which the gods weighed the souls of men in the afterlife, weighed the words and acts of a lifetime against the testimony of the Goddess of Truth.

Officials and slaves swarmed about it now, bringing the tribute, stacking it in piles, counting, weighing, carrying it away.

"Mountain gold from the land of the Naharin, 16 uten;
White gold from the Isles, 46 uten;
Lapis lazuli, two blocks at 30 uten;
Ivory from the land of the Tehennu, 240 tusks..."

The young priest who called the computed weights to scribes of the temple and the Royal Treasury performed his duties with the ease and assurance of veteran service, and with a subtle exaggeration that hinted consciousness of a royal audience. Well, Pharaoh admitted, there were traits of human nature more reprehensible than ambition; when enthusiasm and health were added—the lad had amazing shoulders and legs for a priest —a valuable instrument of the state was in the making.

24

Pharaoh knew him; this was Senmut, Ineni's protégé, the farmer's son, over whom Ineni and Aahmes warred continually. The boy had promise, whom both Royal Architect and General of the Armies fought to sponsor. Aahmes' interest stemmed from the fact that, he said, there was leader-material in the boy, clear-thinking, remarkable ease with weapons, all of which would be wasted in a priest. Ineni claimed that the youth would not long be a simple priest, that he had natural administrative ability, that, besides, when he graduated from the College of Priests he had chosen him, Ineni, as master. And Pharaoh, daring Aahmes' wrath, agreed with Ineni.

Pharaoh commanded the Royal Fan-bearer, and in a moment the Lord Ineni, Steward of Amon, Overseer of the Overseers of the Works of the King, bowed before him.

Pharaoh smiled at his friend. "Neb-taui brought me a writing this morning."

"Yes, Majesty."

"You have seen it?"

"I gave it to Neb-taui."

"So." These were the things he treasured in his Chief of Works—simplicity and directness. "It is descriptive of the Princess Hat-shep-sut?"

"It was so intended, Majesty."

"And was written by ..."

"Yes, Majesty—by Senmut, son of Hat-nefer."

"Hum-m-m." And son of a farmer, eh? Perhaps Ineni was correct in his assumption that the gods favored both poor and rich; Ineni was a priest and it was his business to know. And it seemed as if Amon might have guided this Senmut from the first. Ineni had brought him from the country, a child and unschooled, and in eight years the boy had graduated among the leaders in his class. That proved Amon's favor. And there were other signs; Pharaoh remembered the shooting of the lion. And now Senmut was an able draughtsman, he could turn a neat phrase, he had got him a rich wife and influential sponsors. And ...

Pharaoh nodded. He said to Ineni, "Come to the palace after the evening service, and tell the same to Aahmes and Nefer-peret and the High Priest."

There need be no more dallying; the creaking of his ancient

25

joints warned that there could not be too much time left in which to so buttress the throne that the wobblings of a witless heir would pass unheeded. The answer was in strong ministers. Strong ministers who would be loyal—not to a weak king, but to the king's wife. A woman might not, by law, sit on Egypt's throne, but with wise counsel she could govern. And he had prepared, cunningly, for years, since the ineptitudes of his son had become obvious, to fit Hat-shep-sut into his picture of the future.

From her childhood he had found traits to admire, among them sincerity, subdued gaiety, self-discipline. He remembered an incident when she was nine, the year of his last great campaign in the lands east of Egypt, the year old Aahmes had taken the son of the king of Mitanni captive. That year Thothmes had set his stone on the eastern boundary of Two River Land, thus stretching the frontiers of Egypt, the priests said, farther than any king before him. He told this to the child—Egypt now master of the world, he said; and this he had done for her sake, to make her Queen of the World.

She had listened gravely. She was a serious child—not solemn, he hastily assured himself, mature, rather—accepting the grown-up world about her and trying to adjust her inexperience to its puzzling inconsistencies. She watched him with thoughtful eyes, her tiny jeweled sandals neatly aligned, slim hands folded, composed.

"You will like that?" he urged. "The people of all nations calling you 'Queen'?"

"Will this mean that Your Majesty can spend more time here in Thebes?"

"Perhaps," he said, surprised. "There will be need of limited police action only in the conquered countries."

She had smiled, then, a flicker of lips and eyelids, and slipped a white hand into his gnarled fist. "I will like that," she said shyly.

A strange and unpredictable and very dear child, he had decided; Egypt's hope, and the world's.

As daughter of the Royal Wife, Hat-shep-sut was of direct solar descent, and, to double the divinity, he had caused a fiction to be published: that Amon himself had presided at her conception. He had begun her schooling early, had ordered that she be

26

trained in government and finance, in law and politics and history. And when she was grown, he had married her to her half-brother.

That had seemed little less than brutal—the uniting of beauty and intelligence with grossness—but the laws of succession demanded marriage of sister to brother when possible. The only sign when he told her his decision had been a further tightening of her thin lips. "For Egypt," he said, and she nodded.

He sighed now, remembering. Where did a king's duty end, and a father's begin? Amon would favor the union; the heir to the throne would be a boy, for Pharaoh was lavish with promises to the god, of heifers and smoking altars and gold. He worried a little—she had not the figure for child-bearing. What had the priest Senmut written? "To look upon her is more beautiful than anything; her splendor and her form are divine; she is a maiden, beautiful and blooming." It described her—dignity, delicate refinement. This Senmut had an eye and a courtier's tongue, and daring. Favored of Amon? Perhaps. Ineni was seldom mistaken.

Pharaoh chose for the evening meeting the semi-privacy of an alcove off the audience-chamber, where intimate conversation could be enjoyed publicly. It was in that vast hall with its brightly painted columns that he and his captains had planned, and celebrated, the campaigns that had made the world his footstool. Then, the palace had been a soldiers' camp and his companions, men who were afraid neither to die nor to live; as he listened now to the decorous murmurs of courtiers milling about the apartment, he wondered whether his values of things important had changed or if the softness of the times really bred citizens of lighter bulk. He was old, he decided, and the change he thought in others was in himself; he was not the man he had been, when a day's hard hunting could be followed by a night's feasting and riot. Now it tired him to superintend a simple temple ceremony. He would be glad to rest—almost glad, he thought with a shrug, of the quiet and eternity of the tomb.

He had dwelt much, lately, on death; without hysteria, as was his nature—acknowledging the enemy, consulting the experts, formulating his plans. The priests agreed that peace of the soul after death was dependent upon several factors, chief being the

27

preservation of its earthly house, the body in which it had lived. The rites of mummification, subject of study and experiment since earliest times, insured successful coping with this problem, provided—here was the real difficulty—the place of burial could be kept secret. Rifled tombs were constantly coming to light, even the tombs of his fathers, with the royal limbs torn apart, fragments scattered in frenzied search for the rare metals accompanying the burial. He froze with horror at this evidence of brutal selfishness in man—for a few bits of gold, to cheat a fellow-being of the gift of eternity.

He had said to Ineni, "Dig my tomb in a hidden place and swear that the burial shall be secret." And Ineni had sworn and that satisfied Pharaoh; there was no need to pry or to fret of means, for his Overseer of Works was given to the keeping of pledges. And the tomb was nearly finished, in a remote canyon of the hills across the Nile from Thebes, and prisoners of the wars of Pharaoh did the digging, guarded by the soldiers who had won the wars.

He signed his Fan-bearer to bring the four waiting ministers to the alcove: Ineni, his Overseer of Works; Aahmes, the General of the Armies; Nefer-peret, the Royal Treasurer; and the First Prophet of Amon. Four friends they were, rather than subjects or servants, gifted each in his way, old like himself, soon like him to start the dread journey to the Underworld. It would not be easy to replace them, but this was one more task before he rested; younger men were needed, young men familiar with the problems of his daughter's world, young men with old heads. It would not be easy.

As they approached, a fifth joined them, Penati, one of Ineni's architects who had been newly placed in charge of work at the tomb. He was a wisp of a man, prematurely dried and shrunken by years spent in the deserts searching for fine stone; fussy, competent, without ambition but to provoke Ineni's smile of approval. Did Penati's presence here in the palace, his nervous whispering in Ineni's ear, mean trouble at the tomb? An uprising of the slave-workers? The secret of the tomb's location betrayed?

"Well?" said Pharaoh uneasily, disregarding the prescribed genuflections and formal greeting by which royalty is honored.

Ineni answered, "Majesty, an annoying delay, nothing more.

Penati reports bad rock in the first tomb chamber that will necessitate a change of plan."

"Another site, you mean? The digging abandoned?"

"No, Majesty, the bad rock is spotty and we can easily pass around it. It will not affect the efficiency of the tomb."

"Are you sure?" Pharaoh tapped his chin nervously. This tomb was to be his spirit's living place on earth for eternity, and spirits might be sensitive to irregularities. If the prescribed arrangement of tomb chambers was in a straight line, chamber succeeding chamber, who knew what evils might result from variations? "What do you think?" he said to the First Prophet.

This put the priest at a disadvantage. He wanted to please his master, but no sane man courted an argument with Ineni. The First Prophet puffed his fat cheeks, solemnly studied his toes, cleared his throat and drew upon his richest belly tones.

"It is a matter for close consideration, Your Majesty," he fumbled. "As my esteemed colleague, the Lord Ineni, says, and with experience to support his statement, the presence of rock of unsound quality precludes adherence to the original plan. On the other hand, it is a plan carrying the sanction of long use, and it may be that the ancients, upon whose authority the plan is based, knew of certain idiosyncrasies to which the soul is subject, and that any irregularity in the arrangement of the chambers would cause discomfort to the soul."

"Your advice, then?" said Pharaoh.

"With the Lord Ineni's approval, refer the problem to Neb-taui for further study."

This made sense, and Pharaoh nodded. Neb-taui was one of the most learned men of the kingdom, Keeper of the Temple Library, versed alike in the wisdom of the ancients and the mysteries. Ineni could not object to his advice.

"So be it," said Pharaoh, avoiding Ineni's eye and ending the discussion.

He drew a hand across tired eyes and settled his old bones comfortably. "Late at night," he said, "and on special feast days, an old man is permitted the luxury of sentiment. Surely no king ever knew friends more devoted and no country such unselfish sons; what Egypt will be without you four, I cannot guess. The ancients tell us that some few are privileged, in the after-life, to sail with Re across the heavens in his shining sun-boat, to work the ropes and oars. I like to think that we will be so privileged, and can look down on familiar scenes and faces—watch over the Egypt that we love. And I like to think, too, that we will find it prosperous and healthy and wisely governed—and it is for us, now, to insure this."

He had spoken his plans years before, he reminded them— each to select one from among the youths of Egypt to watch and guide and train to fill his place. As he, Pharaoh, had guided and trained his daughter Hat-shep-sut. Now the preliminaries were finished, and if each was satisfied with his selection, the youths could be told and the polishing started, the grooming for the specific duties and offices involved.

"Aahmes, my friend," he continued, "you are satisfied with your Menti?"

The General of the King's Armies rubbed his knotted skull and then loosed a rumbling plaint.

"Would Your Majesty judge the worth of a new bow without drawing it? How can I guess Menti's whole value without the test of combat? Give me a campaign, Majesty, one campaign."

Pharaoh shrugged. "Fighting at our age? Come, be satisfied; you've had sixty years of it. Menti pleases you except for this— unknown quantity?"

"Good enough, Majesty. The men like him, I've drilled him myself in weapons, and he can drive and shoot with anyone. You've seen him hunting."

"Well, Menti then, for protection of the borders. Now for financial matters. Nefer-peret, do you consider the youth Thuti ready?"

This Thuti—in spite of family, breeding, background, acknowledged ability, there was something, indefinable, that Pharaoh did not wholly trust. Silly, perhaps; the boy had a splendid record. Pharaoh listened to Nefer-peret's enumeration of his virtues—salting them with the knowledge that Nefer-peret was the lad's uncle and prejudiced—and nodded.

"Hapu-seneb, now; he shows great promise, I understand."

The First Prophet bowed with impressive gravity. Pharaoh sometimes wondered, from his manner, if this representative of the chief god did not occasionally confuse his identity with that of the exalted name he served, take as personal tribute the praise and adulation aimed at Amon. His strut and his booming

30

bass awed the humble and amused his equals, but while affairs in the god's house ran smoothly, Pharaoh asked no more.

". . . and excellent presence," the First Prophet was saying, "which, Your Majesty agrees, coupled with resonance of voice, adds the requisite dignity. His acquaintance with the mysteries is profound for one so young, and his earnestness . . . Why, his father (you know him, Majesty—Hapu, Governor of the Fish Province), his father assures me . . ."

Yes, yes, thought Pharaoh, the lad never swears, touches neither beer nor wine, has never known a woman—bah; he will die young and be lost to our need.

"Yes," he said aloud, "yes, yes. Now, Ineni, your upstart, if he is to control the wealth of Amon, must combine many virtues in his body. Name them for us."

Ineni appeared to ponder, Ineni the sly one, drawing his wrinkles into knots, fingering his chin, frowning, shaking his head. "They escape me, Majesty. Senmut is ambitious; he quarrels with his wife; his father was a farmer; he is given to unbridled enthusiasms; he is willful. I set him the task of copying tax lists and find the papyrus scrawled with plans of shrines and offering tables. On an errand to the Temple Library, he detours by way of the Shops and shows Tet—Tet, Your Majesty, Overseer of the Workmen—a new hinge he has thought up, or the ingredients for a new glaze. His nose is in everyone's business, he asks questions faster than tongues can answer. . . ."

With one hand Pharaoh stemmed the flood, with the other smoothed the satisfaction from his lips. These four—Egypt would be safe in the hands of men chosen by friends of hers and his, friends like these.

"Begin the final schooling tomorrow," he said.

CHAPTER IV

Year 4 of the Reign of Thothmes II

Hat-nefer, breathless with her hurrying and from the weight of her basket, paused inside the gateway, searching the little garden for movement.

"Is he here?" she called. "Husband, has he come yet?"

A stooped figure came slowly from behind the trellis.

"Who?" said Ramose.

"Who? Senmut, of course. Have you forgotten the messenger from the temple?"

Ramose poked at the basket. "What have you there?"

"A fine bulti. See." She exposed the fish for her husband's admiration. "For supper; he likes it boiled in a cloth."

"Extravagance," said Ramose. "We have cabbages."

"But it will be his first meal at home in months."

"So we beggar ourselves. And beans—don't tell me that you bought beans."

He was not himself since they had left Tu-shennet for Thebes to live with Senmut and his wife. Hat-nefer, stirring the coals in the alcove-kitchen and setting the pots to boil, admitted that perhaps their leaving the farm had been a mistake. No man is whole whose heart is wanting, and his was buried in the soil; he was like the frightening spirits of which Senmut told—though dead, they could not rest. For the thousandth time she wondered which was the better: to kill oneself with overwork, or to die of fretting over something lost. Ramose was not dying, but his mind was sick for the things which a lifetime had made familiar to him, and nothing pleased him here. The crowding in the city stifled him, street noises kept him awake, the sun's course had changed, the north wind no longer blew from the north. The house, even, with two stories and a garden, this fine house loaned for their living by the Lord Ineni and better than the mayor's house in Tu-shennet—Ramose longed for the two-roomed shack in which he and his sons had been born.

When Senmut's brothers died, one from the goring of a neighbor's bull and one from a sickness that swelled his belly, it had seemed right to leave the farm; even with her help Ramose could not handle half the work. And Senmut needed her; she had known from the start that his marriage was ill-starred, for the daughters of wealth do not bed comfortably with the sons of farmers. Min-Hor was a pretty little thing, but she wept night and day and she refused stubbornly to give Senmut a child because, of all senseless notions, it might ruin her figure. "The queen has two girl-children," Hat-nefer argued, "and she still is slim and pretty. And if your mother had felt as you feel . . ." And Min-Hor would cry, "I wish she had," and stamp and weep again. Hat-nefer clucked her tongue; she was a child, and spoiled, and time would give her the sense to know that a man's patience is a brittle thing.

In the room reserved for living, Hat-nefer righted a stool, picked threads from the coarse rug, straightened the hanging, dusted the household god and replaced him in his niche. Sometimes she wished that Senmut had not told her that there were many gods, some good and some evil. This was but a lump of clay, but it was older than Ramose and the shining pebbles that were its eyes gleamed wickedly at times as if plotting mischief for them. Which was it, evil—or good? She remembered that all their lives there had been misery and want, and she thought of the death of the two sons, too young for dying. But now there was this fine house, and Senmut was coming home, safe from a dangerous journey.

The curtain that hid the stairs to the sleeping chambers parted and Min-Hor entered; and Hat-nefer thought, Perhaps her great-uncle is General of the King's Armies and another uncle is Prince of Nekheb, but with her hair disordered and her dress wrinkled she looks like the servant in a house. She was small and pale, and Hat-nefer sometimes could not wonder that Senmut once had fallen under the spell of such wistful innocence; until, that is, she remembered to look for the hardness of the mouth, the petulant curve of the lips. Here, the mother

33

knew, lay no softness; rather, the ruthlessness of a completely self-centered woman.

To Hat-nefer's mild reproach, "Senmut will be home any time now," the girl shrugged.

"What is that awful smell?" she demanded.

"It is fish; he likes it, boiled in a cloth."

Min-Hor made a gesture of repugnance. "Peasant's food."

It was as cruel as a slap, and as deliberate, and through the pounding of blood in her ears, Hat-nefer heard her voice exclaim shrilly, "That is fine talk for a girl to her elders, and your mother would be proud to hear it." And for some time after Min-Hor disappeared through the curtain, Hat-nefer stood biting her lip. She and Ramose were peasants and they pretended to nothing more; but Senmut—he was an honored graduate of the College of Priests and on the way to becoming an important man, and would it be ignored and only this remembered, that his parents had been farmers? Which was important, she wondered dully, the class into which a man was helplessly born or the intelligence he used to lift himself above his birth?

Suddenly she felt old, ancient as the ageless god in his niche, and the stairs were a weariness as she climbed, and she sank heavily to a stool in the small chamber shared with Ramose and beside Min-Hor's chamber. She often wondered why Senmut had married the girl; at such times a distressing inner voice reminded her of the obvious advantages to one of their class of an alliance with the noble house in Nekheb, and of Senmut's custom of seizing advantages and squeezing profit from them. The marriage had been the Lord Aahmes' idea. He and the Lord Ineni were flattering in their praise of Senmut and saw honors in his future, and skills that a mother's eye missed. And it was all right, of course; Senmut was an honorable man and loved Min-Hor in his way. He worked too hard, men had many things on their minds that their women never guessed. . . .

She sighed and hurried clumsily through her toilet. Her hair was thinning alarmingly; she had used warm castor oil with no effect, and now was trying a remedy proposed by a neighbor, the tooth of an ass ground to powder and mixed with honey and smeared on the head. And what could she do about her weight? The ease of city living had not helped; it seemed that

34

every new dress, however carefully measured in the making, was too tight at the hips, and it was embarrassing in a city of slim women.

As a final touch, she tinted her nails and the palms of her hands and soles of her feet with a reddish paste made from the crushed leaves of the henna plant, a city refinement that offended Ramose but which Senmut applauded. And she wondered, as she descended the stairs, what thing could be named that she would not do if it brought pleasure to her remaining son.

Then she heard his whistle, and from the gateway saw him striding through the dust and refuse of the street, tall in his white linen, half hidden behind a dozen parcels and bundles and followed by a boy sweating under the burden of a huge jar. His arm on her shoulder, his voice, his funny twisted smile—the world was right again.

"Here," he called to the boy, "set the jar here. A gift to the household," he cried, catching her hand; "beer, and a goose, and oil—a bonus above my salary for good work done. Here, Father, onions, peas, cucumbers, dates—did you grow grain like this on the farm? Oh, yes, and these flowers for Min Hor, lotus from the marshes of Per-haa. . . ."

It was a noisy, exuberant meeting. The boy ran laughing with his payment of a handful of dates, the father sifted the kernels of grain critically and wagged his head over their fatness, and Hat-nefer, close to tears with joy and pride at this fine son burned so black by desert heat, hurried between garden and kitchen, babbling like a girl. Senmut followed his mother, sniffing.

"Do I smell fish?"

"A bulti, boiled as you like it."

"A feast, a real celebration! See, Father, I should go away oftener."

Ramose, always out of tune with humor, grumbled, "An expense."

Hat-nefer wished uneasily that her husband would not quibble and fret; it annoyed Senmut. The latter's earnings now were princely if measured against the limits of their former living, but the old man clung to economies made foolish by changed conditions; his mind had been too long squeezed by

35

poverty to change the pattern of its thinking. She pushed him from the kitchen. "This is an occasion, your son home again. Put on one of the fine aprons Senmut gave you."

When Min-Hor came, the mother breathed a thankful prayer to the household god. The girl, in a new yellow gown, was dressed and painted to honor her husband, and received his gift of flowers with no hint of the afternoon's temper. So Hat-nefer heaped the god's portion and placed it before him in his niche, and when Ramose returned, she set the wick of the lamp aflame and called brightly, "Come, the meal will be cold."

In Tu-shennet they had squatted on the floor and each dipped his food from the common pot; but in the city, in this house with its refinements, they sat on mats about a low table and the mother served the portions on thin slabs of bread. She ate nothing, content with the privilege of watching and listening; loving her son's thin darkness, marveling at his sureness of phrase and gesture, indulging the mother-instinct to worship. Working with his great and noble friends had not spoiled him; when he patted her hand and drank a toast to her in the sweet beer and praised the bulti, and swore in his joking way that if she had cooked for the expedition there would have been no straggling in the marches—her heart ached with the weight of its pride.

"You know," he said, raising his cup to Min-Hor, "your husband may yet be famous, if the boasting of the Lord Ineni will help."

"You found a place for the tomb, then?" the mother exclaimed.

He nodded. "The queen's tomb will be hidden and inaccessible; and Ineni gives me the credit."

The throbbing of her pulse quickened. The Lord Ineni—since the old king's death, he was the queen's most trusted minister; Senmut said so. Anything was possible for the good friend Ineni—the queen listened to his voice, and if he said a thing, that thing she believed. If he said, "The priest Senmut found the excellent site for your tomb," Senmut's name would be placed in her mind beside a pleasant thought and good might come of it.

"Can you tell us?" she said.

"Not yet." Senmut squeezed her hand. "Except that no journey that a dead spirit makes in search of the Underworld can be rougher or more dangerous. Jackals—not one or two, but bands of them. But we came through safely, and Ineni says that I found the site. That is the thing to remember, Mother. He must report to Queen Hat-shep-sut, and has requested audience for me as well. Think of that—your son in private audience at the palace! The queen will be pleased; it's as if the gods made it especially for Her Majesty—a perfect site, and Ineni's story of the search will lose nothing in its telling."

He leaned back from the table and beamed at all of them. "It was incredible luck—Ineni's taking me, I mean, the chance that might not come twice in a man's life. It can mean—well, anything and everything."

Hat-nefer hardly heard, her mind was so troubled by his brief picture of the dangers in a man's world. And he talked as if this was normal work for a scribe. She shivered, and opened her mouth to remonstrate, to urge against rashness, when Min-Hor spoke.

She had been wordless, listless, with the irritating half smile which a sophisticate adopts toward the prattle of children; it was almost as if her husband or his adventures held no interest for her. There had been a critical puckering of the brows, too, when Senmut, in his enthusiasm, talked with a mouth too full or gestured too widely.

She said now, "What honors of importance does the Lord Ineni expect from Pharaoh from this expedition?"

"None from Pharaoh," said Senmut, "and perhaps none from the queen." He smiled at her, sipping at his cup. "You've never understood, have you, the necessity of grubbing for favors, of passing no smallest opportunity that might bring your name to the thought of one of importance?"

She shrugged. "Of course not. My family . . ."

"Exactly. The men of your family have known preference for generations. Position, wealth, honors have been theirs automatically, without the asking or earning."

"How can you say that?" Min-Hor said hotly. "Paheri is Draughtsman of Amon, and that is a title earned."

Senmut shook his head. "Oh, come. The gods made your cousin lazy. He draws because he enjoys it and because he can sit while working."

"Well, when his father dies, Paheri will be Prince of Nekheb and will govern the Southern Provinces; he does not have to work, and you are jealous of him."

"No," said Senmut, grinning, "I am not jealous of Paheri; I'll get my share of honors and wealth, and not by standing on my father's grave."

That was unkind, Hat-nefer thought. Whenever they are together, bicker, bicker; they agree on nothing, there is no meeting ground, of mind or of spirit.

Min-Hor sat with downcast eyes, nibbling at her lip in anger, while Senmut refilled his cup.

"I don't mean this," he said to soothe her. "Paheri is my friend, and Egypt owes more to Aahmes Pen-Nekheb, your great-uncle, than it can pay. You've heard, of course, of his latest honor?"

His wife glanced suspiciously and shook her head.

"The queen has named him tutor to the Royal Daughters."

"To the Princess Neferu-Re and the Princess Meryt?" Hat-nefer clapped her hands. "He must be happy."

Senmut shook his head. "He's furious. You see, it's not intended as a reward." He dodged his mother's elbow while she heaped another portion of the boiled fish before him. "When the old king died, Aahmes was determined to take the young Pharaoh on a campaign, but Hat-shep-sut opposed it. She finally agreed to one last campaign when the general convinced her that the world would be watching to see if the father's fighting spirit lives in the son. So Aahmes fought the Nubians in the south, and while he was about it he also fought the Libyans in the north—this against the queen's strict orders. Well, she summoned him to audience, thanked him sweetly for his zeal in protecting Egypt's borders, and announced his appointment as Royal Nurse."

The mother saw no reason for the general's anger at this signal honor, and Min-Hor agreed. "It is his due," said Min-Hor tartly, "in recognition of service to the Royal House. Every Pharaoh since my uncle was fifteen has given him honors."

Senmut folded his hands patiently. "All this is acknowledged," he said. "For any other man in Egypt, appointment as Royal Nurse would be the crowning of a life's work. But for Aahmes—can't you see? The lion, the dreaded warrior whose frown spells death to strong men—to be made responsible for the education of two girl babies? It's—well, ludicrous."

Hat-nefer smiled. Men, she thought, with their vast knowledge of the working of a woman's mind. Of course the queen chose a powerful sponsor for the health and development of her children. . . . She remembered Pharaoh's son by that awful concubine called Aset, and asked, "Wasn't it in the south that the young Pharaoh met—that woman?"

Her son laughed. "The world does not know it, but Pharaoh fought the southern campaign from his headquarters—in bed. His generals defeated the Nubians, but he subdued the daughter of the local mayor."

"What he sees in her," the mother sniffed; "a common face, big hips. . . . Will General Aahmes oversee the training of *her* son, also?"

"Oh, yes, yes. Hat-shep-sut can hardly prevent that, since it is her husband's son and not hers. The old man already is excited about the boy's training in weapons; he'll turn out a warrior king fit to rule Egypt."

"The son of a concubine—king of Egypt?"

"Pharaoh's son by the concubine Aset can reign if married to Hat-shep-sut's eldest daughter. And Pharaoh already has demanded betrothal of the babies to insure succession."

"Before they are two years old, even." Hat-nefer shook her head. "Poor little Princess Neferu-Re."

"Well, Queen Hat-shep-sut must consent first, and there will be no marriage until the prince is sixteen."

Min-Hor had been frowning, picking with nervous, angry fingers at a hem of her gown. Now she flared. "Is it Pharaoh or Pharaoh's women who make decisions? Who is king of Egypt?"

Senmut nodded agreeably. "A good question, which many are asking. Hat-shep-sut is the real ruler. Her husband, Thothmes, sits on the throne, frets about his pimples and his concubines, and leaves governing to the ministers, who, in turn, are loyal to the queen. The old king," said Senmut, "saw that his son was a fool, so he trained the daughter. She has great natural ability; she is the power in Egypt, and all the ministers know this, and they take their problems to her, and her decisions are law. It sounds incredible, but it's true."

This was interesting, Hat-nefer admitted, but she was tired

39

from the excitements of the day, the preparations and the home-coming, and her attention wandered. Ramose, under influence of the food and beer and dullness of conversational topics, was frankly asleep, punctuating pauses with a rhythmic wheezing.

"Come," said the mother, "that is enough sober talk, and you children want to be alone. Come."

Min-Hor rose without a word, without raising her eyes, and the curtains swung behind her slim figure. But when Senmut stretched and made to follow, the mother sought a pretext to keep her son beside her a moment longer.

"A last cup of the good beer," she said. "There . . . The place of the queen's tomb that you just found—it is not secret as was the old king's?"

"The queen would not allow the cost in lives that secrecy of that kind demands."

"How 'cost in lives'? Were men killed in its digging?"

"The serving of kings can be a grim business, Mother," said Senmut carefully. "It was the old king's wish to be buried secretly, and Ineni's and Aahmes' duty to insure this. Prisoners of war were chosen for the digging, and guarded by Aahmes' veterans. When the tomb was finished—well, Aahmes made arrangements, and the ghosts of a few hundred foreigners will guard that valley of the dead."

Hat-nefer shuddered and Senmut added, "The guards were pensioned; they will not talk."

The mother's eyes were wide with horror. "Prisoners were driven past here a month ago—tall men with yellow hair and white skins—their elbows bound cruelly behind, some of them limping from untended wounds."

"Libyans"—Senmut nodded—"from Aahmes' northern campaign."

"Will—will they be . . ."

"No, no. The queen would never allow it, I told you." He patted her hand in reassurance. "I do not think you will see many more wounded prisoners paraded through Egypt for some years. Not while Hat-shep-sut has power to interfere. She has effectively sheathed Aahmes' claws, Menti will not have the strength to defy her, and Pharaoh's son will not be of age to rule or fight for some time. So you are not to worry. The prisoners you saw will be sold as slaves and will probably be happy."

40

Hat-nefer sighed and rose. "It—it is so good to have you home. You do not have to leave for a while?"

"That is for Ineni to decide," he told her gently. "I'm taking over more of his duties, and we must check the affairs of Amon's estates in the north, neglected during the trip into the desert."

She felt cheated. "We never see you, and Min-Hor gets lonesome. Be kinder to her, Senmut."

In the uncertain light of the lamps she thought that the lines about his mouth tightened. "Does she complain to you?" he asked.

"No, no. We miss you, all of us, and—well, she is young and it is natural that— I wish she had a child, Senmut."

"So do I," he exclaimed, and suddenly his face was drawn and somber. "I suppose our marriage was a mistake; it's quite a change for her from the palace in Nekheb to—this."

"Nonsense," the mother snapped. "This fine house, and a walled garden, and trees . . . Come, you must get rest. Help me rouse your father."

"She'll have all that again," said Senmut, "servants and dancing girls and singers and delicacies, and a litter. . . ."

Later, Hat-nefer lay wide-eyed in the dark listening for voices from the adjoining room and hearing nothing above her husband's horrendous snores. ("How can so small a man make such frightful noise?") There had been no greeting; it was a bad marriage, a thoroughly bad marriage, and he would kill himself with overwork, and this chit would accept the sacrifice—of his health, even—as her due, and . . .

Hat-nefer sighed heavily, nudged her husband to still his uproar, and drifted to troubled sleep.

41

CHAPTER V

Year 4 of the Reign of Thothmes II

Stepping carefully to avoid soiling his fresh dress, Lord Ma-herpa, Steward of Her Majesty Queen Hat-shep-sut, paraded back and forth in the narrow room reserved for his use in the palace. He was a fleshy man who took a serious view of the exalted position he held in the state—that of official buffer between the real ruler of Egypt and her subjects. As Hat-shep-sut's representative, he must be example and leader in all phases of deportment—as well as in such minor categories as taste.

"You are sure that this is new?" he asked of his valet, shaking his hips so the tassels of the girdle-tie swung free.

"Positive, My Lord. Lord Thuti's had a single knot, and the tassels were short. Your double knot with tassels to the hem of the apron will be a sensation."

"The mixture of gold and silver threads helps, too."

"Exactly." The valet squatted with head held to one side admiringly. "Everyone in court will copy it within a week."

Ma-herpa nodded. "And every petty official and merchant in Thebes within a month. Then you will have to dream up something new, Renni."

His personal scribe scurried through the doorway, leafing anxiously through a fistful of bits of papyrus. Ma-herpa swung his stick and posed again. "How do you like it, Beta?"

The scribe, startled, dropped a flutter of notes. "The—oh, the stick, Master? Exquisite."

"The girdle-tie, fool!"

"Ah—of course. It is new, isn't it?"

He dropped to his knees, still fumbling with his notes.

"What have you lost now?" Ma-herpa exclaimed.

"Misplaced only, Master—not lost. The name of the foreign envoy demanding audience with His Majesty."

"Have you explained that His Majesty sees no one? That *Her* Majesty is now . . ."

"Twenty times, Master. But still he sits."

"Let him sit. Who else is waiting?"

"The farmer from Abdu. He has a petition for Her Majesty's ear alone. This is his twelfth day, Master . . ."

"Her Majesty is indisposed. Who else?"

Beta rattled his slips. "Lady Sit-Re sent a messenger."

Ma-herpa sniffed. "What is the noble Sit-Re indignant about now?"

"A gown of Her Majesty's was improperly ironed. One of the pleats *is* crooked, Master; shall I . . ."

"Bring it here; I will speak to the overseer myself. Renni, we may have to make changes in that department."

"Yes," Renni agreed, "there have been too many . . ."

"Let me see," Beta interrupted. "Lord Ineni has an audience with Her Majesty, but that is later. . . . Oh—Pharaoh's Herald is waiting to see you."

"Lord User?" Ma-herpa pounded his stick on the floor. "You have kept Lord User waiting? Are you insane?"

Beta scampered from the room and the Queen's Steward resettled his wig with an angry jerk. "The dolt. I can learn much of interest to Her Majesty by keeping User in friendly mood. The old days, Renni," he sighed, "when there was but one king to satisfy."

"Ah, but think of the weight your name carries now. Now you are a power in the kingdom—in the world."

"That has its embarrassments."

"In the old days, would Pharaoh's Herald wait outside your door?"

"You are right, of course. . . ."

"Sh-h-h," warned Renni, and bowed as the burly figure of the Royal Herald darkened the doorway.

Ma-herpa bowed also, but less elaborately. Once he had looked with awe upon this fighting companion of the old king, but conditions now were changed. Now Ma-herpa, the queen's man, with his hand upon the reins of government, could exert subtle pressures—modest, perhaps, but effective—while the king's man sat in idleness, chewing his nails, dead as far as influence on policies was concerned.

43

"A friendly inquiry after your health, My Lord," said User, "nothing more."

"Honored, My Lord. A stool, Renni. And perhaps Lord User will accept a cup of wine."

User lifted his cup. "The king. Life, health, and strength."

Ma-herpa's reply was: "To Her Majesty."

User laughed ruefully as he set his empty cup aside. "I hope the old king is not watching the Egypt that he and his fathers rescued from barbarians, now broken into two camps."

"I have never understood," countered Ma-herpa, "why you alone of the old king's close favorites adhere to the weakling son rather than follow his choice, the daughter—as did Lords Nefer-peret, Ineni, Aahmes and others."

User frowned. "I can never agree that the woman, however brilliant, should govern while the man, however ill, lives."

Ma-herpa bowed. "An honest opinion, My Lord. Let us drink, then, to Egypt. . . . And now—His Majesty is improved, I hope?"

"He will never improve," said User bitterly; "the body, perhaps, but the mind is a festering sore. You have seen in the temple services with what malevolence he watches his sister; it is worse in his rooms, for there he abandons all control, and his . . ."

An interruption startled them both; Beta's head showed in the doorway. "I found it," he announced.

"What?"

"Mazipalali."

"You found *what*?"

"The name of the foreign envoy." Beta disappeared.

"My Lord," said Ma-herpa, abashed.

"Scribes are all alike," said User, smiling. "By the way, I understand that Ineni has returned, and, knowing him, I am sure that his search was successful."

"I have not heard, My Lord."

"They went into the mountains from Per-haa, I believe. It looks formidable from the Nile. You do not know how deeply they penetrated?"

"No, My Lord."

"It takes courage to march into the unknown that way. I was terrified the one trip I made with Aahmes into the valley where the old king is buried. A forbidding place. It connects with the valley to the south that Ineni explored—did you know that?"

"No, My Lord."

"He said nothing about passing between the two valleys?"

"Not to me, My Lord."

User looked at him sharply for some moments, said, "Humph," and presently took his leave.

"Now, what was . . ." Renni began.

Ma-herpa rubbed his hands, laughing quietly. "I think I know. Yes, Her Majesty will enjoy this. Send Beta in now, and call me when Lord Ineni arrives. I will conduct him myself to the queen."

The next hour, while he battled with the novel spelling and sentence arrangement by which Beta sought to enrich tedious official documents, Ma-herpa spent in good spirits. These were somewhat dampened when, summoned by Renni, he found a stranger waiting with Ineni, a nervous young priest whom Ineni called Senmut.

"I am sorry, My Lord," Ma-herpa explained patiently to the old Steward of Amon, "the order is quite specific: 'Admit Lord Ineni to the Presence.' You see, no mention of this Senmut. He can wait here. My stick, Renni . . . Follow me, My Lord."

In the passage to the audience-chamber, he fell into companionable step beside the old priest. "Her Majesty will be delighted to see you so fit after your ordeal. You penetrated the mountains behind Per-haa? The valleys there, I believe, are a continuation of the great northern valley where the old king is buried."

"Indeed?" said Ineni. "There must have been a cataclysm of fine proportions since last week, then."

"You found no such passage? My informant seemed quite positive."

"Not as positive as the man who has explored both valleys, my friend."

"Good. I guessed as much. . . . In here, My Lord."

Hat-shep-sut had chosen an antechamber for the informal greeting with her father's friend and hers, and her greeting surprised Ma-herpa by its warmth.

"We have missed you, My Lord. It is our hope that hereafter you will delegate these arduous labors to younger men so we will not be deprived of your presence and counsel."

45

"You are generous, Majesty, and younger men are in train-ing—one in particular. And soon I should be able to turn affairs which you have entrusted to me into his capable hands. *Then* I can rest."

"Do I know him?"

"Senmut, Your Majesty, son of Hat-nefer."

"I thought as much."

Ma-herpa, seeing the queen's smile, felt sweat trickle down his back. The youth left waiting . . . Senmut! He had heard the name, but where? In what connection?

"He is young," said Hat-shep-sut, "and ambitious, and"—Ma-herpa thought that a rare gentleness showed for a moment in her eyes—"not without pleasing qualities of the spirit. Time, and your wisdom, My Lord, may fashion him into a useful minister. Has he shot more lions?"

Lions! Of course! Ma-herpa recalled the public honoring by the old king—the splendid bow. . . . Strange that Her Majesty should remember so trivial an incident.

"He has done better," said Ineni. "He was with me in our search, and it was Senmut who discovered a perfect site for Your Majesty's tomb."

Ma-herpa dared to interrupt. "He is waiting, Your Majesty; shall I introduce him?"

"Immediately."

Senmut seemed neither surprised nor agitated. The nervous-ness that Ma-herpa had noticed was gone, and he apparently was not offended by the period of waiting; in fact, he followed the steward with an air of anticipation and quiet dignity as if audiences with royalty were a pleasurable daily occurrence. Not a handsome youth, Ma-herpa decided; capable, probably, since Ineni praised him to Her Majesty. And she, too, thought highly of him—"pleasing qualities of the spirit." Now, that was a peculiar phrase. What did it mean exactly?

He smiled confidentially over his shoulder. "You know Her Majesty well? I mean, you have performed commissions for her before?"

"No," said Senmut.

"Your father, perhaps? She knows your family?"

"No."

46

Ma-herpa grunted. Damn the lout! Was he stupid, or arrogant?

He threw open the door of the antechamber, announced, "The priest Senmut," and waited within the room. If permitted, he wanted to see all of this.

Senmut knew his manners before royalty, at least; he bowed from the waist, arms pendant, and remained thus until Her Majesty spoke. She delayed, however, for some moments, appraising the youth through narrowed lids, one hand—Ma-herpa noted the unorthodox position—pressing the handsome pectoral that covered throat and breast. And her voice, when it came, lacked customary incisiveness—it was soft, the voice of a woman and not a queen.

"Welcome home, Senmut. The reports of your activities in our behalf are pleasing."

Again Ma-herpa was surprised at what he heard. Ineni had been leader of the expedition, his the responsibilities, and yet Senmut got the praise. High praise, too, from one of Hat-shepsut's cautious and unsympathetic nature. Ineni was smiling, however, and when the queen nodded for him to tell the story of his search, he begged, "Senmut, Your Majesty; he shared the perils, and it is his tale as much as mine."

So Senmut spoke—and well, Ma-herpa admitted—of the members of the party: Lord Ineni, Penati who was familiar with conditions in the wild places, and himself. None knew this wilderness of mountain and ravine behind Per-haa, so food and water must be carried by porters, and sufficient guards to protect against whatever danger might lurk.

While Senmut talked, a strange feeling came to Ma-herpa; his spirit seemed to leave his well-fed body and stumbled beside the three adventurers and their porters and guards, toiling through sand and over boulders, plunging into a nightmare of frightening canyons, ever deeper into the unknown. On every side cliff-walls rose straight and high, and the party struggled through a furnace of heat; and at night their fire was a single star in a heaven of black and numbing cold. Days and weeks were spent in examination of lateral valleys; the site they needed must include an almost impossible variety of natural advantages, and Ma-herpa shared, vicariously, the shadings of excitement and despair with which each location was considered, and abandoned. Dwarfed in a loneliness of rock and sand, he crawled with them, scanning the sides of precipitous cliffs and hunting the shadows for faults and crevices; shivering beside them, the night wind brought to his ears the sighs of the wandering dead, punctuated by the horrid screams of jackals. And when the floor of the many-branched valley was exhausted, he climbed the cliffs with them and followed the rim, continuing their search from above.

"And there we found it," Senmut concluded. "I saw a notch in the rim's edge; a porter held me while I leaned far out and saw, halfway to the bottom, a small shelf in the perpendicular face of the cliff, a shelf hidden from below so we had missed it."

"That is the site, Majesty," Ineni interrupted eagerly. "We were lowered by ropes—it's a hundred and thirty feet from the top and two hundred above the floor of the canyon—and there is good rock; a corridor can be driven into the cliff and rooms cut for the tomb. And Senmut found it!"

With difficulty Ma-herpa returned to the present, to the comfort and security of the brightly painted anteroom in the palace. Hat-shep-sut, also, he thought, seemed to lack ability or desire to leave the dream world of Senmut's making; she lay back in the throne-chair, eyes shaded by a hand, motionless for the space of several breaths. Then she murmured, "The efforts—perilous efforts—that one thoughtlessly demands of friends!" She sighed, and straightened in the chair. "The work will not be too dangerous?"

Ineni answered. "Every precaution will be taken, Majesty. The tomb will not be secret, as is your father's, but it will be hidden and difficult of access."

"The gods love Your Majesty," said Senmut with quiet emphasis; "they will never let harm come near you, in this world or in the next."

Well, well, thought Ma-herpa, our friend will bear watching; he is neither stupid nor arrogant, he is clever.

Hat-shep-sut, from her expression, also appreciated the sentiment, but her next words were thoughtful. "As a child I shunned mention of the tomb, until Pharaoh my father explained that it is but a convenient house for the spirit, a comfortable and familiar dwelling to which one returns after a journey. Make my tomb such a place, Lord Ineni."

48

Ineni bowed. "A house of peace where your soul, when wearied with the councils and feasting of the gods, will know joy. It is a command, Your Majesty."

"You do understand, my friend." She smiled. "And you, Senmut. And Lord Ma-herpa. Three whose loyalty is a staff."

Ma-herpa was touched; the queen was seldom so generous.

"May I speak, Your Majesty," he said, "on a matter which may be disagreeable to your ears? Pharaoh your husband published an edict that none but kings of Egypt might have their tombs in the valley where your august father is buried."

The queen and Ineni nodded.

"I was approached today by Pharaoh's agent, who implied that the king believes this edict about to be violated."

Hat-shep-sut's face whitened with quick anger. "He would not dare suggest . . ."

"He does, Your Majesty."

"But how ridiculous," Ineni stormed. "There is a range of mountains between the northern and southern valleys."

"His Majesty believes that a passage exists through those mountains; that—apologies, My Lord—the party hunting a site for Her Majesty's tomb may have blundered into the forbidden area. Shall I inform the agent of his error?"

"Under no circumstances," Hat-shep-sut replied sweetly. "Such action would deprive my dear husband of something tangible to fret about."

She stared moodily before her. "I can never forgive the last campaign he ordered, the one against Libya—a needless abuse of power, a piling of misery upon a neighbor whose only error is weakness."

"I understood that there had been violation of the borders, Majesty," said Ineni.

"You have listened to General Aahmes, My Lord. There were minor infractions, yes, but nothing that police action could not handle. There was no need for armies and invasion and slaughter and wholesale destruction. I consider it Egypt's privilege and duty to lead and to protect, not to destroy.

"General Aahmes chose to disobey my express command, and"—she smiled thinly—"I have felt it necessary to take mild disciplinary action; he has been appointed Nurse to the royal daughters, and I hope that he is unhappy with the honor.

49

"This, however, does not correct a great wrong. What of the countless prisoners—men and women and children? Are they to be sacrificed to the whims of that witless half-man, my husband? Are their lives to be ruined because a professional warrior wishes to test a new bow or a new design in chariot wheels?"

"They will be happy in Egypt, Majesty," Ineni assured her.

"As slaves? Come, My Lord—you would enjoy being torn from family and home and forced to dig in some rich man's fields for your remaining days? Knowing that your wife and children were suffering like indignities, or worse? You would be happy?"

Ma-herpa carefully kept his mouth closed. He could have argued that slaves were necessary to the economy, that there always would be slaves in Egypt, but she would not hear his logic. And nothing but discredit would be gained if he could prove her natural woman's bias but the product of sentimentality.

Senmut, however . . . When Ma-herpa heard the young priest's voice, his thought was: No—no; don't ruin a good impression already established!

Senmut said, "Your Majesty, cannot your and Lord Ineni's hopes be reconciled? If these prisoners of war are not slaves, may they not be happy in Egypt?"

Ma-herpa saw the queen's face brighten with interest. She leaned forward in her chair. "Speak your thought, Senmut."

"It is with those prisoners taken in Pharaoh's campaign in Libya that Your Majesty is most concerned now. If their families were kept intact, if they were settled on lands belonging to the crown—a small holding of land to a family—might they not in time accept our culture and our gods, become Egyptians? I have seen a list of spoils taken in the campaign—cattle, skins, weapons, boats, jewelry—all this now in the Royal Treasury. Could this be considered as payment for state lands so used?"

Hat-shep-sut nodded thoughtfully. "The plan could be presented for Nefer-peret's consideration."

Ineni exclaimed, "Tell Nefer-peret, Your Majesty, that these Libyans are excellent farmers and weavers; let him ask Aahmes. The taxes collected by his men will in a few years reimburse the Royal Treasury ten-fold."

"Lord Nefer-peret is a shrewd bargainer where state funds

are concerned. I shall need your presence at the audience. Lord Ma-herpa, do you approve Senmut's suggestion?"

Ma-herpa bowed. "I am expert neither at finance nor philanthropy, Your Majesty. But I do venture an opinion: our young friend will not long be known merely as 'the priest Senmut.' "

"Well spoken, My Lord. Such is also our belief."

CHAPTER VI

Year 6 of the Reign of Thothmes II

The General Aahmes Pen-Nekheb was essentially a sober man, and ninety-two years of living, eighty of them spent in violence or the pursuit of violence, had cast his features in a forbidding mask of uncompromising severity. With that face, roaring was expected, so he roared; bursts of temper were feared, so he erupted; a smile would have upset the entire geography of consummate harshness, so his smiles were secret.

This morning his limping progress across the parade ground from the stables was accented nasally by a queer tumult which a broadminded person might have accepted as humming. He admitted that there were inconsistencies in his behavior; to another this day would have been given over to cursing, for his favorite horse was lame, half a dozen of his old wounds troubled, he had slept perhaps an hour in the previous night, and decisions were being forced upon him by the Royal Palace that racked his very soul. Today, however, he pushed all these into a corner to make room for dispassionate examination of an idea which, at that morning's rising, had exploded with stunning violence upon his consciousness.

As he walked, the part of his brain dedicated to technical matters approved of the multiple activities of the camp: the wrestling, leaping, running and marching, the practice with sling and bow and throw-stick, the charioteers exercising their horses, the blacksmiths, wheelwrights, cooks, guards—no man sweating, yet all employed. Morale was a tricky element, doubly important in peacetime and difficult always to maintain near a city. "Keep them active," was his motto, if it meant nothing but moving stones from one side of camp to the other.

Menti was Captain of the Captains now, but Aahmes' eye

wandered professionally—the habit of a lifetime impossible to break—and he beckoned a young charioteer to him, a recruit. The frightened boy drove close and saluted, from his expression uncertain whether slow torture or sudden death awaited, such were the tales of the general's ferocity fed juniors by the veterans.

"Your reins are tied too short," said Aahmes in his conversational growl, "so your arrows miss the target; loosen the reins and let your weight be squarely on the right foot. That's it, straddle the apron—left foot on the pole between the horses for balance, right foot in the car for support. Now tie the reins about your waist. You see? When you drive, the pull on the reins should guide the horses without distorting your aim at the target. Try it."

He watched the chariot gather speed and approach a leather shield nailed waist-high to a post, watched the lad draw and loose, saw the arrow quivering in the shield, and grunted. Good stuff in these youngsters.

As he approached the camp's gateway, a tall and heavily muscled man detached himself from a group of officers and came swinging toward him—the General Menti. Aahmes scowled as he watched the youthful vigor of the other's stride; once he, too, had walked that way.

Menti pointed to a dust cloud that hung over the road between camp and city. "Here comes Khem, now, with the boy. Did I tell you, Master, he wanted to drive yesterday? Four years old—and I swear I think he could do it! He's afraid of nothing. I'm going to have a small chariot made, and gentle a pair of ponies—white ponies, perhaps. . . . Can't you see him leading the festival procession of Amon?"

Aahmes grunted. "Is that the bow we talked about?"

Menti, accustomed to the old man's vagaries, handed him the stick without comment. It was a war bow in miniature, tapered at each end and nocked, polished, beautifully balanced. Aahmes strung it and tested its pull.

"Sweet drawing," said Menti, "and an added two pounds of pull as you suggested. If he continues to shoot as he did yesterday—you know, it won't be a month before he will pierce a copper target. I'll wager on it."

"You will lose," said Aahmes.

53

"A month from today—the twentieth Pachons," Menti insisted stubbornly. "You stand behind him today and watch those back muscles when he shoots. Come, is it a bet, Master?"

For answer Aahmes pointed toward the gateway.

The old charioteer, Khem, pulled his sweating horses to a stop, tossed reins to a waiting guard and scuffled toward the two officers.

Menti started. "Where is Prince Thothmes?" he called.

"I was refused admittance at the palace, General," Khem reported.

"By whose order?"

"The queen's, General."

Menti turned to his master, who nodded. "Word was brought me last night, my friend," Aahmes said. "No more training in arms for the young prince."

"But—but . . ."

"I know. I have arranged audience with Queen Hat-shep-sut for this afternoon, but I look for nothing."

Menti scowled at the useless bow in his hands; slowly he bent it until the tough wood splintered with a snap—and Aahmes nodded understandingly. "I felt the same at first. If her pretty neck had been within my reach . . ."

The old man stumped beside the younger, each fumbling amidst the wreckage of plans and hopes. At the gateway grooms held restive horses hitched to Aahmes' chariot; he gathered the reins, made his withered leg comfortable, and looked down moodily at the younger man.

"It's not the way the old king would like it. I'm leaving you a sorry legacy. We can always hope, of course, that some heathen upstart will let impatience smother memory and invade Egypt, but . . ."

He braced himself, waved his hand, and whirled through the gates on the road Khem had recently quitted.

The Egyptian war-chariot, though feather-light, was of the toughest construction, and the speediest—if not the safest—method of locomotion. Rocking and bounding in the rutted road, progress was a series of flights and crashes that tested the skill of the most practiced, and which only the hardiest could pretend to enjoy.

Aahmes drove like a bald-headed demon, and perhaps the

children working in the fields that bordered the high road thought him one, for they screamed as he tore past with a thunder of hooves and a twisting tail of dust. And their fathers on the way to market screamed, too, but in dismay and anger, as they dumped their burdens and leaped to save their skins. If the queen forbade his harrying foreigners in their native lands, the general retaliated by making the roads of Egypt unsafe for Egyptians.

Exercise, Aahmes called it, and he pressed the straining horses, and flexed his muscles to absorb the shocks and to anticipate the erratic leaping of the car, cheating death. "By the gods— he wanted to drive! Four years old and he wanted to drive...."

By the time the city gates were reached—without casualty— his steady weight on the reins had slowed the animals to maneuverable speed, and as long as citizens dove for doorways and flattened themselves against walls, there were few incidents; an old crone was tumbled in the dirt, but judging from the stream of healthy curses, the only damage was to her dignity. If she were a man, he thought, with that spirit and that vocabulary I'd make her a captain.

At his gateway, the groom who took the steaming horses whispered that his grandson Paheri and the priest Senmut awaited him; his gatekeeper, gardener, doorman and personal steward all confirmed this news in tones hinting that they knew his habits and that guests in the house were an oddity. He confused them all by greeting the young men warmly, by calling for beer, and by shooing them to the garden while he bathed and changed.

Aahmes did not claim to understand Paheri, any more than he understood the rest of his family. All but one of Aahmes' sons had disappointed him by dying in youth, defying the extravagant plans with which parents greet a new arrival. The son who lived, Ateferu-Re (Paheri's father), infuriated the old man by refusing to remain in Thebes in the court atmosphere of fawning insincerities, and returned, with a rich wife, to Nekheb.

A little of the general's hurt was salved, however, when the rich wife laid a grandson in his arms; and when, some months later, the old Pharaoh appointed Ateferu-Re Royal Nurse to a newborn heir to the throne, Aahmes' wounds were healed.

He saw in his own red mite a future general who, with the help of the gods, would lead the armies of the royal red mite to victory over mites unborn.

And then the gods must have napped. The king's son died, and Paheri became an artist!

He was a good artist, Aahmes admitted; you had to be, to earn the title "Draughtsman of Amon" under Ineni. And if Paheri could not be a general, at least his name would be remembered while the walls of the Great Temple stood, for on those walls were texts and drawings, worked by the royal artists from Paheri's careful drawings. He was now putting the same careful work into the decoration of Aahmes' tomb in the hills behind Nekheb, listing the battles and wars in the old man's adventurous career, the prisoners taken, the honors given by four kings.

The voices of the young men sounded from a screen of vines that made a shady arbor, and Aahmes ordered his steward to serve the noon meal there. He shared his garden with few people—a place of quiet and rest, of dreaming, of loosening the strings of memory. Here he relaxed body and thought through the drug of homely sounds, and mingled with the hum of insects and chatter of birds and whispering of the leaves, sometimes he heard, as faint echoes, voices dear and long dead. It was a place of magic; here his soul escaped its prison and its world and wandered in far countries and through lost years, and returned to its scarred body strengthened. He told the magic to no one.

The meal was brightened by nonsense and laughter. Paheri and Senmut were young, the furious ride had rinsed Aahmes' mind of bitterness, the food was plentiful, the wine excellent. Paheri imitated Hapu-seneb's reading of the evening service in the temple, mimicking his impressive belly-tones; Senmut described the tricks of farmers to evade a just reckoning of the taxes; Aahmes retold, with gestures, a novel expedient by which a Kushite princess saved her army from annihilation.

Aahmes compared the youths, and from surface appearances a stranger could not have distinguished prince from commoner, artist from priest. Paheri, perhaps, with his knowledge of inherited position and wealth, showed a hint more sureness in his manner—Senmut, perhaps from lack of background, more aggressiveness. Mentally they were equals; Aahmes, no scholar, lost his way in their discussions of basic principles of architecture, or creative genius, or such—to him—wordy froth. But their voices calmed him. It was cool in the bower, restful after his exercise and the meat and wine; the play of light on the fretted surface of the pool held his eye . . . the drifting fragrance of a flower . . . Aahmes snored gently.

Faintly he became aware of Paheri's voice.

". . . four necklaces, an armlet, six golden flies, a golden axe . . ."

"*Two* golden axes," the old man snapped.

"Oh, you are not asleep, Grandfather?"

"Nonsense. The light hurts my eyes. What are you reading?"

"I was telling Senmut of the rewards for valor given you by the old king—the list that I am preparing for your tomb."

Aahmes nodded. "Start it again and don't mumble."

Paheri consulted a scrap of papyrus in his hand. "From the first Aahmes, he who liberated Egypt—you were too young, I suppose, to receive great reward. But from Pharaoh Amenhotep —here it is: a dagger, an armlet, two necklaces, two bracelets, a headdress and a fan."

Aahmes checked the items on his fingers. "Right. And the dagger was one that Pharaoh himself plucked from the belt of the Nubian chief, after smashing his head with an axe."

"From the old king, Thothmes," Paheri resumed, "I find two bracelets, four necklaces, an armlet, six golden flies, a golden axe . . ."

"*Two*," roared Aahmes, "two golden axes. Of what value is a record if it be faulty? Two golden axes and three golden lions."

Paheri wetted his pen in the bottle of water that hung from his girdle and blackened the point in the charcoal on his writing palette and corrected his script. "*Two* golden axes, and three golden lions. Thanks. Now, from the present Pharaoh the list shows six necklaces, three armlets, three bracelets and one silver axe."

Aahmes shrugged. "All the rest were won under fighting kings, but from our present Pharaoh—only my rank of General of the Army gives me title to his rewards."

"You are modest, General," said Senmut. "Menti says that you are a raging lion in battle."

Aahmes chuckled, obviously pleased. "A hyena, perhaps; only kings are 'raging lions.' And someone had to get Menti out of that swarm of Libyans. He won't get himself surrounded again."

Paheri put away his writing equipment. "Thanks, Grandfather, for the corrections and for hospitality. If you will excuse me, the Lord Ineni expects Neb-taui and me for conference on plans of a new chamber for the temple."

When Senmut sought to follow, Aahmes waved him back to his seat. "Unless you too must go, humor a lonely old man." The idea which had so stunned him with its brilliance at the morning's waking involved, besides himself, Senmut. But he must think it through. So he closed his eyes and let the problem simmer.

One distasteful fact had to be acknowledged: he was past what men call the "prime of life." He had been too careless with the lives of other men to set an inflated valuation upon his own; like all Egyptians, he knew just where and how eternity would be spent, so his whole concern was with the present, with those who must carry the burden when he surrendered it.

Menti now was standing ably on his own feet, so there was but one bit of unfinished business in which he still felt vital interest, and that had been removed from his control by Hatshep-sut's order of yesterday. Aahmes labored sulphurously upon this. What did abandonment of the weapon-training of the child prince accomplish except delay in the development of a natural fighter? Once the double crown was firmly on his head, Aahmes predicted that the boy would find immediate excuse to start pushing Egypt's borders outward, and there would be costly lessons and delays if he cast himself, untrained, upon seasoned enemies. A fool could reason this, yet the queen listened to her heart, set her thin lips in a line and said, "War is evil," believing—Aahmes credited her with a bemused sincerity—her voice the echo of Holy Amon's will.

He was tired, he told himself bitterly, of playing adviser to a deaf woman. His flesh, too, cried for rest and ease. Since the queen's dictum that training of the prince must stop, he had been plagued by a picture of old Nekheb set in its semicircle of barren hills, the place of his birth and the site of his tomb. His had been a stormy life, and suddenly the quiet that was contained within the crumbling walls of the ancient fortress seemed important to him.

Well, then, there remained but to say to Hat-shep-sut, "Majesty, my work is finished. Egypt is powerful and rich, no enemy threatens, and a man loyal to your interests guards the borders. The royal daughters are in health and I have found one who, better than an old soldier, can prepare them for living in today's complex and changing world."

That was all that need be said. "Majesty, my work is finished."

Senmut was drawing with a finger in the dust of the garden, and Aahmes remembered another garden and a thin urchin squatting in a circle of awed buzzing. Magic, he had then thought, to watch him writing, and magic it seemed now that the thinness had grown to strength and the farmer's brat to distinguished manhood. There was nothing ornamental about Senmut, for already, at twenty-one, his face was etched with the tell-tale lines of application and of hours of late study; but humor was there, a lightness of spirit that balanced soberness, and there was honesty and inner strength.

"Scribble, scribble," Aahmes said roughly. "What will you write when all the words that are in your skull have been written down?"

"Rearrange the thought," said Senmut, smiling over his shoulder, "and write it a second and third time. Rewrite the legends, invent stories . . ."

"Pish! There is enough falsehood in the world without inventing more."

"No." Senmut settled back on his heels and prepared for argument. "Say, rather, that there is too much gloom and unhappiness, and that a tale, well told, lightens the load, amuses or instructs."

Aahmes shrugged. "Like the fancies you mentioned the other day for the queen's daughters? I would be ashamed to fill their heads with silliness."

"They are children, not adults," said Senmut patiently. "Light and fanciful things are real to them. They hear the murmur of wind passing through a tree; well, tell them that the leaves are tongues and talk a hidden language. Children can understand that and it delights them. Tell them that birds

59

are the souls of the dead, returned for a brief visit—and then watch their pleasure in every bird they see."

"I tell them what I know," Aahmes argued, "of fighting, battles, how to fortify a camp. I cannot manufacture tales any better than I could teach dancing or playing the harp."

"Well, then, *tell* them what you know, only translate it into simple terms which their small minds can grasp. Like this," said Senmut, warming to the theme. "They know only the flat land of Egypt with its single mighty river, its endless sun. Think how tales of the strange land of the Naharin would delight them—wooded hills, streams and waterfalls, storms of rain, the winter season when the white clouds break into small pieces and fall and bury the earth in a blanket, and men and animals die beneath its cold. You've seen how eagerly Paheri and I listen when you tell your experiences? The children can be taught, too—history, geography, building, art, religion, even death. It can be done, Excellency, and they will be impressed and instructed, *and* entertained."

Aahmes shook his head—not, as Senmut thought, in stubbornness, but rather in secret appreciation of the younger man's dexterities of thought and invention. Senmut was the man. Aahmes was doubly assured now. If Senmut became Royal Nurse, the education of the two princesses would be liberal and exact. Were there no limits to the youth's ability? Ineni no longer sang his praises, he shouted them; the boy's grasp of the intricacies of finance, his understanding of tax problems, the range of his interests, his wealth of technical skill—no parent ever boasted more monotonously of a son's perfections than did Ineni of his pupil's.

"How are you getting on as Steward of Amon?" Aahmes asked suddenly.

"The appointment will not come for a while yet," Senmut reminded him.

"You've done all Ineni's work for a year, though?"

"The work on the estates of Amon, yes. With his supervision."

"You work well with Tet? And Penati?"

"Of course." Senmut's tone showed surprise at the question. "That is part of Ineni's training, teamwork."

"Does your wife like your absences from home on temple business?"

"Well..." Senmut made a helpless gesture. "You know women, General. Position and wealth are important to Min-Hor—she was raised in a palace, you know—and so her husband makes his name big in the land, I doubt if the methods worry her."

"For yourself, however"—Aahmes smoothed his chin reflectively—"fame and wealth are unimportant, eh?"

"Oh, now, see here," Senmut began, then caught the other's twinkle. "I want these more, I think, than anything else in this life. Why else do I work as I do? Titles do not drop into my lap like figs, as they did into Thuti's and Hapu-seneb's; my father was a farmer, and that will not be forgotten, however high I climb."

"You have aids that less fortunate men envy already; Amon's favor, for instance, your name familiar to the queen, and a friend or two."

"Acknowledged, General, with honest appreciation. But because of the envy, my labor and its results must be doubled."

He was right, of course; everything he did must be done faster and better than another could do it. Aahmes glanced at the sun, sighed and got heavily to his feet. "I must dress for the audience," he said. "Walk with me to the house."

They went a few steps in silence, then the general said, "I fear only the impatience of youth and, heed an old man, there is no need of hurry for you. The king's son is four and it will be twelve years before he can rule, even if Pharaoh his father dies of his sores. For twelve years Hat-shep-sut will govern Egypt, and your name is familiar to her. Use those years to prepare yourself exhaustively in administration, building— what you wish—and when the new king ascends the throne you will be an indispensible minister. Think this over, Senmut; meanwhile—can you get a fat goose?"

"Yes, I can get you one, General."

"No, for yourself. Offer it this afternoon to Amon, with a prayer for his special favor this day."

The Royal Palace, in contrast with earlier days, seemed like a house of death; where once its chambers resounded to the clack of a dozen heathen tongues and the walls bulged with the glittering retinues of visiting emissaries, now there was little to recall the vigor and brilliance of the court which, a few short years gone, had dominated the thoughts of the world.

Pharaoh sulked in a wing of the palace, busied with his pretty serving maids, fretting at his physicians, dying slowly and hopelessly at the age of twenty in a crescendo of little rages and revilings against the gods. For a while officers and ministers of the kingdom, for form's sake, had brought the business of government to his door, and then even this pretense stopped; now what could be called a court was to be found in the ante-rooms of Hat-shep-sut's apartments. Aahmes' approach to these, for his audience, was a walk through echoing emptiness, a walk with ghosts.

Ma-herpa chatted amiably during the passage of chambers and corridors to the queen's boudoir. He was fastidious and correct, and the old soldier, disliking everything about the man, was obliged to admit that behind that unctuous mask lay incorruptible loyalty, and intelligence sufficient to satisfy a queen who brooked no fumbling. Perhaps the success of his stewardship lay in the shrewdness of his appraisal of Hat-shep-sut's character, once expressed to Aahmes. "She is a beautiful and strange person," Ma-herpa had said, "with the mental strength, the will and the wit of a man. But never forget that she is all woman, My Lord, and that women cannot be driven; they fight the bridle that seeks to direct their going or curb their will. Sometimes, however"—and his broad face had beamed in innocence—"sometimes they can be led."

In the council room where Hat-shep-sut customarily met the ministers, Ma-herpa left the general alone with the painted pillars and painted ceiling and painted decorations on the walls. Then a curtain was drawn and Aahmes was ushered into a luxurious chamber with great silver ceiling lamps and costly fabrics, with bowing female slaves, with music and heavenly fragrance. Hat-shep-sut, reclining on a couch while the nurse, Sit-Re, brushed her hair, lifted a hand for him to kiss.

Aahmes was an old man, with sons and grandsons, yet he felt his pulse stammer, as always, in the presence of Hat-shep-sut. It was not alone her loveliness; that was for all men to admire— slim and milk-skinned, thin-lipped and proud, and with haunting blue eyes that held unfathomable secrets and sorrows. For Aahmes—and perhaps for a handful of others—the lips unbent and the eyes softened; goddess and queen became a woman for Aahmes and he shivered like a youth.

He made his bow, back bent and arms pendant from the shoulders, and then he kissed her hand, alabaster-white and smooth and smelling of perfumes reserved for the gods. He spoke her names, and continued in the ancient formula—"Thou art the rising sun, lighting the world with thy beauty. . . . Thy rays penetrate into all lands. . . . Thou art eternal, everything acts according to thy designs, everything obeys thy words. . . ."— subtly complimenting her, for the attributes he named were customarily applied only to a throned Pharaoh. And the flattery pleased her—the woman was not hopelessly buried beneath a frigidness of ceremony and convention; she welcomed him warmly, with simple and kindly words.

These disarmed him. She knew well his reason for seeking audience, so he was braced for a formal exposition of policy, for reservations, excuses, even hostility—not, certainly, for the intimacy of admittance to the family circle. He waited, his mind in taut expectancy, for her speech.

She signaled her maids who brought a stool and cups of wine. "Be seated, My Lord, and forgive informality; Sit-Re is unhappy if she cannot brush my hair at this hour."

Aahmes mumbled that Sit-Re's was an enviable task, and Hat-shep-sut nodded in delighted surprise. "Come, My Lord, a soldier with pretty compliments?"

Sit-Re sniffed with elaborate emphasis. The Lady Sit-Re enjoyed a unique niche in life, since she refused to remember that Hat-shep-sut was no longer the baby she had nursed, the child she had comforted; others might see a queen to be obeyed or feared, but she saw only a girl to be protected. All men she appraised with a hard and suspicious eye; old or young, prince or farmer, if it was a man, his actions were to be watched and his motives suspected. This attitude, since the queen had been forced into active participation in government, kept the good nurse in a perpetual boil.

"Pay no attention to Sit-Re's hysteria," the queen murmured. "Nefer-peret and his assistant just left, and she is in foul temper after a meeting with Lord Thuti."

"That one," said Sit-Re hoarsely, "could learn manners from a goat. The way he looks at a woman."

"Thuti is young," said Aahmes, "but he is more in love with power and with himself than with women. Bear with him, Majesty; feed his vanity and he will make you a conscientious and efficient minister. Your father knew. 'An old head on a young body' was what he said of Lord Thuti. And of Senmut, too . . ."

"The farmer!" Sit-Re exclaimed.

"Exactly. Senmut the farmer. Now Senmut the priest, and soon to be Senmut the Steward of Amon. And if you listen to Ineni . . ."

"I have." Hat-shep-sut laughed. " 'There is no post in government that Senmut cannot fill,' says Ineni. 'There is no title within Your Majesty's power to bestow to which Senmut will not bring honor.' I begin to think him a monster, this Senmut; no single vice, and a thousand virtues."

"Ineni gave to the old king your father much good counsel."

"I know, but it seems improbable that in one man, a youth, there should be centered so much genuine ability."

Aahmes forgot himself so far as to rub his crooked leg thoughtfully. "I felt as you feel, Majesty. Then I remembered something Neb-taui once said of the limitless hidden power of the gods. Now, if Senmut has Amon's favor, will that not answer all questions? Amon's will, working through a receptive intelligence? I wish I had Ineni's tongue—or Senmut's, for that matter."

"You do well with your own, My Lord."

"How do you know," Sit-Re interrupted, "that it is Amon's favor? It sounds more to me the sharpness of an unprincipled adventurer."

Aahmes glared at the nurse. "You have talked with Senmut? Ineni and I are two fools? Two babes? Unable to distinguish between falseness and truth, pretense and sincerity? We are so unskilled in the world of men . . ."

The queen lifted her hand. "You have been answered, Sit-Re." Then to Aahmes: "I agree, My Lord, that Amon's favor works strongly in Senmut. He, of all the young men trained under my father's orders, sees most clearly and deeply into a problem, gives unselfishly of his thought and efforts to Egypt's needs. I seek his counsel frequently."

"He will fail Your Majesty in nothing. I know Senmut. And

64

your appreciation of his ability makes the subject of my request for audience easier to express."

"Yes?"

"The years remaining to me are few," said Aahmes, leaning forward in his earnestness, "and I await Your Majesty's command to spend them in Nekheb, the town of my birth."

Hat-shep-sut's lips struggled to suppress a smile; she obviously guessed the hidden reasons behind her general's demand. "Egypt cannot spare you yet, My Lord. Come, you are angry because I do not place the same value on battle-training for Pharaoh's son that you do."

Aahmes bowed and recited his speech stubbornly. "My work in Egypt is finished. The borders are safe, no enemy threatens, General Menti is a capable and trustworthy servant. My work is finished."

The queen took some time to reply, and when again she looked at him, he saw that her eyes were troubled. "My Lord," she said, "we cannot quarrel, for you are as much Egypt as Pharaoh my father ever was. If we appear on opposite sides of a problem, it is because I think with my heart and you with your head. We both seek security and prosperity for our land; perhaps my secret desire is too inclusive, for I would offer that same security to the world outside Egypt. Cannot Egypt set the example among nations, practice humility and friendliness, be the wise mother? Must we, just because we are strong and others weak, continue to rob and ravish and destroy? Tell me that I am not a hopeless visionary."

Aahmes shook his head. How could he make this gentle, dreaming woman-child see that the world, already weary with a lifetime of pettiness and self-seeking, would read into such proposals nothing but evidence of weakness, would strap on its armor and sharpen its spears and plot to disembowel and destroy its "mother"?

"Majesty," he sighed, "everything that I remember from a long lifetime of contacts with Egypt's neighbors tells me that you are wrong, but I am weary and my judgment is not now to be trusted. Remember these two things, however—that Egypt once was overwhelmed by foreign neighbors and it took two centuries and the lives of thousands to disperse them; and this—that men living today in Naharin plot and scheme how they may bring it again to pass. Remember this and keep your armies strong—not for conquest, but for protection.

"One day," the old man continued, "the child Thothmes, as husband of Princess Neferu-Re, will sit upon the throne. For some years you will supervise his training and can indoctrinate him with your ideals, but I cannot give you hope of results."

"The priest Neb-taui, a gentle man, will oversee the schooling; I have faith in his influence."

"No, Majesty," said Aahmes firmly, "the instant the checks are removed, the lad will bolt. I know his kind. This is why I hoped to forearm him with at least the rudiments of . . ."

He broke off as Hat-shep-sut shook her head in stubborn negation. "Then, Majesty," he said, "your permission to withdraw from a task as arduous as any set me by your father, that of Royal Nurse to the princesses."

"I wondered if you had forgotten your obligation to the children."

"On the contrary. I have sought and found one better qualified than myself to superintend their education. One of sensitiveness, of imagination, of ambition. A man wholly devoted to Your Majesty, and who, with or without royal favor, is destined to leave his mark in Egypt."

"You mean—Senmut, again?"

"I speak of the priest Senmut, son of Hat-nefer."

Hat-shep-sut's eyes narrowed in quick irritation. "You carry your enthusiasm to extremes, My Lord. Senmut has many admitted excellencies, but the post of Royal Nurse requires a man, not a youth. A man with position, with background, with . . . The assignment carries grave responsibilities, My Lord," she ended weakly.

Aahmes bowed. "My grandson Paheri, now, a prince of the noble house of Nekheb—would Your Majesty, perhaps, consider him more eligible for the honor of Royal Nurse?"

"Certainly. Far more."

"Good. Now, here is something that I have hardly owned to myself, Majesty. The two youths, Senmut and Paheri, lunched with me today, and as we talked, as I watched them, the thought came, 'Which of the two is noble and which humble?' There was no choice in deportment or education, and the differences were those one might expect between brothers. However, for character and intelligence—I say this soberly and honestly—I would be prouder of Senmut for a grandson."

The queen was listening; he had captured her reluctant interest. He retold Senmut's ideas by which the children's minds could be stimulated, led step by step in growth. When he saw Her Majesty's nod, he decided upon a bold stroke.

"But Your Majesty knows best, of course. The wise leader gives as close attention to criticism as to agreement; closer, if he would have harmony in his house."

"Criticism?" The queen's eyebrows lifted.

"Many men, some of them of influence, remember Senmut's obscure parentage. They watch his every act, hoping to catch him in error so they may wag their heads and say, 'What can you expect of a farmer?' And you must see the parallel here, Majesty; for you, a woman on Egypt's throne, are also watched, and if one of your appointed ministers errs, the heads wag again: 'What can you expect of a woman playing king?'"

If he anticipated outburst and angry words, he was disappointed. Hat-shep-sut nodded thoughtfully and murmured, "A parallel? A bond, My Lord, another bond." She smiled at him, her eyes bright with mischief. "These head-waggers will talk, whatever I do?"

"You may plan on that as on Amon's love, Majesty."

"Then let us give them exercise." She nodded brightly. "Old Lord Ani died without heir, and his estates are crown property. They should be adequate, I think?"

"You mean . . ."

She offered him her hand to kiss, and her warmest smile. "My Lord, your precious Senmut will not be neglected. Go you to Nekheb and take with you the affection of Egypt and her queen."

CHAPTER VII

Year 11 of the Reign of Thothmes II

With Senmut and Penati beside him, Ineni rested in a shadowed place high on the southern arm of hills opposite Thebes.

There were several reasons for the feeling of satisfaction which, in recent months, he had found growing in his heart: the pressures of half a hundred duties now were being shared with able men trained to his exacting standards; he need no longer flog unwilling muscles to feats of endurance; his tomb was finished, and now he could relax a little. A sigh of rich contentment escaped him, and he answered the others' glances of startled concern with a nod.

"My soul will know happiness here."

His planning had been good. In life a rich man spent lavishly to surround his body with comfort and good things. Should the same thoughtful care be denied the soul, when the tomb is to be its house for eternity?

He waved his arm to indicate the scene below. "Look, everything that I have loved best in this world. The half-circle of cliffs, like a giant's bow with the Nile for its cord. Northward the river, a writhing serpent bearing the commerce of the world on its back. Eastward, close-packed to the far hills, mighty Thebes, king of cities."

He nodded again. "The gods have been generous; I have feasted, and nothing in and beyond life has been denied me. Family, wealth and titles and honors, and above everything the friends like you two and Tet, like the old king and Aahmes. And now this fine tomb . . ."

Senmut the loyal, Penati the faithful. Few of the monuments to Ineni's industry that were seeded throughout Egypt could have reached successful completion without these two. Many times in his career Ineni had been humbled by realization of his dependence upon others; his were the titles and to him went the praise and rewards for accomplishment, but often the mission would have died in its planning stage but for a Penati, a Nebtaui, a Nebiri, a Senmut.

He continued the thought aloud. "It is a valuable tool that I have fashioned for Hat-shep-sut's use—Penati's knowledge, Tet's skill, Senmut's vision. You three work together like fingers on a hand, with a dovetailing of talents that surprises even me who encouraged the development. You three will do good work for Her Majesty, and my spirit will watch from the fine tomb you built for it. . . ."

"Do not talk so, Master." There was desperate earnestness in Penati's cry. "You have years of useful work ahead."

Ineni said gently, "Death is not an ending; rather is it a beginning, the friendly opening of a door to stillness and to rest. Pictures are painted in the tombs, of nobles hunting and fishing, resting in flower-filled gardens, feasting with lovely women and enjoying tranquility, but in a prince's life these moments come rarely. There are compensations for royal favor, but there also are endless labors which the master alone must oversee.

"Aahmes felt as I feel," he continued, "when he left for Nekheb nearly five years ago. He said, 'Comforting to one whose work is finished is thought of the peace of the tomb.' And with a stupid king on the throne, Penati, zest has gone from living. And Aahmes said this, too; the world that we loved, Aahmes and I, died when the old king died."

Ineni realized that at times he missed the old general desperately. For all the surliness, he had been the best of companions, a friend to whom one brought moods with the certainty that they would be understood. A violent man, yet one capable of gentleness, of amazing personal sacrifices. He had voluntarily retired from the office of Royal Tutor because the princesses could learn from Senmut. "And," he had told Ineni, "there must be intimate contacts between Senmut and Hat-shep-sut if the boy is to reach the heights planned for him by Amon."

"You said you found a great change in Aahmes when you visited Nekheb two years ago?" asked Senmut.

"The same tough body, but a slackening grip on the day's affairs and preoccupation with those of the next life. He sat hour after silent hour within the portico of his splendid tomb in the hills, watching over the village of his birth. Storing memories against the solitude of death, Senmut." Ineni nodded slowly. "I was not surprised when word came that the fighting soul had slipped its earthly sheath and begun its journey to the Underworld."

He became conscious that Penati was watching him, worrying in his silent, puckered way, and felt shame for the selfish abstraction into which his thought had fallen. He roused himself and pointed to the bay of sand far below that filled the space between river and cliffs.

"Sometime," he said lightly, "you and Senmut go over the ruins of the old temple down there. The masters of six hundred years ago had a sound knowledge of engineering principles, and Senmut can learn something of the joining of limestone blocks, of placement of the blocks to avoid strain. And it's a curious plan for a temple—combination of terrace and pyramid. Sometime when you both need relaxing."

"Of course, Master."

"How is your tomb coming, Senmut? I meant to look at it with you today."

"Save your strength, Master. Tet was saying only last week . . ."

"Yes, yes." Ineni was touched by the constant solicitude for his welfare displayed by his friends. "I know, I am falling apart."

"No, Master, but—well, your head is always full of plans and your legs race to keep up. You must rest occasionally."

Ineni patted the younger man's knee. "Of course. See, I am resting now. What of your tomb?"

"The corridor is half dug, and the portico and supporting pillars are rough-finished. It will be a fine tomb."

"It will be if Penati oversees the work. The best artists only, when it is ready for decorating; you will become an important man and your tomb must be worthy."

He brooded silently for some moments and then said, "I confess to selfishness in urging that your tomb be near mine. While you live, my spirit can superintend the details and finishing, and

70

later there is the pleasant anticipation of association of souls for a thousand thousand years, here in this spot. You are a son to me; with faults, perhaps, and I may criticize the ethics involved in some of your operations, but I do find much to admire."

Penati nodded soberly. "We all know who work with you, Master, and we know your ambitions for Senmut; he will never disappoint you. He is young, of course, only twenty-six, but . . ."

Ineni chuckled easily. "You speak of my ambitions for Senmut, but apparently you know little of his ambitions for himself; for all his youth, he approaches the future with mature vision. Senmut, repeat for our friend the conversation we had last night. It will explain why my worries are few concerning your future."

"Well," said Senmut, smiling, "I see 'my future,' as you call it, as divided into two unequal parts: one influenced by Queen Hat-shep-sut's regency while her husband lives, and the other, and greater part, as minister to the young Thothmes when he assumes the throne, as he will when of age and married to Princess Neferu-Re. At present, of course, I am concerned with holding the queen's favor and establishing my worth in her eyes."

"In the past five years," Ineni interrupted, "he has made progress: the queen acknowledges the increased revenue from the estates and particularly the health and mental advancement of the princesses. Tell Penati what Her Majesty said to you last week, Senmut."

"Her Majesty is generous, Master. 'They are seeing for themselves, My Lord,' she said, 'thinking, and interpreting what they see, in terms of childhood, of course. There is a new and intelligent awareness in their reaction to happenings in their small world, and this awareness you gave them.' "

"Also," said Ineni, "Senmut's methods of teaching impress his own personality indelibly on the children's minds. You see, Penati? When Neferu-Re is Queen of Egypt, she may be expected to exert influence on Pharaoh's thinking, and Senmut, as a friend of her childhood, can hope for strong recommendation to her husband."

Penati was impressed. "You planned thus, Senmut?"

"With the master's help, of course. Also, I reason that material wealth will be important to a youngster coming to the throne—full granaries, impressive herds; the boy will see these evidences of prosperity and remember the official responsible for them. It will be seven years before Thothmes is sixteen, but I have a scheme already in operation."

"Explain it in detail, Senmut, as you did to me."

Senmut nodded and settled himself comfortably. "Well, Amon's estates and those of the princesses are found all over Egypt, as you know, Penati. So I prepared a map—both banks, from the marshes in the north to the cataract at Yebu—and colored the lands belonging to Amon in yellow and those of the princesses in green, each holding designated on the master-map by a number. All other lands, estates of the crown or of private owners, are uncolored as being of no interest to my need.

"Then I prepared a smaller detailed map of each one of the numbered districts, showing occupants, boundaries, roads, canals, and in a corner I noted the principal products of that district—wheat, a cheap wine, woven cloth, hoe handles, and so on. If there is a bad Nile, adjustment of the tax can be made without leaving Ineni's office; if there is a boundary dispute, the original placement of the stones is marked for our judgment."

"Now, Penati," said Ineni, "attend to this; this is the really ingenious part of his planning."

Senmut saluted his master with mock seriousness, and continued. "Each harvest-time I compare yields with the earlier reports of the assessors and plan the next year's crops accordingly. For instance, let us say that a farmer, A, with three grown sons to help, and with well-watered land, produces only eighty bushels, while the farmer B with one son and inferior land turns the same amount into the treasury. At the next planting, B will be established with his single helper on the well-watered land of higher yield and A moved to the poorer site. B, with his better knowledge and greater industry, will increase A's yield on the good land, and the latter's quota will be unchanged."

Penati frowned. "It is like uprooting a plant to move a farmer from the soil he knows; you will have stone-throwing and riots and strikes and worse."

"Not Senmut," said Ineni comfortably. "Thuti, now, Thuti could not do this, for he was born a prince and to him farmers are clods and scum; Thuti would sit in his office and issue orders—and then there *would* be trouble. But Senmut is not Thuti; Senmut was born a farmer and he knows how the poor

72

think and he knows the arguments to inspire them. He takes one like A aside and says . . . Tell him, Senmut."

"I say to him, 'I am looking for a good man who can handle a difficult farming problem north of here, and not just any man will do, but one who, like you, has studied and made himself expert. And there are two goats that go with the place. . . .' And on my trips I often take Ramose my father with me. The old man knows soil, and he digs in the earth with a toe and says, 'Wheat here,' or 'Beans here'; and he looks across the fields and says privately, 'The yield from these fields a hundred bushels.' Then I say to the farmer, 'Give me this year a hundred and ten bushels from these fields, and all above that amount is yours, tax free.' "

Penati shook his head. "Well," he began doubtfully.

"Now as I said"—Ineni spoke hurriedly—"some of Senmut's methods I do not approve. Once his position is established, however—he is kindly by nature and I am sure will not demand exorbitant sacrifice from anyone. He drives himself, you know that, Penati, harder than he drives those serving him."

The old man's voice faded to stillness in contemplating the amazing facets of character of his prized pupil. "Lord Senmut" now, with a modest palace, gardeners and maids and cooks, a personal steward and a harpist, an income which, to the mother and father, must seem like the limitless wealth of kings. A fine barque with captain and rowers, a chariot and horses, a pretentious tomb in the process of building—these last would do much to impress a society that rated a man's worth by the loudness of his claims and the exhibiting of his wealth.

Ineni, thinking thus, felt a surging of pride, and he thought, Senmut, this Senmut beside me now, is my real gift to Egypt. The temples and the shrines that I have built, the massive pylons and the obelisks, all raised for the glory of the gods and of their sons on earth, these are but symbols of the past, while Senmut is a living force and a promise for the future. And the future, for Egypt and for Senmut, looked bright from every view that Ineni could gain of it.

For some minutes Penati had been fidgeting. "Excuse me, Master," he said, "if we are to sail with the first light, I should be at the Temple Shops now. The queen's sarcophagus must be loaded on the barge tonight, and the gear, and Nebiri contacted to be sure the men are ready, and there's the food to check and . . ."

"Yes," said Ineni. "Yes, yes." He climbed stiffly erect. "Senmut can learn lessons in slave-driving from you," he grumbled affectionately. For a moment longer his gaze wandered far over the scene spread like a banquet for the refreshment of his spirit. "Of the three seasons of a year," he said quietly, "this, the growing season, is my favorite, I think, symbolizing the never-ending battle between Nature and man. Do you see the analogy, Penati—the waste-lands versus the farms, barrenness versus fertility, death versus life?"

"I like the season of flooding best," said Penati; "then the Nile runs full between its bank and stone can be loaded directly to the ships without hauling and lifting."

Ineni slapped his hands together in feigned irritation. "A practical man! . . . Come, Senmut, give me your arm."

A little over three weeks later, Ineni stepped from the stone-barge with Penati and Nebiri, three dirty and tired men, and shouldered a way along the crowded quay that reached into the Nile from a point near Amon's great temple. Their backs might ache and their legs sag, but, home in Thebes from a mission accomplished, their eyes were bright and they surveyed the multiple activities of the waterfront with the interest of strangers to the scene. Ineni sniffed and said drily, "Three weeks in the desert makes one critical of city smells—or does a dog lay dead in the neighborhood?"

At the place of parting Penati said, "You will want to rest a day or so, Master. I will bring a report, and later . . ."

"You visit the king's tomb tomorrow?"

"Just a routine inspection to see the work finished while we have been at the queen's tomb."

"I will meet you at the quay at daybreak."

"But, Master . . ."

"Now, the king's tomb is important, too, and you know his jealousies; I cannot work three weeks for Hat-shep-sut and then refuse to spend one day in Pharaoh's interests. Do you want him to have another of his spells?"

Bath and a shave and fresh linen revived in Ineni a greater need for gossip and news than for sleep. And it was easy to argue himself into attending the Temple's evening ceremony; Senmut would be there, there always was business to talk with Neb-taui, and drawings or inscriptions to check with Tet. . . .

Ineni never entered the great House of Amon alone. Beside him walked always a memory and a ghost, a bent figure with corded legs, and wearing the enameled apron, the towering white and red crowns of royalty. And the thin and reedy command of the old king sounded in Ineni's ears: "Make for my Father Amon a house of stone, a house befitting the dignity and the majesty of the King of all the Gods."

Before the days of the old king there had been a building where Amon was worshipped by the king's fathers, a place of scant significance, little more than a chapel. Ineni had added to the chapel, following laws older than the ancient written records. These laws required that all Egypt's temples be constructed on the same general plan: a progression from light to the mystery of total darkness (from life to death), from a lower to a higher plane (from earth to heaven). Thus, on entering a temple from blazing sunlight, one mounted a step into a cool and shadowed portico, then another step into a dim-lit hall. Pharaoh and the high orders of priesthood alone were privileged to mount the third step to the secret chambers, where, in the blackness and silence of a tomb, the god dwelt.

Ineni went in by a side portal, greeting the ancient attendant who presided over the ablutions which all who visited the House of the God must perform, passed chambers where vestments and temple furniture were stored, and came to the vastness of the inner hall. It was a quiet hour between ceremonies when Amon brooded.

The great wall lamps were not alight and there was no sound or movement to disturb the pleasant drifting of Ineni's thought. He, as Overseer of All the Works of the King in the Temple of Amon, had been responsible for everything that now met his gaze; almost, he sometimes thought, to the placing of every stone in each of the three pylons, to the erecting of every column in the colonnaded halls, of every statue in their planned niches.

As he paced the shadows, his mind sampled tidbits from a diet of rich experience, and one embraced Senmut's astonishment, almost revulsion, when, on the occasion of his initiation into the priesthood, he learned from Ineni that the god hidden behind the veil, who owned great houses and vast wealth, for whom thousands labored and whose name millions feared—this god was a lump of heavy stone, roughly shaped and a foot high and blue in color!

Ineni had explained that the stone was but the emblem by which the god was recognized, the inanimate shell in which the god's soul sometimes dwelt. Senmut's idealism was shaken and Ineni hurried to explain further: like the mummy of a man, stiff, inert, a shell without the power of breath or movement. Like a boat, a skiff without a rower, Ineni said—that was a good comparison to the stone when the god's spirit was absent. A skiff, alone, could not direct its course, it was an empty thing and useless, prey to wind and current, drifting aimlessly. But when the rower entered, it pushed against the river and gathered riches from far lands and went here and there at the will of the rower and became alive. So with the stone. The High Priest, by his magic, could tell when the god was within; for others, it was safest if they treated it always respectfully and reverently.

The subject was not mentioned again, and perhaps Senmut accepted the fiction; he served the god with enthusiasm and profit, and Ineni was not inclined to question whether or not his pupil's beliefs were orthodox. Many priests—Ineni himself—although submerging themselves in study of the deeper mysteries, remained skeptics regarding certain phases of doctrine.

An under-priest moved silently along the walls igniting the huge lamps, and grotesque shifting shadows added their touch of solemn mystery calculated to give extra significance to the parade of the god. Early comers, mostly initiates and the lower orders, arrived and gathered in buzzing groups along the sides of the great hall, whispering, giggling, pushing, pinching—the restrained horseplay by which youth in all ages has declared its timid defiance to authority. Mainly they were good boys. Sometimes they fought among themselves, or drank too much beer; a few, fancying a necessity to prove themselves men, might steal in shamefaced groups to some brothel, swaggering a little, hiding their shame at contact with debauchery and disease. But in the main they were good boys, the priests and the merchants and the princes of tomorrow, and they bobbed their heads as Ineni passed, and he spoke their names. When Neb-taui, kher-heb and

76

reader of the ritual, emerged from the shadows, Ineni stepped across the hall to greet him.

There was affection and respect in the meeting between the two old priests. Ineni's admiration for this friend of a lifetime was heightened by his ability—which Ineni envied—to shut non-essentials out of a busy life. Activities of temporal significance had little meaning for Neb-taui; hosts of servants might care for the god's daily needs, other praise him with song and dancing, with wordy prayers and exacting ritual, still others foster his wealth. Neb-taui's work, to which his existence was devoted, was the study and understanding of the demands made by all the gods on men, and interpretation of his findings. Living in this rarefied atmosphere accented the sweetness and serenity of a naturally gentle nature; he was loved, even by politicians whose piety was a feeble thing and subject to pressures.

Tonight the customary serenity of his expression was broken by signs of inner tumult; after the greeting, he tucked his arm through Ineni's. "Your return today is an answer to prayer, Ineni. Walk with me until time for the service."

They paced slowly between the gathering rows of white-robed priests, and Neb-taui's agitation became increasingly apparent. "I really need your counsel. You have seen how ill is our king— unable to walk without assistance, demanding constant attendance of the physicians. . . . I have had recurring dreams, Ineni, of disturbing significance. Once I saw a hawk flying erratically, lurching from side to side with heavy and uneven wing-beat. It was in distress, fighting for breath, dying in the air. As I watched, it plunged to earth, struggled, and was dead."

He wiped his shining pate.

"Another time I saw a nest, and in it a half-grown hawk of noble plumage. It could not fly for cords that bound its wings against its body. Its spirit was untamed, however, and it fixed me with fiery gaze. And still another dream, most vivid: the young hawk fighting its silent battle for freedom, while rats and other vermin attacked the nest, nibbling and tearing until it was destroyed."

The old man's voice slowed to silence, and Ineni felt his own blood congeal in his veins; such a vision coming to Neb-taui must not be ignored. "Have you told this to Her Majesty?"

"Not yet; I wanted your advice. You understand it as I do?"

"It is a warning direct from the gods," Ineni agreed. "The king is dying, and no heir has been appointed to succeed him."

"And the rats . . ."

"Egypt's enemies, swarming, picking her bones."

"Exactly." Neb-taui nodded vigorous delight over his friend's agreement. "Why does Her Majesty delay? I sympathize with her reluctance to sacrifice a daughter to the son of one she holds in contempt, but the gods must have planned it so. There is no substitute for Pharaoh's son, and the law—the law says that Pharaoh's son by a common woman can never become king unless married to one of solar blood."

"I know. If Pharaoh should be called to his fathers this night . . . She must be made to see. Your dreams are not enough in themselves—they must be augmented by some display of the god's direct intervention."

A golden thread of sound, the first faint chanting signaling start of the ceremony, wound from the darkened recesses of the temple and Ineni had but time to whisper, "Say nothing to the queen until I talk further with you." Neb-taui nodded and the two priests hurried to their respective stations.

The sides of the great hall now were lined solidly with white-robed participants. Everyone was there, Ineni noticed—priests, ministers, princes, the great and the near-great. The queen had not arrived, but at the end of the hall farthest from the altar was the prince, the king's son, at his station Pillar-of-his-Mother, one of the lesser offices in temple hierarchy; short for his nine years, with the large family nose, and with the Horus lock, worn by young princes in honor of the god, plaited and hanging below his right shoulder.

Senmut made a sign of greeting, edged near and whispered, "Welcome home, Master. No trouble?"

Ineni smiled. "The queen's sarcophagus rests in the corridor of her tomb, bound in hides for protection. Penati will move it to the tomb-chamber when the artists are finished there."

"Tet can sleep again. After all, months of work in hollowing and smoothing the stone and cutting the inscription, his anxiety is . . . is . . . is . . ."

Ineni looked up in surprise. Hat-shep-sut was entering the hall and Senmut, until she reached her place beside the altar, forgot to breathe. The old man had seen this reaction in his pupil before when the queen came into a room suddenly, and it worried him. This was more than reverence for royalty and she would be offended if she noticed; he must warn Senmut. . . .

A whisper of astonishment sounding through the hall broke his thought. Pharaoh, leaning heavily on the arms of the Royal Steward and the Royal Physician, entered and advanced toward the Station of the King. Not in months had he left his bed to officiate at a temple service, and it needed no second glance to tell all present that illness was not feigned. The emaciated body rode precariously on legs that seemed incapable of bearing even this feeble weight, and the towering double crown added an intolerable burden; his expression was one of tortured wonder that the gods could so misuse one whom they set so high. In startling contrast, Hat-shep-sut stood, regal in bearing, contained, possessed of an unearthly and shining beauty that lent credence to the popular story of her divine origin. Certainly, seeing the two together, Pharaoh and his queen, no one could reasonably doubt which the gods favored.

Neb-taui, as kher-heb, began the reading of the ritual, speaking in the true voice which alone commanded the ear of the god. The voices of the unseen singers, men and women both, grew in volume: "Amon is the rudder of truth. . . . Thou art he that giveth bread. . . . Thou art our strong defender, our Bull, our Mighty One." Amon's concubines appeared, the gayest and fairest of the daughters of the princes of Thebes, followed by the dancers of Amon. Then the altar smoked, and a roaring thunder of chanting: "Amon the King of the Gods. Amon the Sun. Hail to Amon the Strong Bull. . . ."

The god entered, borne in his golden boat on the shoulders of solemn, slow-paced priests who swung their arms to the measured rhythm of the chanting, to the beat of tambourines and the silvery chatter of sistrums. "The beginning of wisdom is the way of Amon. . . . Strong is Amon, fulfilling desires. . . ." The god was hidden behind a drawn curtain, and his coming produced a progressive undulation in the ranks of worshippers as backs bent in reverence or fear.

Ineni forgot the ceremony in watching the pitiful shell of the man who, with the First Prophet, fed the altar's flames and poured the libations. As always, Pharaoh's attention wandered and tonight it lit with a fevered wildness on his queen; there

79

was no doubt that Pharaoh hated, with the smoldering viciousness of the weak, her mind and strength and health, the very ground she touched. Ineni had seen it grow, this hatred, fattening, eating the king's heart like a poison.

The ceremony neared its end. Ineni bowed with the rest as the god's barque, finishing its circuit of the hall, crept slowly past; there was a pause before the altar while Neb-taui intoned the words of the ritual and while clouds of incense bathed the barque and its bearers. The concubines disappeared, and the dancers—and then Ineni stiffened. Something was wrong. Instead of following the escort into the recesses behind the altar, it was as if a powerful hand pulled the bearers to the left to begin the march again!

There were murmurs, then exclamations from all sides; Ineni stretched on tiptoe. The bearers seemed as surprised as the audience—he saw sweat and terror on their faces, and their ordered step, in which they were drilled daily, was broken. Someone screamed.

It was unprecedented. The barque jostled and rocked as the frightened bearers sought to guide it, to control its jerking progress. Men of dignity and learning prostrated themselves to cries of "Beware the wrath of Amon," "Be merciful, O Amon our Protector!"

Ineni felt a tugging at his arm. "Look—look, Master," said Senmut. "Look at Pharaoh."

The king, oblivious of the commotion, the shouts and prayers that enveloped him, stood with neck outstretched, burning eyes fastened on Hat-shep-sut, hatred straining every taut muscle.

Senmut whispered, "A trick of some kind; he'd be first to frighten, otherwise."

A fresh outburst of shouted prayers drew Ineni's attention to the far end of the hall. The barque was motionless, and now the bearers, strain and pull as they might, could not move it. If this is a trick, said Ineni to himself, it was superbly rehearsed. The barque stood squarely in front of the station Pillar-of-his-Mother, in front of the king's son, the boy Thothmes, who remained rigid and white-faced, staring with fear-filled eyes at the veil that hid the god. The boy does not know, Ineni thought; he's as startled as the rest of us. There came a shout—Hapu-seneb's bull-throated roar: "It is a sign!"

A cry echoed joyously by a hundred throats. A dozen of the highest in Pharaoh's court hurried to the prince's side—and miraculously the barque moved again, the bearers stepping with their customary measured pace.

Pandemonium broke in the hall. The boy was advanced to the altar, and through the uproar Ineni heard the sick king pronounce him heir to the throne of Egypt, "by order of My Father Amon, King of all the Gods."

Who? thought Ineni in his bed as he surrendered himself at last to earned rest. Not Pharaoh—he has not the wit. Not Neferperet—he lacks the courage. Hardly Thuti or Hapu-seneb—they are young. But—would they dare? It was planned, well rehearsed. No, not Amon the god, but a mortal who can command or bribe the bearers. . . .

"Anyway," he mumbled drowsily, "the succession now is assured; the queen now must agree to betrothal of the princess to young Thothmes. She may defy convention and the king, but she dare not defy Amon."

CHAPTER VIII

Year 12 of the Reign of Thothmes II

The two girls, intent on their exciting new game, did not hear Lord Senmut's approach.

Meryt leaned far over the parapet that rimmed the palace roof; Princess Neferu-Re, eight years to the other's seven and conscious of this gulf that never could be crossed, watched her sister with amused tolerance. She kept carefully to the shade cast by the gay awning of the pavilion, an erect figure, with her mother's eyes and a slimness and frailty of her own.

"It *is* a fowling skiff," Meryt called.

"A farmer's raft," Neferu-Re repeated with quiet insistence.

"How can you say that? I can see the recurve of the prow."

"What you see is probably a pile of vegetables."

Meryt, with fine disregard for her freshly laundered gown, scrambled across the intervening space and snatched a writing board which leaned against an awning support. "I identified it, so that allows me two marks."

"Meryt, you're not sure. It *could* be a farmer's raft."

"May I help, ladies?" said Senmut.

Neferu-Re, instantly composed, smiled her welcome, while Meryt caught his hand and pulled him toward the parapet. "Lord Senmut, she is simply poisonous," Meryt cried. "And blind, and stubborn as Lady Sit-Re. Look—to the north, on the other bank of the river, half-hidden in the reeds. It *is* a fowling skiff. See?"

"This is a momentous decision?"

"Of course. Neferu-Re saw the boat first, so she is allowed one mark; but the first to identify it may make two marks. See, I have . . . Wait—I have drawn twelve marks already, and Neferu-Re . . ."

"I will count my own," said Princess Neferu-Re. "Here.

There are thirteen marks on my board," she announced proudly.

"You see?" Meryt hopped up and down. "It *has* to be a fowling skiff!"

"I'm afraid . . ." said Senmut slowly. "Yes, I must disappoint you both; he just cast his net, and that is a fisherman in his boat. Who invented this excellent game?"

"Meryt did," said Neferu-Re generously; the younger sister, deprived of victory, looked as if she might burst into tears. "It passes the time very well," Neferu-Re added gravely, remembering that her mother the queen might consider this simple amusement trivial for a future Queen of Egypt. "You look tired, My Lord," she added in her best conversational tone. "Sit here, on this stool between us, and tell us what affairs of state have occupied you."

"Tell us another story," Meryt demanded, recovered from her pique and hitching her stool nearer. "About the magician who drained the Nile to find Pharaoh's lost pearl, or . . ."

"Perhaps Lord Senmut is not in the mood for stories, Meryt."

"On the contrary," said Senmut. "It is refreshing to the spirit to think of something other than tax reports and building plans, while resting with two of Egypt's loveliest ladies."

Meryt clapped her hands with delight. "That is the way he talks to Her Majesty!" she cried.

"Oh—I forgot," Neferu-Re exclaimed in dismay. "You asked us to remind you to take offerings to Lord Ineni's tomb."

"Thanks, Your Royal Highness." Senmut bowed and smiled at her. "I left a jar of his favorite wine there this morning, and some of the figs he liked best. He chose the site well, and I know that his soul is satisfied. There are flowers growing beside the tomb—did I tell you? About two months after he died I found that a small desert shrub had rooted in that dry place. I watered and tended it, and now it is blooming, for the master's enjoyment."

"Can Lord Ineni really see the flowers and smell the fragrance? His soul, I mean?" Meryt's eyes searched his anxiously.

"So the students of the mysteries assure us. The magic of the burial ceremony restores life to the spirit; it may be invisible to our eyes, but it achieves the journey to the Underworld, you know."

"Is it a difficult journey? Does the dead soul ever lose the way?"

"A guide for the soul is included in all proper burials. Perhaps I could tell a story about such a journey. Would you like that?"

"About Lord Ineni's journey?" asked Neferu-Re doubtfully.

"No. A story about the Mayor of Tu-shennet, the town where I was born."

"Oh, yes, yes."

Meryt wiggled closer and propped her chin on two small fists. Neferu-Re smoothed a wrinkle from her dress and folded her hands.

"Don't use big words, will you, My Lord?" Meryt cautioned.

"I shall be careful," Senmut promised. "Now, the Mayor of Tu-shennet, you should know, was a fussy man, so his modest tomb on the west bank was ready and arrangements with the local priests completed long before he died. Linen was set aside for his use in the Underworld, his finest staffs, a favorite pot or two, a bed—familiar objects with which he was comfortable. He even paid a local artist to carve a half-dozen Ushab-ti figures, the servants of the dead who, at their master's call, perform all labors assigned him.

"He had asked many questions and felt that he knew what would be expected of him. There would be a papyrus, said the priests; he needed but to follow its instructions. Will the papyrus be in my hand? Yes, the priests assured him, it would be in his hand. So the mayor was comforted and forgot the matter.

"Then years later he sickened and his body was filled with torment. The physicians tried to help, but he felt himself drifting—drifting.

"He awoke from what seemed refreshing sleep, and noticed that someone had extinguished the lamp that always burned in his chamber—also that he felt no pain. He lifted a hand to the place where the pain had been, and heard a crackling sound. A roll of new papyrus was clutched tightly in the hand.

"He lay a long while in the dark and quiet, thinking. For the first time in months his body was free of pain. If he was still in his small palace at Tu-shennet, someone would enter presently and light the lamp, and he would have to move and leave this newly found comfort—the utter silence and peace. Wonderful, he thought, and sighed.

84

"It was the sigh that roused him. Some word of the priest spoken years before: 'When you waken . . .'—that was it. The kingdom of the dead lay to the west of Egypt, the priest had said. 'When you waken, go to the west.'

"He sighed again and arose, still clutching the precious roll in his hand, shuffled in the darkness with hands held before him —and passed through the wall of the tomb into the blinding light of day!"

"Right through the wall? Without hurting himself?"

"He was a spirit," Neferu-Re whispered.

Senmut nodded. "He looked about him, blinking. There, across the river to the east, were the distant sycamores of Tu-shennet—home and family and friends, the familiar. To the west were gorges and mountains and desert—the unknown. He sat in the sun beside his tomb to think this over. And saw two women approaching.

"The mayor recognized them as residents of Tu-shennet whose father had died some time earlier. One carried water in a jar and the other a small bundle of vegetables, and he waited until they were near and then waved to them. They paid no attention, so he called, 'Hallo.' They looked about in a startled manner, and he called, 'Over here, by my tomb.' And the women shrieked and fled."

"Why?" said Meryt.

"They could not see him, silly," said Neferu-Re. "He was invisible. Isn't that it, Lord Senmut?"

"His mummy rested snugly within the tomb." Senmut nodded. "This was his ka, his invisible spirit. Thoughtfully, the mayor unrolled his papyrus and read that the soul must climb the mountains to the west and search there for the guide that would lead him to the Fields of Aahlu. He glanced upward and saw that Re in his sun-boat was approaching from the east, a child yet in his brief day. By noon, Re would be grown to the vigor and strength of manhood, and by evening Re would be wizened and ready for the tomb of night. Time was wasting. The mayor rerolled his papyrus and turned his back on Re in the sun-boat, and stepped toward the mountains that rimmed the world on the west. And as he walked, he felt youth renewing in his body, and he strode along, whistling the tune of a song nearly forgotten, a song of the inundation. Do either of you know the words of the song?"

"Wait," said Meryt. "Yes, these are the words:

" 'When the tanks are full of fresh water,
  And the earth overflows with god's love.' "

"Good," said Senmut. "That was the song the mayor whistled. Then he stilled his whistling, for ahead he saw two figures walking like himself toward the west, a large man with a belly and with spindly legs, and a child."

Meryt clapped her hands again. "How old is the child?"

"Let me see," said Senmut, "a pretty boy, about six years, with an eagerness in his eyes that the mayor liked to see in children. He did not know the boy, but he recognized the man as a master carpenter of Tu-shennet."

"Were they also spirits?" said Neferu-Re. "And can the spirits see one another?"

"The mayor was not sure, so he waited until he neared them. Then the master carpenter stopped and looked at him sourly and said, 'So you do not speak to a friend now that you wear a fine apron with a gold thread worked into it.' "

"The spirits can see one another!" Neferu-Re said happily.

"So it seems. 'You can see me? You are a spirit, then,' said the mayor, 'you and the child here?'

" 'Aye.' The master carpenter sighed. 'After a year's sickness. It is good to be rid of the sickness.'

" 'And the boy, here—this is your son?'

" 'No, he joined me after we left the burial place.'

"The three faced the mountains again, and the mayor felt a hand steal into his and saw the child smiling up at him. 'Well,' said the mayor, and rubbed the boy's head playfully. 'How did you get here?'

" 'A serpent bit me. See, here is the mark, on my leg.'

"They were entering rough country and there was little breath for talking; these were the foothills of the mountains that rimmed the world—deep gullies, canyons pinched out of weathered rock, boulders that blocked the way. Re passed them, flaming, brilliant in his manhood, and they labored—yet the mayor felt no fatigue. He even helped the others, the boy with his shorter legs, the master carpenter with his huge belly. This one carried his belly in both hands, lifted it as he climbed, and groaned at each step.

" 'There is still pain, friend?" asked the mayor.

" 'No, no, but the bonds of habit are strong. I have groaned with every step for over a year and I forget that it is no longer necessary.'

"The mayor nodded understandingly. 'You have a holy writing to guide you to the Islands of the Blessed?'

" 'No, a writing might be lost and then where would I be? No'—the master carpenter tapped his forehead—'it is all here. I paid a priest of the temple to read it to me, over and over, till it was firmly in my memory. It took some time.'

" 'I should think so,' marveled the mayor, showing his papyrus. 'Your head must feel stuffed with all this inside it.'

" 'No, really.' The master carpenter hitched his belly. 'A little each day—the priest was a patient man.'

"The mayor shook his head. 'Come now, how well did you learn? What shall you watch for, beyond the mountains there, to guide you further?'

"The master carpenter stopped, and screwed his face. 'Wait, now. One thing at a time. I cannot think while I am walking. Beyond the mountains? Hum-m . . .'

" 'Is it a bee?'

"The master carpenter beat his hands. 'No—no. I almost had it. Hum-m . . . No, not a bee . . . Ah, a butterfly. Or a bird . . . No, a butterfly, I am sure.'

" 'My holy papyrus says it is a grasshopper.'

"The other's face strained with the effort of his thinking. 'No, I am sure; a butterfly—or a bird.'

"They moved on, stopping occasionally to argue.

" 'A butterfly . . .'

" 'A grasshopper . . .'

" 'The priest . . .'

" 'My writing . . .'

"And came at last to the heights and gazed eagerly, stared in dismay.

" 'Sand,' groaned the master carpenter. 'More sand and heat. We have no water, no food. We shall perish.'

" 'The writing,' said the mayor, 'tells of a sycamore tree in the

87

desert to which a grasshopper shall lead us and where food will be found.'

" 'It was a bird—or a butterfly. And—yes, now I remember the sycamore.'

"Then came the heat in shimmering waves from the desert and a wind driving fine sand against their faces. The child cried and the men shielded their eyes and hurried and watched on all sides. And Re was far ahead of them now and growing feeble as he neared the end of his day.

"The child was the first to see it, a small brown grasshopper that whirled past and tumbled to the sand, gathered its legs and leaped again. The master carpenter followed unwillingly where the mayor and the boy led in eager pursuit of the heaven-sent guide. To right and to left, in erratic flight, the mayor and the child darting, calling, the master carpenter toiling in the rear and lugging his great burden and sweating. If they lost their guide they might never see the magic tree with its promise of shelter and sustenance—to left, to right, over rocks, deeper into the heat, into the curse of the stinging wind.

"Again the boy was the first to see it—the tree, hidden in a basin, green in a waste of gray. The three hurried, stumbled into the basin and fell on their faces in the tree's shadow. And presently, when the mayor rolled to his back and stretched, he saw a woman's face smiling from the depths of the leaves. The goddess of the magic tree was like a flower for loveliness, and her arms, when she leaned and offered fruits and sweet-cakes and water, were slender and of the grace of reeds tossed in a breeze. And while they ate their fill and drank of the sweet water, Re died and the world slipped slowly into night.

"Suddenly the master carpenter groaned. 'I just remembered,' he said. 'We should not have eaten the food offered by the divine one; now we can never return to the land of the living without the gods' permission.' "

"What a beautiful story, My Lord," said a voice from behind them. "That is not the end?"

"Your Majesty!" Senmut and the girls scrambled to their feet and bowed. Hat-shep-sut stepped through the doorway of the pavilion, and Meryt ran to her.

"Did you hear, Your Majesty? It was the little boy who saw the grasshopper, and found the magic tree, and saved them all!"

"I heard." The queen, followed by Lady Sit-Re, seated herself on one of the stools, and Neferu-Re adjusted a cushion to support her mother's feet. "Be seated, My Lord; the children will be comfortable on these cushions. Your tale, My Lord Senmut, suggests an astonishing acquaintance with the mysteries."

"Superficial, I fear, Your Majesty, and gained more in listening to Neb-taui than from study."

"You repeat the details well, and I feel that I could recognize your mayor of Tu-shennet. Were all the characters of the story drawn from life—for instance, the goddess in the tree?"

"From life, Your Majesty."

Neferu-Re thought that her mother was so beautiful when she allowed herself to smile that way, the lips, usually so straightly drawn, softening, and little crinkly lines spreading for a moment from the corners of her eyes. "You like the story, don't you, Your Majesty?"

"Very much, child." Hat-shep-sut touched her daughter lightly on the cheek and then nodded to Senmut. "Continue, My Lord."

"But, Your Majesty, it is a tale intended to amuse Their Royal . . ."

Lady Sit-Re interrupted dryly. "The queen also chooses to be amused. You heard her command."

Hat-shep-sut sighed and said to Senmut, "That was an idle wind blowing, My Lord. You will ignore it."

"If you insist, Your Majesty." Senmut bowed and Neferu-Re thought for a moment that he was laughing.

"To continue the tale," he said soberly. "Four days they rested beneath the tree, while the mayor read aloud from his papyrus and the master carpenter checked his memory—this to be said to the crocodiles, this to render passable the lakes of boiling water, this to paralyze unknown monsters. The master carpenter's memory was a stubborn thing and moved only after vigorous prodding, and then often in the wrong direction and must be coaxed and led and pushed until at last it stumbled over the correct answer.

"They worried about the boy. He had come unprepared to face the perils of the journey, with neither writing nor priest's whispered words. The mayor decided to keep him always by his side, and when emergencies arose, to read the words and let the boy repeat them.

"On the fifth day the goddess of the tree loaded their arms with all good things, and they started again on their travels. Beyond the tree they found a fat land with lush meadows and lazy rivers, with marshes bright with darting birds, a peaceful land. But here, within an hour, the worth of the papyrus was tested.

"A serpent glided from a thicket and stretched its evil length across their path, and it was a frightful thing, with reared head and lightning tongue, with death in its golden eyes. The writing shook so in the mayor's hands that he could not read; when he found the words, his tongue was stiff and he could not utter them. The serpent advanced, swaying, weaving its flat head; it towered above them like a palm and its mouth widened. The child screamed and the master carpenter beat his head to gather the words the priest had taught him and which would drive off the monster.

"The mayor found his tongue at last and spoke the words written on the papyrus. But his voice was thin with fear, and not the true voice which was required to make the magic effective. He read: 'Hail, thou serpent; advance not hither. . . . Thou, god Shu, behold the being who is about to eat me. . . . O serpent, depart from me, for I am the god Shu. . . .'

"The serpent withdrew its head a little and swayed and watched with its cruel golden eyes, but because this was not the true voice, it came again with jaws agape to devour them. And the mayor found his voice, the true voice, and repeated the magic words: 'Hail, thou serpent; advance not hither. . . .'

"And the serpent hissed in anger and circled them—then darted at the child who had not spoken. The mayor made him repeat the magic hastily; the master carpenter also, using his richest tones. And the serpent left them, writhing into its thicket, and was gone. And they wiped the sweat and thanked the gods and praised the good papyrus.

"And one thing they had learned—that the magic protected only him who spoke it.

"Other adventures they had—a beast higher than a house with a tail at both ends, a monster that destroyed trees of the forest as if they were reeds, disappeared in a fury when they recited the passage which dealt with strange monsters. Crocodiles, too, waiting in the river and submerged like the trunks of dead trees, snapped their jaws and lashed the river with their tails when the correct passage was intoned.

"Walls of flame rushed upon them and surrounded them, leaped high above their heads and reached hungry tongues and roared with the sound of a thousand demons. But the magic was stronger than the fire, and a path opened in the flames and they passed beyond the burning. And came, at last, to the great river where the apes cast their nets for the souls of men.

"The apes were hairy monsters with great arms who walked upright like men, and even talked among themselves in a curious, chirping language. They waded hip-deep in the shallows, and there was no way to cross but to wade with them. The three companions hid long in the bushes rehearsing the magic words.

" 'Hail to Thoth,' mumbled the mayor, and the others repeated after him. 'Hail to Thoth, who didst snare the enemies of Osiris with their own nets. I am Horus, the son of Osiris, and I have come to see my father Osiris.'

"At last the mayor sighed and untied his girdle. 'Come. Make your clothes into a bundle, and keep beside me. Here, I will carry the child on my shoulder.'

"They entered the water boldly, for the magic had not failed them yet. But the apes also were bold and came wading from all the river, hurrying, with muzzles outthrust, and uttering cries. The apes fought the magic with shouts and great splashing, trying to drown the true voices. Some sought with their nets to snare the unhappy travelers, but Thoth heard the true voices above the din and spoiled the cast of the nets, and the friends gained to the middle of the river.

"Then the master carpenter, striking at the nets with his stick and shouting, 'I am Horus, I am the son of Osiris,' stepped into a hole and disappeared. The mayor struggled through the press of apes but saw, when the master carpenter reappeared, that the soaking had done his memory no good; he looked about wildly and opened his mouth, but no sound came. Then the child and the mayor both screamed, 'Hail to Thoth!' And the other repeated the phrase mechanically and then with full voice, and Thoth smiled and caused a hopeless tangle among the nets.

And the three dragged themselves, sick and spent, to the reeds on the far shore.

"The dangers of the journey were past, for presently the goddess Hathor, Lady of Heaven, appeared as a cow and took them on her broad back and carried them over marsh and mountain to the shores of the Lake of Kha. And a magic boat received them there; the sails filled and the rudder creaked and they flew over the mirrored lake like a bird soaring. And thus they came at last to the Islands of the Blessed, to the judgment of the king of the dead, Osiris."

Meryt hugged herself with glee. "Oh, I am glad. They were saved; all three were saved!"

"That master carpenter!" Lady Sit-Re spat the words. "That one is a weak and stupid fool, and does he deserve paradise?"

"My Lady!" Hat-shep-sut looked at her in surprise. "A fable, told to amuse children and simple folk like your queen? And you enjoyed it?"

Sit-Re mumbled, "The priest tells it well."

"Then silence while My Lord continues."

"There are more dangers?" said Neferu-Re nervously.

Senmut reassured her. "The dead soul that survives the journey to the Underworld and then proves itself worthy before the throne of Osiris, that soul becomes a god and lives eternally."

"And if it is found unworthy?"

"The wicked and the evil souls are known no more, in heaven or on earth."

"These were good souls, weren't they? Please, Lord Senmut . . ."

Senmut nodded gently. "And Osiris is just."

"Of course." Her fingers interlaced tightly. "I—please continue, My Lord."

"The mayor," said Senmut, "had guessed all along that Heaven was a wonderful city—like Thebes, with its palaces and temples and throngs, only grander, of course. But he was not prepared for long avenues paved with shining gold, pylons that touched the stars, splendid banners, and gods and goddesses attended by kings and princes. And neither had he expected that these divinities would conduct him, and the master carpenter and the child, in solemn procession to the Judgment Hall.

"Osiris sat on his throne at the far end, brooding, in a mysterious twilight and within a shrine of gold and dully gleaming stones. Motionless, awful in majesty, in secret power. His eyes were closed, yet the mayor knew that the god watched him. Deliberating, weighing. The mayor chanced a glance and felt the skin crawl over his bones. The stern face, green in color, topped by a white diadem and plumes; the green hands, crossed and holding the crook and scourge of sovereignty; the tight, white bandaging from chin to toes; the red necklace, pendant on a breast that knew no breathing.

"Osiris, King of the Dead.

"The mayor and the master carpenter and the child fell on their faces, 'smelled the earth' before the Presence. Someone lifted the mayor and led him forward; someone placed an object in his hands—his heart, accomplice of his earthly sins and virtues, and offered now for Osiris' clemency. He heard his own voice from afar, making the recitation demanded of the dead before the Judge of the Dead.

" 'Hail to thee, great god, Lord of Truth.' This was not the true voice, but a weak and stumbling thing. 'I come before thee; I see thy beauties. . . .' Osiris made no movement and the voice grew in courage: 'I know thy name; I bring thee Truth; I have destroyed sins for thee. I am pure. There is no crime against me in the land. . . . Save thou me from the gods who are with thee in the Hall of Judgment, for I am pure. I am pure.'

"The mayor turned to the forty-two judges who squatted before the throne of Osiris, each judging one of the forty-two sins man might commit in his life on earth. He stopped before each in turn, reading the god's name from the papyrus and disclaiming participation in the crime which that particular god considered.

" 'Hail, thou who art embraced by the flame, I have not robbed with violence. . . . Hail, thou whose legs are long, I have not committed theft. . . . Hail, thou double source of the Nile, I have not uttered evil words. . . . Hail, thou who goest backwards, I have not defiled purity. . . . Hail, thou who givest knowledge, I have not judged hastily. . . . Hail, thou whose head is holy, I have not cursed the gods. . . .'

"Before each of the forty-two the mayor offered the Negative

Confession, then returned to Osiris. 'Grant, great Lord of Truth, that the deceased may come unto thee, he who hath neither lied, nor done evil, nor committed crime; who feedeth on truth. Speak not against him, for his mouth is pure.'

"Before the throne of Osiris, the acts of the mayor already were being weighed in the great golden balance. Thoth presided, placing the mayor's heart in one pan of the scale and the feather of truth in the other pan. Each of the forty-two judges in turn laid his act beside the feather and Thoth made a mark on his record, crediting the mayor when the beam tipped one way, assessing the mayor when the heart weighed heavy. The mayor watched with his breath between his teeth and groaned whenever a mark was set against him. Thoth saw his agonies and in compassion touched the scale occasionally to make it bear in the mayor's favor. When all the acts were weighed, Thoth cast the total, figuring with his reed on a leaf of the palm tree. The mayor, hot and cold by turns, waited in numbed terror.

"Thoth finished with his reckoning and spoke before the throne. 'Thus saith Thoth, scribe of the Great God, to his father Osiris: "Behold the deceased in this Hall of Truth. The heart of the deceased hath been weighed in the golden balance in the presence of the great ones. The heart of the deceased hath been found true." '

"Then Osiris reached his right hand and touched with the crook the place on the mayor's breast where his heart had been. And made of the mayor a pure soul, a god among gods, living forever."

There was a moment of silence in the pavilion, then Meryt whispered, "Oh, yes—yes. Oh, My Lord, that is the best story you ever told us."

"The others, too, My Lord?" said Neferu-Re. "The child and the master carpenter?"

"All three, yes."

"Are you sure, My Lord?" Hat-shep-sut looked a little shocked. "Kings and commoners both? The scholars say this?"

"In the earliest times, Your Majesty, it was taught that divinity was accorded members of the royal family only, but now it is generally agreed that all who pass the judgment live in equality."

"But that is stupidity and nonsense," scoffed Sit-Re.

"No," the queen interrupted, "the golden balance would not weigh falsely, and in the heart of Osiris an honest man, whatever his birth, would be considered worthy. Yes, My Lord, I like that. Your mayor lived happily, then?"

"In happiness beyond dreams, Your Majesty. An estate was given him, houses and fields, cattle and geese, beer and wine and cakes. He walked in his gardens and sniffed the fragrance of the lotus in his pools. And when there was labor to be done, he called The Answerers, those slaves of the dead. He called, 'O Ushab-ti, fill my canals with water from the sacred river; reap my harvests. Come, Ushab-ti.' And these answered, 'We are here; command us, Master.'

"He met friends of his earthly days, and they chatted pleasantly of times gone, of this one and that one, still living. And on special occasions he was permitted to ride with Re in the sun-boat, with other pure souls, and saw the Nile winding like a silver ribbon, saw Tu-shennet, his own house, even. And sometimes he saw his wife, his sons and daughters, and their continued health filled his heart and he knew the peace that all find in the Islands of the Blessed."

"Thank you, Lord Senmut." Hat-shep-sut's voice was vibrant with feeling, and Neferu-Re thought that she had never seen her mother's eyes so gentle. "Thank you for a happy day."

CHAPTER IX

Year 13 of the Reign of Thothmes II

A final check showed all the equipment for the lesson ready: pens newly pointed, fresh ink moistened with gum and water in the palette, sheets of clean papyrus on the table. Neb-taui moved a stool, the tall one with its seat polished by the bottoms of three generations of restless scholars, to a place beside his short stool. A poor place in which to entertain the king's son, perhaps, but clean and well lighted, and the boy's father and grandfather had studied here, and countless youths of lesser consequence.

While awaiting the arrival of his illustrious pupil, the old priest stood thoughtfully fingering several ancient rolls which a subordinate had brought from files in the adjacent Temple Library. The enthusiasms of children would forever amaze him; this infatuation of Prince Thothmes for an ancestor dead five hundred years was a case in point. It was as if kings since Sen-usert had not lived, their wars but tales of idle imagining. Sen-usert was living hero and god for him, the model upon which his own life must be patterned.

Neb-taui cocked an ear as voices from another chamber broke his thought, stepped to a doorway and drew the curtain aside.

"In here, My Lord Steward," he called. "Come in here and help me wait until the prince arrives for his lessons."

It warmed his old heart when a former pupil, full now of worldly cares and responsibilities, remembered to visit him. He drew Senmut into the room and seated him on the low stool, relieved him of his stick and laid it carefully on the table.

"Do you know," he said, sliding his finger caressingly down the stick's tapered smoothness, "to what you owe possession of gold armlets and royal linen and this fine stick? To your ability, as a child, to think of more questions in one day than a master could answer in a month, *and* to make use of information received. There never was a questioner like you, Senmut."

"Nor a master like you for feeding curiosity." Senmut smiled slyly. "I haven't changed. I brought a question with me today."

"Good! Out with it, and see if I am still good at answering."

"Penati and I have been poking about the ruins of the old temple across the Nile, in the bay of sand, you know, close against the cliffs where Ineni is buried."

"The mortuary temple of Neb-hapet-Re Mentuhotep."

"That's it," said Senmut. "Ineni used to say that it possessed architectural features that would bear study, and it does. Now, I came across something yesterday that I cannot reconcile with what I remember of your teaching of that period. If I remember, you said that the temple was built during a time of unrest and confusion?"

"Exactly. The country divided under two Pharaohs—one ruling the north and one the south."

"Well, Penati showed me a shrine of alabaster, the stone coming from Hatnub in the north—and columns of tawny sandstone from the quarries of Silsileh in the south."

"Stone from both north and south, eh?" Neb-taui nodded and searched for his pen. "This indicates—let me write this—the presence of stone from the north in the temple across from Thebes implies that the country was united under the southern Pharaoh Mentuhotep. Interesting."

He looked at the younger man with pleased surprise. "Imagine your remembering my teaching on that obscure point. I shall begin to agree with Her Majesty, that you forget nothing you have heard or seen."

"Hat-shep-sut said that?"

"In effect. Our conversation dealt with experiences of the soul in the afterlife, and when I mentioned the night journey of the sun, she said, 'That is when the dead appear to us as stars, I suppose.'

" 'Stars, Your Majesty?' I said.

" 'Lord Senmut recited the passage to me,' she answered. " ' "The sky has given birth to thee and to Orion. . . ." ' "

"The ancient text," said Senmut. "You remember it, Master—from one of the old pyramid temples."

Neb-taui chuckled. "Later I remembered, but at the time . . ."

This was not all Her Majesty had said, Neb-taui thought, but with her eyes rather than her tongue. There were few, he knew, of her age and intellectual level with whom she could exchange ideas, and it rejoiced his simple heart that she had one of Senmut's honesty and worth to lighten the tedium of governing.

He reread his notes with satisfaction. "A contribution to the records, Senmut. A period of prosperity followed Mentuhotep; this pins it more exactly. There began a sort of golden age when art and architecture flourished, lasting until after the time of Sen-usert."

"Prince Thothmes' hero, eh?"

Neb-taui nodded. "I try to impress the prince that Sen-usert's concern was with the over-all welfare of Egypt, that he considered a healthy and vigorous internal economy as essential as frontier forts."

"He probably quarrels with that picture of the 'great conqueror.'"

"He doesn't hear me, Senmut." Neb-taui sighed and tapped the papyrus rolls laid ready on the table. "At the end of yesterday's lesson he said, 'Tomorrow let us study the Pharaoh Sen-usert's Nubian campaigns.' Fighting, strategy, tactics—his mind is full of these, and Her Majesty is furious." Neb-taui repeated his sigh. "As a priest, I am in sympathy with Her Majesty's ideals of a world at peace. But I also understand, as she cannot, the boy's absorption in warfare. And here are two strong natures already at war, and there will be troublous times ahead. One does not have to be a seer to know that."

"He cannot become king for another five years at best," Senmut said by way of comfort. "Much can happen in five years, Master; your influence is strong."

"Menti's is stronger," returned the priest with a wry smile. "Menti is a soldier and it is natural that he be delighted with the trend of the boy's thinking. Oh, Menti is loyal to Her Majesty, but he sees, too, the advantages to him of a warlike king."

"What I'll never understand," said Senmut, "is why our prince goes so far afield for his hero. Sen-usert died five hundred years ago, but men of as great or greater influence in Egyptian foreign affairs—Aahmes, for instance, or the prince's own grandfather, the old king. . . . A legendary figure, perhaps."

Neb-taui nodded, absently riffling the sheets of papyrus that covered a corner of the table. Suddenly he smiled, drew one of the sheets from the pile and spread it before his guest. "Give me your opinion of this, Senmut."

It was a drawing, carefully and expertly rendered, of a huge harp nearly the height of a man and with fourteen strings. The base was what captured Senmut's particular interest—a man's head wearing the tall plumes of the headdress of the god Amon.

"A ceremonial harp. This is good, Master—a nice conception, nicely balanced. Who made the drawing?"

"Read the writing on the back."

Senmut held the papyrus toward the window and spelled the schoolboy's scrawl with difficulty:

> "For the praise of the beauty
> of my father Amon at his ap-
> pearances in his temple."

He looked at the older man in astonishment. "Prince Thothmes?"

"An amazing and unpredictable child, isn't he?" Neb-taui rubbed his chin reflectively. "Imaginative, intelligent . . . This search for beauty, for expression—how is it reconciled with the urge to destroy?"

"At least, there are thoughts in his head besides blood and violence." Senmut patted the drawing. "May I show this to Tet? He may have an idea . . ."

"Of course." Neb-taui, his mind still occupied with its problem, rolled the papyrus and laid it in the other's hand. "I wish that I could foresee the end, for there will be trouble. Her Majesty is long-suffering . . ."

"But her hands will be tied once Prince Thothmes is sixteen and married to Princess Neferu-Re."

"Hum—yes, perhaps."

"How 'perhaps'? He is heir to the throne—you saw how Amon publicly expressed his choice."

"Of course. But Hat-shep-sut is resourceful, and if the boy remains obstinate . . . Wait—isn't that—yes, here is the prince now. More of this later. . . . Ah, greetings, Your Highness."

Prince Thothmes, son of Pharaoh and the Lady Aset, hesitated inside the doorway, surprised to find an unexpected third person present in the classroom. He ignored the low bows, standing rigidly erect and with chin outthrust, a pose that Nebtaui recognized as characteristic of his annoyance. Even at the early age of eleven years the prince was careless of the feelings of others; he would make a strong, if not the wisest, king.

He had the short stature and the large nose of his father, but resemblance ended there, for his body was firmly muscled and quick of movement and his eye alert. It shone now with suppressed excitement; forgetting momentary displeasure, he launched into impetuous description of the morning's activities.

"General Menti ordered a special drill. You know, Master—running, wrestling, single-stick, the exercises used to condition men for a campaign. And javelin throwing, and shooting at copper targets with heavy war bows. General Menti says competition is important in peace time; he says General Aahmes taught him that. He's always quoting General Aahmes. He must think General Aahmes the greatest warrior that ever lived."

"Many others are convinced of that, Your Highness, including most of Egypt's former enemies."

The prince stiffened. "You mean greater than Pharaoh Senusert?"

"Aahmes Pen-Nekheb was not a god, Your Highness," Nebtaui reminded him gently, "but among mortal men he ranked high as warrior and leader. A fierce fighter, yet gentle."

"How can a really fierce man be gentle?" said the prince scornfully. "I can remember him, short and limping and scowling and swearing. I don't think that I was afraid of him, but I was very careful. He never seemed gentle to me."

"Lord Senmut can tell you more about him, Your Highness; he and Lord Aahmes were particular friends."

"Friendly with a priest?" The prince sniffed.

"Lord Senmut was Aahmes' first choice to succeed him as General of Pharaoh's Armies."

Prince Thothmes stared uncertainly at his old teacher, and at the white-gowned Steward of Amon, and flushed angrily. And Senmut interposed. "This is truth, Your Highness," he said with simple directness. "From motives best understood by himself—kindness, altruism, experiment—the general took a paternal interest in me from the first and trained me in shooting and wrestling and driving. He found certain qualities that he thought worth developing, but I disappointed him by choosing Lord Ineni as master. The title 'Steward of Amon' fits me better than 'General,' and I am happy in administrative work."

Neb-taui nodded ready agreement with this speech, and added softly, "There are many skills involved, Your Highness, in the serving of one's king."

The prince tapped a foot in fretful disbelief. "It doesn't seem possible. Such a choice? Deliberately?"

Senmut ventured a smile. "I confess," he said, "that a bow is comfortable to my hand, that I enjoy a good hunt, but these do not make a warrior. To excel in any trade—and fighting is a trade—there must be enthusiasm, a conviction that this thing you must do, or die. I never saw Aahmes smile, but the veterans tell of his singing in the crash and roar of battle, sword-arm bloodied to the elbow, a raging panther. Fighting was the breath of his living; he ate and drank it, admitted no other thought to his mind, studied the fighting methods of all nations, was a rigid disciplinarian, and allowed no man's foot ahead of his on a march."

The prince had listened with growing interest, and now he nodded eagerly. "A good general leads his troops. Pharaoh Sen-usert led."

"Of course," said Senmut. "Sen-usert was a great Pharaoh, in war and in peace. There was a hymn written of him—you know it, perhaps:

" 'He is a bower, letting every man lie down in the mid-day heat;
He is a screen, like walls built of sharp stones;
He is a refuge, shutting out the robber;
He is an asylum, shielding the timid from his enemy;
He is a shade to provide coolness in the summer;
He is a warm corner of shelter in the winter;
He is a rock, shielding from the blast in the stormy day.' "

Neb-taui watched excitement and ecstatic delight growing in the boy's eyes. "Why," the prince exclaimed, "he—he knows Pharaoh Sen-usert!"

"The measure of a king's stature, Your Highness," said Senmut, "is in the esteem of his subjects, not in the number of countries he subdues."

Come, thought Neb-taui, Hat-shep-sut shall certainly hear of this.

"Egypt's internal health and prosperity," Senmut continued, "were as much concern to Sen-usert as its borders. So he was loved by his people and feared by his enemies, and there is no higher monument."

Neb-taui recognized with appreciation the simple expedient by which Senmut had set his image indelibly in the boy's thought; having accomplished this, Senmut retired. Regardless of later developments, the boy would remember him as a man of discernment, of sympathy and understanding; thus, Neb-taui knew, do we remember those who champion our cherished theories.

The prince still bubbled after Senmut disappeared through the doorway. "Imagine! A priest who knows Pharaoh Sen-usert!"

"You will come to find Lord Senmut more than a priest, Your Highness. Besides superintendence of Amon's wealth, he is steward to the princesses, your sisters. He studies building and is a capable artist and, in Lord Ineni's place, oversees work in the Temple Shops. He is dependable and resourceful, and you will come to appreciate men like Senmut."

"When I am king, I shall find an important position for him."

"You will find him worthy of any trust, Your Highness, and capable."

"While I am fighting the heathen," said the prince, "Egypt will have to be governed wisely. Perhaps Lord Senmut will make a good vizier."

Neb-taui hid his smile. "That is a post of great honor and responsibility. Your ministers will help you decide on the right man."

The prince scowled. "When I am king, I will decide."

"Of course, Your Highness."

"It is all right for ministers to make reports and suggestions, but I will make decisions."

"Yes, Your Highness."

The scowl left the boy's forehead. "Of course. The king is the king, you see. Now, Master," he continued eagerly, "today you said we could see records of Pharaoh Sen-usert's campaigns."

"Ah, yes." Neb-taui sighed. "Here, Your Highness, here in these rolls. Now, here is Yebu at the Cataract, here is Nubia. . . ."

102

Year 14 of the Reign of Thothmes II

At last Senmut was satisfied to sit quietly, lost in contemplation of the shadows creeping across the valley floor. This was almost the first moment of inaction in the whole day and Paheri thankfully eased his aching limbs to the doubtful comfort of the rocks that edged the path. He respected Senmut's silence; this had been Ineni's favorite lookout, near to his tomb and overlooking the world he had loved. Perhaps his spirit had watched them all the morning as they climbed and burrowed in the ruins on the valley floor below; perhaps his spirit sat with them now in mute enjoyment of their company.

Paheri should have known what the day would be like. He enjoyed his ease and never walked when he could ride nor stood when he could sit—and he knew Senmut and Senmut's tireless energy. Yet when the latter said, "Let's explore the ruins across the river," Paheri found himself agreeing—and regretting the foolishness within an hour. The six-hundred-year-old temple embodied unique features, no doubt, and exceptional workmanship, but the task of ferreting them called for the muscles of an ox. Then, when all Paheri's bones cried for rest and his feet were like hot stones, what had Senmut said. He said, "While we are over here, you must see the new decorations on the wall of my tomb." So Paheri, the uncomplaining friend, had hoisted his sweating bulk up the trail that was like a ladder for steepness and admired the drawings.

Now that he had regained a part of his breath, he admitted that the drawings were good and the subject was well chosen. A year ago an envoy from the distant Isles in the Great Green had brought tribute to Thebes, and Senmut, as Steward of Amon, had officiated in weighing and counting the god's share.

It was an event important in his career, and Tet's artists detailed for posterity in faithful and accurate line the peculiarities of foreign dress and countenance: kilts, and gaiters bound round and round the legs by thongs; long wavy locks falling to the shoulder; straight noses; small-waisted figures.

Paheri saw that Senmut continued to stare into the lengthening shadows. Were his thoughts of past honors, of problems incident to his many offices, worries about the future? Of the stubborn Min-Hor? Of Hat-shep-sut? Her Majesty was demanding more and more of his time—not always, Senmut confessed with surprise and gratification, on matters of business. Paheri thought he understood. Senmut could be the most delightful of companions, witty and intelligent—the queen valued his opinions and the originality with which he expressed them.

Also, from remarks Senmut had made, Paheri guessed that the Steward of Amon was something of an enigma to Her Majesty; where most officials were satisfied to accomplish work assigned them, Senmut spent his leisure prying into the secrets of a hundred obscure fields of knowledge—with results that overwhelmed those conscious of the deviation. "How," she had said to him, "can you anticipate and influence the arguments of men from remote districts, the priests and mayors and farmers who distrust Thebans?" And: "Your exact knowledge of the mysteries—why does the subject so interest you, and how can you know where to search?" Tonight, Senmut said, he was meeting with Her Majesty to consider the possibility of strengthening national pride in the thought of young Thothmes, to formulate some project so engaging that it might lessen the boy's passion for war.

He seemed strained and intense, Paheri thought, even in repose. Already, at twenty-nine, there were lines graved deeply in Senmut's face, lines that told of concentration, exhausting hours of study, determination to "succeed." Paheri understood, in the abstract, poverty and hunger and struggle and ambition, and there was nothing but admiration in his thought for one who, with no springboard but intelligence, could leap from mud house to palace, to distinction among men, to envy and respect. His cousin Min-Hor was a fool if she could not see the worth of her husband; too selfish to help, and pouting and whining . . . A succession of babies, now, as fast as she could bear—that was a prime antidote for the poison that was eating Min-Hor's life.

Senmut's voice in a curious strained tone broke his thought. "Paheri—did you see it?"

"I see spears of sunlight piercing the haze. Is that . . ."

"It's gone now—it was long, and low against the cliffs, filling the space north of the ruins."

"A trick of the shadows?" said Paheri.

"With terraces like the ruined temple. Remember, Paheri? But without the brick pyramid; low against the cliffs . . . Pharaoh Amen-hotep's chapel would be in the way. Would the priests allow removal of Amen-hotep's chapel, do you think?"

"Whatever are you talking about, Senmut?"

"It was like a vision," said Senmut, his voice rising with excitement. "It seemed to grow as I watched—a beautiful shining temple, filling the northern end of the valley, building in terraces, but the accent horizontal and not in conflict with the towering vertical cliffs behind."

"H-m-m," said Paheri. His artist's eye approved the concept offered it, but instead of a finished temple, his imagination showed him rolling clouds of dust hiding thousands of workers, gangs emptying fleets of ships of the stone dug in far quarries by other gangs; overseers, water-carriers, artists, stone-cutters. There would be staggering labor and expense, and not for a year only, but for ten years, twenty years. . . . The Royal Treasury was well-filled, but there was a bottom to it.

Senmut struck his palms together. "This may be what we want. A mortuary temple, Paheri—a mortuary temple for Prince Thothmes. Look"—he drew in the dirt—"a long avenue of approach—the cliffs must be a mile from the river—perhaps with sphinxes lining the avenue. A gateway at the end of the avenue, and a wide flat terrace like the one we found in the ruins. Then a ramp to another terrace—perhaps a third with statues. There's nothing like it in Egypt, Paheri."

Paheri was dazzled by the magnitude and daring of the conception, and by its completeness. From slight shiftings in the afternoon haze, Senmut had visualized in the space of a dozen heart-beats a monument unique and of startling beauty. He looked at his friend with new respect. Some of Senmut's enthusiasm stirred in his own veins and he heard his voice saying, "I should like to help with the drawing."

Senmut grasped his hand. "I hoped you would—I hoped you would!"

And too late Paheri realized that his tongue had talked him into work.

"It will be costly," Paheri warned, "maybe prohibitive. Penati and Tet will know; we'll make a rough drawing. They'll have suggestions, too. . . ."

Senmut stared for a long minute into the twilit chaos of rock and waste that lay below them on the valley floor. "Am I a fool, Paheri? I have studied, but what do I know of building? With you and Penati and Tet to help . . . But . . ."

"You have not failed in anything you've started," said Paheri.

"I . . ." Slowly Senmut's frown changed to an expression of boyish gratification. "You *are* a friend, Paheri." His animation returned. "You remember the tree pits we found in the ruins of the old temple? Some of the roots looked like sycamore-figs . . ."

"Tamarisk. Tamarisk and sycamore-fig."

"Ah," said Senmut, and waved a hand toward the valley. "The region is sacred to the Goddess Hathor; the temple could be dedicated to her, and trees planted to make a garden for the goddess."

"Good. With careful tending, they would live even in that desert."

Senmut stood up. "Are you rested, Paheri?"

"Oh, yes."

"Then . . ." Senmut hitched his apron. "If we hurry, we can get a look at the old quarry before it's dark."

Paheri smothered a groan. His next friend, he decided, would be a cripple, with sedentary tastes.

Paheri's impression, as he entered Senmut's office a week later, was of a crowd of people all talking at once. It was a small room on the ground floor of the dormitories behind the Sacred Lake and near the Shops and the Temple Library, Ineni's old office, a simple room and homely. Senmut had not changed its furnishings since the master's time: stools, a table, lamp, shelves, a worn mat, a pan of coals, and numerous tall clay jars for the filing and safekeeping of drawings and accounts. And, as in Ineni's day, a bed in the corner where Paheri knew that Senmut often slept when duties engaged him beyond the hours of reason.

Her Majesty was enchanted, Senmut had told him, with his description and wanted a plan with as much detail as they could devise. Neb-taui and Penati were now seated at Senmut's table with a rough sketch before them. Leaning across the table were Tet and Nebiri—Tet the hard-working Overseer of the Temple Shops, Nebiri the tough and boisterous foreman of Penati's work-gangs. It was Nebiri who was making the noise. For hours daily he chanted a call that controlled the rhythmic step of his pullers of weights, and habit rendered him constitutionally unable to regulate his full-throated roars to the confines of a room.

"See now," he bellowed, thrusting a stubby forefinger at the plan, "if the new causeway is to parallel the old one, here's the old quarry close by to the north. Good stone in here for the grading and fills. And a short haul. See? And on the other side, a depression between the causeways where workmen can build their huts. If they live on the spot . . . See what I mean, Penati —the time saved, and cost of carrying them across the river twice daily?"

Paheri saw Senmut then, squatting in a corner with a scribe and dictating from a sheaf of notes, oblivious of the tumult. Paheri joined those at the table, and Penati saluted him.

"Ah, Lord Paheri. We were saying that time and expense can be saved if the new building is confined to the present graded space; within the old courtyard, you see. You're planning on a smaller building than the ruined temple, anyway?"

Paheri nodded. "We used a scale of five palms to the cubit for the drawing."

"There will still be plenty of filling needed. The whole area is badly cut up; been used as a cemetery for a thousand years, I guess. Mostly we can fill over the tombs and graves and not disturb them."

"Will there be trouble about removal of the small chapel?"

"The one built for the great-grandfather of His Highness? Neb-taui thinks permission can be obtained."

"The young prince," said Neb-taui, "is strangely indifferent to all his ancestors except Pharaoh Sen-usert. If the matter is properly presented, he should make no objection."

Paheri felt a hand on his shoulder, and Senmut said, "The temple records will have to wait; I can't see you men having all the fun while I work."

"Ah, Senmut," said Penati, "are you free at last? Look—we can cut costs further if we save the bricks from the small chapel and use them later for scaffolding."

Senmut nodded to him and turned to Paheri. "Aren't they a wonderful group to work with? Oh, Tet, there's a good Osiride motif in the chapel that I want you to see. We can use a series of giant figures across the front of the topmost terrace—figures of the mummified Osiris, you see, with Pharaoh's face. Painted sandstone, probably."

"I'll make drawings of it," Tet promised. "What other statues have you planned?"

Senmut laughed. "It's early for all the details. Sphinxes, I suppose—from the landing, the full length of the causeway to the gateway, and perhaps sphinxes on the two lower terraces. There should be a colonnade and portico on each side of the ramps to mask the elevations of the second and third terraces, but the important statues will be on the third terrace, the temple proper."

"Senmut plans a series of chapels on the third terrace," Paheri explained, "to Amon, to Hathor, and to other gods."

"The principal chapel will be dedicated to Amon as the state god, and the sanctuary will be cut deep into the mountain behind it. At least, that's the way I see it now. And I thought of kneeling statues of Pharaoh offering incense to Amon and lining the way to the sanctuary. Red granite, perhaps."

"Good, good. Excellent," said Neb-taui. "And statues to Hathor and the other gods each in his own chapel. Good; the young prince will like it."

"Well"—Tet shook his head—"he may not not like the expense. Limestone, sandstone, and red and gray granite . . . No quartzite or alabaster?"

"Perhaps," said Senmut. "Better plan on them. Can we use the local limestone, Penati?"

"Only for filling. The fine blocks we'll have to get from Kaw. And sandstone from Silsileh, and red granite from the east bank near the Cataract. Nebiri will like that; easy to transport."

Nebiri hunched his thick shoulders. "You find it and I'll get

108

it out. But get all you can from the south; you can float stone from Yebu to Thebes in two days—when the Nile's high, I mean. That's a saving."

"Yes," Penati agreed. "The other hard stones must come from the northern Hammamat quarries, and that means a big expedition, an overland haul of fifty miles."

"Now, don't worry about the hauling," said Nebiri, snapping his fingers and grinning about the table. "Get me men enough and I'll haul the mountain down here for you."

"I worry about the cost," said Penati drily. "Extensive quarrying in the desert means guards and their captains, a thousand, two thousand laborers with their overseers, every man in the expedition to be supplied with two jars of water and twenty small loaves a day. And then ships for transport; it will take a fleet. . . ."

"Any leaky tub will do," Senmut protested, "or rafts, even. Small blocks can be ferried on a raft."

"We'll want the largest blocks that can be handled comfortably," Penati insisted. "In a composite building it's a good principle to have as few joints as possible. Ineni used to say that. Makes for strength."

"What about a rubble core?" said Senmut. "The wall around the base of the pyramid in the old temple used facing blocks and rubble, and it's still strong after six hundred years."

"Only where the walls are thick enough. For the southern retaining wall as you've planned it, a rubble core might do as well as solid stone."

Neb-taui interrupted in his gentle manner. "Did I hear you say, Senmut, that you found evidence in the ruins of Mentuhotep's temple that trees had been planted there?"

"Yes, Master. Pits in which we found the decayed roots of tamarisk and sycamore-fig."

"I wonder if myrrh trees would grow under similar conditions."

"They should, if properly planted and tended. Incense trees? Why do you ask?"

Neb-taui smiled apologetically. "You know that an old man's mind is a depository of odds and ends of irrelevant learning, half-forgotten and generally useless. Your repeated mention of 'terraces' stirred a dormant memory of a phrase read years ago in an ancient papyrus, one dealing with a voyage to Punt, the God's Land, and telling of the presence there of 'Ladders of Incense.' This was reference to the fact that incense trees grow there on terraces, and . . ."

Paheri exclaimed, "A terraced garden of incense for Amon!"

"A garden of myrrh trees—bringing Punt to Thebes! Master," said Senmut, "this is the idea I've been searching for, the novelty that will capture Prince Thothmes' imagination."

Punt, the God's Land—a year, two years distant to the east and south. No one in the memory of the oldest had been there, but Paheri had heard tales of wonders, tales pieced from fragmentary reports of ancient missions. No one was sure, even, where the country lay, but the journey would require a huge expedition, hundreds of men, two or three years. . . .

Neb-taui was saying, "There is no record of trade with Punt in recent years, the last expedition of note being in the reign of Pharaoh Sen-usert."

"Sen-usert!" Senmut exclaimed. "Prince Thothmes' hero. Now he will insist on the mission."

"Do you remember what routes were followed in the old days?" Paheri asked.

"All the early expeditions with which I am familiar," said Neb-taui, "left the Nile at Koptos and marched overland to the sea and built their ships, and then sailed south. Sen-usert, however—we have positive evidence that he caused a canal to be dug connecting the eastern arm of the Nile with the Bitter Lakes. He probably sailed all the way from Thebes to Punt."

"That's it," said Senmut. "Thothmes will do as Sen-usert did. I'll wager on it. Let's get Nehessi's ideas on such an expedition."

He called the scribe to bring papyrus and pen, and scribbled a note and dispatched it by runner to Nehessi's house. "This is it," he said jubilantly. "It's just different and mad enough to appeal to the boy, and he will . . ."

" 'Mad' is the word," said Penati with a sour expression. "Have you any idea, I wonder, what all this—the temple *and* a voyage to the ends of the earth—will cost?"

"Work up an estimate for us, Penati. But don't forget that a successful expedition to Punt should return rich tribute in gold and ivory and pelts and precious woods, besides the aromatic gums and incense."

"A drop," Penati declared, "that would not offset the cost of new ships and wages of the crews. Look, now: overseers, stone-cutters, laborers, barges with crews and captains, master-artists and apprentices, scribes, sculptors, finishers; wages in beans, oil, fish, beer, barley, onions, cloth; tools, grinding powder, paint, rope, sledges—not just for a month, you know; as you're planning it, the temple will not be finished in ten years...."

Senmut had returned to the plan and did not hear Penati's grumbling. "Plant the trees here and here, perhaps," he said. "And couldn't we send artists with the expedition, Tet? It will be an important event in the reign."

Neb-taui joined him in study of the plan. "The holy-of-holies, I believe you said, is to be excavated in the mountain behind the highest terrace? Your plan is good, Senmut, embodying the principles laid down by the ancients—progression in three steps from lowest to highest, from light to darkness."

It was excellent planning, Paheri knew, the long horizontal lines of the building offering no competition to the towering cliffs that formed a natural background; instead, each complemented the other. As seen from the river, when completed it should be a spectacular monument and credit to the architect and to his king. It would be costly, but perhaps it could gain Hat-shep-sut's support if it replaced war in her nephew's mind.

All this—incredible, thought Paheri—from the son of a peasant. Aahmes, in his life, had insisted that Senmut was no ordinary man, that in those the gods marked there were resources of the mind beyond normal understanding, and this Paheri was ready to concede. Already the farmer's son was Steward of Amon and Chief Guardian of the Queen's Daughters; Paheri could think of no sensible reason why he should not gain the envied title "Overseer of the Works of Amon."

Nehessi arrived, Captain of the King's Ships, a little on the sulky side for being routed from his rest, and his petulance doubled when he heard the word "Punt."

"The God's Land? A myth, a legend. Who knows the country? Who knows where it lies? Don't tell me that you called me here tonight to ..."

"It is not a myth," said Neb-taui; "many expeditions visited the God's Land in ancient times and I will show the records to you."

111

"Penati knows the desert marches and the caravan routes, but I am a sailor. Penati is your man."

Senmut, with patience, told of the reported canal connecting the Nile and the Bitter Lakes. "That's why we need you, Captain," he said. "You're the man with experience and knowledge to determine if the old canal can be made usable. If it can, ships can sail all the way from Thebes."

Nehessi sighed impatiently. "It's easy to sit here and say, 'Here's a ship, Captain; bring us incense from Punt.' How many of you have sailed the Great Green? Have you fought seas like mountains, and raging winds, and rocks that reach from shores like fingers to claw the bottom from a ship? It's not like sailing the Nile, you know. And what reception can you expect if or when you find Punt? Are the natives savage or friendly? And what of wild beasts? Why, I'd need an army for protection—and such a voyage would last three years. Or more. And the cost— Now this is a mad scheme hatched in a madman's brain. Look —the crews must eat, they have to be paid. Have you figured the salaries of three hundred men, and the captains, for three years? And six or seven new ships . . ."

Tet was nodding agreement, and Penati said, "The captain is right, Senmut, and the whole venture is impractical. The temple, even. The plan of the temple has its interesting points, but . . ."

Senmut listened, but when Penati finished he said, "Work up an estimate to cover costs for fifteen years—labor, salaries, tools, stone, ships—everything, Penati."

"But why, Senmut? Why?"

"Because," said Senmut, "when the temple is finished it will be a monument to the greatness of Egypt, to the divine majesty of Pharaoh. A monument for eternity."

There was a long moment of uncomfortable silence. Then Tet struck his palms together smartly and spoke. "Well, if Nehessi cannot find Punt with his ships, that leaves Lord Tura's proposition, Senmut. He is Viceroy of Kush and perhaps Punt comes under his jurisdiction. Too bad; his caravan cannot return a tenth the treasure the ships could, and Pharaoh will be disappointed . . ."

"Wait," said Nehessi. "Tura? Old Tura of Nekheb? He is

taking a caravan half across the earth—to Punt? Now look, at his age he will not live through twenty days of desert heat."

"Here"—Senmut pointed to the plan—"a record of the expedition will be drawn on the walls of the portico, here and here. Artists will be sent and a record preserved for posterity. It will be a great event in the reign, and Tura's name will be remembered as leader."

Nehessi was watching the faces about him sharply.

"Perhaps a caravan is better," said Senmut. "It will be cheaper, and the hazards of desert travel are known and can be reckoned."

"How 'cheaper'?" said Nehessi suddenly. "With five or six ships, stout sea-going ships, I can return treasure that a caravan of a thousand could not carry. Five ships, now."

"Well..."

"And two years at the most. Come, I promise, two years. I'll go north and look the canal over; it happens that relief for the border garrisons is due and..."

When the room was empty at last except for Senmut and Paheri, the former laughed. "I shall have to check Tet's accounts more closely; that tale of his about old Tura proposing a caravan to Punt!" He studied the rumpled working drawing on the table. "We'll prepare a fresh drawing, one including the details mentioned tonight, and then show it to Hat-shep-sut."

"The queen? Kings build temples, my friend."

"Her Majesty will be my king for a few years yet, Paheri, and all work is offered for her consideration. Besides"—he rolled the drawing slowly—"I cannot forget something that Neb-taui hinted a year ago—about Hat-shep-sut's resourcefulness if Prince Thothmes continued obstinate...."

The queen's reception of the two servants of the god, the Steward and the Draughtsman of Amon, was gracious and flatteringly informal. She admired the drawing, listened attentively to their description of the scheme, asked an occasional pertinent question, laughed gently at Senmut's enthusiasm. It was the first time Paheri had seen the two in conference and he was puzzled. This was not queen and minister, it was—sister and brother? They forgot him; there was a lightness that bespoke enjoyment of each other's company, sympathy of outlook. It was a new Hat-shep-sut that Paheri watched, a different Senmut. He wondered at what he saw.

And at the end the queen sighed. "Friend, priest, administrator, and now architect and engineer. When will I learn not to be surprised by you, Senmut? Your temple is a jewel, a beautiful, beautiful conception, skillfully planned. I wish I could promise that Thothmes will be as excited with it as I am."

"We know the boy's appreciation of beauty, Your Majesty. If we can make him see this as a monument of which his people will be proud . . ."

"I will try, Senmut. But I have talked much with Neb-taui, his tutor. The boy will build, of course; it is the duty, and privilege, of every Pharaoh to contribute to the cultural growth of our great land. But Neb-taui assures me that first will come war and conquest; the prince is determined to follow in the exact footsteps of his hero Sen-usert: enslavement of Egypt's neighbors, and then attention to the art of peace. It is a pattern, Senmut; my own father followed it."

"I understand your discouragement, Majesty; your example disregarded, the plans and hopes . . ."

"Discouraged!" She shook her head, smiling, at Paheri. "Our friend does not know me, even yet. And neither," she continued softly, and Paheri saw that her hand gripped the chair arm tightly, "do others in Thebes, selfish men who speak fairly to my face and secretly urge the young prince to defiance."

Paheri was thoughtful. "Your Majesty," he said, "may not other noble houses feel in this matter as do the princes of Nekheb? We serve with unqualified sincerity the Pharaoh placed on Egypt's throne by the gods. Despite his deficiencies, Thothmes your husband is our king while he lives; his son will be our king when the father dies. Meanwhile, we applaud Your Majesty's inspired handling of affairs of government in the name of your husband and of the child prince, knowing that the gods also approve."

"Thank you, My Lord," said Hat-shep-sut simply. "The loyalty and support of families like yours of Nekheb give me needed courage. Unfortunately, not all my husband's subjects are as generous. Many, weighing material benefits to be gained from war against the less dramatic rewards of peace, poison the child against the policies which I am convinced are essential to a friendly world and, therefore, to Egypt's well-being."

"Surely, Your Majesty . . ."

"I do not exaggerate. Men who swear love for me—Senmut, name them for My Lord."

So Senmut named them to his friend, the opponents to Hat-shep-sut's hopes for peace.

"The High Priest of Amon, whom the old king trusted. As chief priest of the state god, his influence is felt in all the temples of Egypt. He speaks against Her Majesty, saying that war will bring gold and slaves to the priesthood.

"General Menti. Peace in the land is like slow dying for him and for his armies.

"Lord User. A man of action, he is weary with playing nurse to a sick master and longs for the excitement of conquest.

"Lord Thuti is ambitious for Egypt, and for himself. He will be Royal Treasurer when his uncle retires; to him, full granaries and bulging storehouses, however acquired, are the blood of a nation.

"These are the chief opponents to Her Majesty's policies. There are others, little men of confused loyalties—like Hapu-seneb," said Senmut, "little men who sway one way and another, their support available to the highest bidder."

Paheri was thinking stubbornly: Well, is it wrong to praise the youth who, in four years, will sit on his father's throne as Pharaoh? Is that treason?

And again: Who can say with assurance that Hat-shep-sut's plans, and not Thothmes', echo the wishes of the gods for Egypt and the world?

My grandfather was right, he decided; she mistakes her dreams for the commands of Amon.

"Your Majesty," he said aloud, "the prince is the divinely appointed heir; we three were present on the night when Amon's wishes were miraculously expressed. Once on the throne, may we not expect Amon's interest to continue? May we not consider all the new king's decisions to be but extensions of the god's will?"

Hat-shep-sut was silent for a long moment, and Paheri, fancying a new sharpness in her glance, felt the sweat start on his forehead. Yet when she finally spoke, her voice was controlled, her manner calm.

"I find fault with two words only in your speech, My Lord—the words 'divinely appointed.' You may not realize that some minds question the authenticity of the event which caused the boy to be named heir. There was evidence which strongly hints foreknowledge of the happening. These are not accusations, you understand, but the memory is unpleasantly active.

"In the time remaining," she said, "I shall continue my efforts to impress the prince with the importance of building if his reign is to be remembered by posterity—your plan, for instance, Senmut, and other temples and shrines. My hope for success lies in Neb-taui's reports of his intelligence; if, however, he refuses to listen"—she shrugged and smiled brightly—"I have faith in Holy Amon's continued solicitude for Egypt's welfare."

CHAPTER XI

Year 1 of the Reign of Thothmes III

The darkness of the sanctuary in which the god Amon lived pressed like a hand on the boy's back, pressed his body against the cold stone of the temple floor. Prostrate before the holy-of-holies, Thothmes waited for a sign, a whisper, alone in the dread presence of the King of the Gods.

He tried to pray, but his jaws were locked with the rigid tension of waiting, of listening. Would Amon come as a voice, a presence felt and heard but unseen? Or, on this important day, would he clothe himself in the form and flesh of a man, shining like the glory of the undimmed sun, awful in divine majesty?

His ears, straining to catch any tell-tale movement that would betray the presence so strongly felt, heard only the sweet faint chanting in the outer halls, the thin murmur of the multitude that packed the streets of Thebes leading to the temple. It was an important day for them, as for him, this day of coronation. There had been a few shouts of acclaim as he drove his chariot that morning—like a victorious general, he thought, at the head of captains and warriors. There had been curiosity, and admiration at the skill with which, a boy, he handled the nervous horses. Heads had bowed at his passing but there was no surge of enthusiasm—as if they thought, these heads that stared and nodded briefly: We have managed without a king—except in name—for years; let the boy prove himself.

By an effort, his teeth unlocked and lips moved stiffly. "Make me a good king," he prayed, "like Pharaoh Sen-usert—and I will bring the wealth of the world to Thebes, the people of the world as slaves to your gardens."

Thus, perhaps, his father had prayed on the day of his coronation. And now his father was dead. Dead after thirty years of tortured living; now his father was a name only, a shell over

117

which at this moment the priests labored with their magic to form into an imperishable home for the departed soul. Stifled cries of alarm echoing in the palace at night—this had been the sudden warning from the king's chambers. The boy had found his aunt the queen in an anteroom with Pharaoh's ministers hurriedly summoned from sleep, conferring in whispers, watching with nervous expectancy the curtains that shut them from the struggle between physicians and the forces of evil that dwelt in Pharaoh's body. He had felt little emotion beyond a tingling excitement; after all, Pharaoh had meant but a title to him, never a father, and now if Pharaoah died . . . He was fourteen, and in two years more, if Pharaoh died, he would be undisputed Lord of Egypt and commander-in-chief of Egypt's armies! Thus he thought, and then the curtains had parted and the Royal Herald had appeared from the inner chamber with the expression of one who has witnessed a scene better forgotten, and knelt at the boy's feet and kissed the pavement before him.

The king, then—the king was dead. And in two years . . .

He had questioned Neb-taui endlessly on the queen's powers as regent, and the master left no doubt in the boy's mind that, until he was sixteen, he was little more than a show-piece, wearing the crowns and sitting the throne, being seen at ceremonies and festivals, performing the functions of an unimaginative and docile child. This was the unchangeable law as established in the beginning by Re, Neb-taui said. The law further provided the regent with full administrative powers, control of the Royal Treasury, authority over the ministers and government agencies and priesthood, over building, taxation, boundaries—in short, his aunt the queen would for two years be Pharaoh in all but name. Well, two years would pass, and there were many times two years beyond when his least wish would be law. Neb-taui said that, too; he could wait without fretting.

He could not really know his aunt the queen. Perhaps she was a kindly person, though it was difficult to pierce the armor of formality with which she clothed all speech and action, and no one could tell from watching when she was pleased or angry. Even during the ceremony of marriage that morning when he and the older daughter Princess Neferu-Re had been joined, the queen's expression had betrayed no particular interest, certainly no emotion. Nor, for that matter, had the daughter displayed anything like enthusiasm at becoming his bride; stiff and color-less as a statue, and probably as cold. . . . Neb-taui had hinted delicately that he must be kind to her, that she was young and timid and not too strong, and he had agreed without second thought; after all, he was interested in the throne and not the girl. The law required that, if he was to be Egypt's king as ap-pointed by Amon and by his father, he must marry Princess Neferu-Re; if the law had said, "To be Pharaoh, thou must marry a crocodile," he would not have questioned the law.

The marrying was done, and General Menti had staged a spectacular acrobatic show—customary at such ceremonies—and soldiers had wrestled and fought with the single-stick. He ac-cepted Menti; the general was aggressive and a stern disci-plinarian, and if his was not the most brilliant mind in Egypt, that did not trouble the boy, who planned to do his own think-ing, in military and in other matters. . . .

A faint sound—the slither of naked feet on stone. He peered about him in the blackness, heart fluttering. The god? A hand felt for and touched his shoulder: "Come, Your Highness, it is time for the ceremony." Not the god, but priests of the temple; it would have been something to tell if he could say, "Amon visited me while I prayed." He sighed in disappointment and followed the priests.

They led him to a chamber lighted by tapers; bathed and anointed him, dressed him in royal apparel, the great jeweled collar that covered shoulders and breast, a pleated linen skirt with the jackal's tail behind and a stiffened apron of gold and enamel in front. Sandals with peaked toes were laced to his feet. And then they bowed before him and escorted him by narrow corridors to the great Hall of Columns.

Except for a space before the altar and a narrow aisle for the passage of the god, the vast hall was as jammed with princes and ministers and clergy as were the streets outside with commoners. He looked into a sea of eyes, some friendly, some questioning, some critical, and stiffened his spine against a moment of panic, reminding himself that his days of comparative obscurity were ended, that from now to the day of his death every glance and gesture and muscle-twitch would be noted and appraised. Then he saw Neb-taui's smile of gentle reassurance and the tension drained from him; these were his friends. These, when he became Pharaoh, would look to him for prosperity, for protection, leadership against the enemies of Egypt, for life itself. A prayer formed in his mind: "Make me a powerful king, O Father Amon, and I will cause the flowers and the fruits of the earth to overflow your house."

The god's place was ready beside the altar, hidden by curtains stiff with their gold. No one knew, Neb-taui had told him, when a god might choose to appear in person, at what hour of the day or night; meanwhile, priests, specially trained, stood ready to play a god's part in any ceremony, and you could never be sure whether the figure you saw with a hawk's head and body of a man was the god Horus in person or a priest masked to represent him. True, a god's visits to earth were rare as jewels in a fish-wife's hair, but it was safest, Neb-taui cautioned, always to show respect and reverence.

The boy would know, he told himself confidently. Egypt was the special concern of the gods, and an event as important as the crowning of a new Pharaoh would not be ignored. The gods would officiate in person, and he would know them. His heart leaped as the swelling chant announced the approach of the highest moment in his fourteen years of living.

Priests bearing Amon's barque circled the hall and then disappeared behind the curtain that hid the shrine. The chanting thundered and the altar smoked and slowly, slowly the curtain pulled aside, while all in the building prostrated themselves before the awful majesty revealed upon the golden throne—the King of All the Gods. The boy's stolen glance showed an imposing figure in the shape and flesh of a man, but blue in color, blue from sole to shaven pate, and topped with the towering double plumes of Amon's distinctive headdress. Rigid, with stern and unwinking gaze . . . "Thanks, Father Amon," the boy prayed; "this day every year I will make a feast day in honor of thy coming."

Then from secret chambers paraded other gods and goddesses (or priests and priestesses dressed to impersonate them)—Horus with the hawk's head and the crowns of Upper and Lower Egypt, Thoth with the head of an ibis surmounted by crescent and disk, Atum as a man wearing the double crown, Khonsu swathed like a mummy and with the sidelock of youth, the Lady Hathor with a cow's head, divine Nekhebt with a vulture's head, snake-headed Buto of the north, fierce Sekhmet with the head of a lioness. . . . These grouped before Amon's throne and made obeisance, and the boy studied them anxiously and refused to admit uncertainty; on this important day the great ones of heaven must see the necessity of personal attendance, of participation in the ceremony that invested a mortal with powers almost divine. This is Holy Amon, he told himself fiercely, and these are the lords and ladies of his court, and I know this because—because I know! And he thought joyfully, The like of this is not known to man before this day—and straightened his back and waited, content.

At a sign from Amon, Horus approached the boy and led him before the throne and sprinkled on him water that had been blessed, and Horus said, "Thou art pure, together with thy soul." And the god Khonsu approached and sprinkled water and said, "Thou are pure, together with thy soul." The ladies Sekhmet and Hathor led him to the god Atum; the boy knelt and Atum said, "All life and well-being and health are given thee, beloved son," and touched the boy and said, "Set his diadem upon his head."

The goddess Buto approached from the north bearing the red crown of Lower Egypt, and she said, "Presented to thee is this red crown which is upon the head of Re."

The goddess Nekhebt brought the white crown of Upper Egypt: "Presented to thee is this white crown, mighty upon thy head."

Thoth led him, then, wearing the double crown, to Amon, and Amon spoke the boy's new names aloud, the boy repeating them and Thoth, god of scribes, writing each name upon a leaf of the sacred persea tree:

"HORUS: Mighty Bull, Shining in Thebes.
FAVORITE OF THE TWO GODDESSES: Enduring in kingship, like Re in heaven.
GOLDEN HORUS: Mighty in Strength, Splendid in Diadems.
KING OF UPPER AND LOWER EGYPT: Lord of the Two Lands: Men-kheper-Re.
SON OF RE: Thothmes, Beautiful of Form, living forever and ever."

Now a stone tablet was handed to the young king, a tablet on which had been carved his new names, and on his knees he pushed the tablet across the floor of the temple to a place beneath the god's feet, thus placing himself wholly in Amon's power and securing, in return, the god's promise of life everlasting.

Fresh offerings were heaped upon the altar and the First Prophet said, "An official sacrifice which the gods give to the Horus, the King of Upper and Lower Egypt, Men-kheper-Re, Lord of the Two Lands."

The royal cloak was spread over the boy's shoulders, the symbols of sovereignty, crook and flail, placed in his hands, and while men surrounded him bearing the standards of all the provinces of Egypt, he squatted with his back to Amon. And the god reached his hand and touched the king's neck and caused the divine fluid, the blood of the gods, to flow in his veins.

Then Amon raised the king and embraced him before the company and summoned all the gods of the south and all the gods of the north, and said to them, "Behold ye my son Thothmes, living; be ye loving toward him, and be ye satisfied with him." And the gods bowed before the boy, and they said, "This is thy son who liveth, and we are satisfied with him. The lands are his, the countries are his, all that the heavens cover, all that the seas encircle."

And Horus led the boy in a circuit of the hall that all might bow to him, and the ceremony ended. Thus the boy Thothmes, third of that name, came to sit in the place of his father as King of Upper and Lower Egypt and Lord of the Two Lands, though for two more years his aunt the Queen Hat-shep-sut would rule the country in his name.

The first of the two years of what the young king called his "probation" was excitingly different from any previous period of his existence. There was a new and exhilarating sense of importance; if his duties were minor, they were royal duties, performed only by Pharaoh. He presided, for example, over the daily ritual of attendance on the symbol of Holy Amon in the sanctuary. It was his hand that dressed the lump of heavy blue stone which the records proved to have been discharged by Amon from heaven to this spot; his hand that perfumed the

122

image, offered it incense from the south, alum from the north, vases of red and of ordinary water. In the public worship of the god, he, Thothmes, stood in the Station of the King, and his aunt Queen Hat-shep-sut took a subordinate position, with Queen Neferu-Re, behind him. His appearance in the streets of Thebes was occasion for instant loosening of taut features in appreciation of his youth and splendor. At least, Menti said this. And Menti said that the country rejoiced that the sun was again risen, that Pharaoh again moved among his people.

The Annual Harvest Festival gave him the first real test of officiating at an important ceremony before throngs of the curious and the critical. As the son of Re and as the corn-god, he symbolized sun and earth, bestowing rich benefactions upon his people. Surrounded by priests and lords and officials, by pomp and glitter, by piles of grain rising in pyramids of abundance, the young king Thothmes sat in a high place. Here he received reports of the grain supply from stewards of temples and treasury, and in thanks to the gods made public offerings of slaughtered animals, of incense and wine and flowers and sheafs of corn and coils of the cord used in measuring the fields. There were four days of celebration, four days of exacting ritualistic posturing and recital, with every eye in Thebes and in heaven, he was convinced, watching for the wrong gesture, every ear tuned to catch a false intonation. He came through the ordeal without error and even Queen Hat-shep-sut was satisfied, and he knew secret exhilaration in the thought that she must see that he was ready for the task of governing.

His new confidence was shaken, however, when, his aunt the queen beside him, he sat enthroned in the Council Chamber. The palace swarmed with officials of the kingdom; where for years there had been darkness and silence, now there was light from a thousand lamps, sweet scents, the rippling chords of lute and harp, a lively bustle and chatter. Ministers paid him court, judges, governors, dignitaries of the temples; all bowed before him and pledged their lives to his service. And all brought petitions—for repairs to temples, for the restoration of monuments, for new roads, new canals and dikes, for protection from beasts of the desert, for establishment of new colleges of learning, for permission to dig stone in the Royal Quarries.

The boy's mind reeled under the impact of the diverse prob-

123

lems, the need for detachment and balance, of detailed knowledge to permit wise decisions, yet his aunt the queen said "Yes"
to this and "No" to that and "Perhaps" to another, with hardly
a hesitation or a shifting of her level glance.

There were so many things about his aunt that awed him—
the alertness of her thinking, her quiet strength and dignity, her
single-purposed devotion to Egypt. She was not human, he
thought, but a being remote as the stars; a cold, white statue,
almost one of the holy goddesses. Then, as when the audiences
were ended and they were alone in the Council Chamber, the
mask of divinity sometimes slipped and the eyes of a thoughtful
woman watched him.

"I understand that Your Majesty is inclined to think unkindly
of ministers," she said. "You heard the requests put to you this
morning; will you be able, unassisted, to answer all such questions wisely?"

"I shall need overseers, perhaps," Thothmes admitted, "men
who investigate and report. When I am king I will make the
decisions."

"I act in Pharaoh's name, Your Majesty, and no one questions
my decisions."

Her remark was gently spoken, but it irritated him—partly
because it was logical and unanswerable, and partly because the
fierce independence of his nature met criticism or advice with
antagonism.

"Pharaoh your grandfather," she urged, "used ministers to
help fashion the Egypt which you inherit, a healthy and prosperous and happy community of a million and a half subjects.
He chose men friendly to his purpose, who saw through his eyes
and who applied his thought-processes to problems as they arose.
General Aahmes, for example, and Lords Ineni and Nefer-peret
and User—men of strength and integrity, Your Majesty, united
in a common cause."

This lecture bored him. Old men did not fit into his plans;
their thoughts were buried in the past, their reasoning clouded
by dead issues. He knew what was needed in Egypt, and young
men, guided by his inspiration, would build the shining temples and palaces with which his vision lined the Nile—all
erected by his order as substantial bribes for divine favor, and
financed by spoils from his campaigns.

124

He shifted restlessly in the great throne chair. "If I must have advisors, I shall choose young men who are not afraid of change. They will learn with me—friends sharing the new adventure."

The Queen shook her head. "The world is essentially a lonely place, Your Majesty, particularly so for kings. Pharaoh can have no friends, only subjects, and you must learn this in another few months. At best you may find a few capable men of agreeable tastes and of reasonable unselfishness." In her earnestness she leaned forward. "Youth is a fine asset, but its value is temporary and cannot replace that of experience. Use the men trained by the ministers of Pharaoh your grandfather for the special duties of serving Your Majesty wisely and efficiently."

He was prepared to agree to this, in part: he would use anyone who satisfied his immediate need—and discard him when a better appeared. Sentimentality in government, he thought, was a dangerous indulgence.

Menti, for instance, would do for now; the army was Thothmes' own private department, and not even the old warrior Aahmes Pen-Nekheb, with his record of battles won and foreigners enslaved, would have satisfied him.

Senmut—here was a man to watch. He had ordered the fashioning of the great harp to impress his king; it was now in use in the daily worship of Amon, a royal gift to the god, of silver and gold and blazing stones. Everyone knew that it was made from the king's own drawing, and all expressed wonder and joy in its shining beauty. And he remembered, too, Senmut's understanding of Pharaoh Sen-usert. Neb-taui praised the Steward of Amon, the queen consulted with him daily. . . .

He addressed his aunt impulsively: "Neb-taui says that Lord Senmut could have been General of the Armies instead of Menti. Why do you think he chose to be priest?"

The Queen smiled. "It was Holy Amon's choice, not his, Your Majesty. The gods anticipate Egypt's needs—you have read enough history with Neb-taui to see this proved in a thousand ways. Senmut . . ." She hesitated so long that the king looked up in surprise. Her Majesty recovered her thought. "Lord Senmut, I should say—you must ask Neb-taui sometime how Amon drew Lord Ineni's attention to him; it is an amazing tale. And from that moment his progress has been spectacular. He performs the most difficult commissions brilliantly—Your Majesty

125

saw an example during the Harvest Festival. As Steward of Amon, Lord Senmut must keep the god's storehouses filled with the riches of Egypt, and Your Majesty saw the abundance of grain, reaching to heaven."

It was expedient, probably, to keep the business of temple prosperity in the hands of one familiar to the god. "I made a promise to Amon," Thothmes said, "to fill his house with the fruits and flowers of Egypt. Senmut, now, since he is Overseer of the Granaries of Amon . . ."

"Excellent, Your Majesty! 'Overseer of the Storehouses, of the Fields, Gardens and Cattle of Amon' is the title of the office. It will be fitting reward of effort in your behalf."

Thothmes had heard the whispering campaign against Hatshep-sut's regency. Some said that, given a taste of power, she would swallow him, but he had to admit that her advice sounded little like that of one planning treachery. Indeed, the working arrangement between them had become almost as if she was a wise and competent scribe, leading his inexperience with suggestions and recommendations, guiding his unsteady steps with a sure hand. He watched for signs in the early months of his first year as Pharaoh, but there were none. Never did she pretend to more than the title allowed her by law— "Divine Consort."

She herself introduced the subject of Lord Thuti's promotion. Thuti was one of the few of his aunt's ministers that he was determined to keep, so when she said, "Lord Nefer-peret requests permission to retire from the office of Superintendent of the House of Silver, and I hope that you will consider Lord Thuti in his place," he was surprised and pleased. He knew all about Lord Thuti, his private wealth, his appreciation of pretty women, his devotion to the problem of developing Egyptian prestige in foreign countries. Thothmes wondered if the queen realized how much of his own knowledge of the economics and resources of other nations came from quiet hours in Thuti's company. Thuti would be Royal Treasurer when Lord Nefer-peret retired.

It was pleasant to be consulted thus—a conversation between equals, the boy thought with pride. He seemed to be striding toward independence daily. His aunt even deferred to his judgment in temple affairs of the most vital and secret nature when

Lord Hapu-seneb requested private audience one day. He was Third Prophet of Amon, but Thothmes knew him only as an earnest man with a rich rolling voice and an impressive manner, and he brought a fantastic proposal involving reorganization of the entire priesthood of Egypt.

Hapu-seneb admitted that the idea came to him in the most holy sanctuary—therefore, direct from Amon himself. The present system, he pointed out, allowed duplication of effort and waste of revenue, since every temple, large and small, operated as an independent unit, sought to fatten at the expense of its neighbor.

Exactly, said Hapu-seneb, as the princes of Egypt had quarreled and raided when His Majesty's great-great-grandfather was Pharaoh. And His Majesty's great-great-grandfather saw the evil and abolished the feudal system by attaching the lords of Egypt to his court and absorbing their scattered holdings into the lands of the Crown.

"Now," said Hapu-seneb, "Holy Amon is the King of the Gods. And if his subjects (the lesser gods who acknowledge his sovereignty) persist in their evil ways and retard Amon's plans, should not balance be restored by appointing his First Prophet as Chief Priest of All the Gods? Amon's order, issuing from Your Majesty's divine lips, would be obeyed."

Thothmes' thought was numbed by the prospect of the chaos that must follow such a decree. He managed, "Thank you, My Lord; your proposal shall receive our attention," and waited until the priest bowed and departed. Hat-shep-sut sat silent, watching him with sober intensity.

"The man is mad," he said at last.

"Or ambitious. Lord Hapu-seneb is Amon's Third Prophet, you know." He was annoyed that his aunt remembered a fact that momentarily had slipped his mind. "Of course," he said, frowning. "The scheme might benefit Amon, but wouldn't every priest in Egypt, except Amon's, descend in wrath on the palace?"

"It could prove a dangerous experiment," the queen agreed. "Pharaoh my father rejected a plan of like nature years ago."

"Of course. If all the priests of Egypt were unified under one head—why, it would be a state within a state." He was delighted with the phrase and repeated, "A state within a state." And when his aunt nodded as if convinced, and said, "Your Majesty is right, and perhaps the proposal should be given study to see if it can be made workable," he felt a surge of elation. She might have listened to the priest's madness if he, Thothmes, had not stopped the fool.

He tried to keep his satisfaction from showing too openly, but her agreement signified, he thought confidently, a willingness to shift her burdens to his young shoulders. His aunt might nurse peculiar and womanish ideals, but once he had made Egypt fat with tribute from conquered nations, when she saw his triumphal processions and the slaves and plunder, when the temple storehouses bulged with foreign gold as well as domestic grain, then she must admit that man's vision was wider than woman's and that he was competent to lead Egypt to its great destiny of world power.

It was perhaps a month later, just after the public celebration of His Majesty's fifteenth birthday, that Hat-shep-sut gave further demonstration of her wish to be of help to him. "It is not too early," she said, "for Your Majesty to think of the monuments by which your reign can achieve lasting glory and distinction. Lord Senmut has suggestions, and with Your Majesty's approval we should visit and talk with the authorities in the cities involved. Your Majesty needs a change of scene," she added, "and your subjects will welcome the chance to entertain their king."

It was a holiday for Thothmes, a gay and leisurely invasion of another Egypt, foreign to the disciplined austerities of court and temple living. And there was no disguising the delight and excitement caused on both banks of the Nile by the appearance offshore of the brilliant pageant of ships.

The time of inundation was nearing and the river, for months confined to narrow, twisting channels, now reached muddy fingers across the dried flats toward the farm lands. Peasants, harvesting late crops and strengthening dikes against the coming flood, waved sickles and hoes and shouted to wives and children and pointed.

First came the ships with soldiers and their spears and banners and standards, then the splendid golden barge of Thothmes, and, only slightly less magnificent, those of Queen Hat-shep-sut and Queen Neferu-Re. Behind these the river was filled with color and movement—barques of princes, kitchen boats, galleys, tenders. For Pharaoh's court traveled with him.

For a while, when the procession passed a village, the young Thothmes sat stiffly in lonely grandeur so the poor of the land might view their king. He saw their pointing and how the children danced with excitement, and a vagrant breeze brought their cries and sometimes the voice, but not the words, of the mayor who shouted a speech of welcome. In larger towns the quays were massed with shopkeepers, and artisans of every trade, with priests and farmers and fishermen, and the roar of the throng filled the Nile valley.

The greetings seemed spontaneous, but Pharaoh knew that the Royal Herald had warned of His Majesty's approach. And at the city of Koptos, where the party spent its first night, they found ample evidence of his labors. Here a royal pavilion was erected to receive, in comfort and reasonable privacy, the entire retinue—great tents furnished with necessities of the household, and the luxuries without which royalty is unhappy.

This first night set a pattern for the others. A guard of picked warriors led the parade from the quay through a respectful crowd that lined the streets and house-tops. Pharaoh Thothmes appeared driving a golden chariot and its spirited horses, followed by the two queens in their carrying-chairs. A host of nobles and ladies in chariots and litters, more soldiers, and then an army of cooks and maids and stewards and retainers. Gifts and speeches of welcome were offered before Pharaoh's pavilion, and the crowd settled patiently to wait and watch, to discuss what it had seen, to admire at a distance the elegance of equipment and the arrogance of these Theban soldiers who guarded it.

One more public appearance was made when the court, led by Pharaoh and the queens, bore offerings to the temples of Min and Isis, deities of the city, and then returned to the privacy of the tented enclosure. A mob of the curious remained, determined to extract the last ounce of interest. They huddled beyond the patrolling guards, sniffed the exotic scents which escaped the women's tents, wagged their heads to match the faint throbbing rhythm of harp and tambourine, pointed to the laden trays of food and vine-wrapped jars of wine carried by hurrying servants, argued over the importance of individuals seen moving among the tents, whether one wearing two gold armlets was of higher rank than another with one armlet and a jeweled necklace.

After the evening meal Pharaoh and Queen Hat-shep-sut received a few of their friends in comfortable informality—Neb-taui, Lord Thuti, Senmut, Ma-herpa, General Menti among others, and Thothmes asked Neb-taui why the caravan route which led from here to the eastern sea was no longer used.

"In the old days, Your Majesty, the road served three purposes—the shortest route to splendid granite quarries, to prolific gold mines, and to the eastern sea from which ships trafficked with the God's Land in Punt." Neb-taui ticked the three uses of the road on his fingers. "The gold mines no longer give a paying yield; those east of Nekheb and in Nubia are richer. The quarries—some of the finest hard stone in the temples of Egypt came from there, and excellent stone remains for the cutting, but the quarries are three days' march from the Nile. When large building projects are in operation, gangs of two and three thousand workers must live in the desert and food and water must be brought them daily, and the quarried stone must be hauled here across the burning wastes. New quarries have been developed in the south at Yebu near the Cataract, stone of excellent quality which can be hauled to the river in an hour."

Neb-taui smiled at his king. "The short haul is important to bear in mind, Your Majesty, when you begin your building. In the old days a king seldom considered the cost, in gold or in labor, but now . . ."

Hat-shep-sut interrupted the old man with a kindly nod. "Egypt has grown mentally and morally since those days, Your Majesty," she said. "Today Pharaoh considers his subjects' welfare as well as his own desires. This is good governing."

"Why?" said Thothmes. "Is Pharaoh king, or not? Does he think of one group of men or of Egypt? A king," he said fretfully, "has responsibilities which few can guess."

Neb-taui bowed. "Your Majesty is right, of course. As the gods' representative on earth, may not your responsibility be to interpret their wishes correctly? To the gods, Egypt is more than a river lined with temples; it is the home of countless souls, the meanest of which has a place in their plans. I hope that Your Majesty will consider this.

"Now," said Neb-taui, "the third reason why the caravan route from Koptos is no longer needed—Lord Senmut can give a better account than I."

Senmut the priest? What, Thothmes thought, can he know about trade routes? He nodded careless agreement.

"The early kings," said Senmut, "when they wished to trade with Sinai or the incense lands in Punt, marched an army for five days across the desert from Koptos, built their ships on the shore of the eastern sea, and sailed from there. Then one of the great Pharaohs of history—your ancestor Pharaoh Sen-usert, Your Majesty—dug a canal which connected the waters of the Nile with those of the Bitter Lakes and the eastern sea. He was able then to sail all the way from Thebes to Punt without an army or a caravan."

Thothmes' eyes glistened. "Sen-usert? He did this?"

"Yes, Your Majesty. So today Koptos has lost much of its importance; it is still the center of worship of the harvest-god Min and of Holy Isis, but it no longer plays host to armies."

General Menti leaned forward eagerly. "With permission, Your Majesty—Koptos will, however, always merit Your Majesty's generous consideration. When the hated Shepherd Kings overran Egypt, they never got south of Koptos. I do not know if there were forts or battles, but General Aahmes Pen-Nekheb told of being garrisoned here in his youth. The city still is important to memory, Your Majesty."

The next day Neb-taui rode in Pharaoh's barge, and on following days sometimes one, sometimes several, princes at a time conversed with Thothmes, answered his many questions, informed him on details familiar to their work or experience; and at night in the seclusion of the pavilion, while his aunt listened and offered occasional friendly comment, the talks continued and the boy's curiosity was led subtly in paths strange to his thinking. Many of the arguments explored subjects on which the queen had expressed strong prejudices, and the boy wondered sometimes if, perhaps by signs, she directed the conversations.

"What did you mean last night," he asked one morning of Senmut, "when you said it was questionable practice to force a son to follow the father's trade? Doesn't apprenticeship insure a steady flow of young talent to replace the old and wornout? Isn't that good planning?"

"In theory, yes, Your Majesty, but it also can be wasteful of talent. A method whereby the whole economic structure of Egypt would be gradually strengthened is preferred. A controlled apprenticeship, yes; forced, no."

"What is 'controlled apprenticeship'?" A plan that developed gradually held little interest for Thothmes; he wanted immediate and showy results, ideas that would impress and astonish. He wanted people to say, "Pharaoh—truly the son of Amon! Who else could do this?"

"My duties as steward of the estates of Amon and of the princesses take me into all corners of Egypt," said Senmut. "Wherever I go I watch for the unusual worker, the gifted man or boy —perhaps it will be just the way he smiles as he works, Your Majesty. I talk with him, ask others about him. I find what he likes best to do, how he accepts instruction; I find if he asks questions, and if he hears the answers. I describe him to Tet, Overseer of the Temple Shops, and perhaps bring him to Thebes and settle him with the family of a worker of the same trade. And soon we have a good sculptor or leather-worker instead of another bad farmer or disinterested carpenter.

"This has been my program for years past in Thebes, and if the same system were adopted in the shops of the other temples of Egypt . . . You see, Your Majesty? Multiplied a hundred times in a year, an evergrowing corps of skilled workers, boys favored by the gods and with special aptitudes—the master-artisans of tomorrow."

"Have you thought where this army could be employed?" said Thothmes impatiently.

"That will be the responsibility of those appointed as heads of departments. I know Your Majesty's intentions to make his reign brilliant, praised by posterity, and nothing assures this like an aggressive program of building and reconstruction. The whole land is stimulated, there is work for all the trades, a free flow of goods, health and prosperity throughout the land—can Your Majesty guess the joy with which your every appearance would be greeted?"

"I shall build, of course." Thothmes nodded and waved his hand to include both banks, the barren fields awaiting the Nile's fructifying silt, the drowsy villages. He liked Senmut's phrase "praised by posterity"; it sketched a picture to his mind of awe-struck crowds standing before a magnificent shining temple and whispering the words of dedication:

> "Men-kheper-Re Thothmes, he
> made it for love of his father
> Min (or Re, or Amon, or Osiris)."

A hundred, a thousand years from now his name still would be remembered and praised, for *his* buildings, of enduring stone and startling beauty, would outlive the work of ordinary Pharaohs.

Perhaps he would need an army of master-workers such as Senmut proposed—when he was ready to build. Besides new structures, there were the restorations his aunt mentioned—shrines, chapels, damaged chambers in existing temples—neglected during more than a century of occupation by the foreign Shepherd Kings. There would be much to occupy his thought in Egypt—when he was ready to build.

As the holiday advanced, he spent more and more time on Hat-shep-sut's ship. She surrounded herself daily with a congenial group whose talk was free and relaxed—with few of the tensions, Thothmes noticed, that attended an audience on the royal barge. She was charming, gracious; the boy thought now not of a stone goddess but of a woman of gentle wit, one of rare loveliness whose glance stirred warmth and happiness in the heart. The change surprised him; heretofore he had seen only the queen.

The conversation on such days ranged far: control of the Nile flooding, peaceful trade with foreign countries, tax collection methods and the rights of peasants, use of criminals in mining operations, the development of the turquoise mines in Sinai, certain problems in building. . . .

One day she said, "My Lord Thuti, I am not sure that I approve of the practice of beating farmers in order to extract the taxes levied against their land. Surely there are methods less—emphatic, shall we say?"

"Not if Your Majesty wishes to keep your government alive and prosperous," said Thuti easily. "Lord Senmut should be able to offer evidence of the stubbornness of farmers; as Steward of Amon he quarrels with them daily."

"It is not easy," Senmut agreed, "to convince a farmer that a tax which leaves him bare subsistence is a just tax. Since he cannot read, the written laws bearing Your Majesty's seal carry no meaning to him; he sees every official as an enemy, a thief motivated by selfish greed who will steal his donkey and his daughter if unwatched. Such a man, as Lord Thuti hints, is difficult to persuade."

"Yet without farmers," said Hat-shep-sut, "Egypt would have no existence."

"The farmer knows that, Your Majesty, and it adds to his bitterness. Further, he knows that he has been exploited in times past and is convinced that his rights always will be ignored."

Thuti waved a careless hand. "I think that you exaggerate the situation, My Lord. These are not thinking people; they answer to impulses and urges, offer blind resistance to fancied wrongs. The gentlest horse will kick when irritated—but the stick tames it to the master's will."

"My Lord Thuti," the Queen said severely, "we speak of human beings, not of beasts; men of great practical value to their community and their country, a steadying influence on the economy of Egypt, as the bowrope steadies a ship. If they fear the collector of taxes, this is our fault and not theirs. Is there any law which says that they cannot be taught their honorable place in society? Would not everyone benefit from a gradual raising of people's intelligence throughout the land?"

"Not a country of scribes and priests, surely!" But Lord Thuti's attempt at humor did not amuse the queen.

"Your Majesty," she said to Thothmes, "I urge a long-range plan. The cities which we have visited—Your Majesty has found them centers of cults and prejudices, each holding to its local traditions, each blindly contented with ignorance of affairs outside its borders. Does this make for a united and prosperous Egypt? Does it not, rather, reveal to the visitor from another country that our boasted 'civilization' is an empty word? Think of this, Your Majesty; there are many ways by which Pharaoh can make his name live through eternity."

To his surprise, Thothmes found much of stimulation in these talks, though their effect was somewhat lessened by the shifting scene, the ever-changing Nile valley—now crowded where eastern and western hills pulled together, now broadening to accommodate acres of gently rising fertile lands on either bank. He had seen it all many times, but not with this leisure or with the maturity of viewpoint which, he assured himself, he now brought to it. After all, a few months would find him sole master of the potentials of Egypt, responsible for the health and prosperity, the very lives of its masses; he found this a sobering thought, at odd moments.

Menefe was exciting as usual; it had been one of the earliest capitals of the Pharaohs and its monuments were easily the most spectacularly massive in the land. As Thothmes and Senmut approached Khufu's great pyramid on the sloping avenue from the River Temple, the Steward told Thothmes how the ancient king had been a real benefactor to his people. He gave work and wages to thousands every year for twenty years during the months of inundation while the waters covered the farms, using this period for the ferrying of a surplus of stone from the quarries and dragging it to the pyramid site for later use by the stone-cutters.

With General Menti the boy inspected the border fortresses in the Delta, and the general told him of the war with the Libyans in the western Delta region, the last offensive operation by Egyptian soldiers, when Thothmes was an infant.

"It was Your Majesty's father's second fighting. His first was in Nubia. All Pharaohs campaign first in Nubia, you know."

"Why?"

"It has always been. Perhaps because it gets the men into quick condition—marching and maneuvers. There are usually just raiding parties, no real fighting. And Your Majesty comes to know the feel of your bow, and of the horses in rough country. General Aahmes said that he understood that Pharaoh Senusert's first campaign was in the south."

"Neb-taui did not tell me that."

"Oh, yes, Your Majesty. And he built two splendid fortresses above the First Cataract. They are in ruins now, but they were strategically located. . . ."

"Can they be restored?"

"Well, I am not an architect. I do not know, Your Majesty."

"Take me there to see them. Now."

135

"Why—yes, Your Majesty. If the queen approves."

"What has she to do with it?"

Later he stormed into the queen's presence. "Menti is taking me south to Yebu, Your Majesty. With Senmut. Today."

"You will enjoy the trip, I am sure."

Hat-shep-sut's smile spoiled the beautiful argument that he had prepared, left him stammering. "Two fighting galleys—for speed, you know."

His aunt nodded. "The royal barge and Lord Senmut's barque can return to Thebes with the rest of our party."

The king sailed within the hour.

There was nothing leisurely about this return voyage. Though the inundation was gaining daily and the valley between the banks was already a swirling, muddy torrent, yet with the good north wind behind to fill the sail, and with the captains calling a fast stroke, the two ships flew southward.

The speed and danger exhilarated Thothmes. Traveling so swiftly, it was impossible to follow a channel or to sight hidden sandbars in time to avoid them; at any moment the ship might crash at full flight, tossing its mast and occupants into the river. There were narrow escapes, but Amon's finger guided his favorite and they swept past Thebes without incident.

Thothmes had been thinking of Her Majesty's failure to question this impulse of his to end the pleasant holiday. He decided that this was proof of her growing faith in him and in his maturity. She might disagree with certain of his policies once he was alone on the throne, but he would say, "I am Pharaoh," and that would end it. They could remain friends, and there doubtless would be matters of local importance on which her advice would be useful.

With Senmut beside him, he studied the towering cliffs opposite Thebes which encircled the great bay of sand. "The causeway of your proposed temple would start here, I suppose, and lead straight west toward the cliffs."

Senmut bowed; he seemed surprised that the king remembered details of a plan seen but once and summarily discarded.

"Aren't there many early burials there that would be disturbed in the digging?"

"Probably, Your Majesty; the site was popular with your ancestors some five hundred years ago."

Pharaoh nodded. "It is an impressive setting for a temple, but I would not wish to offend the powerful dead. Besides"—he turned away to indicate loss of interest—"when I build, I shall draw my own plans."

They passed the town of Per-haa and entered a relatively unproductive section of the valley where rocks and waste lands crowded the river, where arable lands were confined to narrow strips on the two banks. The province was barely self-sustaining and he asked Senmut for ideas of how conditions here could be improved. This apparently was like asking a mother if she had ideas on child-care, for Senmut was still talking when the signal flags of the Nekheb lookouts were sighted, announcing their approach to the town.

They stayed only long enough for the king to sound Lord Tura, his Viceroy of Kush, on conditions south of the frontier. The answers were straight and enabled Pharaoh to reach a decision.

"The Kushites are warlike," said Tura, "but they lack cohesion." The old man spoke slowly, choosing his words. "A display of force would but scatter them and result in endless and annoying border incidents. Your Majesty's real enemies are in Rutenu and the east; if you wish to concentrate on them, you will need a quiet southern border. Do I understand that Your Majesty asks my advice?"

"I do, My Lord."

"No campaign in the south, then, Your Majesty."

This argument made such sense that, despite Menti's scowls and mutterings, the king abandoned the subject. He was in a fret of excitement as they neared Yebu, and even the deafening tumult of the waters at the Cataract and the perilous inch-by-inch passage through the raging flood interested him only momentarily.

He attacked the crumbled fortresses as if to rebuild them with his own hands. They were so placed as to command the river and nothing could pass that would not be swept by arrows. Once they had been impregnable, he decided—sheer eighty-foot walls and shrewdly placed covering walls and counter-forts of crude brick reinforced by massive beams.

"Can they be restored?" he asked eagerly of Senmut.

"Oh, yes, Your Majesty. It will be costly, but . . ."

"Prepare me an estimate of the cost. And the dedication shall read:

> " 'The Good God, Men-kheper-Re, made it as a monument for holy Dedun, presider over Nubia, and for the Pharaoh Sen-usert.' "

He felt the exhilaration of one who has kept a cherished vow; his mind was ready, now, to focus on events that would blaze his name like a meteor across the heavens for all to see and fear. No campaign in Nubia, he decided on the swift return to Thebes; his first fighting would be in Syria.

He threw himself enthusiastically into review of the knowledge necessary to assure complete domination of the nations east of Egypt to the great River-that-flows-backward. This was the land of herds and grains and minerals subdued by his grandfather; fear of the latter's name had worn a little, however, and the princes of the region now sent more excuses than tribute.

With his maps before him, he planned for the day of "liberation" as he called it, the day when he need no longer say, "This I will do if the queen approves it." His first act, on the very day the regency was dissolved, would be to issue a decree of conscription on the governors of districts, demanding of each his quota of recruits. Thirty thousand would be called, of which fifteen thousand would be kneaded into shape and equipped from the royal arsenals as light infantry. Chariotry, the aristocratic branch of the army and composed of princes and their sons, was always drilled and ready.

Attainment of his ultimate goal might require several campaigns. The cities of the coast, some of them fortified, must be subdued before the eastern countries could be conquered. Resistance, however, was not likely to be strong; differences of race and speech and religion kept the small city states in jealous discord.

Lord Thuti pointed out that besides complete conquest there must be permanent occupation. Therein, Thuti said, had His Majesty's grandfather failed; he had slaughtered and pillaged and set a stone on the banks of the River-that-flows-backward, and then withdrawn, and for a while men saw the stone and

138

remembered; and then the sons, without memory of the evil that had befallen their fathers, threw down the stone, saying, "Who is this Mighty Bull, this Son of Re who lives eternally?" And other nations, seeing that Egypt did not strike the offenders, withheld in turn their tribute. A permanent occupation, said Thuti.

Lord Menti described the country as recited to him by General Aahmes. Instead of the one river as in Egypt, a river which flowed from south to north, and one valley enclosed between two ranges of mountains, the land of the foreigners was a confusion of mountains and streams. Also there were forests, and broad plains fertilized by torrents of rain, there was stinking heat and killing cold—and, Aahmes had sworn this, there was that winding, sluggish, chocolate-colored River-that-flows-backward, from north to south! This Thothmes knew that he must see to believe, for to credit it was to admit that the gods had not created Egypt as the pattern for the universe.

One day he told his determination to see this foreign river to his aunt the queen, and she said "Yes?" and looked at him with thoughtful steadiness for a while.

"I wonder if I understand Your Majesty," she said presently. "It is unfriendly territory and you will need a strong escort."

"My escort will be strong enough," he boasted, "and I shall march at its head."

"An army? You plan a campaign against the Rutenu and the Naharin? You know my feelings regarding aggression, Your Majesty."

"I will be Pharaoh, then," said Thothmes firmly. He was a little frightened by his own words, but continued. "It is planned to the last dagger, to the last bag of onions and water-jar. Nothing can stop it, you see."

The queen's lips pulled to a thin, straight line.

"I see," she said, and bowed, and left him.

CHAPTER XII

Year 3 of the Reign of Hat-shep-sut
(also reckoned as the Reign of Thothmes III)

It was not needed that a man holding Tet's office, Overseer of the Shops of the Temple of Amon in Thebes, be also a seer to know that some unusual development was building in those last days of Hat-shep-sut's regency, in the weeks just prior to the young king's sixteenth birthday.

By nature of the office, Tet often guessed secrets hidden from others of wider acquaintance or activity; not because he was an inquisitive man—he was interested only in his work, and happy if that work when finished was as near perfection as human patience and skill could make it—but because, a simple man and sensitive, deviations from accustomed procedures intruded upon the orderliness of his mind, alerted his attention.

As the New Year approached, the feeling grew that strange and hidden forces were in movement. It was the custom at New Year's that gifts be offered by Pharaoh to the gods, and by the princes to Pharaoh. Each year the Temple Shops were flooded with commissions—from statues and boats to gold-tipped canes; this year was no exception, but there was an unbalance that puzzled Tet. Pharaoh ordered for Amon an offering-table wrought in gold and silver and two silver ceremonial pails, while Hat-shep-sut, for Amon, ordered a barge of new cedar imported from the terraces of Lebanon, pink granite jars of ointment, an ebony harp inlaid with silver and gold, and jars and vases and necklaces. The queen's offering would outshine Pharaoh's, and this, Tet worried, was not done.

There were further perplexing circumstances of which the good man could make no sense. Whereas other princes ordered lavishly of statues and war helmets and gold axes and chariots and fans and sticks and vases for Pharaoh, Senmut, of all men,

140

ignored Pharaoh and ordered for Hat-shep-sut only—dishes of gold, jeweled necklaces, a costly ceremonial barque, a statuette, an inlaid game-box, and so on. As if Hat-shep-sut is his king, Tet thought. He is committing political suicide. Usually the decisions of the Steward of Amon could be trusted, but Tet found himself watching the younger man with affectionate anxiety. And he soon found other details to puzzle him.

Senmut had been disappointed when the plans he and Paheri prepared for the elaborate mortuary temple across the Nile from Thebes were ignored. Now suddenly the drawings were spread all over his office, and he worked on them daily, changing, erasing, redrawing; he even took them to the palace with him at night, and if Tet needed the master, he must go to the palace and send word by a servant to the queen's chambers. And now, also, Nehessi, Captain of the King's Ships, was frequently closeted with him, and Tet remembered the proposed expedition to Punt, the God's Land, for incense, and when Senmut ordered quantities of cheap knives and beads and necklaces and hatchets, articles used as trade goods, Tet was really confused. For Nehessi, if General Menti's stories of preparations for Pharaoh's coming campaign were not fantasy, Nehessi would be occupied with the ferrying of troops and supplies for the next several months.

Fortunately for Tet's peace, scant time was allowed him to indulge uneasiness; the night before celebration of the New Year found him in the Shops superintending a last polishing, and the packing of the more fragile pieces. He had been there since dawn, and now the midnight hour was past. He yawned and rubbed his smarting eyes and stepped outside.

The temple loomed black and silent through the trees that bordered the Sacred Lake, and he paced slowly, snuffing the chill air deep into his lungs. The stars blazed with frosty brilliance—holes let into the iron lid that covered Egypt at night, a priest once had told him. A light showed as usual in Senmut's office, but the rest of the world could have been dead. Then a distant moan sounded and Tet shivered. The hour when the dead walk, he thought, and turned to re-enter the Shops. And at that moment the gong within the temple was struck, stranger to hear at this hour than howl of beast or spirit, a persistent urgent hammering that signaled emergency.

As he waited, wondering, torches appeared at the temple gates and messengers sped into the city; an under-priest came panting and almost collided with Senmut who ran from his office.

"What?" Senmut called.

"The god, Master," gasped the priest, "in the holy place—the god's voice, Master."

Other priests stumbled from the nearby dormitories, yawning, cursing the breaking of their rest. Neb-taui passed, an aged white-gowned ghost.

What, Tet thought, could this be? What message could Amon have for Egypt that would not await the day? Lights already were showing in the streets; and presently a jostling litter disgorged the Governor of Thebes, another the Royal Treasurer, and with a rattle of hooves Pharaoh himself drove up in his chariot, accompanied by General Menti and guards. The whole city, Tet thought—the queen, even, Queen Hatshep-sut with her steward, Lord Ma-herpa.

He shrugged curiosity aside; this was not getting his work done and there remained two hours, probably three, before he could rest. Occasionally, in a momentary hush of the Shops' clamor, he caught the continued solemn chanting, and thought, Whatever it is, it's important; then, he had no idea what the hour, he saw Lord Senmut in the doorway of the Shops.

The Steward of Amon looked worn, but there was a light in his eyes of something like triumph, and his tone was unwearied.

"The king's order, Tet," he said. "Prepare a slab of fine-grained sandstone four fingers thick and two-and-a-half spans wide by five spans tall. When it is ready, Neb-taui will give you the exact wording to be carved—from this."

He passed a strip of papyrus to the Overseer's hand, and the latter read:

> "Royal command to the king's son, the governor
> of the south countries, Tura triumphant.
> Behold, there is brought to thee this command
> of the king in order to inform thee that my
> majesty has appeared as King of Upper and
> Lower Egypt upon the Horus-throne of the
> living.

142

Make my titulary as follows:
HORUS: Mighty of souls;
FAVORITE OF TWO GODDESSES: Fresh in years;
GOLDEN HORUS: Divine of appearances;
KING OF UPPER AND LOWER EGYPT: Ma-ka-Re;
DAUGHTER OF RE: Divine Consort, Great Royal
Wife, Princess of the Two Lands, Hat-shep-
sut. She lives eternally.
Cause thou oblations to be offered to the gods of
Yebu of the South.
Cause thou that the oath be established in the
name of my majesty.
This is a communication to inform thee of it.
Year 3 of the reign, first month of the first season,
first day, the day of coronation."

Midway in the reading, Tet thrust a startled glance at the other, then finished hurriedly. He turned the papyrus over and over, scowling, and reread it slowly.

"B-but," he stammered, "you said 'the king's order.'"

"A new king sits Egypt's throne, as of this night," said Senmut. "King Ma-ka-Re—she who was Queen Hat-shep-sut. The coronation ceremony was just performed."

"King Ma-ka-Re?" Tet's mind refused to accept the absurdity offered it. "Two kings? Pharaoh Thothmes *and* the queen?"

Senmut shook his head. "I don't know all the details," he confessed. "Amon's voice was heard calling from the sanctuary, demanding the presence of Pharaoh and Hat-shep-sut. You heard the alarm, remember? The Chief Prophet conducted them to the secret presence, and when they returned, Thothmes was as white as my apron, and the Chief Prophet announced Amon's appearance in person naming Hat-shep-sut king for her lifetime in the place of her nephew. . . ."

"Wait, wait." Tet struck his head as if to knock the ideas into understandable form. "A woman king? This is nonsense, Senmut. '*Her* Majesty, the King.' How will that sound? How can a woman rule Egypt?"

"Hat-shep-sut has done well in the years since her father's death."

"Yes, yes, as regent; but as king . . . Will a woman lead Egypt's armies in the wars?"

"There will be no wars, my friend."

Tet saw that Senmut made this statement in sober earnestness. "I see; no wars. The queen—the king, I mean—that is, Hat-shep-sut—she is thirty-three years old, I think. She is to be king while she lives, say another twenty, twenty-five years. Well, it's a pretty dream, but—how does she expect to hold the loyalty of the heathen princes overrun by her father? By love?"

Senmut shrugged the problem aside. "I think that we can depend on Amon in the event of need; it is his will, you know, that she be named king."

"I wonder," Tet murmured, but Senmut did not hear.

"We have our own work," said Senmut with an effort at casualness. "Amon also ordered Her Majesty to send an expedition to Punt for incense . . ."

"Senmut!" Tet exclaimed.

". . . and to build for him a terraced temple on the West Bank . . ."

"After your plan!"

". . . and in a generous moment Her Majesty named me 'Overseer of the Works of Amon,' to conduct the building."

Delight as genuine as if the coveted honor were his own leaped to Tet's eyes, then he checked himself and bowed formally. "Congratulations, My Lord; it is a title honestly earned."

"Oh, come," said Senmut roughly, "between us? I remember a youngster to whom your friendship was important as bread. He hasn't changed, Tet."

And Tet, to hide emotion and to demonstrate the extremity of his pleasure, beat his superior on the back and babbled, "Let me tell Penati—he'll rejoice as I do. And the master—Ineni knows—I feel it; and he'll be there—his spirit will be with you on the West Bank. Can we—you're exhausted, of course, but let's glance again at the plans; a causeway with sphinxes, I remember, and three terraces. . . ."

The new-born sun was peering over the distant mountains when Tet threaded the busy streets homeward, his mind a tumult of excited planning. A hundred and fifty to two hundred statues, Senmut said, of limestone, sandstone, black and red granite—there were years of work ahead for the master sculptors and artists and their apprentices. It was bigger than any single project that Ineni had handled, and the Shops would have to be enlarged. He must see Penati tomorrow—today, that is. He could not make it seem possible that so much of importance could happen in the small handful of hours since he had walked by the Sacred Lake.

"Amon's will," Senmut had said. All the little hints and signs that had bothered him in recent weeks fell neatly into a pattern, but Tet decided that if Senmut wanted to plot with Hat-shep-sut, it was Senmut's business. After all, a boy or a woman on the throne—in a month, who would remember? Carpenters still would shape their boxes and stools, and gold-smiths solder their delicate necklaces; leather-workers, brick-makers, butchers, fishermen, all the complements of a robust and versatile society would re enter their ruts, beat their wives with customary abandon, bribe the gods, sing or curse according to habit. "Her Majesty," "His Majesty," one or both—did it matter?

In the next week the river before Thebes wore a festive air, with dozens of gilded barques bringing princes of the south and north to pledge support to King Ma-ka-Re.

From what Tet could hear, relief seemed to be the general reaction; governors of provinces and other officers had become used to Hat-shep-sut as head of the state, while no one could guess in what direction the boy Thothmes might leap when the controls were lifted. Many expressed the belief that she was inspired, and the story of her divine birth, invented by that canny politician, her father, was revived and quoted in the city. She gained immediate favor, also, by insisting upon inclusion of Thothmes' name with hers on royal decrees, and by directing that the regnal years be numbered from his accession. This indicated, people said, that she considered the arrangement as temporary, perhaps until the youth grew in years and balance— a wise precaution, most agreed. It was not known how Thothmes thought on the matter; he was in Yebu with Tura, the Viceroy of Kush, restoring the fortresses of his dead hero.

Penati already was somewhere in the desert hunting stone, and Senmut spent every daylit moment that he could steal from other duties on the West Bank with Nebiri. Tet, if he would consult him, must be ferried across the river and search in one of the score of dust clouds that marked preparations for the eventful day of "stretching the cord," the ceremony of laying the foundations.

From the river, the site was an ugly and forbidding waste of rock and sand, and the prospect of beauty blooming there seemed remote and fantastic. Attempts were being made to smooth and level the road that led for a mile across an ancient cemetery to the planned gateway, for the formal procession must pass this way on "the day," and later the road would be a paved causeway. Surveyors drew their lines around the boundaries of the future building, and at each important angle and corner a pit was being dug to hold the foundation deposits.

In Thebes, among a dozen duties of varying magnitude, Tet was responsible for preparation of some of these deposits. Included were miniatures of the tools that would be used in building the temple: axes, mallets, chisels, crucibles, brickmakers' molds, wooden picks, sieves—each inscribed in blue ink with King Ma-ka-Re's cartouche. Also platters and small saucers intended to hold samples of food offerings. A number of little jars, beautifully carved from alabaster, were prepared to hold ointments, and on each a skilled workman engraved:

"The Daughter of the Sun-God, Hat-shep-sut.
She made this as her monument to her father
Amon at the time of stretching the cord over
the Temple of Amon Zeser-Zeseru. May she
be living."

Then handfuls of gemlike scarab seals were carved, of exquisite workmanship and design. Most of these carried the full names and titles of Hat-shep-sut; some bore Thothmes' name, "The Beautiful God, Men-kheper-Re," and some read "King's Daughter, King's Sister, and Divine Consort, Neferu-Re."

Then, in the midst of fevered preparations, Senmut dragged Tet out of the Shops on a half-holiday. Nehessi, Captain of the King's Ships, appeared before Thebes with the five new ships built for the hazardous expedition to the God's Land. If Tet needed further proof that "Amon's will" had been anticipated by a margin of months, this was that proof, for ninety-foot

146

ships are not produced, equipped and shining, by snapping the fingers.

In their structure they combined the acknowledged features necessary to sea-going ships and certain refinements that Nehessi feared might go unnoticed, and he explained them to any listener. Tet made a good audience.

This day his audience included Her Majesty whose presence, with members of her suite, confused the honest captain. He bustled and perspired, herded his precious charges with the seriousness of an artist offering a masterpiece to the vulgar gaze.

"Over here, if you please, Your Majesty." He pointed over the side of the ship. "See here, the deck beams pass through the skin of the hull. This new construction strengthens the ship. On the Great Green—waves as high as the mast-top, Your Majesty. A weak ship can be crushed by them."

"This is your idea?" said Hat-shep-sut.

Nehessi bowed. "My idea. And the mast—I have stepped the mast exactly amidships. It is a fixture; it cannot be lowered. Heavily stayed; you can see the forest of strong ropes fore and aft."

"How can you know one rope from another?" Senmut marveled.

Nehessi ignored the remark. "Look at those yards," he said to the queen. "With sail and gear they weigh eighteen hundred pounds! You need a stout mast, well-stayed. . . ."

"Indeed, yes," Her Majesty agreed. "And some of the ropes are to raise the sail quickly when a wind hits the ship?"

Nehessi faltered. Tet guessed from his expression that the captain's thought might be, How can one so stupid be King of Egypt? Tet also caught an exchange of glances between Her Majesty and Lord Senmut that signified a sharing of some pleasantry hidden from the others.

"*Raise* the sail? To furl it?" Nehessi sighed "No, Your Majesty. On the Great Green where the winds change without warning, you do not empty a sail by raising a lower yard. On ships that sail the Great Green the lower yard must be stationary; the ropes are to raise the *upper* yard, so then, in emergency, the ropes are cut and the sail drops by its great weight, you see, and the ship does not founder."

147

"Most ingenious," the queen murmured. "This also is your idea?"

"No," Nehessi admitted, "it has long been in use. But here, Your Majesty—this *method* of raising the upper yard, this is mine. You see those two heavy single ropes fastened near the two ends of the upper yard? See how they pass through that box at the mast-head and then down to the stern of the ship? Now, follow them along the rail—on each side of the ship, and past the rowers' benches. Now. Here, My Lord"—he directed Senmut—"you are a rower. Sit on the bench—no, facing the stern, so. And you"—he snapped his fingers and pointed at Tet—"sit here. You are rowers, and the command comes to raise the sail. There are thirty rowers, fifteen to a side. You grasp the ropes—without leaving the benches, see—and pull together, and up goes the sail. Now. Ingenious, eh?"

Tet heard subdued laughter among the lords and ladies watching, and he guessed how incongruous the scene was—a prince of Egypt with rich dress and fine stick and wig, and the Overseer of the Temple Shops, playing rowers on a sea-going barge! Her Majesty controlled what amusement she might feel, though her eyes were suspiciously bright.

Nehessi, delighted that anyone showed any kind of interest in his enthusiasm, led his distinguished visitors from pointed prow to incurved stern. A few facts of nautical purport were reaching Tet's understanding; at least, now he could tell a "yard" from a "deck beam," and this was an accomplishment which, an hour earlier, would have seemed to him fantastic. "Well-stayed mast," Nehessi had said—the phrase had meaning now. Tet tested a heavy rope that ran the length of the ship, from stern to mast and on to the bow, and found it taut as a lute-string. He nodded in comprehension and answered the captain's inquiring glance, "Well-stayed indeed; it would take a strong wind to topple that mast, wouldn't it?"

Nehessi glowered. "That is a truss. A truss and not a stay. It prevents the ship from breaking in two parts. River ships do not need it. A truss is found only on sea-going ships. It has nothing to do with supporting the mast."

Tet guarded his thoughts and tongue until the end of the visit.

He took another holiday on the day of sailing, and so, he

148

thought, did the rest of Thebes. The boats were ready, trim, provisioned, ballasted, and the crews in their places. A few men on Nehessi's ship appeared apprehensive; these were artists commissioned by royal command to return a pictorial history of the expedition. And a grim reminder of lurking dangers was seen in the presence aboard of a captain and his dozen heavily armed soldiers.

The ceremony ashore was simple; Amon and his priests, Her Majesty the King and the officials of her court. Hat-shep-sut arrived in a litter to the lively rattle of drums and resonant sticks and blare of trumpets. The people of Thebes loved a show, and there were cheers, and clapping of hands to the rhythm of the march of her bodyguard, and then a respectful quiet during the offerings and incense burning and the prayers to Hathor, Goddess of Punt, that she send kindly winds.

And presently a hush. Nehessi in the leading ship raised his hand, the captains of each of the ships did likewise, the sailors settled on the benches and grasped their oars, the soldiers ashore saluted, the waiting throng held its collective breath—and loosed it with a roaring shout as Nehessi's arm fell and the oars bit froth from the Nile. The captains' voices called a smart stroke, and like five straddling bugs skimming the surface of the water, the brave ships swept to the channel, dwindled swiftly to shining specks, and dissolved into the nothingness of distance.

The ships disappeared. The Nile could have swallowed them for all the word that came, and in the months that followed, the same thoughts stabbed sharply into many minds: Where are the ships? Where is Nehessi now? How is it with them? What terrors pursue them? Tet, safe in the familiarity of his beloved Shops, thanked his private gods for work that kept specters to a dimmed background.

It was still dark when Tet crossed in a temple barge carrying materials for use in the ceremony of "stretching the cord." Already the Nile was thronged with craft of every description bringing early-risers to the show; their torches dotted the waters like stars in an uneasy heaven, and ashore a mile-long thread of lights moved slowly inland to the base of the frowning cliffs.

Here surveyors had set their marks to indicate the boundaries of the future temple; at gateways, at angles and important corners, pits were prepared to receive dedication deposits, pits three spans square by five deep, and lined with mud bricks, and Tet made the round of the pits with temple slaves, leaving at each a collection of articles and a slave to guard them from theft by the milling holiday-makers.

Tet heard his name called and saw Nebiri shouldering his way through the press. He carried a bundle of rags under his arm, and bawled: "The master. Have you seen the master?"

"Senmut and Penati were back by the quarry when I passed. Something is wrong?"

Nebiri snorted. "Come here."

He pulled Tet away from the crowd and in passing caught a torch from the hand of one in a nearby group, and when the man cursed and tried to snatch the torch, Nebiri thrust him back and said carelessly, "You'll get it back, friend."

He drew Tet apart from the watchers and laid the bundle of rags in his hands and held the torch close, and Tet could not conceal a start of loathing when he peered within the folds. It was a shrunken human forearm, the arm of a mummy torn from its body, jeweled rings still on its fingers and circlets of gold and gems still clasping the withered wrist.

Nebiri rewrapped the gruesome object, tossed the torch to its owner, and took off toward the river with a swinging stride that Tet found difficult to match. There was the beginning of dawn in the east, and a forerunner of the wind that came with dawn fluttered the lights and made staggering shadows across the sand.

"I could have told the master," Nebiri grumbled. "There have been burials here for a thousand years, rich burials, princes and their women. It will take an army to guard them all. And can you blame a poor devil, when he sees gold in a hole, if he puts in his hand and helps himself?"

"Robbing the dead is an evil thing," said Tet piously.

Nebiri spat with savage violence. "You temple prigs with your soft living, what do you know of a poor man's hunger— not of the belly alone, but of the gnawing, aching hunger for a taste of the soft things of life? He doesn't see the dead man; in the gold he sees six months of ease and drunkenness, perhaps a pretty young slave, perhaps a bit of well-watered land and a mud house. Those are the dreams of your laborer, who, year in and out, carries sand and hauls stone for a few figs and onions, and once a year a piece of cloth and a pot of cheap ointment."

"All right," said Tet, "I can hear without the yelling." It was strange to find in Nebiri sympathy for the men he drove in the gangs.

"I mean that I see *why* he did it," Nebiri said earnestly, screwing his forehead, "not that I think he should. Thieving's thieving, I guess, but . . ."

"I should think so, tearing mummies apart."

"He'll be branded, probably, and sentenced to slavery in the mines. Just because he reached too far for a bit of beauty. Well, I take the master's pay, so I must report it, but I swear, Tet, sometimes I wish . . ."

"Is that Senmut, just leaving the quarry?"

It was the master, in his finest ceremonial dress and wearing the badges of his many honors, in conversation with Penati and surrounded by scribes and by slaves carrying blackened torches from which, with the coming of daylight, the flames had been extinguished. On this great day of his career, Senmut was calm, as if strolling in his garden with a friend, and when he saw Tet and Nebiri running, he waved his stick in greeting and smiled.

Nebiri passed his bundle to Senmut's hand. The smile turned to a frown and he said sharply, "Where?"

"South of where the second terrace is planned, Master."

"A gang?"

"One man only. At least, I searched and found no other. He had a hole and was coming out when . . ."

"Where is he now?"

"I beat him on the head with my fist. He'll wait there for you. Anyway, I set a man to guard the hole."

Senmut nodded and turned to Penati. "That answers our question of how soon thieving would start. Menti has promised guards, picked men; we'll open the prince's tomb you located yesterday and store everything we find in it. That should limit the stealing. Thanks, Nebiri, for watchfulness. Bring the man to me after the ceremony, and I'll see Menti."

A faint blare of horns was heard from the city, and they saw the god's barge, ablaze with gold and silver in the new sun's light, starting from the east bank and followed closely by the royal barge. Senmut and his group hurried across sand and rubble toward the place of landing.

The procession was forming when they arrived, the god in his shrine, Hat-shep-sut in her litter. Senmut made his bow, and she signed him nearer and held private conversation with him for some minutes, a mark of honor that told as certainly as a proclamation his place in her favor. When the procession moved, he walked with other nobles close behind the litter.

Picked guards led with their drum-beaters, then officials and priests and temple dancers and Amon's concubines, the god with his thirty bearers, Hat-shep-sut escorted by the Royal Fan-bearer and Lord Ma-herpa. Behind the princes were other guards, and treading on their heels was Tet and a mob of sight-seers, crowding and jostling in jealous competition for a view of the show.

The actual ceremony was disappointing, Tet thought. There were involved prayers by Amon's First Prophet, chantings, burning of incense; then Hat-shep-sut, accompanied by a priest-ess dressed to impersonate the goddess Seshat, held the cord on lines already laid by the surveyors, lines marking the axis of the proposed building. Each held golden hammers and pegs, and Hat-shep-sut said, "I hold the peg. I grasp the handle of the club and grip the measuring-cord with Holy Seshat. I make firm the four corners of thy temple."

A stop was made at each of the prepared pits. Here there were endless prayers and scattering of holy water, and the Chief Prophet dropped in the head, a leg and a rib of a newly slaughtered ox; and beside these were laid loaves of bread and little plates of barley and figs and grapes, or dates and bundles of celery. Tet's small jars were added, and the models of the tools to be used in the building of the temple; a handful of the exquisite scarabs cut and glazed so carefully by Tet's artists was tossed in, and the pits one by one were filled with sifted sand.

The sun was still hours high when the last of the priests and royal party pulled across the river, leaving on the West Bank a mass of quarreling humanity, disputing, wrangling in shrill discord over return passage to their homes. Oblivious of the uproar, a knot of men listened to the words of one of their number: "Grading of the causeway first; we'll need a stone bed to facilitate pulling the heavy stone for the terraces. Get your men at it tomorrow, Nebiri. Before you bring the stone already squared and smoothed, Penati, how about dismantling the shrine of the old king's father and setting the bricks aside? Remember—you spoke of using them later as scaffolding. And, Tet, your immediate worry will be finishing the paving blocks to keep up with Nebiri's grading."

Senmut sighed with satisfaction, tapping a gold-laced sandal with his stick. "Nothing can stop it, now," he said quietly; "and there'll be nothing like it in Egypt. And we four"— he smiled at his companions—"we four will build it. Come," he added briskly, "I have a jar of wine from Her Majesty's own pantry. Today is a day to celebrate. Come."

CHAPTER XIII

Year 5 of the Reign of Hat-shep-sut
(also reckoned as the Reign of Thothmes III)

The first real feeling of again being in Egypt came to Nehessi when, from the prow of the leading ship, he watched the pyramids thrusting their polished white sides out of the desert wastes behind Menefe. This, the broad main body of the Nile, was home and familiar, as the narrower and twisting fingers that felt north and east for the sea could never be.

Two years almost to a day—without the memory of storms and strange lands thick in his consciousness, it would be difficult to realize that the scene unfolding before him had been twice repeated since he last viewed it. As when the fleet sailed northward, the captured waters of the inundation again silvered canals and ditches on both banks, and farmers everywhere ploughed and planted, and the broad bosom of the Nile was unmarked by islands and shifting bars.

He asked the lookout, "Is there a channel close to the West Bank?"

"Do you want to stop at Menefe, Master?"

"No, but sail near so the people can get a view of the ships. It will be something to tell their grandchildren, you know."

The lookout considered. "This is the twenty-fifth Thoth; there should still be a safe channel within four boat-lengths, Master."

"That will do it." Nehessi rubbed his hands; they would give these country-dwellers, these provincials, something to wake them up. He could imagine their excitement when the messenger he had dispatched from the Bitter Lakes had told Egypt of the expedition's return; the Governor of Menefe would probably be offended because Nehessi could not stop, but he'd have to be satisfied with what he saw from the quay.

The buildings of Menefe seemed rushing toward them. Nehessi told the captain to signal the other ships to close in, also to order the rowers to their stations so the boats would give a trim appearance. These were no common cargo carriers, he reminded the captain.

He admitted to himself that, to the un-nautical eye, the ships might seem cluttered, with bales and tubs and chests and crates piled and tied to every inch of available deck-space, but it was a confusion made necessary by the unexpected variety and quantity of goods pressed on them by the innocence of the natives of that far country. When a cheap hatchet would buy a yearling ox, when for a handful of colored beads men would fell an ebony tree and deliver its heavy logs to the shore, it had seemed criminal to Nehessi not to take full advantage; the holds of the five ships were bursting with treasure and rarities, and the decks dangerously loaded. It was a magnificent "tribute" that he was bringing Pharaoh, and Pharaoh would see the wealth and, in fairness, acknowledge rare qualities in the man who accomplished difficult missions without fuss, and returned a profit. Especially, Nehessi reasoned hopefully, when Pharaoh saw the bonus surprise so ingeniously conceived and executed.

He passed an order to the captain, and presently a man emerged from the gaudy pavilion near the stern. He was tall, thin and fair-skinned as an Egyptian, and he wore the ordinary Egyptian dress, loin-cloth and beads and dagger, but there the similarity ended. For his right leg was ensheathed from ankle to knee in gold rings, and from his chin there sprouted a narrow upturned beard, identical with that ascribed to the gods. This was Parihu, Chief of the people of Punt, part of the surprise by which Nehessi hoped to impress Pharaoh; the rest of the surprise was hidden inside the pavilion in the form of Parihu's monstrously fat wife.

The lookout found a safe channel that paralleled the west bank and the five ships, sails full-bellied by the wind, bore in proud column past the outskirts of Menefe. Nehessi strained his eyes but could find disturbingly little evidence of interest in their approach; nowhere could he see crowds assembled. There were no shouts, no horns; it could have been a city of the dead except for the glimpse, now and then, of a bustling marketplace.

Nehessi swore. The captain edged nearer and cocked an

admiring ear to the flow of rich invective. Then he spat over the rail.

"You really expected a demonstration of some kind, didn't you?"

"Why not?" snapped his superior. "How many times during *your* life have expeditions like ours sailed into the unknown, and returned?"

"I know, but consider, now: was the scheme hatched in Menefe?"

"Of course not."

"Were men from Menefe included in the expedition? Any of the sailors, say, or a soldier, or just one of the artists?"

"No."

"Then for Menefe there was no expedition."

The captain was right, of course. Menefe, once great, was fiercely jealous of the rise of the sister-city in the south, jealous of Amon's displacement of Ptah in the public eye; determined, in short, to admit no good in any Theban or in any program sponsored by a Theban.

"Look at it," said Nehessi, waving his hand. "A city? A dead thing sprawled in the sun."

Chief Parihu, forgotten beside them, watching with fascinated awe the mile on mile of close-packed buildings sweeping past, spoke for the first time. "Cit-ee?"

"That's right, 'city.'" Nehessi grinned. Slack hours of the voyage home had been spent in teaching the chief Egyptian and he had proved a gratifying pupil. "Big city."

"Beeg cit-ee," repeated the chief. "Thebes."

By the time Nehessi had explained in blasphemous detail the enormity of the latter's error, the farmlands south of Menefe appeared and the ships were again in the safer channels of mid-river. The Nile stretched its gleaming sinuous length before them, empty except for a clumsy leaking tub so laden with blocks of stone that the steersman was unable to maneuver the twisting course of deep water and had driven it onto a hidden bank of mud. The crew were overboard in water to their waists, heaving and straining, while a disconsolate man sat amidships bailing with an earthen jar.

Stone for the new temple, perhaps? Nehessi had wondered often in the two years if Lord Senmut had been able to start as planned, and how the building was going. And who was king, now, Hat-shep-sut or Thothmes? The god had changed his mind once and could change it again; in two years a thousand calamities could come to Egypt—some enemy could have swallowed Thebes, even. He worked himself into a fine nervous state, ordered lookouts aloft, kept the five ships within hailing distance of each other, set a watch when they moored for the night, and spent the days pacing and peering.

Then on the third day from Menefe the lookout reported ships rowing from the south, war-galleys, and Nehessi's heart stopped until he identified them as Egyptian and the sailors as Egyptian marines. Ten ships—a welcoming party! His messenger had got through and everything was all right. A welcoming party! Now, this was better. He beat Chief Parihu on the back, dug his captain in the ribs, bustled the sailors to their stations, changed to a fresh dress. A fleet of war-galleys to welcome him home!

He watched their approach critically. Precision rowing, every blade lifting and dipping with a short, sharp stroke that kept a curl of foam under the prows. Presently the ships split into two files, five to the east and five to the west; as Nehessi came between them, the welcoming fleet swung about, dipped their flags in salute, raised their huge sails, and the three files, escorters and escorted, rushed southward in gallant and impressive parade.

A royal welcome! Nehessi forgot the impudence of those monkeys of Menefe in the excitement of this outstanding honor, though his pleasure was modified by the presence of Prince Thuti as leader of the escorting fleet. Thuti, with but the movement of an eyebrow, could make him feel like a farmer masquerading in fine linen. The mere sight of Thuti, poised and aloof, always gave Nehessi the feeling that he himself was somehow misshapen, of inferior clay—sensations unpleasant to a man of ambitions. Hidden behind his mutterings—Nehessi admitted it to himself—was envy over Thuti's inherited wealth and his inherited position in society. Anyone with that start, Nehessi reasoned, could have armies of slaves, country estates, favor at court, friends—anybody with that background could be Royal Treasurer.

He sniffed now to see the prince pacing the narrow deck of

the leading ship. Lord Senmut, now—if Senmut were in Thuti's place, he would have come aboard at once and now be rummaging through the plunder, exclaiming, exchanging gossip for news of the expedition, congratulating. Senmut was a man like one's brother. But this Prince Thuti ...

The Chief of Punt was impressed by the size and style of their welcome, and as the sun flashed from the gold and gems of Thuti's dress, he made a reasonable mistake. "Keeng," said Chief Parihu, and bent his back in humble obeisance.

"No," Nehessi shouted, "not the king!" He explained less vehemently that Thuti was just a trusted minister—like himself, Nehessi boasted—one who did the king's bidding. The king awaited them in Thebes.

"There," he exclaimed somewhat later, "on the East Bank. First farms, then villages, now houses closely packed. Inland, too, to the mountains. Solid. Carpenters' quarter, leatherworkers' quarter, fishermen's quarter ... There's the city wall ... And look, where I'm pointing—the temple. See—the royal palace, and palaces of the princes of the court. And look, the throngs lining the bank and on the house-tops—and soldiers on the quay—and priests—priests with Amon's barque! A welcome, a royal welcome home to Thebes, to Heaven on earth!"

Nehessi confessed afterwards that he had no memory of the docking. One moment he was in mid-stream, the sail was coming down and the sailors checking the ship's way with oars; the next, he was kneeling and meeting Hat-shep-sut's smile. Hat-shep-sut? She was still king, then? Nothing was changed? Familiar faces, friends, slender women. With something of a shock he realized that he had forgotten—perhaps never appreciated—how beautiful Egyptian women were. Daily association for nearly a year with that—that elephant the Chief of Punt called "wife" had all but eliminated interest in the fair sex. Now, confronted by the piquant charms native to Theban girls —slim ankles, graceful hands, small breasts, vivacity—it was like being suddenly introduced to a high heaven of bliss. And when he surprised envy in the eyes of the princes of Hat-shep-sut's court, men who customarily ignored him, he knew that Nehessi the sailer of ships was suddenly Nehessi the explorer, the hero. And he tried not to swagger as he returned along the quay to superintend unloading.

Soon files of temple slaves were shuttling between docks and temple, carrying, pulling, driving the fantastic cargo past a court that forgot to be blasé, whose murmurs broke into exclamations and were echoed by shouts of startled wonder from commoners massed in the streets and on house-tops.

The first bearers staggered under the weight of logs of ebony and of fragrant incense woods, tusks of ivory, balls of myrrh-resin, heavy ingots of gold. The living incense trees followed, with the roots balled in mud and packed into tubs, thirty-one of them. Bales of skins, bundles of throw-sticks, pots of eye-cosmetic, baskets of fruits strange to Egypt, and animals—a seemingly endless flow of apes and monkeys and greyhounds, of fierce leopards and amazing giraffes, oxen and miscellaneous small cattle.

For the climax, Nehessi had saved the triumph of the day. Night was thickening, and by the uneasy light of torches the watchers saw him swing past at the head of his small army of sailors, veterans of adventure nearly two hundred strong. A growing murmur of approval was shocked to silence by the appearance behind them of the Chief of Punt and that monstrous offense, his wife. Chief Parihu, except for his beard and massive leg-ornaments, could have been Egyptian, but the woman was like nothing human, a mass of great sagging rolls of flesh; in a land of slim women, an affront to dignity. Exclamations burst from the lips of solemn officials, hoots and jeers from the less restrained populace. If Nehessi had hoped to create a sensation by the pageantry of his home-coming, before he reached the temple gates he knew that no one present would forget this day.

The ceremony ended within the temple, where in the presence of princes, the god's portion was counted and measured before the king. Lord Thuti stood before a great pile of myrrh-resin that reached to twice his height and declaimed: "Behold, the best of the marvels of Punt are offered to Amon, Lord of Thebes, for the sake of the life, prosperity and health of King Ma-ka-Re, given life, stability, health. Amon gave the king the Two Lands, for he knew that the king would offer them to him." The great rings of commercial gold were officially weighed in balances ten feet in height and the count was entered in records by Temple and by Treasury scribes, and piece by piece all the

159

wealth brought by the five loaded ships was carried before the image of Amon.

Senmut found a chance to whisper, "If you're interested, come to the Shops in the morning, and then we can inspect work on the new temple. And dine with me tomorrow night and tell your experiences."

Nehessi nodded eagerly, flattered by the invitation. Chief Parihu tugged at Nehessi's dress. "Keeng?" he whispered.

"No, no," said Nehessi, and bobbed his head guardedly toward Hat-shep-sut, serene in royal splendor of enameled ceremonial apron and high crown.

The befuddled chief gaped. "But," he said, "your keeng is *woman?*"

There was no time to relieve the poor man's confusion; at this moment Hat-shep-sut demanded Nehessi's presence before her chair, acknowledged his obeisance with charming friendliness and thanked him publicly before the great lords of her court.

"It is done," she said, "as my father Amon commanded me in the holy place of the temple, and I will make for my father Amon a Punt in his garden, and it shall be large enough for him to walk abroad in it."

And she pronounced new honors for Nehessi, and henceforth his titles read: Hereditary Prince, Count, Wearer of the Royal Seal, Captain of the King's Ships.

Nehessi heard the praises of his king. But he knew that his expression was one of strained embarrassment, that his worker's hands hung from the thick arms of a toiler, and he thought, If, now, I had Lord Thuti's distinguished appearance, Lord Senmut's ease of manner . . .

Nevertheless, a happy day, a day to remember.

The Temple Shops bewildered Nehessi, with their fury of sound and activity, much as the unfamiliar rigging of the ships had mystified Tet. The captain stopped inside the doorway, and tried to reduce the chaos of chips and dust and noise to order.

The large room seemed crowded with stone of every size and color upon which a grubby army pounded and sawed and ground and rubbed, tongues vying with busy hands.

"Fill the hole with plaster; when it's painted, who will know?"

160

"The Number Two chisel, the Number Two, stupid."

"This paint is thin; a pinch of the yellow earth, boy."

"I know red wine of Kakem, don't I? It was red wine of Kakem."

"Easy with the grit, the stone's about thin enough."

". . . so I said, 'Who'll tell your husband,' and she said . . ."

Nehessi grunted; perhaps this was efficiency, but a ship run in this fashion, with more wind on the decks than in the sails, would make little headway. He wound a cautious path between partly finished statues in red, black and white stone, dodging hammers and elbows and paint-pots and surly glances, feeling as out of place as a fish in a boat. He spied Tet at last and found him examining a massive sarcophagus which two laborers were hollowing from a block of fine-grained quartzite.

"Keep the sand a little wetter," said Tet, and acknowledged Nehessi's salute. The latter saw that the bed of the sarcophagus was covered with powdered gleaming sand over which the men rubbed a pair of rounded stones.

"Do you mean," said Nehessi, "that that great block of stone has been hollowed just by grinding it that way? By two men? Just with muscle and sand?"

Tet smiled and shook his head. "We bore holes with tubular drills—this side is not finished yet and you can see the marks—and dress it to reasonable smoothness with hammers. The sanding is the last step before polishing. It will be soft as the flesh of a maid when we're done, Captain. The best only for the master, you know."

"Who?"

"The master—Senmut."

Nehessi stared. This magnificent, gleaming sarcophagus, as fine as any he had ever seen—as fine as the old Pharaoh's, certainly—for Senmut?

"A royal gift," said Tet.

"Ah." The incredible cost, Nehessi was thinking: quarrying the rock in a forgotten corner of some desert, long and arduous hauling to the river and transportation by boat, months of tedious grinding and polishing. The ministers of King Ma-ka-Re were well paid, he decided; or perhaps a woman-king was more generous than a man-king; or—was Hat-shep-sut unsure of the firmness of her seat on the throne, and hoping to buy loyalty? He rubbed his thick hands; now, he was not above accepting a bribe of this kind. Senmut certainly lost nothing by favoring the queen, and Senmut was a smart man. He said, "Lord Senmut is quite a favorite with Her Majesty?"

"He should be," said Tet shortly. "He's a lot like the old master—like Ineni; not afraid of work, and he doesn't pretend. The men like that, they break their backs; but he's still working while they sleep. And when he finds something he doesn't understand, he sits down and listens. You get a lot out of your men if they like you, Captain. And Her Majesty sees results and values a man accordingly."

Tet clapped his hands together suddenly. "Excuse me," he said, "I forgot my manners. Congratulations, My Lord, on your new honors. And the sketches that the temple artists returned—superb, My Lord. A record of the whole expedition can be painted from them in the portico of the new temple."

This has been Senmut's promise, Nehessi remembered; perhaps, too, his own name would appear there: "The Captain of the King's Ships, Nehessi, brought trees from the God's Land." Why, a monument for eternity! A thrill of pleasurable excitement tripped his heart. "You mean—Lord Senmut might persuade Her Majesty?"

"Senmut saw the sketches last night, and I heard him instruct Puy-em-Re to prepare scale drawings to fit the wall spaces of the portico. Come, the master told me to bring you."

Senmut, the good Senmut and his promises; he had the queen's ear; he could do anything. "Puy-em-Re?" said Nehessi. "Should I know this Puy-em-Re?"

"He's a remarkable boy, Captain, the kind of pupil one dreams about. Son of the Governor of the Northern Oasis. Newly graduated from the College of Priests, and chose Senmut as master. Newly graduated, mind you, but already an accomplished artist—you know, the clean sure line, the single expressive stroke of brush, a quality of work that normally comes after years of practice."

Nehessi knew that, next to royal favor, the highest compliment that could be paid a man was his selection by sons of the rich as master. Often, if the pupil was gifted, he succeeded the master in the chosen profession—as Senmut had become Steward of Amon in Ineni's place, as Thuti was now Royal Treasurer after Nefer-peret. He said, "Is Senmut grooming him for a particular office?"

They were threading the narrow aisles, Tet's eyes missing no detail of a hundred varying activities.

"Senmut follows Ineni's method of teaching," he said, "acquainting the pupil with a number of fields and watching for special aptitudes. Puy-em-Re seems—oh, excuse me for a moment, Captain."

Tet stopped beside an elderly artist who, with palette and pot of water before him, was drawing an inscription in black ink on the polished side of a statue. Each character was precisely and beautifully formed; later the sculptor's chisel need but follow his careful lines. Tet talked for a moment and rejoined Nehessi, shaking his head.

"These old ones—habit is strong with them. To them a king means a man, it always has, and they have difficulty remembering that King Ma-ka-Re is a woman. And when they do remember, the result can be surprising. His lettering read:

> " 'The king made this monument for
> his father—as her offering.' "

Nehessi agreed that the new order was confusing and cited the perplexity of the Chief of Punt when told that Egypt's king was a woman. "It's only temporary, of course, until young Thothmes forgets his schemes of conquest."

"H-m," said Tet. "Temporary. Of course, of course . . . Here they are now, Senmut and Puy-em-Re."

They were squatted in the dust of the floor, Senmut in his fine linen, a boy in the dress of an under-priest, and a frowning master-sculptor naked except for loin cloth, grouped about a pair of small half-blocked limestone sphinxes. The boy Puy-em-Re looked up with a smiling, alert expression and then resumed his conversation—or argument—with the sculptor. Senmut listened with amused detachment.

"If you want a proper sphinx," the sculptor was saying, "it will have a lion's body and a human head. I carved my first sphinx better than forty years ago—for Her Majesty's grandfather, it was; he was a man that knew a proper sphinx."

"All the other sphinxes in the temple will have the usual human head," said Puy-em-Re patiently. "These are gifts from

Hapu-seneb to the queen, and it is his order that they be different."

"All that hair around the face? It will look like Her Majesty never had her hair combed."

"It is Hapu-seneb's order. He is paying for it; he liked my sketch and he ordered it carved like the sketch."

The old sculptor was enjoying his stubbornness. "Everyone knows the work of my chisel. It will be known as my cutting and I'll be laughed out of the Shops for not carving a proper sphinx."

"That's just it," Puy-em-Re argued. "Your work is known as the best in the Shops; that's why you were commissioned to do this unique portrait of Her Majesty."

"The queen's face looking out from the mane of a lion . . . No!"

For the first time Senmut entered the conversation, his voice quiet, neither wheedling nor commanding.

"These sphinxes," Senmut said, "are planned for a special place—on the balustrade."

The artist looked at him doubtfully. "You, Excellency? You ask me to forget forty years of . . . Where in Egypt, in the world, will you find such a sphinx?"

"They will be placed prominently; all who see them will praise the ingenuity of the sculptor."

The old man shook his head, grumbling. "Freaks. Caricatures. I'll be driven from Thebes." Then he sighed. "All right, give me the sketch. And get away from me. You'll have your monsters."

Senmut, his arm about Puy-em-Re's shoulders, led the boy away. "Good work, youngster. It is easier sometimes to move Amon's temple than to change a man's habit of work."

"But you did it, Master."

"No. Your arguments were the hammer that wore him down."

Anyone could see the affection that existed between the two, Nehessi thought—the expression close to worship in the boy's eyes, the master's exaggeration of his pupil's powers of persuasion.

Tet and the boy excused themselves and hurried to other duties, and even Senmut's return through the Shops with Nehessi was a series of delays and small detours. "Over here,

164

Master"..."Look at this, Excellency." Outside, walking through the temple courtyard on the way to the quay, Senmut shook his head. "Never build a temple, Captain, unless you're ready to sacrifice your sanity. I used to think that I had problems as Steward of the god, but that was before I tried to satisfy the separate creative urges of half a hundred master-artists."

"There is noise and crowding in the Shops," Nehessi admitted, "but work seems to be turned out."

"Tet's organization," said Senmut. "As if he didn't have trouble enough, lack of room puts him on a close schedule; there's little space to store raw materials—woods, stone, paints and the like, yet he must feed finished work to the site as needed. There must be no idleness, nor can a man be pushed beyond his ability.... Here's my barque, Captain.... Without Tet," said Senmut, "and Penati, there would be no new temple."

"Puy-em-Re can be trained, perhaps, to relieve your responsibility."

Senmut, watching the progress of their boat across the river, was slow to answer. "It's early for that," he said at last, "until he decides whether to be artist or architect; he favors artist at the moment. He's a remarkable lad, a real child of the gods, specially favored; there can be no other explanation of his great talent. A pity," he added as if to himself, "that they did not also give him better judgment."

At Nehessi's expression of surprise: "His father," said Senmut, "supports the young Thothmes against Her Majesty, King Ma-ka-Re, and Puy-em-Re is a dutiful son and thinks what his father bids him think."

"I wondered how the old houses would accept a woman on the throne. Thothmes has many supporters?"

"A few, at least, that have influence," Senmut admitted. "This will surprise you. Thuti, Her Majesty's Royal Treasurer, stands openly behind young Thothmes. Even Paheri, my friend Paheri, thinks Hat-shep-sut has denied Thothmes his divine right to reign on the throne of his fathers. Also, they complain over the cost of building this new temple, and it's useless to point out that if Thothmes were Pharaoh they'd be supporting armies in the field at this moment."

"How does the priesthood stand? Their organization is strong, I know."

"Oh, they fear any change, every change. Also, it was Amon's High Priest who announced the displacement of Thothmes by King Ma-ka-Re, so as a whole the priesthood goes along with the new order."

"Where is young Thothmes now? I did not see him at the temple yesterday."

"Sulking in the south," said Senmut, "rebuilding the fortresses beyond Yebu."

He broke off to point, and Nehessi saw that they neared the West Bank at a place where a broad ribbon of stone, dividing fields just emerging from the waters of the inundation, led inland and tapered to a distant pile of gleaming stone.

"The causeway!" Nehessi exclaimed. "Why, your causeway is finished. Already."

"We have not been idle while you were in Punt." Senmut laughed. "But that's not the causeway. It's a temporary road, an inclined plane built over the causeway so heavy weights, statues and building blocks for the temple can be hauled to the site."

In the next hour Nehessi heard many things, a tenth of which he understood, but he was enormously impressed, as in the Shops, by evidences of a smoothly functioning organization for which Senmut alone must be responsible. It seemed that weights of twenty tons and more must be hauled a mile to the temple site, and some of them brought to rest at a level fifty spans above the river. It seemed, further, that the inclined plane was the cheapest method of lifting such great weights, provided the gradient was easy and its surface smooth to allow free hauling of the sledges on which the weights rested. When all the heavy stones and statues were at their respective levels, Senmut explained, then the stones and rubble grading of the inclined plane would be removed, leaving the paved surface of the causeway.

"There have been problems," Senmut confessed as they landed. "For instance, Her Majesty decided to triple the size of the original plans, and new drawings and details had to be made, new foundation deposits prepared and the foundation trenches extended. But this will be a real monument to Her Majesty's reign."

A long file of water-carriers passed and repassed, laborers and foremen and police and scribes swarmed everywhere.

166

Nehessi remarked that the farmers scratching in their fields nearby seemed little concerned by this intrusion on their solitude, and Senmut agreed. "At this time of year it would take more than the building of a temple to distract a good farmer. Plowing and seeding, my father would tell you, are important."

As they progressed, the hauling road lifted gradually higher and higher above the exposed rim of causeway; at regular intervals they looked down on pairs of imposing sandstone sphinxes about which sculptors and polishers worked. Nehessi pointed down to such a pair. "All the carving is not done in the Shops, then," he said.

"Only the important statues that need the skill of a master. When possible, we save extra unloading and loading and bring men to the work instead of work to the men. Even in the quarries," said Senmut, "Penati keeps stone-cutters to rough-dress the stone so extra weight need not be hauled."

Ahead of them on the inclined plane Nehessi saw a slow-moving gang and heard the unmistakable leather-lunged chant of Nebiri calling the step. The lower two-thirds of a giant statue was being hauled up the gentle slope, a roughly blocked shaft of stone twelve spans high and fresh from the quarries. Senmut pointed out that the purely decorative monoliths were hauled piecemeal to the site, carved and assembled. As they drew abreast, Nebiri, from his stand atop the stone, waved a greeting without disturbing the measured cadence of his call. A man stood on the sledge below Nebiri's position and scattered oil from a jar to ease friction between sledge and roadway, and overseers ran up and down the lines of laboring men, prodding, slapping with their sticks. Nehessi counted thirty-five men to a rope, and there were four ropes, but the circumstance that amazed him was that on no face did he find strain or exhaustion; rather, good spirits were in evidence and little jokes were called back and forth. The sticks of the overseers, then, were to rouse the lazy and not to drive the willing.

Senmut explained: "The ancients calculated a man's walking-pull over the period of a working day. It's about a fourth his weight. So we figure the angle of ascent and the weight to be hauled and assign enough haulers, and no man is wearied. It is hard work, but no harder than carrying baskets of rubble on your back from the quarry all the day."

The first terrace, seen from the point at which the inclined roadway ended temporarily, was a broad and flat expanse of polished stone where scattered crews of stone-cutters and sculptors worked on varied projects. It was bounded on the west by two recessed porches some ten spans high, the porches divided by a long ramp which led to the middle terrace. Flanking the ramp, Senmut showed Nehessi the pits prepared to receive the sacred incense trees brought from Punt, and two rectangular pools in which a lush stand of papyrus plants would be grown to form a garden for the god. Planting would wait for dismantling of the inclined plane which, Senmut explained, was needed until the last of the great statues and roofing stones of the top terrace were in place.

The middle terrace was a repetition of the first—broad and flat, with a ramp dividing twin colonnaded porches. The southern porch held particular interest for the captain, for here would be drawn on the smoothed back wall a history of the Punt expedition. Since the God's Land lay south of Egypt, Senmut explained that pictures of the country would be at the extreme south end of the wall, a drawing of the outgoing fleet facing south, that of the home-coming, north.

This was what Tet had said. Nehessi swallowed, and furtively wiped the sudden sweat from his palms—his name in so prominent a place in this splendid temple! "All the boats?" he said. "All five, unloaded and loaded?"

"Probably one of each in detail, and the others suggested. Lack of space, you know."

"But the drawing will be careful, accurate?"

"The same artists that made the sketches. Their work was acceptable?"

"As art, yes," Nehessi admitted. "There are unique features in the design of the boats, revolutionary, little things—only a sailor would understand the importance, the significance—you see?"

"Suppose I instruct Tet that all work is subject to your corrections, Excellency. That should insure accuracy?"

"Thank you, thank you, My Lord. For Her Majesty, you know . . ."

"Of course. The best only. Her Majesty will be pleased."

Nehessi wiped his palms again and followed Senmut to the

168

southern parapet, beaming. There was a sheer drop at this point of about thirty spans to the uneven desert floor. Here and there a fragment of ancient masonry showed, a wall, part of the ruins of the old temple, that source of Senmut's inspiration and where he had dreamed his dream. It was in the hills above that temple that Ineni was buried. Nehessi remembered the ceremony, and the splendid inner coffin of beaten gold, gift of Hat-shep-sut. All his life Nehessi had heard of the uncertainty of the memory of kings—but here was a king who remembered.

Somewhere he lost the sense of Senmut's discourse on the building of retaining walls and on the protection of old tombs from rape, the greater portion of his thought being given to what it was like to be favorite of a king, and how one gained to that enviable distinction.

Birth was not a consideration, apparently—since Lord Thuti had it and Senmut did not. There were scores of princes in Thebes handsomer, better dressed and of better presence than Senmut. Senmut was able, but so was Menti, so were Ma-herpa and Paheri and a dozen he could name. . . . Or it could be, he thought, just a whim. Perhaps kings were given to unpredictable fancies, like normal people. Perhaps all that was needed was to be in the right place at the right time—near Hat-shep-sut, in short, at a moment when she felt generous, or wanted to be amused, or instructed.

Well, his new honor, Wearer of the Royal Seal, gave him access to the palace; a little patience, and some day Hat-shep-sut would see him and the rest would be easy.

Senmut was pointing to a depression in the desert below where workers and their families lived, and quoting figures of time and cost saved by this expedient, and Nehessi nodded politely, hiding his yawn.

"Ah," he said, "ingenious, My Lord, ingenious . . ."

That night at Senmut's house Nehessi had the chance to see how one favored by a king lived, and he was impressed unpleasantly. Why, his own house was as good as Senmut's, his wife as pretty—and without a puckered frown of discontent, his table as varied; he could offer a guest choice of six kinds of meat, too. The wines were excellent, he admitted, and the linen bore the mark of the royal weavers. The cups, fragile as egg shells and ground to lucent thinness from blocks of alabaster, also carried Hat-shep-sut's cartouche, and there were splendid plates of gold worked with an incised design. There were cooks in the kitchens, waiting-maids to serve each member of the party, a blind harper whose deft fingers wove a background of melody for the conversation, and Senmut's private steward, called Antef. And Senmut's mother and father, of course.

The steward, a sober and intense young man, welcomed him at the gateway in a manner that hinted flatteringly of admiration and respect. He supervised everything, during the meal directing the serving-maids, anticipating all needs. When Nehessi praised a sauce, Senmut said, "Antef's specialty." A treasure, the captain thought, and wasted in this house.

For Nehessi was disappointed. A man of Senmut's importance—Steward of Amon, Royal Tutor, Chief Prophet of Montu, Overseer of the Works of Amon—surely a prince with these appointments rated a palace spectacularly decorated and staffed. Nehessi had no understanding of a man of substance who did not boast of his wealth; in Senmut's place he would have surrounded himself with luxuries, slaves and concubines, rarities from all countries, possessions that called loud attention to the owner's prominence.

He guessed shrewdly that the household was divided on this subject; Min-Hor's bitterness well could arise from the fact that, scion of a noble house and accustomed to opulence, she resented niggardliness in the house-mother Hat-nefer. But the caution forced on Hat-nefer by years of poverty was not readily overcome. Senmut, of course, being master, could demand what refinements he thought necessary, but it was plain for anyone to see that Senmut spared his wife little thought, that the mother held first rank in his mind and household.

From the way the family hung on his words, Antef and the harper Harmose, too, Nehessi decided that little entertainment came to the house; this was an event for them, and he a person of importance. His tale lost nothing in its telling; modest embroideries were added here and there when their effect was noted, especially when moments of danger had threatened the expedition and a frightened crew cowered behind the broad shield of his daring. Early in the trip, he said, after passage of the eastern arm of the Nile and when they entered the salt sea south of the Bitter Lakes, trouble began.

"That is a most treacherous sea," he said, "unpredictable currents, shoals, vicious winds, long unbroken calms.... One storm held for fifteen days and nights—waves higher than the mast pounding, beating, tossing the ships as if they were sticks. The men were crazed by fear and begged me to return; the gods were angry, they said, that we sought their secret land, the gods would crush the ships, drown them in angry waters. All would perish, they said; no man could withstand the wrath of the gods.

"All this and more they said while the ships shuddered and groaned and leaped and wallowed, fought like live things for their lives. I refused to turn back. I had made the king my promise. Besides"—Nehessi allowed a smile of modest pride to wrinkle his lips—"I made the ships, and strength was built into them. I, alone of all the company, was unafraid."

"Naturally," said Senmut politely, and Nehessi bowed.

"We watered at the port opposite Koptos, eastern end of the overland trade-route, a spot of green in red desolation. Then weeks, months of slow working southward. Sometimes the wind beat us back, sometimes it failed entirely and the heavy ships must be rowed under a burning sun. Often we could not anchor at night, for the coast is treacherous and good shelter rare. But at last—you see, the good Hathor led us—we found a broad river that emptied into the sea and deep enough for careful passage. A strange land opened to us, a green land, haunted, filled with shadows and bodyless voices."

Senmut leaned forward in his interest. "Bodyless voices?"

"Chatterings, My Lord, a tongue foreign to our ears; continuous, on all sides and from the tree-tops. And screams in the night; cries that would stop a man's blood."

"Land of demons," said Senmut.

"You are a brave man, My Lord," said Harmose.

"The unburied dead!" Hat-nefer exclaimed, shuddering. "We've heard such screams—remember, Husband, from the hills behind the farm?"

Ramose snorted. "You say spirits, I say jackals."

"Pardon me," said Antef; "my old teacher in Abdu ..."

"The wandering dead," Min-Hor interrupted with contemptuous finality. "They are common in the desert beyond Nekheb."

"Jackals," Ramose muttered.

Senmut frowned in thought. "No habitation? No sign of man or his work?"

"Not till the third day," said Nehessi. "Then, where the water was no longer salty, we rounded a sharp bend and saw houses."

"Ah?"

"Round houses of twigs and branches and set high on poles, a village scattered in sleepy peace amongst palms and great sycamores and with cattle grazing beneath the houses, women at work and children playing in the grass. When they saw us, what a clamor—what dashing about and scrambling up and down ladders! Their warriors came running with shields and spears, and with feathers in their hair, but I landed with eight bowmen, and the warriors dissolved in the shadows of the forest."

"They gave no fight?"

"Even savages may recognize superiority, My Lord, and eight Egyptian fighters with drawn bows are not to be trifled with. I caused a table to be set on the bank and covered it with shining gifts—bracelets, collars, a dagger, a battle-axe, strings of glass beads. By signs I invited the heathen to approach, and they are a gentle people, and their fear vanished. . . . You noticed a distinctive feature about Chief Parihu, My Lord?"

"His pointed beard?"

"When we saw the beards of these jungle heathen, we knew that the good Hathor had led us directly to the God's Land. They, in turn, marveled to see us. 'Have you come out of the sky, out of the sun?' they asked by signs, and prostrated themselves, and I accepted their homage. For Her Majesty, of course."

Chief Parihu came, Nehessi continued, with his monstrous wife and attendants, and a feast of Egyptian delicacies was prepared for them—vegetables, bread, meats, beer and wine.

"The chief marveled at everything, our dress and weapons, our language, the ships. . . . I showed him our trade goods, the knives and beads, and by signs indicated that we wished to trade. He clapped his hands and shouted orders, and soon treasure began flowing into our camp. I passed a strict order—

payment always to be made at the moment of purchase; that way, no one could collect twice for an article."

"A wise precaution," Senmut agreed.

"The things they offered us ... well, My Lord, you saw the procession of tribute yesterday—ivory, gold, skins, cattle. In exchange for cheap knives and beads and hatchets; perhaps I should have been ashamed. . . ."

"No," said Senmut. "They are a primitive people and their reasoning is simple; the forests, they would say, are full of skins for the hunting, incense wood for the felling of a tree, cattle for driving them from the ranges, but who among us can make such a knife, such beautifully colored beads? If these crazy foreigners, they would say, offer us articles of such value, shall we also be crazy and refuse to trade? Don't you worry, Nehessi, they are satisfied that they beat you at bargaining."

"A truly primitive people," said Antef.

"Wait." Ideas filtered slowly to Ramose's thinking. "Are you saying that for a knife or a few beads they sold you a cow?"

"A hundred," said Nehessi, "and ivory, and logs of ebony, and apes, greyhounds, giraffes . . ."

"Wait, wait." Ramose looked around the room to see if others shared his disbelief in such a tale. "All these things— cows, ivory, ebony . . . What are giraffes?"

"A kind of cattle," Senmut instructed him.

"Found only in the God's Land," said Nehessi, "very rare, with a slim neck longer than your full height."

"Yes, yes." Ramose nodded his head slowly. "You saw all these things—the trading of valuables for worthless beads, and these rare beasts—you saw all this with your own eyes?"

"I was leader of the expedition," said Nehessi.

"Now, perhaps also you saw a certain strange beast that the General Aahmes used to tell of—big as a house, he said, with a tail at either end and teeth as long as the neck of your rare cow. You saw such an animal in your God's Land, perhaps?"

"Oh, elephants." Nehessi laughed. "Yes, elephants too. I told you, Punt is a strange country."

"I see," said Ramose. He glanced indignantly at his son, arose and beckoned to Hat-nefer. "You will excuse us," he said, bowed stiffly and left the room.

"Have I offended?" Nehessi whispered.

"He lived in the country most of his life," Senmut reassured him hurriedly; "this is a late hour for him." He turned to his wife. "Perhaps you, also, are tired?"

She stood erect. "So kind, My Lord, to remind me that I, too, am from the country."

Her departure left a moment of silence, broken awkwardly when Senmut clapped his hands and ordered fresh wine.

"I should go," said Nehessi.

"Just when we have a chance for serious drinking? Nonsense. I want to hear more of Chief Parihu and his awful wife. How do you get them back to Punt?"

While Nehessi explained that traders of his country were to pick him up at the port east of Koptos, he was thinking, Well, what does he have, this Senmut, this favorite of a king? I have a better house and more costly furnishings. I have more servants. My mother can keep her wig straight, my father is not boorish, my wife does not hate me. I do not have a fine sarcophagus, but neither do I work sixteen and twenty hours in a day, as a favorite must, until my bones are on fire.

He thought further: I like the good Senmut but I do not envy him.

And again: The seat of a favorite is unsteady, for every man seeks to replace him. But who wants to be Captain of the King's Ships?

Nehessi sighed. He felt as if a weight had been lifted from him. He could stretch, scratch when he itched, he could forget the awkwardness that had been built into his body; if he was not to compete for favors, he could be his comfortable, ordinary self.

He emptied his cup and held it for refilling.

"A toast, My Lord," he said. "To the fulfillment of all your desires."

He was still wondering, the next day, why at that moment Senmut's face had burned scarlet.

CHAPTER XIV

Year 8 of the Reign of Hat-shep-sut
(also reckoned as the Reign of Thothmes III)

A beam of sunlight, more daring than all its fellows, investigated a slit between the thick curtains that formed the pavilion on the royal barge, thrust deeply into the gloom and awakened the King of Egypt on her couch.

For some minutes Hat-shep-sut lay puzzling sleepily, trying to explain the curious gentle rocking of her bed and to account for the absence of city noise. The muffled thud of a spear-butt dropped by a careless guard roused her to fuller consciousness; the barge, of course, and anchored miles north of Thebes before the ancient cliff tombs. A startled glance assured her that the disordered chamber held no other occupant, and she sank again into the cushions, the wonted stiffness of her lips relaxing to a rush of poignant memories. Normally she was ready for a day the instant her eyes opened, but today everything was different—today she was content to savor the new peace that pulsed through every nerve and fiber of her body, that weighted her limbs with pleasing lassitude and lighted hitherto unsounded depths in her eyes. Today she loved, and was loved.

Strange that she had not seen it building. The indications were so clear: a great and increasing restlessness, beginning soon after Senmut sailed north to supervise restorations of the ruined Pakht shrine, fretfulness, indecisions, a sense of emptiness. Unlike her usual self-contained sufficiency, the rigid control by which she ordered her thoughts and actions. Perhaps Sit-Re had recognized the signs; the queen remembered her nurse's worried mouth and the extremes sought to provide amusement and distraction—poetry, new perfumes, acrobatic dancers, a stream of foreign scholars. . . . Still Hat-shep-sut remained irritable and bored, and at last Sit-Re snapped, "You need a man."

Hat-shep-sut had slapped her. She was shocked by the woman's grossness, by the inference that she, King of Egypt, with the blood of gods coursing through her veins, should be subject to the shackles that bound ordinary mortals, that divinity should not be above the laws of Nature. From infancy she had been educated by her father for a life of selfless service. In early years the dedication had been welcome—a young girl's love of dramatic sacrifice; later, habit and a sense of duty stilled any questioning voice.

And why Senmut, she asked herself. She could name a dozen princes of the court who were handsomer, wittier, many as capable, as devoted to Egypt. It was fantastic, it was common, she had told herself fiercely, but the aching had grown and filled her throat.

A scratching at the curtain of the pavilion caused her heart to leap painfully, but it was Sit-Re who slipped inside, Sit-Re looking innocent and ordinary as water, certainly not as one who had knowledge of the world's changing in a night. Hat-shep-sut held no secrets from Sit-Re, but she hid her eyes now with a white arm; she could not yet show another evidences of the heaven from which she was slowly returning. The nurse took no notice, hurrying about the chamber and straightening the disorder, humming discordantly, finally summoning attendants for the ceremony of bathing and feeding and dressing the king.

Shrewd, wily Sit-Re! How had she known something of which Hat-shep-sut herself was not sure? It was Sit-Re who had proposed the trip northward. "Summer heat is on the city," she had said, "and the northern breeze is cooling. Besides, Thebes is not the whole of Egypt, and other cities must be allowed to see their king."

Hat-shep-sut pretended hesitation, though the suggestion answered unvoiced prayers. "Tomorrow," said Sit-Re firmly, and the king nodded and ordered offerings in the temples as bribes to the gods for safe-guarding.

The Nile was low and its channel narrow and winding, and one or another of the attending ships—bearing ladies of the queen's chambers and guards and cooks and entertainers and the motley crew that must go where a king goes—was always fouling on a hidden bar, and the trip, to the queen's fevered anticipation, seemed endless.

What could she say to him? For all she knew, Senmut was indifferent to her; by no glance or action had he betrayed more than respect and friendly interest. If he sought her presence oftener than did other princes of the court, it could be that the offices he held required closer cooperation between ruler and official. Other men desired her; she had seen it in their eyes, read it in their thoughts. But Senmut never presumed, never offended. He had always seemed sensitive to her moods—but this was no mood that sympathy or a careless caress might cure. She loved him with the resistless passion of a healthy body and mind long in leash; only love as deep, as honest, would answer. And by what right could she expect that? Desperately she assured herself that nearness to him would suffice—and knew that she lied.

When the little fleet passed the town of Hatnub on the East Bank, she called to Sit-Re and her maids and allowed herself to be bathed and scented and dressed as carefully as for a court affair. She decided upon a simple dress of sheer gauffered linen, and she chose to be wigless; she also discarded rings and bracelets and wore a single jewel, pendant between her small breasts. This would be Hat-shep-sut the woman, not Hat-shep-sut the king. Almost for the first time in her thirty-eight years, she realized, she was allowing herself the luxury of being human. It was a heady experience. Surveying herself in the polished silver mirror, breathless as a girl, she remembered what Senmut, years before, had written of her:

> "To look upon her is more beautiful
> than anything; her splendor and her
> form are divine; she is a maiden,
> beautiful and blooming."

What would he say of her now?

At last his barge had come to view, anchored beneath the cliffs of the East Bank, before the rocky trail that led inland to the small shrine which he was restoring. She had purposely sent no warning, hoping that surprise might prove her ally. But as they neared, a figure appeared on the deck of his ship— Senmut, dressed in finest wig and apron and sandals and with his staff of office. Presently Sit-Re had introduced him to the queen's pavilion and left them.

Senmut bowed and waited. From under her brows, Hat-shepsut gave him swift and critical inspection. He seemed as always; never one to parade emotion, he had maddening control of his features and she could not guess whether turmoil or indifference hid behind the smiling glance. Distinguished, she decided, almost handsome, worthy of admiration, of . . . She kept her eyes lowered lest he read their secret.

"How did you know, My Lord?" she managed at last.

"Holy Amon looks after his favorites, Your Majesty." Then he added, "Penati is in touch with me, and when his messenger reported that you had sailed north from Thebes, I did not know—but I could hope."

She signed him to sit at her feet and searched nervously in her mind for conversation: tribute falling off—taxes inadequate —work on the new temple. . . . Growing resentment, she told him, new pressures by the priesthood and others against the expense of the new temple were becoming annoying. She needed his counsel.

Senmut nodded. "This I *did* know, Majesty; my spies, and Penati, of course, keep me informed. Now, my days are busy with the restoration work here, but the nights"—he shrugged— "at night there is little to do but think. With your permission, I can outline suggestions for your study."

The queen relaxed in her cushions. His matter-of-fact acceptance of her presence was typical of qualities that she admired—an independent spirit that allowed equal independence to another. As she had guessed, the mere sight of Senmut, the rationality of his thinking soothed for a while the tumult in which she had been living.

As he talked, there unfolded a masterly plan, one which, with luck and Amon's help, might silence opposition to the new temple at Thebes for all time. Senmut reminded her that the valley where the temple was being built was separated by high cliffs from the valley in which her father and husband were buried, that the temple backed against these cliffs, with sanctuary and altar recessed into them. She was king now, and it was time, he reminded her further, that a site be chosen for her royal tomb. And, since she was king, where could she be more suitably buried than in the valley reserved by her father for the tombs of kings? And where, still further, more logically than directly beneath the altar of her great mortuary temple? They could tunnel into the cliffs from behind; there was much bad rock in the neighborhood, but ways could be found around that.

This, Senmut suggested, would give meaning to the temple, for no one could with justice deny her the right to make offerings on the altar for the welfare of her soul. And if they should . . . "I urge this for your consideration, Majesty—let the resting place of your father be opened and his august mummy laid in your new tomb, to rest beside yours for eternity, both to receive the full benefits of all temple ceremonies. And," he continued, "appoint Hapu-seneb overseer of work on the entire project."

The resonance of his voice, the remembered manner of his speaking shook her almost out of her control, but she heard enough to recognize this as a plan of magnificent proportions. It would kill all opposition with one stroke, for Thothmes her father had been greatly loved and his memory was revered; such an act might well receive universal endorsement and be hailed as an example of filial devotion. And to thus gain the support of Hapu-seneb, ringleader of her opposition—this was inspired thinking.

Senmut misinterpreted her hesitation. "Believe me, Majesty, Hapu-seneb is a strong man, and I make another suggestion: Pharaoh your father often considered consolidation of the entire priesthood of Egypt under a single head. Unification of control, you see a cut in administrative costs. Hapu-seneb again; appoint him Chief of all the Priests of Egypt."

The queen allowed herself the thinnest of smiles. "You are not, of course, in Hapu-seneb's pay?"

"Nor Thuti's, Majesty," Senmut replied easily, "but I recognize both as brilliant and dangerous men whose good-will it might be well to own, even by purchase. I confess," he added, "my dismay when I learned in youth that there are men of flexible conscience whose loyalties are marketable. Perhaps I wrong Hapu-seneb . . ."

"Neither Hapu-seneb nor Thuti, I think. Let me reflect on what has been said, My Lord."

Sit-Re had come then with attendants bearing food and

drink. The sun had gone to its tomb in the western hills, and Sit-Re lighted the lamp beside her mistress' couch, drew the curtains close against the night's chill, and withdrew. Music, the tinkle of a sweet-toned lute, sounded from beyond the curtains. She was alone, at last, with Senmut.

For an instant she thought—so violently did she want to see it—that something stirred deep in his eyes, a shifting and gathering of impulses, then he smiled in polite disbelief.

"Dine? With you, Majesty? What a great honor!"

"Earned, My Lord."

She accepted a cup of wine, sipped and smiled at him over the cup's rim, but refused the food. Quite suddenly a heat, like that of raging summer in the desert, enveloped her; she heard her voice as from a distance: "Eat, My Lord, and tell me of the restorations to the shrine."

She never had thought that a man could make her feel like this—the meaning of his words was lost.". . . supported by four pillars . . . established your great name like the heavens . . ." She was confused, shaking like a girl. And Senmut—he was not unmoved; she saw his hand tremble as he refilled her cup. She groped and touched his hand, and their touch lingered. He was staring at her, and she returned the gaze steadily, careless if he saw this unfamiliar soul-searing ecstasy in her eyes. For a long moment she struggled. What was she doing? She was not free, she was Egypt. This could happen to any other woman, but *she* was a god. . . .

The cup fell unnoticed as his touch burned her flesh. He leaned and extinguished the lamp. She seemed to be sinking, sinking under the weight of darkness, under the exquisite violence of his kiss.

Now sunlight flooded the pavilion, Hat-shep-sut's chamber, expelling the vapors of night, surprising the queen in an exercise alien to habit. She stared with unblinking abstraction past the open curtains, seeing nothing of the wilderness of reedy bank and tomb-pocked hills, lost to the present in a torment of soul-searching. Even the sibilations of Sit-Re in directing removal of toilet and breakfast articles by slaves went unheeded. A single phrase pulsed in her brain: "What now? What now?"

Love? What could she know of it? A weakness, a disease, an

evil magic that promised heaven—but the fruit of its blooming was misery. This she had said, seeing the cruel wrongs often done in its name. The men in her life, father, husband, nephew —not one had she loved; they were symbols of state, as statues in the temple are symbols of the gods.

Her father had possessed qualities which she admired— strength and intelligence and devotion to Egypt. There were times when she sensed the loneliness in which he lived, and it would have been easy, in those times of brooding, to touch the war-worn hands of the old king her father, to smile and whisper, "Be comforted." It would have been enough, a suggestion of tenderness, of understanding. But—she had been young, then, and the new-found dignity of her divinity allowed no hint of emotion; the gods, reason told her, thought with the head and not the heart. So the old man died, alone as he had lived, leaving a nation free from enemies of consequence, a son without wit, and a daughter who hid, beneath a determined composure, a host of small regrets. Too late, she knew that she could have loved her father.

Her husband—no one could love a vicious incompetent. There were some who had professed sympathy for her half-brother—son of her father and a slave woman—calling him frustrated, a king in name but without power; but her father knew that the high places were not for fumblers and weaklings, and he had trained Hat-shep-sut in governing. The marriage, of course, had been a political expedient, since heirs were necessary; she submitted, too, for Egypt, to the revolting but necessary mechanics of procreation. There was no question of love here; her life with him was a horror, and she made secret and lavish thank-offerings to the gods when he died.

Antipathy for her husband carried over, perhaps wrongly, to his children, to her own daughters, and to the young Thothmes, born of Aset. She watched them with a critical detachment, saw them not as normal children but as instruments of government, potential queens and kings. She anticipated a repetition in them of the father's faults and vices, and when these failed to materialize, she was grudgingly pleased. Thothmes, indeed, showed promise of strength and leadership and she laid early plans of guidance, convinced that her policy of non-aggression in a world at peace was sound. The boy, however, did his own thinking, and while she admitted that this was admirable in a man, until he learned to balance ambition with judgment he must be reined. So she caused herself to be named king.

Senmut, of all her ministers, had shown her how to accomplish this legally and without suspicion, for he knew the tricks by which priests manipulate the will of the gods. He knew an astonishing number of valuable secrets—among them that of fitting himself tightly into one's memory. His had been one of the earliest names impressed upon her consciousness as queen, above those of the scions of wealth; and once established, his name had grown, until today—today . . .

What was Senmut's position today? To the world he was Steward of Amon, Royal Tutor, Chief Prophet of Montu, Overseer of the Storehouses, of the Fields, Gardens and Cattle of Amon, Overseer of the Works of Amon. He was thirty-eight years of age, a prince with sprawling estates and a fine tomb. What the world did not know, must never know, was that he was favored above all other mortals, that in addition to conventional honors he enjoyed one of singular magnitude—that he was the accepted lover of his king.

This was one more secret for Senmut's store, and for Sit-Re's. They could be trusted—Hat-shep-sut knew this with certainty—but could she herself be trusted? A thoughtless word, a sudden blush . . . For the first time in her life she doubted her ability to control whatever situation arose. For the first time she envied other women, who need not guard every gesture and expression. This was silliness; she was a woman, not a child without will or subtlety. She would practice; tonight when Senmut returned to her she would be cordial, and while light lasted they would chat on subjects of common interest as if he were any other of her ministers. While the light lasted . . .

"Sst!" said Sit-Re.

. . . she would guard tongue and thought; she must learn to be casual in his presence . . .

"Sssssssst-t!" said Sit-Re, pointing.

She saw Senmut poling a skiff from the reeds, a skiff piled with blossoms. An ecstasy swelled her heart. She had thought him superintending work at the shrine; instead, he had been stripping the marshes of flowers. For her.

Resolutions were ignored. She knew that she was leaning

tensely, watching his approach, and she knew that others, the members of her court on the barge, saw her eagerness and the flaming of her cheek, and she did not care. This man, bending his lithe strength against the pole, was no prince or minister, but a lover hurrying to her side. She began to tremble. If he touched her . . .

He vaulted the rail, leaving the skiff to the attention of slaves, strode across the deck and, wordless, offered her a single fragrant bloom. She brushed it across her lips, searching his eyes and finding worship, veneration, passion; enough, surely, to satisfy god or king or woman. At her sign he sat, still silent; hidden by the draperies of the couch his fingers sought hers, clung and intertwined. The sigh that wandered from her lips signaled death of any small lingering doubt that might have harbored in her thought. Senmut loved her, indeed.

Three nights and a part of three days remained of their holiday. Afterwards, in Thebes, Hat-shep-sut remembered that she had not seen the shrine, a few minutes' journey from the barge, nor had Senmut thought to invite her inspection. They were much too occupied with exploring hitherto unguessed harmonies of taste and opinion to reckon with the mundane, though Senmut, to her momentary pique, occasionally lapsed into thoughtful silence. He was oppressed, she knew, by problems of financing the work on the new temple opposite Thebes, but she wished—well, this experience eclipsed everything that had happened in her life and she wished that its effect could be as all-powerful in him.

In the main she could not complain of his ardor. One particular happening became her dearest memory, supporting in times of distress her belief that once, however briefly, the gods had looked with kindness on this adventure. From her couch and screened from the rest of the barge by a hanging, they watched the death of a day. It was a moment of peace and solemnity; the sun's dying was a pageant—shadows in the western cliffs changed to blue, to violet, and the rocks were a burning gold; then the mountains became greenish-gray, sharp against the fevered sky, an arch of blue crept from the east, crowding brightness from the west; stars appeared, with only a scarlet ribbon where the sun had been.

From beyond the hanging came the tinkle of a lute, spilling its muted harmonies over darkened waters. She pressed Senmut's hand: "A love-song; Sit-Re's doing." He kissed her shoulder, then in guarded voice for her ear only he sang the words of the lute's song:

> "Oh flower of henna,
>> My heart stands still in thy presence.
> Oh, Lady of my heart, sweet is this hour;
> When I behold thee, I fly to thee, Beloved.

> "Oh flower of marjoram,
>> Thou art a garden in which are planted
>> Flowers and sweet shrubs;
> Here let us walk, hand in hand,
> Our hearts overflowing with joy.
> Better than food, than drink, is it to behold thee,
> Beloved."

Darkness had come, filled with the clamor of crickets and frogs. Then a soft and mysterious light flooded the heavens, and Hat-shep-sut whispered, "A benediction, my Senmut, from the dying sun-god!" The glory held, thinned to a long beam, faded, disappeared. She stirred in his embrace, gave him her lips.

The mold of another golden memory was formed on the day she sailed for Thebes. The last night had been a restless one, neither being reconciled to a parting; they talked late and she wept a little, then chided herself for weakness.

"You see your power, My Lord," she said with affected lightness. When she returned to him, she sighed. "I do want to share with you, Senmut, your work, your troubles."

"You shall, My Lady."

"No, everything, I mean. Your pleasures, too." She leaned her head against his shoulder. "You have looked tired for months past; I know you work too hard."

He laughed gently. "My mother's theme."

"It is all in my interests; you kill yourself for me. Well, it must stop, Senmut. You must take some recreation."

"I do, I do, My Lady."

"What, for instance?"

"Oh, a hunt in the deserts behind Menefe sometimes, or fowling with Nehessi. . . . Ineni taught me the value of relaxation, change of scene and activity; it really works, you know."

Why were men so inhuman that killing could be counted as recreation? Even Senmut, to whose gentleness she trusted her heart, her body, her love—even Senmut found entertainment in slaughter. Still—would she change him, if she could?

"I wish I could go with you," she said.

"Hunting?"

"Well—fowling, anyway. They do not suffer—too much, do they? It is a quick death?"

He gathered her close in his arms and murmured, "Poor gentle spirit in a world of evil. Let me confess something to you," he said, "a thought that I have voiced to no one. The gods, now, are at home in the wind and sunlight, surrounded by stones and reeds and flowers and wildlife, all these of their own making, and they are happier in the lonely places than in a temple; I do not believe they enjoy the glitter and artificiality of man-made ceremony. And—this is my confession— neither do I. I, too, am happiest in the lonely places; and I go there, not to hunt, but to worship."

She should have known; from the first Neb-taui and others had told how he supported her opinions on needless warring, even before the prince who one day would be his king. Gentleness and strength; an amazing man—her man!

"Take me there with you," she said impulsively, "now."

"In the night?"

She clapped her hands smartly together. "Sit-Re will be furious. . . . In the south, my love, who knows when the chance will offer? Besides, it will be light soon and we can watch the world waken, just we two. . . ."

Sit-Re appeared with a taper, rubbing sleep from her eyes, and listened to her mistress' instructions that the fowling skiff be secured alongside and that her ladies be roused.

"What foolishness is this, My Lady?" she cried. "It is black night."

Hat-shep-sut sighed. "Some day I hope to make a request that you will hear without argument. Come—move your feet!"

"There is mist on the river," said Senmut. "Bring warm wraps for Her Majesty."

185

Sit-Re bent the full glare of her displeasure on him and spoke evenly and with great distinctness: "You are not king yet, My Lord, to give orders here."

This small triumph apparently restored her good-nature; lights appeared, and before Hat-shep-sut could consider a change of mind, she found herself bundled warmly and adrift with Senmut in the skiff. He stood near the stern and wielded the long pole with the ease of practice; the lighted barge seemed to dwindle, then the mists crept between and they entered another world, a ghostly world, white and clean and bounded narrowly by cloudy vapors that stirred with their passing.

She lost herself in a new sensation of bodiless movement. They could have been floating in the air; she thought of the blessed dead who crossed the heavens daily with Re in his sunboat—they would feel this same leisurely drifting in space. The analogy was strong, and when she heard a voice, seemingly nearby, she thought, Of course—the spirits of the dead that accompany the god on his travels. The voice sounded again, at her elbow—a disembodied voice, for nothing was to be seen but floating leaves and shreds of mist.

"Senmut," she gasped, "what is it?"

"Fishermen on the far bank, My Lady; the mist magnifies sound and plays strange tricks. . . . See—it is lighter already and this is far enough."

He urged the skiff through protesting reeds until they were hidden, then caught her in a sudden, close embrace. When at last they were settled comfortably, he still held her hand in both of his. "I must remember," he sighed, "that we are here to watch the wild things for whom this is home."

She lay beside him, hardly breathing. The man-made world seemed far away; this silent, narrow, dim-lit room was like the chamber of a tomb, and the occasional voices could be those of invisible wandering souls. She imagined in the swirling, twisting mists the figures of dancers at a burial feast; it was almost as if she were watching, through the great painted eyes on a coffin, the ceremony of a burial—her burial. . . . Then a fish rolled on the surface of the river, a frog cleared its throat sleepily after its night of singing, and Senmut pressed her hand and pointed guardedly to an opening in the thicket.

A gaily painted duck paddled noiselessly into view, threading intricate waterways through the reed clumps, and tailed by a dozen balls of yellow down. The mother viewed the trespassers in her domain without alarm, busy with the multiple problems of guarding and feeding her brood. These darted here and there among the reed stems, nibbling at root and leaf, quarreling, leaving a thing half tasted to snatch a larger morsel from a brother. The mother guided them with minute whispers and murmurings scarcely audible, the little ones instantly obeying; something alarmed her and she muttered briefly, and all disappeared, swimming in a compact body, all but one, a glutton who stopped for one last bite, one frantic wrenching at an obstinate tidbit, then foamed through the water with head and wings outstretched in pursuit.

Hat-shep-sut was charmed. Small splashes and scuttlings told her that a new day was beginning in the marshes, a bird attempted a few drowsy scales, a breeze, forerunner of the morning wind, stirred the tops of the tufted papyrus. A great crane hesitated outside their "chamber," stepping carefully and peering, like an old man with rounded shoulders and hands clasped behind, and passed silently in search of breakfast.

Warmth pressed on her shoulders like a hand and Senmut poled the boat forward. The mists had dissolved and it was day.

CHAPTER XV

Year 9 of the Reign of Hat-shep-sut
(also reckoned as the Reign of Thothmes III)

When Hapu-seneb had planned the office in which work of the new Chief Prophet of All the Gods of Egypt was to be done, Khet, as Chief Scribe, had thought the arrangements admirable. It was of decent size, adequately lighted, near to the Temple Library, and with a large table for Hapu-seneb and one only slightly smaller for Khet. There was space for a dozen scribes in which to slave comfortably; his table was placed conveniently between Hapu-seneb's and the doorway, so all incoming correspondence passed through his hands, and set at such an angle that he could oversee the activities of the under-scribes.

The ideal conditions continued, but something had happened to the rest of the plan. As soon as King Ma-ka-Re's ambitious program to reorganize the priesthood of the country was fully launched, and the novelty of real work sampled, Hapu-seneb lost interest in the office. His stool and his table remained empty, while Khet, in addition to other duties, must prepare a daily report of official business for the great man's leisurely digestion.

This still need not have crippled the enterprise if the original complement of workers had been maintained. But Hapu-seneb felt the need to show immediate results in the drive to reduce expenditures; and Khet, lifting a weary head above the pile of rolls that cluttered his table, now saw not twelve but six scribes in the room, five of whom were employed industriously, while the sixth rubbed at his eyes with one hand and dibbled his pen in the water-pot with the other.

Khet opened his mouth to summon him when an under-priest entered the door and laid a rolled papyrus on the table beside him.

"Another?" groaned Khet.

"From Nekheb," said the priest.

"Paheri, too." The Chief Scribe shoved the roll with his elbow to join the pile on the table. "I know without reading it: his temple is falling apart, his priests must beg their bread in the streets."

Cries and protests were being received daily, from every temple in the land, and all voicing the same complaint: Hapu-seneb was draining their blood, destroying them. The Chief Priest chuckled happily when he read Khet's reports of this widespread discontent; the great in the land were learning his name, feeling the power which Her Majesty's appointment gave him.

Khet dismissed the messenger. This was no time for idle dreaming, for Pharaoh's wife had died in the night, and a thousand new tasks were laid on his shoulders as a result. He was not prepared to say that it was a bad day for Egypt, for in six months who would remember Queen Neferu-Re? She had been a colorless child, obedient, a nonentity in the court—and now she was dead, at this inconvenient time. Now he must interrupt important state matters to fix the date of her burial, to plan the funeral rites, to list for all the temples precisely what extra supplies might be drawn from their magazines to advance these solemn ceremonies. All this with only six scribes, one of whom played with his pen and did no work. The Chief Scribe shook his head; this day Egypt might soon forget, but it definitely was a bad day for Khet.

He called to the idle scribe, "Bring me the calendar of feast days, Nibi."

When the latter placed the roll of papyrus before him, Khet ignored the devices by which Nibi advertised his unhappiness, the sighs, the dabbing at his eyes with a rag, and said, "Figure for me the date of seventy days from this day."

The scribe performed clumsily with his fingers. "The twenty-fifth—wait—yes, the twenty-fifth Paopi, seventy days from now. I think."

"H-m-m," said Khet; "in the middle of the Feast of Opet. Well, the funeral of Queen Neferu-Re must be delayed." He studied the papyrus. "Good—the month Athor, the fourteenth Athor has no important festival. Take a sheet of new papyrus, Nibi, and write carefully. A letter to Her Majesty King Ma-ka-

Re, saying that the fourteenth Athor is suggested as propitious for the temple rites of burial. Then . . ."

"I—I can't, Master."

"What?"

"My eyes. I can't see. That is, the light is bad in my corner, and when I try to copy . . . It's the old script, perhaps; it has been corrected many times, and at the end of a day . . ."

Khet folded his arms on the table. "What does the physician say about your eyes?"

"I have not seen a physician."

"Well, of course there are simple remedies that one can prepare, incense and crocus, for example, equal parts and mashed to make a poultice. That soothes an inflammation."

"Can I afford incense?"

"Goose grease and pond water, then," said Khet sharply. "You can afford pond water?"

Speaking of sore eyes, Khet thought, his own felt as if they had been boiled in a pot. Ordinarily Nibi was a good worker, methodical, accurate, writing with a neat precision that rendered each of his letters models of perfection and brought credit to the office of the Chief Prophet—and to Khet who had found him. He could be replaced, but not readily.

Khet pulled a stool to a place beside him. "Sit here, Nibi, so we can talk. . . . Now, how do the eyes feel? I mean, do they burn and itch?"

"Yes."

"As if there were little sticks scratching them?"

"Yes. How can you know?"

"Yours are not the only eyes that are tired, Nibi. Have you honey at home?"

"No, how can I . . ."

"Send your son to my house tonight and I will give him a pot of honey and some fresh onions. Have your wife press the sap from the onions and mix it with the honey and make a poultice. Do this for a night or two and your eyes will be well. Will you do this, Nibi?"

"Well . . ."

Khet resisted the impulse to kick some life into the man. Instead of violence he tried reason.

"While the old king lived," he said, "Egypt was a land of

plenty, in which every man, high and low, shared. You remember the waste and liberality, Nibi—three men to do the work of one, the master growing rich and the servant fat. This was when gold and silver and slaves from the wars poured into Egypt like the flooding Nile.

"Now that the old king is dead, rich tribute no longer floods Egypt. As every man once shared in the wealth, so now each shares in the economies. Does this sound reasonable to you, Nibi?"

Nibi blinked and said nothing.

"Of course." Khet answered himself. "Now, it is unfortunate, perhaps, for everyone suffers, the temple and government offices, even. You feel the difference here, for there is work for a dozen scribes and only six to do that work. I, myself, must labor twelve and fourteen hours in a day. So all over Egypt."

He touched the rolls piled at his elbow. "By Pharaoh Ma-ka-Re's order, the supplies which may be drawn from temple storehouses for daily needs have been reapportioned. All temples in the land, Nibi. All temple staffs have been reduced, so the labors of those remaining on each staff have been doubled. Now, each man's house is important to him, and every Chief Priest thinks that his temple has been discriminated against, and blames Lord Hapu-seneb. So they write these complaints, all of which must be answered, and that adds to *your* work. So, Nibi"—he leaned back, watching the scribe—"everyone in Egypt must work harder, every day, for less. It is Pharaoh's order."

The scribe had seemed to hear, but Khet, remembering the time being wasted while the man sat picking absently at a mended place in his apron, thought, He will have to go; it is too bad, but . . .

The under-priest who served as Hapu-seneb's messenger interrupted from the doorway. "The Chief Priest—at once, Khet. In his private office."

This happened fifty times in a day. He has misplaced his bundle of magic seals again, probably, Khet thought. And to Nibi, aloud, "Go home for the day and rest your eyes. And send your son for the honey; the eyes will be better."

The quarters appropriated by the Chief Priest of All the Gods as his private sanctuary were in a remote and quiet corner of the temple grounds, removed from his office. Here he could

191

formulate his weighty decisions, or sleep if the pressures of his great office bore too heavily; here, guarded and buffered, he could emphasize to the world an impression of the hidden, the mysterious, the superior.

Khet found him in a fine rage. His fortress had been breached, his dignity assaulted. He strode about the sumptuously furnished room, kicking furniture, scattering papers.

"Who is this upstart, this Senmut," he bawled at Khet, "that he orders my movements? Can a mere Steward of the God command the Chief of all the priests of Egypt? Did Her Gracious Majesty assign to me the honor of preparing her tomb in the valley behind the new temple—of supervising the reburial of her august father? Am I a child that he must stick his farmer's thumb into my affairs, order me like one of his unwashed, grave-robbing ploughmen?"

"What happened, My Lord?"

"A letter." Hapu-seneb made a show of searching by scattering and kicking papers about generously. "A letter demanding—well, requesting, it is the same thing—my presence in his office regarding removal of the old king's mummy. With all this work before me—preparations for the marriage of Princess Meryt, and . . ."

"M-Meryt?" stammered Khet. "Marriage?"

Hapu-seneb pierced him with the glance reserved for inferiors, particularly those whom the gods had forgot to give brains. "You *did* know," he said slowly and distinctly, "that Queen Neferu-Re died in the night? And that she has a younger sister named Princess Meryt? And that the young Pharaoh cannot reign unless married to a daughter of the royal blood? Surely, these facts are familiar to you?"

"I am sorry, My Lord. The pressure of business . . ."

"*You* are pressed! Come, get your stick."

Khet knew the folly of argument. Besides, his work was so far in arrears now that another hour mattered little. And he rather anticipated being spectator to a clash between the Steward of Amon and the blustery Chief Prophet; Khet was no friend to Senmut, but he acknowledged the latter's weight in Egypt and his gift for tact, for control in circumstances that shattered the dignity of lesser men.

The table in Senmut's office reminded Khet of his own, piled with rolls and strewn with notes and memoranda—the table of a man acquainted with more than the sound of the word "labor." He greeted them pleasantly, himself set stools for their comfort, and suggested, "A cup of wine, My Lord, to refresh the spirit?"

But Hapu-seneb was in no mood to bandy civilities. "Affairs of the utmost urgency crowd my days, and leave no time for indulgence. What is this nonsense, now, about the old king's sarcophagus?"

"Nonsense, My Lord?"

"I hold Her Majesty's letter authorizing me to arrange for the reburial of her august father. . . ."

"I saw the letter, My Lord." Senmut smiled. "If I neglected to congratulate you upon the appointment, let me do so now."

Hapu-seneb waved the courtesy aside. "Then what, I say, is this nonsense that the sarcophagus cannot be moved? Has Her Majesty changed her mind?"

Senmut shook his head. "It is Her Majesty's fondest hope that the mummy of her father may sometime rest beside hers in the new tomb which you are preparing."

"Then this is your idea of a pleasantry, to call me here for nothing. I do not think Her Majesty will enjoy the humor. Come, Khet."

"Another moment, My Lord." He waited until Hapu-seneb, with a petulant flounce, reseated himself. "In your inspection of the old king's secret tomb, you noted no feature that might make it difficult—or impossible—to move the sarcophagus?"

"Certainly not. The tomb was exactly as left the day the old king was buried. A passageway, an upper chamber for storage of the funerary equipment, steps cut in the stone to a lower chamber for the burial. The sarcophagus, a beautiful work in yellow stone on an alabaster base, was intact, its lid in place."

"Did you remove the lid?"

"No; this was a preliminary inspection only."

"Too bad, My Lord. If you had removed the lid, you would have found that this seeming block of yellow stone is but the thinnest of shells. A real triumph of the stone-worker's art, My Lord. It was lowered down the steps and then finished in the burial chamber—its sides ground so thin that light penetrates. The sarcophagus cannot be moved from its base or up the steps without danger of smashing it beyond repair."

Hapu-seneb sat in a lump, mouth agape, his jowls slowly purpling. "Her Majesty knew this? You deliberately . . ."

"You do Her Majesty grave injustice, My Lord," said Senmut severely.

Hapu-seneb mumbled, and sat fumbling with his stick. "Then —a new sarcophagus must be made for the old king's coffins and mummy. Is that what you suggest?"

"Much too costly, My Lord. Remember, Her Majesty wishes to cut all unnecessary expenses."

Hapu-seneb had regained some of his composure and with it belligerence. "I made my inspection at Her Majesty's command; you sit here in comfort and theorize. Let Her Majesty judge which of us guesses and which . . ."

Senmut laughed. "I made my own inspection, My Lord, but out of curiosity. You remember that the tomb was dug in great secrecy when we were youths, and yesterday Penati and Tet, who had worked with Ineni on it, took me there. There are features of considerable interest—for instance, the bad rock in the upper chamber which necessitated construction of the lower. The question of moving the sarcophagus came up and Tet, who originally superintended its hollowing, spoke against it. With authority, I think you will agree."

The Chief Priest made no attempt to hide his sneer. "Tet is a good workman, so of course his opinion on any subject is not to be questioned. The old sarcophagus cannot be moved, he says; a new one would be too costly, you say. You propose, then, to move the coffins to the new site and leave the mummy there, unprotected? Her Majesty will consider her duties as a daughter fulfilled?"

"Another solution has occurred to me, My Lord, and I would value your opinion of it."

Hapu-seneb bowed elaborately. "Silence, everyone, while we hear the great Senmut's idea."

The Steward of Amon stared at him for a long moment and Khet noted with interest the angry tightening of a muscle in his jaw. "I had hoped," said Senmut evenly, "to keep our personal evaluation of one another out of this, My Lord, but I find your 'humor' offensive. If you wish to surrender your commission to

194

Her Majesty and admit that you are unable to cope with the technicalities of the problem, then our conference is ended."

Hapu-seneb flushed. "You take a high tone toward a superior; will Her Majesty approve?"

"Ask her, My Lord."

"Be assured that I will. Meanwhile, what of this 'solution'? If it is workable, Her Majesty shall be advised of its source."

"So generous of you, My Lord."

Somehow Khet had not expected this of Senmut, the great prince, Her Majesty's advisor and friend. Showing temper, wrangling like a petulant schoolboy. Khet waited for further violence, but Senmut's voice, when he resumed, carried a more reasonable tone.

"Three sarcophagi," said Senmut, "have been made for Her Majesty's use. One, now in the early tomb prepared while she was Royal Princess, one while she was consort of the second Thothmes, and one which Tet is now finishing and bearing her titles as King Ma-ka-Re. Of these three, the second mentioned is stored in the Temple Shops, and Tet assures me that simple and inexpensive alterations in the inscriptions will make it available for our use."

Hapu-seneb's face mirrored amazement and indignation. "Are you trying to say—the great Thothmes, the Pharaoh of revered memory—to be buried in his daughter's cast-off sarcophagus?"

"I see no other alternative, My Lord."

"It is fantastic, insulting—Her Majesty will never consent."

"I think she will, My Lord."

"No. A thousand times. What would people say?"

Senmut continued, unmoved. "There are a few other minor adjustments. Tet made both the old king's and the queen's sarcophagi, and he says the measurements differ slightly, the queen's being a trifle smaller. However, by cutting a finger's breadth of stone from the inside head and foot ends, the coffins of the old king can be forced in."

"You see? Preposterous. Besides, I remember, now—it is rectangular, a queen-style sarcophagus, the one you talk of using. An insult to the dead, to a noble warrior. No. This is the expedient of a madman. Of a fool!"

"You have a better plan?"

"I shall think of one. And when this 'solution' of yours is known, you will be laughed out of Egypt."

"The matters discussed in this room today are the king's business, My Lord. It will be well to remember that."

"You threaten me, you—you farmer?"

" 'Warn' is the better word. Don't forget your stick, My Lord."

Khet kept well behind his master in their return to his quarters; waited just inside the door. Hapu-seneb stamped into the room and brought his stick down with crashing force on a stool that blocked his path. Stool and staff splintered; the Chief Priest collapsed in his chair and gasped, "Wine!"

He recovered presently, though the hand that held his cup still trembled. "You heard him, Khet; you heard him threaten me. And this scheme to cheat the dead, you heard that, too. What do you think of the great Lord Senmut, now? Do you think him completely mad?"

"I think, My Lord," said Khet, "that Senmut has delivered his future into your hands, to do with as you wish."

"You . . . Sit down. Now—his future, you say? How?"

"Look at it this way, Master. King Ma-ka-Re denies herself nothing. Her new temple eats gold—a hundred and twenty statues thus far, and more to come; the sanctuary doors—wood is not good enough, they must be of ivory; her new tomb; the reburial of her august father . . . All this is a great impudence, to impress the people with *her* majesty, *her* power. 'See me,' she says to the people, 'I am king; I am rich; I am powerful.'

"But what does she say to you, My Lord? To you she says, 'I am poor; cheat the gods a little, but secretly, so none can know.' "

"H-m-m," said Hapu-seneb.

"Have you wondered, My Lord, if the gods might misunderstand why offerings are withheld from them? The grains, fruit, cattle, fowl, wine, beer—the gifts to Egypt by the gods—do they know that you act only on Her Majesty's order? Or may they not think that perhaps—you know, a jar of wine here, a sack of barley, a few figs, onions . . ."

"Khet!"

"Multiplied a hundred-fold. You see, My Lord? There is gold for use where it will show, but for the gods, for her dead father

196

—'I am poor.' And for her favorites, too, there is plenty; for Lords Senmut and Ma-herpa . . ."

"What of them?"

"You haven't heard? You bury yourself in work, Master. New estates and rich gifts; for Senmut a new ship, and promotion to the post of Royal Steward . . ."

"Senmut—Steward to Her Majesty? What has been done with Ma-herpa?"

"He has been raised to the dignity of Fan-bearer on the Right Hand of the King."

"No. You must be mistaken, Khet."

"You squeeze your brain dry, My Lord, so gold may be diverted to add honors to another's name."

"You are right, Khet. My brain is squeezed dry."

"Now, here is my point, Master. All this—denying the gods to magnify herself—this is upside-down thinking and to be expected of a woman. How did the old king her father meet the same problem? In a man's way; Egypt was impoverished when he came to the throne, so he stripped the wealth from a dozen foreign countries and poured that wealth into the temples, and the gods blessed Egypt and him.

"His daughter needs but to nod, My Lord, and the machinery of conquest and of abundance will be set in motion. The armies are ready—young Thothmes strains to lead them, but she refuses to act. So"—he bent forward and whispered into Hapu-seneb's ear—"place a man on the throne."

"Thothmes? But it was by Holy Amon's decree that Ma-ka-Re was chosen in his stead."

"A trick, My Lord, you know that. A trick that worked once and which can work again. Consult with Lord Thuti; he controls the Treasury and he feels as you do. Not today, not this year; prepare slowly. The country is impoverished; when food becomes scarcer and taxes heavier, when the people feel the added pressure, there will be grumbling, strikes, riots. It will be thought that the gods are angry, the priests will present demands on behalf of the gods.

"In the meantime—listen, My Lord. Instead of helping Her Majesty by cutting expenditures in the temples, add to them, cautiously, a little here and a little there. The priests will love you for it; they will do your bidding. You see, My Lord? A gradual undermining of King Ma-ka-Re's regime, of her strength and her favorites—you see?"

Hapu-seneb gave no answer, sat as one asleep. When finally he struggled to his feet he said the one word, "Come," and led through corridors and past the Sacred Lake, to his office, Khet's office, and walked among the scribes who, seeing his dreaded presence, wrote so furiously that sweat gleamed on their heads.

Presently he spoke. "The heat is excessive in here. Let slaves be stationed with fans."

"Slaves, Master?"

"And here, near the scribes for convenience, a jar of wine, a small jar, but good wine. And have these storage jars moved, Khet, to give space for more scribes, two or three more will suffice for now, perhaps."

Khet finally caught his master's meaning and held a hand before his face to hide the breadth of his grin. "Of course, My Lord; three new scribes. I let Nibi go home; he is having trouble with his eyes."

"Good." Hapu-seneb stopped before Khet's desk with its mountain of work. "Perhaps Nibi would be a good Chief Scribe in your place; there would be less writing . . ."

"In my place, Master?"

"Can you be here and in Menefe at the same time? As my steward you will have to travel; a ship of your own, Khet . . ."

"My Lord!"

CHAPTER XVI

Year 10 of the Reign of Hat-shep-sut
(also reckoned as the Reign of Thothmes III)

The three small rooms had become Sit-Re's favorites in the sprawling palace at Thebes, and she rarely left them. They had been Senmut's surprise for Hat-shep-sut while she was in the northern city of Menefe, and he had brought in carpenters and artists and made of this corner of the upper floor a bower, a fresh garden of loveliness.

One room, the largest, was furnished simply, divans and stools and heavy rugs and bright hangings. Here Hat-shep-sut and Senmut relaxed after the day's labor, talked, or played at draughts—Sit-Re could hear their voices now through the open doorway. A second room led off the one in which she sat, and it was like a sun-lit arbor surrounded by brightly flowering shrubs, walls and ceiling painted to represent a trellis from which hung great clusters of grapes. There was a small place of the bath off this, like a reed bordered pool with fishes and water fowl.

And the third room, the one that held her heart and hopes and from which she seldom moved, had reeds and marsh plants painted on the walls, and birds flying and cranes and flamingos stepping carefully. Toys were scattered on the floor of this room, balls of leather, a pot of shining beads. From where she squatted, Sit-Re reached and picked up a cleverly fashioned bit of painted wood on which four jointed figures danced when a string was pulled, and there was a curious softening of her expression as she absently manipulated the toy.

A feeble, whimpered protest came from a basket beside her, and then a bawling howl and a thrashing of small arms and legs. She looked down into angry blue eyes—and Hat-shep-sut's voice came sharply at her shoulder. "What are you doing to the child?"

"See," said Senmut, bending above them, "he is smiling. He is all right."

"Of course he's all right," Sit-Re snapped; "and a true son of his mother; fire and honey."

Senmut shook a pottery rattle before the child, and the old nurse snatched it and thrust it from sight in the clothes of the basket. "He wants to sleep."

The child quieted at last, his mother and father returned to their talking, and Sit-Re remained, patient and worshipping.

Holy Amon must love Her Majesty very much: the quick, easy birth, the fine boy, strong and beautiful, and his very existence still a secret after five months. It was Amon who arranged that Hat-shep-sut's pregnancy coincide with her daughter Meryt's, and Senmut but took advantage of the convenience to transport both mother and daughter to Menefe. It was Amon who focused the world's thought on Meryt, whose child would be heir to Egypt, and Senmut but published a fiction that Hat-shep-sut's presence in the northern city was because of natural concern for a beloved daughter. Both Amon and Senmut had planned well; King Ma-ka-Re's confinement occurred, in private, a week before the public celebration of Queen Meryt's.

Hat-shep-sut called her son Amen-hotep after her grandfather. Meryt called her son Amen-hotep after her great-grandfather. When Sit-Re heard that Meryt's son was blessed by the gods with strength and comeliness, she sniffed; *her* babe had these, and sweetness and intelligence as well, and ready laughter, and temper.

She prepared, now, for a solemn rite that was necessary every morning and evening, one which insured safety for the child in the ensuing twelve hours. Re was the god into whose safeguarding children were placed, Re who lighted Egypt during the day and who fought Egypt's enemies in the Underworld during the night. She washed and perfumed her hands, then, kneeling beside the child's bed, untied a string that bound a tiny amulet about the boy's neck. The amulet was of gold, an open hand with the fingers held together. She recited over it: "Thou settest in the west, O god Re. If thou seest the dead man coming against Amen-hotep, born of Hat-shep-sut, or the dead woman meditating some plot, do not permit them to take the child in their arms." Then she rethreaded the amulet and tied a careful knot and retied the cord about the baby's neck. "The master Re has saved you," she recited; "he will not give you to the thief from hell."

The babe was safe until morning. She washed her hands again and then listened at the doorway.

They were talking of tribute, now, and taxes, subjects that occupied much of their attention these days, and Senmut read from a report of the Royal Treasurer on the newly opened mines at Sinai. They hoped much, she knew, from these mines where the valuable stone, turquoise, was dug from great veins in the earth, and they had built barracks and fortifications and dug cisterns, establishing permanent stations where earlier kings had made camps. The Royal Treasurer wrote of the evil summer season: "It is reported that the highlands are hot in summer, and the mountains brand the skin." In consequence, he wrote further, the yield was disappointing; perhaps, with the cooler winter season . . .

This Thuti! She spat at thought of his name. A snake clothed in fine linen. A treacherous serpent with estates and slaves and slippery manners. She trusted Thuti as far as she could reach and not a finger-length farther, yet Hat-shep-sut kept him in high office. Of course, Sit-Re trusted few men; even her acceptance of Senmut was conditional. So far she could detect no weaknesses, though she watched alertly. (Someone must watch, she argued, or the man would talk Her Majesty out of her throne as he already had talked her out of her senses.) For Hat-shep-sut loved blindly and unreasonably, and if Senmut said it, it was decreed.

And so far Senmut had made no misstep. He filled his many offices honorably and with distinction, he worshipped his king, and he adored the child. If Sit-Re did not set her foot firmly, he would fill the rooms with gifts, idiotic things and useless to the boy for another five years. Like the painting outfit with palette and brushes and lumps of paint, and even fishbones to be dipped in the paint and used for drawing. Like the little bow with its dozen blunted arrows, the game of ninepins—the sandals! Foolish and needless extravagance. Though the sandals were charming, of softest leather and tinted red, and the child

201

liked them, waving his legs in the air by the hour and staring and chuckling.

And Senmut was good for the queen. Sit-Re found his influence in the gentler, more emotional, the human, laughing Hatshep-sut whom she had not known before. She still was cold and aloof majesty before the gods and her subjects, but now this was a dress worn for an occasion and not the only garment she owned. The change gratified the old nurse, and she thought, as she bent over the sleeping child for a last reassurance, The Lord Senmut is a man and therefore unworthy, but Amon prosper him for my lady's sake.

But Amon was busied with other interests, and within a month worries accumulated in the king's heart.

It was the time of feasting and joy, the New Year, and the Nile was swollen with promise—but Senmut frowned. Boats filled the river, lights danced on the shores, and the valley of the river rang with the shouts and songs of revelers. Mounds of incense were consumed on the altars and gifts passed from hand to hand—but Senmut walked unseeing and unsmiling, as if weights crushed his bones. And Her Majesty spoke to Sit-Re, who whispered in the ear of a trusted maid, and that night the king's nurse made her report.

"Vandals have damaged Lord Senmut's tomb, My Lady."

"Seriously?"

"Some of the paintings, and perhaps the sarcophagus."

"But the paintings can be redrawn, and I will make for him a finer . . ."

"That is not all." Sit-Re knew the effect her further news would have, and hesitated.

"Senmut is in health?"

"Oh, yes, Lord Senmut is well . . ."

"Then what else matters?"

Sit-Re nodded glumly. "True," she said. "But—death has visited Senmut's house."

"The old ones?"

"No, a dancing maid, and the ape—from Punt, you know, given him by the king of the Puntites."

"An ape!" Hat-shep-sut laughed with relief. "Why this mystery, Sit-Re? An ape, and a maid."

202

"Well," said the nurse, "it is not known how they died, whether naturally, or . . ."

"Ah-h-h-h . . ." The king released her breath slowly and the color drained from her face.

"My Lady!" Sit-Re exclaimed. She soaked a napkin in scent and hurried to her mistress, but the latter waved her aside. "Poison?"

"It is not known," said Sit-Re, "but . . ."

"You think Senmut is in danger?"

"Oh, who can tell? The tomb—and this—coming so close. . ."

Hat-shep-sut nodded, and Sit-Re saw the old strain, the forgotten tensions building anew in the tightening of her jaw, in the bleakness of her eyes.

"No—I don't know, My Lady—it means nothing, I'm sure."

"Who would harm Senmut?"

"No one, My Lady. Except—Lord Thuti, perhaps?"

"Not Thuti," the king said with finality. "Thuti is a prince."

"Hah! And a snake."

Hat-shep-sut shook her head slowly, unheeding.

"My Lady," said Sit-Re, "this is but another's telling. Ask Lord Senmut."

"He would not tell me." The king sat heavily inert, struck by a torment of apprehension and fear. "He would think to save me worry."

"Well, there are magic spells, powerful amulets that protect from evil."

Hat-shep-sut continued to shake her head. "Leave me," she said.

Senmut came at last, and Sit-Re crept in and out of the chamber on fictitious errands—and was ignored, such was their concentration.

"I hoped you would not learn, Majesty," said Senmut; "there was no connection, really. The girl was a favorite with Min-Hor and had been with her all the morning. And the ape had its own house in the garden. This heat, perhaps—or something they ate, though no one else in the household has sickened. A startling and unhappy coincidence, I am sure."

"You are telling me the whole truth, Senmut?" Hat-shep-sut looked at him levelly.

"I swear it, My Lady."

She touched his arm, and sighed. "I still am frightened. You are—important to me, Senmut, and you take no care of yourself. You dash here and there—at night—in lonely places . . . A man of your abilities creates jealousies and you may have secret enemies. I know," she said in answer to his shrug, "but how do you explain the damage to your tomb? Was that an act of friendliness?"

"Of spite, perhaps," he admitted, "but no more. Some disgruntled workman. I must punish laziness, inefficiency where I find it, and it is the nature of some to call any reprimand an insult, and to avenge by petty reprisal. You must not worry, My Lady, the damage was negligible."

"They will do worse another time."

"I will place a watchman if it will ease your mind. Be satisfied, My Lady," he continued lightly, "it is a good tomb, and so they do not deface the plaster on the walls of the corridor. You remember the portraits concealed beneath the plaster? While these remain undamaged, the gods will remember my name and my soul will know comfort and peace."

"Perhaps," said Hat-shep-sut. "But couldn't you prepare another tomb, Senmut, in some hidden, some safer place? Let me build you one as secret as my father's; you can continue with the other and let vandals wreck it as often as they wish, since it will not be used. Come, a tomb worthy of your place in Egypt."

Senmut smiled and kissed her hand. "You do me much too great honor, My Lady. Besides, such a tomb would take years, and the laborers and artists needed would make a concentration that could hardly be hidden."

The sound of Sit-Re's voice startled all three, since she herself had forgotten that this was private conversation. "Build it where artists and laborers concentrate, then," she said; "build it near the new temple, under one of the courts, perhaps."

The king's eyes widened and she exclaimed, "Senmut!"

"Oh, now—Majesty," he faltered.

"The perfect place. Thousands of workers are milling about . . ."

"But, Majesty, the site has been dedicated to the gods; it would be sacrilege; only royalty can be buried there."

"You are *my* king, Senmut."

Sit-Re quitted the chamber, then. Her Majesty was happy

again, eyes flashing, words tumbling one over another in eagerness to convince. "I wish it; to please me. . . . The old quarry—that is close to the lower terrace—would that do? . . . At once, Senmut; send for Penati and Tet—they can be trusted. Start the plans at once. A gift, Senmut, with my love . . ."

The summer heat was the most oppressive that Sit-Re could remember. Day and night without relief; you accepted the fiery breath of Re when he rode his sun-boat overhead, but when he was absent from Egypt at night, coolness was expected.

When the child became fretful, Sit-Re kept an army of girls busy dipping cloths in water, sponging and bathing him, and other girls fanned the air about his bed. Hat-shep-sut and Senmut were concerned for his comfort, but the heat did not seem to bother them. The king was happy again, for there had been no further deaths in Senmut's house, no recurrence of violence at his tomb, and plans were being readied for his secret tomb under the forecourt of the temple.

They let Sit-Re listen to their plan, though she was near exhaustion from tending the child, and dozed and nodded while they talked. Entrance would be made from the bottom of the old quarry north of the broad avenue that led to the temple; Senmut had workmen secretly clearing a corner of the quarry now. Foundation deposits would be laid, and then steps and corridors and chambers dug, reaching far under the first terrace, and Senmut was preparing drawings of the reliefs with which the rooms would be decorated, and it would be like a royal tomb.

The flies came, then—a pest, a torment of flies in thick, sticky swarms, covering everything, and Sit-Re heard no more for a while of the tomb. She trusted no other to attend the child; left unwatched, his body became a mass of buzzing, crawling flies, they were in his eyes and nose and ears—before food could be placed in his mouth they crept into the cavity and his mouth must be cleaned first, and he screamed and purpled with rage. And Sit-Re, red-eyed and trembling with fatigue, soothed his distress as she could, nodding and jerking to wakefulness, rubbing his limbs with oil, whispering his name, nodding, nodding. . . . When the flies left as they had come, in a body, she collapsed beside his bed and slept a day and a night without

205

stirring; and when she awoke, the sickness had the boy in its grip.

He lay still and pitifully small and weak, neither seeing nor hearing; fevers burned in his body and his limbs twitched with convulsive tremors. The king, terrified, cried, "Call the physicians," but Senmut said, "Not yet; all Thebes would know your secret. Sit-Re knows the cure for fever."

So the nurse gave orders to the king and to Senmut. They offered bread in the temple and they burned incense before the statue of Re. She caused Senmut to bring a green-glazed stone cut to resemble an eye; it was called "Eye of Horus," and she tied it about the child's arm, and recited:

> "Stand thou still, whoever comes! I will
> make thy face become the back of thy head.
> Thy magic profits not, it is not heard.
> Thy limbs shall be weary and thy knee
> painful. But I myself stand up. I am
> Horus, son of Isis."

It was a powerful charm.

She called for dried pods of the mandrake and for cow's milk; she pounded the pods and mixed the powder with the milk, and bathed him with it, and fed a few drops into his mouth to drive out the devil that hid within his body.

She ignored Hat-shep-sut's command that she rest. "Not yet," she said with what firmness exhaustion allowed; "if he wakens he might be frightened by another near him." Day and night became as one to her while she ministered to the boy, rubbing, bathing him with cooling lotions, whispering his name. Then she remembered, and summoned Senmut; and he brought from the Temple Shops a tiny scarab set in gold wire, the scarab cut from a red jewel, and on the reverse was carved a single word, "Khufu," the name of Egypt's ancient king who had built the great pyramid for his tomb. This ring Sit-Re slipped onto the child's finger, thus placing him under the magical protection of the spirit of mighty Khufu. This also was a powerful charm— and within an hour the child smiled at her, stirred weakly, and slept. And Sit-Re slept in peace beside him.

When she awoke, his flesh was cool under her hand, though a thin mucus still dripped from his nose.

While she bathed, the king sat beside her and talked. "When you are rested," Hat-shep-sut said, "you are to dress in your best linen and wig and jewels and come with Senmut and me."

"I am rested, but I cannot leave him yet."

"It will take but an hour or two, and you need fresh air."

"I am still breathing."

Without comment the king passed her a hand-mirror, and she saw reflected in the polished surface the face of an old woman, with faded flesh that sagged on the bones and with streaks of graying hair. This change in the space of a few weeks.

She dressed without further argument and then inspected the child as he slept. He was so small, so thin. She repeated specific instructions to the women in whose care he was to be left: if he wakens, feed him this and this; if he cries, bathe him from this jar; cover him with this if he is cold, but do not let him become overheated. . . .

She rode in her own litter behind Senmut's chariot and the king's carrying-chair and surrounded by Royal Police, and discovered that it was good to be out of prison. She enjoyed the light and movement in the crowded streets, and their small pageant approached Amon's temple before she had fully savored her new freedom.

At the Temple Shops Tet and Penati came and knelt before Her Majesty, and bowed before Sit-Re, and they entered a ghostly, dim-lit place from which Senmut had dismissed the workmen so the visit could be made in peace. It was Sit-Re's first visit in more than a year and she found much to criticize.

A series of great kneeling statues in red granite aroused her instant displeasure. They were alike, each holding a globular vase before it, and were planned to stand face to face in the topmost court before the sanctuary door. They were alike, but subtly different—and the differences enraged her.

"My Lord," she snapped, "these represent My Lady? In the act of offering incense?"

"Every statue in the temple will be a formal representation of Her Majesty," Senmut agreed.

"Then why," stabbing her finger, "does this one have narrow, slanting eyes, this one a thin nose, this one practically no chin at all? Do you find these features in Her Majesty? Is it too much to ask that a portrait look something like the subject?"

"These are representations, symbols of Her Majesty, not portraits," Senmut explained. "Of the thousands of statues of kings of Egypt, My Lady, how many are likenesses? Each of these kneeling statues was carved by a different sculptor, and each idealized Her Majesty in some . . ."

"Does she need idealizing? She is not perfect, but these make her ugly, each in a different way."

"Wait, come over here." He led through a maze of turnings to a corner—and Sit-Re felt the breath catch in her throat. Before her, translated into warm, creamy, marble-like stone, sat Hat-shep-sut. The same exquisite slenderness and grace, the same tender gravity of expression.

"This," said Senmut, "is a portrait statue of Her Majesty."

Yes, Sit-Re thought, this was her baby whom she had tended through girlhood to womanhood; this is a monument worthy of a beautiful woman, worthy even of Hat-shep-sut. But she would cut out her tongue before admitting the thought. "It has a man's dress," she said. "The face is all right, but she was woman before she was king." Secretly she was delighted with the statue, but she muttered, "A 'king,' who bears children!"

She was able to find faults in most of the things she saw that day. "What," she exclaimed, pointing, "are those little monsters? If you tell me those represent My Lady . . ."

Senmut ran his hand caressingly over one of a pair of small limestone sphinxes. "Most sphinxes show the king's head on a lion's body, but these use Her Majesty's face, and framed by the mane of the lion. You remember, My Lady," he said to Hat-shep-sut, "newel posts for the balustrades."

"Designed by Puy-em-Re." The king nodded. "I remember. You have not spoken of him lately."

The steward hesitated. "I loaned him to Thuti, you know; the beautiful shrine they are designing for the sanctuary. And the young king, Thothmes, has taken a fancy to him—the door that he made for Amon's temple was partly Puy-em-Re's work, and the vase of electrum, and other objects of unusual interest and beauty."

The nurse looked at him sharply. "You are losing him. To Lord Thuti and the others."

"No, but he has enormous enthusiasms and creative ability; he sees every problem as a personal challenge. And he does help me here and at the temple."

"Is he helping with your secret tomb?"

"No," Senmut admitted.

And Sit-Re nodded. "You do well not to trust him. Lord Thuti will poison his mind against you."

"My Lord," Hat-shep-sut interrupted, "one more statue, and then we must return to the child."

This decision suited the nurse. She had already lost sense of value, of critical judgment. Perhaps, spaced apart in the temple, each in the setting designed to emphasize its individual size or color or shape, the effect would be of pleasing architectural unity, of grandeur; here, crowded in the Shops, the statues presented a nightmare forest.

They halted before a statue, this one life-size and in sandstone. It showed a woman—the king again, of course, since all the statues were of Hat-shep-sut—holding a child upon her lap. A flicker of interest broke through Sit-Re's boredom: which child would be represented—Neferu-Re, Meryt, or Amen-hotep? She spelled out the carvings by the dim light:

> "May the King Ma-ka-Re and Osiris, the
> Great God of Abdu, be gracious and give
> a mortuary offering of cakes and beer,
> beef and fowl, and thousands of every-
> thing good and pure, to the spirit of
> the Chief Nurse who suckled the Mistress
> of the Two Lands, to . . . to . . ."

It was as if a hand squeezed her heart. For a long moment she held her eyes closed and waited for breathing to begin, then reread the long vertical inscription slowly: ". . . to the spirit of the Chief Nurse who suckled the Mistress of the Two Lands, to Sit-Re, justified."

She stood rigid, fighting for control. She never had wept in her life, but tears of joy, of welling gratitude and pride, abetted by the stunning surprise, were not to be denied. She kept her face hidden, but when she felt the king's touch on her arm, she gasped, "Oh—My Lady!" and seized the royal hand and kissed it.

Fatigue and boredom were forgotten. That Her Majesty, with all the demands on her time and strength; Lord Senmut, with his thousand duties and worries—that they should single her for thought and remembrance, was more than she could grasp. "But why," she said, "but why? . . . but why?"

Hat-shep-sut smiled at her. "Of course you would be the last to guess, silly, that I have you to thank for every happy moment I have known. Memories like mine cannot be bought, but they can be acknowledged. Besides—and this will surprise you, too—I love you, little mother."

Sit-Re, when her unbelief was conquered, was like a child and must touch the statue and examine all its beauty of finish and carving. The babe Hat-shep-sut on her knee was represented as a small adult king—"Majesty should not be portrayed as a helpless infant," Senmut explained. Under the little king's sandals were drawn the nine bows of Egypt's enemies, so these enemies would be under Pharaoh's feet wherever he walked. The statue, Senmut said, would be placed in the chapel of the goddess Hathor, divine nurse of kings, or in the porch dedicated to Her Majesty's divine birth. And when at last their small procession threaded the streets toward the palace, Sit-Re wept again in the seclusion of her litter, the easy tears that wash loneliness from the heart.

They found the child's room quiet, and the maids watching the infant cautioned: "Sh-h-h," they said, "he sleeps." And one said, "His limbs were cold, and I covered him." So Her Majesty and Senmut tiptoed away, and while Sit-Re changed from her finery, she thought, This is a lucky day. And again, With the excellent statue, I am honored above all other women in Egypt. Then she dismissed the maids and sat alone beside the child's bed, to be near when he awoke. And she remembered and composed her features, withdrawing the smile of contentment from her lips, for the gods were watchful and would be jealous if they guessed the depth and breadth of her happiness.

Poor child, she thought, how soundly he sleeps. As soon as he was strong, she would take him to the temple and show him her statue. She bent closer to listen for his breathing, and the glint of gold caught her eye. The golden amulet of protection lay among the pillows, the amulet that always must be bound to the child's neck by the knotted cord—amulet and cord had become loosened. She snatched the covers away. The child stared with sightless eyes, limbs twisted and rigid.

Thus Senmut and Hat-shep-sut found them, the nurse moaning over the small, cold body.

And Sit-Re saw Senmut's eyes in her dreams thereafter, wide with horror and despair—and she heard his cry, "My Lady—Amon's wrath! What have I done to you!"

They buried the boy in a shallow pit dug beneath Senmut's first tomb, in the night. Senmut placed the little coffin carefully; Sit-Re spread leafy branches of the sycamore tree beside it and on these the king laid offerings of bread and raisins and dates in prettily decorated saucers. Tet had made a beautiful Ushab-ti figure in painted limestone; this would come to life in the Underworld and be slave to the boy and do his bidding, and on it Senmut had written:

> "For Amen-hotep, by his brother Senu,
> who causes his name to live."

Then Tet gathered stones with which to hide the burial, but Senmut stopped him and knelt before the opening and drew from his girdle the tiny sandals of red leather and placed them on the coffin's lid.

CHAPTER XVII

Year 11 of the Reign of Hat-shep-sut
(also reckoned as the Reign of Thothmes III)

Kings, Penati grumbled, should be led aside and it should be explained to them, respectfully, that if the energies of a willing servant are diverted into too many channels, the quality of his work suffers. Instead of one task completed, you get six half finished.

Her Majesty knew that he was occupied with the temple, and with the master's secret tomb. She knew that Senmut was abed with an arm and leg broken. And what had she said? Her Majesty said, "A pair of obelisks, Penati, the tallest in Egypt. And they must be in place in Thebes to celebrate the thirtieth anniversary of my appointment to the throne by my father."

And Senmut? He sympathized; he lay on his bed and shook his head. But he said, "Her Majesty's command, Penati. You can do it. You erected obelisks for the old king, and you can do it for Her Majesty. Seven months? Take Tet and Nebiri, Puy-em-Re and Nehessi. Outline the work; each is expert in his line and all you must do is co-ordinate and supervise. Get them together in my office."

So Penati, from experience with the old king's obelisks, prepared a detailed plan of operation—no small feat in itself, since it involved the movements of thousands of workers, their comfort and efficiency.

On the night of the meeting he found Senmut's office alight. He thought that he must have mistaken the hour; but inside, instead of Tet and the others, he found the king's Steward, looking pale and drawn, the bandaged leg propped straight before him and the splints that supported his arm resting carefully on the table.

"Does Her Majesty know that you are out of bed?" Penati scolded.

"She does."

The voice came from the shadows behind Senmut. Penati gasped and dropped the rolls of papyrus he carried. "Your Majesty!"

The king, her slim figure wrapped in a cloak against the chill, stepped to Senmut's side. "Lord Senmut is the most unruly of all my subjects, Penati. And the most important."

The tone of her speech was gentle, and the old architect remembered afterward that her hand had rested, for an instant, in most unkinglike gentleness on the master's shoulder. At the moment his thoughts were scattered, however; he placed a stool, gathered the rolls of papyrus and stacked them on the table, wiped his head with a shaking hand, and bowed.

"Have you been able to learn anything, Penati?"

"Nothing, Your Majesty. Nebiri and I found the place, but there is no way to trace footprints where hundreds of workers tramp about."

Senmut nodded. "It was black night and there were no voices. They tied a cord and waited; when the horse hit it, they ran."

"Ordinary mason's cord, Master, doubled." Penati drummed nervously on the table top and addressed his king. "Someone does not like Lord Senmut, Your Majesty. Someone has observed his habit of checking the day's work late in the evening and then hurrying back along the avenue to his ship. If he will listen to Your Majesty, I hope that you can persuade him to remain indoors after dark."

Hat-shep-sut smiled. "I have ordered him south with you to Yebu, to help with the obelisks—at least until the camp is established. That will keep Lord Senmut away from Thebes for a while."

"Fine, fine!" This sharing of responsibility delighted Penati.

But Senmut groaned. "He's a man of no heart, Your Majesty. You'll see; he'll have me carrying rocks within a week." He sobered, drew a folded papyrus from his girdle and offered it to Penati. "First, however, Her Majesty has been kind enough to insist that I take added and secret precautions that my name shall live."

"Of course." Penati nodded vigorously. "I have said that, too.

213

You have enemies, and you have to admit it now. They will search out your name wherever it is written and destroy it—and of what value is a life honorably lived if there are no records for the gods to read? Your name now is hidden beneath plaster in the old and the new tombs, but those will be checked first." He turned the papyrus over in his hand. "What new place? Have you decided?"

"Her Majesty suggests that it be placed somewhere in the new temple."

Penati rubbed his chin. "Well, no one will think of looking there. Isn't that—irregular?"

"Sacrilege?" Senmut smiled at the queen, and nodded. "Perhaps."

"H-m." Penati wondered how Ineni would have handled a like situation. Still—Her Majesty's command..."Where?"

Senmut pointed to the papyrus and Penati unfolded it. It was a sketch of a kneeling man praying before the gods, and facing it was the inscription:

> "Giving praise to Hathor for the sake of the life, prosperity, and health of Hatshep-sut, by the Steward Senmut."

"You know the small chapels in the upper court," Senmut said, "the closets for housing of the cult statues? There are twenty of them, each with a pair of wooden doors opening inward and folding flat against the walls. The priest opens the doors, performs the necessary ritual, then leaves and closes and seals the doors again. No one is ever inside the chapel when the doors are closed."

Penati nodded; he had admired the space-saving design when it first was drawn.

"Each chapel is dedicated to a different god," Senmut continued. "Well, this sketch with suitable inscription is to be carved on the walls behind the doors, and facing the altars ..."

"And Senmut's name," the king interrupted, "will share in every offering made in the temple. The gods will see his name and remember it."

214

"This is worthy of Ineni!" Penati was impressed by the ingenuity of the plan. "This will work, Your Majesty. Only by the rarest accident will the carvings be discovered."

"I hope so. It is important to me."

"Keep the drawing safe, Penati," said Senmut. "There is no hurry; the obelisks and Her Majesty's Sed-festival require all your thought now...."

"Listen ..." Hat-shep-sut exclaimed. "Yes—they are coming. Remember, My Lord, Penati is in charge now."

It took some time to get the business of the meeting started. Presence of the king served as damper to natural expression of delight over Senmut's partial recovery. Nebiri tempered his roaring; Nehessi edited his curses against those who had waylaid the master, and mourned the loss of Senmut's favorite horse. Tet and Puy-em-Re were more restrained, but their affection reminded Penati of his feelings toward Ineni when, in the old days, he saw his master after an absence.

There was hesitation to sit in the king's presence, even after her insistence, but at last they gathered about the table, Penati at the head.

"My thanks are poor payment for your friendship and loyalty to Lord Senmut," said Hat-shep-sut simply. "My whims seem to bear for him the emphasis of a decree, and you have eased his mind of uncertainty."

Penati could see that the king's words pleased Senmut, though the latter shook his head. "A ceremony like the Sed-festival, occurring thirty years after appointment as heir to the throne, is an honor celebrated by few kings, Your Majesty. We consider its just observance worthy of every effort, and since by custom obelisks are erected to commemorate the event, we are proud to offer our talents. Penati and the others will fail neither Your Majesty nor myself."

When at last it was Penati's turn to recite his plan of operation, he cleared his throat with embarrassment. This part of his duties he did not enjoy. He tried to forget that Her Majesty was listening, and finally addressed the men.

"You all know your work and you know when it's well done. That's all we need, the best work done quickly. We have only seven months, so it means double shifts, day and night. Now, I have located good stone in the quarry about a mile above Yebu, good, flawless granite. One shaft will trim to about a hundred and five feet long, the other about ninety-eight feet, so they'll be taller than the old king's. Ten feet through at the base, and tapering.

"Now, we'll take Tet first. I'll oversee the stone-cutters when they separate each shaft from the mountain, and Tet builds sleds under the shafts. Tet oversees, from then, the finishing and the carving.

"Then Nebiri. Nebiri, you oversee all land transport—getting the finished shafts from the quarry to Nehessi's ship, and getting them off the ship at Thebes and up to the temple. You'll have to build a stone roadway from the quarry to the Nile, and you'll oversee digging the canal across the end of the roadway where Nehessi will build the ship. And you'll also train the hauling gang—about five thousand men, you said?"

"Just under fifty-six hundred; I figured it out," said Nebiri. "Pulling double rank on four drag ropes. With a stone roadway and a down haul and grease under the sleds, they'll pull it in a day, easy."

"Nehessi, you oversee all water transport. You build a barge big enough to carry both shafts at once, and train the crews of the towing-boats. Your Majesty, Lord Ineni stowed the old king's obelisks side by side on the boat, but Nehessi will carry them butt to butt."

"The longer boat is easier to handle, Your Majesty," Nehessi explained. "The going will be bad enough; at that time of year the Nile is in flood and the current strong. We will use drags, and place towboats to keep even tension on the bow."

"It will be a long boat, My Lord, with the shafts placed end to end," said Hat-shep-sut.

"Two hundred and sixty feet, Your Majesty. But it will handle better in the current." Nehessi spoke with confident authority.

"Also," said Penati, "you will transport all workmen and their families between Thebes and Yebu, all supplies of food and tools—wood and rope and chisels and grinding powder—everything that is needed. Tet will set up a magazine in the Temple Shops—see Tet about that.

"Puy-em-Re, you probably have the most difficult task, but you have the full seven months for it. Her Majesty commands that her obelisks be raised inside the temple, between the pylons built by the old king her father. I have been over that with you—the hall must be unroofed, the cedar columns and southern wall removed . . ."

Puy-em-Re interrupted. "Perhaps I should not ask, but—it seems an awkward place for the obelisks. Why not outside the temple, before the pylons?"

The queen and Senmut exchanged amused glances, and Senmut answered the boy. "Her Majesty has her own reasons for her preference, Puy-em-Re. The cedar columns are rotting and should be replaced—the hall itself may arouse distasteful memories. You see?"

Penati remembered—and this had happened before Puy-em-Re's time—it was in this hall that the young Thothmes had been recognized as heir to the throne, through collusion between the boy's father and the priests.

"Besides," Penati reminded Puy-em-Re drily, "it is Her Majesty's command. Also, you, Puy-em-Re, are to dig a ditch at the river's edge where the shafts can be unloaded, build a long ramp of mud bricks south of the pylon, set stone bases in the earth where the obelisks will rest, and arrange for the quantity of gold and silver alloy with which the tips of the obelisks will be sheathed."

He passed the rolls of papyrus which he had brought, one to each of the four men. "Here are plans and details—Tet helped me draw them up—and everything is listed here, I think. If I've forgotten anything, Tet will know where to find me."

As the meeting ended, Hat-shep-sut spoke privately with Penati. "It will not be an easy assignment, but you have developed a sound plan and Lord Senmut and I know your interest and ability. To your other responsibilities I add one more: return Senmut safely to Thebes."

Memories of the next seven months were alive in Penati's mind for the rest of his days. There were highlights of triumph and near-tragedy, but mainly it had been an interesting problem, the solving of which required a concentration of all the knowledge gained in a lifetime of learning. And without the skills of his four helpers the job could not have been done in the time allowed.

He remembered with particular amusement the reactions of natives of the sleepy town of Yebu. Living on the borders of Egypt and far from cities, they were accustomed to peace and order—and the presence of thousands of strangers milling through their narrow alleys drove them to a frenzy of excitement. They crowded the bank watching the approach and unloading of fleets of ships; roof tops were lined, day and night, with rows of staring eyes inspecting the army of porters required to keep the workers' camp in food and beer and water. Penati had to post guards so the quarries would be free of the idle curious, particularly at night when torches and enormous fires lit the place like day.

While workmen crawled over the mountains at the quarry, hacking and chipping and boring at the rock, other hundreds of men, a mile away by the river, dug a great pit and carried the earth away in baskets. The citizens of Yebu concentrated here, and Penati was ready to swear that every able-bodied man, woman and child in Yebu checked the pit's measurements twice daily: ninety-five strong paces in length, thirty in width, and better than twice the height of the Mayor of Yebu—a tall man— in depth.

While these activities took place at quarry and river bank, other gangs graded a gently sloping roadbed between the two, and laborers followed them dragging blocks of stone which, fitted together, formed a wide stone roadway. And all this must be checked, studied, admired and criticized by the citizens of the town at the top of their lungs.

When carpenters arrived at the quays bringing lumber and their saws and adzes and hammers and drills, the populace escorted them to the quarry in a dither of curiosity. Two giant monoliths had been nearly separated from the mountain; they lay on their sides and attached only at the back, the top and front faces hammered to reasonable smoothness and a space cleared beneath each shaft, except for occasional rock supports, the full length and breadth. And in these cleared spaces the carpenters began building two huge sleds.

Then doubt entered the minds of the good citizens as to the sanity of these visitors from the city. They stood in sullen groups, whispering, pointing, muttering spells and making signs to avert the evil eye. And word was passed that the city-livers broke off parts of the mountain, merely to haul them down the fine road and bury them in the pit! Attendance fell to a handful of the more idle and stupid, and the overseers sighed happily and went about their work without escort or criticism.

Penati already had marked a line along the direction of the intended separation of the shafts from mother-rock and had caused a groove three fingers in width and depth to be cut along the line. When Tet's sleds were finished, Penati placed men shoulder to shoulder along the line, each with a chisel and a small iron mallet; at a signal each man in turn, beginning at the left and following to the last man on the far right, beat once lightly on his chisel. This continued hour after hour, day after day, from left to right and beginning again, over and over without violence; shifts of weary laborers replaced by fresh, the blows sounding in quick succession from left to right, over and over—until late on the third day came the shout of the overseers. The shaft had sheared through from top to bottom; its huge bulk rested free on the long sled.

The longest and most tedious operation now began, that of dressing and polishing the four sides of each of the shafts. While the surfaces were being reduced to comparative smoothness, workmen fashioned the special granite blocks used to induce a shining, black, imperishable polish. The blocks were of a size and weight that two men could comfortably manage, shaped like the large end of a pestle with a cavity hollowed out of the bottom, operated by means of sticks lashed to the neck with cords. The cavity was filled with a mixture of powdered grinding stone and melted beeswax, and teams of two men to a block seated themselves at intervals atop each of the great shafts and resigned themselves to the monotony of endless push and pull, back and forth between them twelve hours of a day, a fresh team replacing them for twelve hours of the night.

The carpenters, meanwhile, had established a new camp on the Nile bank. When boatloads of fresh lumber arrived, the carpenters swarmed about the pit and began an infernal racket of sawing and pounding. Here was new excitement close at hand, and all Yebu again lined the edge of the pit and called encouragement and advice, and scrambled about among the carpenters to lift and carry and steady and measure, to help in a thousand ways. Somehow—Penati never knew how—the great ship grew in the pit.

He, meanwhile, as Overseer of the Overseers, tried to keep an eye on all developments and wore himself thin and nervous with his running. He could not forget that his was the responsibility, that one small detail overlooked could spell disaster and shame before all of Egypt. So he worried. He rechecked and remeasured, he dashed to Thebes and back to Yebu, missed meals and sleep, snapped at his friends and barked at his subordinates—until Senmut kidnapped him, carried him for a visit to Lord Paheri in Nekheb.

And later Penati remembered that he had enjoyed himself there. It was like a foreign place, removed from Egypt; life flowed evenly—the days leisurely, the nights black and silent. Like a tomb, he thought. For that matter, Nekheb was dead, and this was as Lord Paheri, Count of Esneh and the South, wanted it. He was a man without ambitions or pretentions. Penati admired without understanding him.

Lord Paheri welcomed them to his palace that lay between the narrow fertile strip and the fortress walls, to his family that included numberless uncles and aunts and cousins, to his excellent wines and to an atmosphere at once stimulating and restful. He listened to Penati's worries: whether Nebiri was training the gangs properly—why Tet had not begun the carving—if Puyem-Re had a large enough reserve of mud bricks. He listened, and offered intelligent comment, sighed, and looked about him with complacence.

"You city men," he said. "I do not envy you. What does this rushing about bring you except wrinkles and gray hairs? You, Senmut, are a rich man; have you thought of retiring to a corner of the world like Nekheb? I recommend it; at least, vandals do not despoil the tombs of Nekheb."

"Oh," said Senmut quietly, "you know about that."

"And of the attempt on your life. You are recovered from that, praise Thoth, but you must see, my friend, that evil forces move against you."

"Little is won without risk, Paheri. I but serve my king with all my heart and intelligence; the 'evil forces' are enemies of my king, and so I fight them."

"You know who directs these enemies, of course?"

"Tell me."

"A hot-headed young prince of our acquaintance whom you, for political reason, have deprived of certain rights which he covets."

"You credit me with extravagant powers, My Lord."

"I but repeat gossip that comes to my ears, that as Her Majesty's first minister you doubtless dictate her policies."

"No one dictates to Hat-shep-sut. Have you tried it, Paheri?"

A smile edged the count's lips. "Aahmes my grandfather did, and retired immediately thereafter. . . . You are comfortable, Penati? Fill your cup and pass the jar to Senmut." He pushed a dish of mixed fruits closer to his guests and then resumed. "My grandfather foresaw all this. He knew Her Majesty's nature, and he knew the heritage of her nephew Thothmes. Both are self-reliant and both are proud and stubborn, and—both are divinely appointed kings of Egypt. It makes a pretty little problem for those who, like myself, sit at a distance and speculate; but for those involved . . . Guilty or innocent, Senmut, it is natural that you be chosen as the victim of Thothmes' fury. He is no longer a child; he is twenty-four, a violent man dedicated in spirit to a profession denied him—that of arms, and I think . . ."

"Yes? Tell me, Paheri."

"This is how I would reason if I were Thothmes: Hat-shep-sut may be Pharaoh, but she is first a woman, and women can be influenced. With you out of the way, he could win her to his thinking. Protect yourself, Senmut, I beg. Suspect everyone, friend or stranger. Thothmes is ruthless. As he sees it, you alone are responsible for the ignominy of the past eight years when he has been reduced to designing temple furniture instead of conquering the world—playing with dolls, in short.

"Now, this is strange hospitality, and I hope you forgive me, Penati; this burned my tongue and I had to say it. The rest of the evening is yours; shall we talk, or drink, or would you be amused by dancing girls? I have . . ."

"If I know Penati," said Senmut, " a breath of night air will be his choice."

"Of course. Nekheb has the best. Your cloaks . . . good."

As they passed through the gateway Senmut said, "Thanks, friend; you have given me much to study. . . . Ah, fill your lungs, Penati; like wine, eh? Min-Hor talks of the air of Nekheb. She did not know that I was coming or she would have sent greetings, Paheri."

"My thanks. By the way, was she frightened because of death in the household—the ape and the maid?"

"She was not disturbed."

"My cousin! Always the selfish little animal."

He kept them for three days and made a festival of the visit, and everyone of importance joined, the Chief Priest, the physicians, the Captain of Police. . . . There was fowling, hunting in the desert beyond the encircling hills, a visit to the tomb of Nekheb's great son, Aahmes Pen-Nekheb. When they left, Penati felt younger by years; it was like leaving a clean and orderly world for one of chaos. The change had refreshed him and he threw himself into the frenzy of the final weeks before high-water.

Then—the day arrived. At the quarry, two sleek stone giants lay on their sleds reflecting the dazzling glare of the sun from polished, tapered surfaces, a long column of faultlessly cut hieroglyphics down the center of each surface from top to base. At the other end of the stone road, a mile away, a great new barge waited in the pit, the deck of the barge flush with the roadway and at right angles to it. The flooding Nile was nearing the top of the embankment that held water from the pit and Penati eyed it anxiously, and hurried to the quarry.

"The water's coming fast; better get your men on those ropes, Nebiri."

Nebiri roared his commands, and the haulers, trained for this moment, formed in four lines, fourteen hundred to a line, and picked up the four ropes that were fastened to the sleds. Priests with jars of oil took their stations on the forepart of the sled, and Nebiri scrambled atop the obelisk. Penati, biting his nails, stood with Senmut out of the way. The haulers shifted their feet, tried their weights tentatively on the rope, settled into position. Overseers, armed with heavy whips to encourage shirkers, stood poised beside the long ranks of waiting men.

Then Nebiri loosed his bull-like roar that could be heard halfway to Yebu, in a chant to fix the rhythm of the step: "Left —right—left—right," and the men, as they had been trained, marked time in perfect unison. "*Left* — right — *left* — right — ca-sy — *left* — right — ea-sy — *left* — right — P-U-L-L — *left*

— right..." At the word "ea-sy," the haulers leaned their shoulders into the ropes; at the word "P-U-L-L," the full pulling-weight of fifty-six hundred men was slowly applied — eased — applied again.... The sled creaked. "P-U-L-L — *left* — right..." The priests slopped oil from their jars. The start was the hardest part. Penati and Senmut strained with the men. "P-U-L-L — *left* — right — P-U-L-L — *left* — right..." The mountain of stone, ten feet through at the butt and a hundred and five feet long, moved — slowly, but with increasing ease. An hour later it was at the end of the roadway.

Next it was worked to parallel the ship with bars and levers and sweat and yelling, and then forty ropes were attached to the sides of the sleds and, a hundred and forty men to a rope, it was inched aboard and brought to rest, lengthwise, in the center of the deck. When the second obelisk was in place and its butt against the butt of the first, they were lashed securely and the dike that held the water from the pit was cut, and the weighted barge floated. Nebiri, to soothe the heat aroused in his throat from continued calling of the chant, drank by himself a small jar of strong black beer; Penati, to assist his friend, swallowed the contents of another. And Senmut found them sleeping despite the thundering of flood waters over the nearby cataracts, an annual phenomenon which promised life to Egypt but shook Yebu like the roaring of a thousand bulls.

The towing of the weighted barge from Yebu to Thebes was accomplished in a single memory-laden day. Nehessi had tested his plans and drilled his men with care, but the vagaries of the boiling current must be met and overcome singly. For towing, he had ready thirty boats arranged in three columns of ten each with thirty-two rowers to a boat. The procession was tailed by three sacred boats manned by priests and bearing holy images of the gods; it was hoped that the gods, finding themselves represented in the show, might take sufficient interest to exert influence if it were needed. The barge was equipped with four huge steering-oars and trailed behind it a broad drag, the latter hopefully designed to keep the bow pointed downstream.

The worst of the whole adventure came a few miles north of Yebu where the Nile, its current swift and eddying, cut through naked sandstone cliffs. Here, for breathless moments, it was not a matter of thirty boats towing an inert barge, but rather the problem of thirty defenseless eggshells keeping beyond the reach of an erratic battering-ram. Penati stood with Nehessi and Senmut and watched the eight men assigned to the work fight the great steering-oars until they won with startling abruptness to the calm of a broad channel.

From here it was a pageant. Drummers on the barge beat a thundering rhythm that echoed through the Nile valley and emptied fields and villages of peasants to cheer the passing. Screaming thousands lined the East Bank at Thebes; Amon's barque came to lead the procession, and King Ma-ka-Re in her royal ship. And when the great barge was inched into the canal dug for it by Puy-em-Re and was supported so it held in upright position, then the end of the canal was sealed and water dipped from it until the deck of the barge was level with the roadway, and the happy ending of the great adventure was in sight.

Puy-em-Re had done his work well. Inside the temple he had made an open court of the huge chamber built by Her Majesty's father, removing roof and pillars and colonnades and porticos and statues. The obelisks would stand here, inside the high pylons, and Puy-em-Re had installed the stone bases, square blocks of granite, in their places. Outside the pylons he had built a long sloping ramp of mud bricks which later would be removed without leaving a trace; on this ramp would be stationed the twelve thousand haulers required to raise the obelisks to an upright position.

All Thebes lined the road to watch the hauling of the great shafts from river to temple, and all Thebes helped with the chanting that set the cadence of the step, Nebiri's "P-U-L-L—left—right . . ." being echoed at the top of ten thousand lungs.

A private ceremony then took place within the temple where Lord Thuti measured the precious alloy of silver and gold by the bushel, and this was applied to the pointed tips of the obelisks; the sun's rays would be reflected from them, and through the years these twin flashing points would be first in a visitor's eye as he approached Thebes from north or from south.

The shafts lay on the floor of the court, the lower edge of each butt protected with a pad of rawhide where it rested on the edge of the stone base, and stout heel lashings were passed around the upper edge of the butt and fastened to stakes to prevent slip and twist. And workmen grouped on either side of the small end of the obelisk first to be erected, some with levers and some with chocks of wood; and when Penati gave the sign, those with levers lifted and the others thrust their chocks into the space gained, holding the small end of the shaft a little off the floor, and other workers packed the empty space with earth. This was repeated until an inclined bank of packed earth formed under the shaft. And when it had reached an awkward height where sufficient leverage could not be applied, this phase of the operation was ended and preparations for the final phase begun.

Now Nebiri climbed to the top of the pylon above the butt-ends of the shafts and arranged his twelve thousand trained haulers in lines on the brick ramp. They faced downhill and with their backs to the pylon, and long, heavy ropes were passed over their shoulders, and the ends of the ropes made fast to the small end of the obelisk below. Penati raised his arm—Nebiri shouted "PULL"—the haulers strained forward on their ropes —the small end of the obelisk lifted a fraction—workmen pounded earth into the space opened beneath—Penati's arm dropped—Nebiri shouted "Ease," and the haulers rested.

The shafts could have been raised in an hour, but Penati was a careful man; there was no need to take chances now, so between each lift he examined the lashings at head and butt before signaling the next pull. As the tip of the shaft lifted, less power was needed on the ropes; indeed, as it neared the perpendicular, other ropes already fastened to the tip were held by gangs of men behind and below to counteract and steady the pull from in front. Thus, slowly, the giant monolith settled squarely on its stone base—and a thunderous shout arose from the watchers.

As with the first shaft, so with the second—except for an embarrassment, a fault of reckoning, that was to eat at Penati's memory like an ulcerous sore for his remaining years. The error was soon hidden beneath plaster, but he could never forget the agony of watching that second shaft twist, beyond his power to rectify, to a full two-fingers' breadth off its base. He was sick with chagrin, with the sense of failure, though Senmut with characteristic generosity ignored the mishap. He crept away; he had failed Senmut, he had failed Ineni. Ineni would know; the spirit of his beloved master lived close beside him and he heard its voice in his ear daily. Ineni would know; he would be angry and would withdraw his counsel and support.

Senmut and Tet found him in his office, buried in reports and sketches and plans.

"You must see the celebration," Senmut said.

"I have work; seven months lost from the temple and your new tomb."

"Her Majesty is delighted, Penati."

"Humph," said Penati.

"She wrote this with her own hand. This will be inscribed on the base of one of the obelisks. Listen:

"'O ye people who shall see my monument after years, do not say, "I know not why this was made." I swear as Re loves me, as my father Amon favors me, as I wear the white crown and the red crown, as I rule this land like the son of Isis, as Re rises in the morning-barque, as heaven abides, as I shall be until eternity like an Imperishable, so surely were these two great obelisks wrought by my majesty for my father Amon, and are of one block of enduring granite without seam or joining. Hear ye! In seven months they were fashioned; never was the like made since the beginning.'"

"Humph," said Penati.

"Rest yourself, my friend," Senmut urged. "After the celebration of Her Majesty's Sed-festival will be time for work. This is a time of joy; not every day is so important a mission so brilliantly concluded."

Penati rustled his papers impatiently. "I am busy."

The days that Egypt rejoiced with its king he spent buried in the depths of Senmut's new tomb, checking progress of work in his absence.

CHAPTER XVIII

Year 12 of the Reign of Hat-shep-sut
(also reckoned as the Reign of Thothmes III)

Yawning, shivering into his clothes by the feeble light of the lamp held by a slave, Antef contrasted glumly in his mind the realities of his existence with the fiction offered him as a youth by his father. "Be a scribe," the old man had counseled, "for a scribe is one who is freed from labor." Antef, young and a fool, had listened. "Be a scribe," the father continued, "for a scribe is one whose limbs are sleek and whose hands are soft, one who goeth forth in white attire, protected from all work."

This program had appealed to his natural indolence, so Antef studied and in time became a scribe and shaved his head and donned the coveted priestly linen. But he had been nicely tricked: work, long hours of exacting toil, was required after all, and now, after fifteen years, his day began before dawn and ended after the midnight hour.

He followed the slave through silent corridors, the stone cold to his bare feet. Other slaves waited before the entrance to Senmut's chamber; he herded them inside and directed the placing of lamps, of pans of live coals and jars of water, then awakened the master.

Senmut was an easy riser; while Antef had been Steward of the Household, he could remember no morning when the master's greeting had not been cheerful, his mind instantly alert; whether his rest had been of one hour or of ten, he awoke refreshed. In an anteroom he now chatted with his barber and with the slaves who attended the bath, while Antef, of the school that resented optimism before breakfast, in moody silence directed by signs the removal of soiled clothing and its replacement with fresh. Then, while Senmut was being dressed, Antef listened to his orders for the day.

This was a formality to which Antef yielded with scant grace. After fifteen years he should know his work, and after fifteen years Senmut should accept the fact that his steward was a responsible person. Yet daily the master persisted in detailing the obvious duties. Today there was an embarrassment of particulars, for a banquet was being given this night to which forty-six guests were invited. What, in the name of all the gods, did Senmut think his steward had been doing these past weeks? Supplies had been pouring into the storerooms: wines, fowl, meats, grains, herbs, spices; new linens had been prepared, the rooms scrubbed, maid-servants drilled in their duties, dancers and singers rehearsed. At this moment the kitchens and bakehouses were bustling, the fires roaring—but Senmut must play the master.

Hiding his scowl, Antef wrote the orders, making a secret check against those that had been anticipated. When dictation was ended, and Senmut was clothed and scented and his jewels and ornaments were in place, the steward rolled the list with a grimace of satisfaction; he had overlooked no detail. And he sighed, again with satisfaction, when the gleaming chariot, bearing the august person of the King's Architect, rolled through the gateway toward the temple. Now he could get about his business without interference or interruption.

Already, in the half-light of dawn, there was activity of a kind in the yards behind the great house; servants dawdled between storehouses and kitchens, slaves of the stables paused in their sweeping and raking to exchange pleasantries with a group of maids of the household, an ancient gatekeeper shooed a file of washerwomen through the portal, gardeners and private police and porters yawned and picked their teeth and considered how best to shirk their tasks. With his thought on breakfast, Antef hurried among the throng, then dodged behind a bakehouse to watch a thin-legged and stooped and sour-faced old man who peered from the shelter of a trellis in the garden. "The old croaker," Antef called him; Ramose, father of the master, who spent his waking hours spying on the household, crying to the steward about theft and waste, creeping, watching, listening. Antef groaned whenever Ramose appeared; if seen, he had to listen to the old man's tales—after all, the master's father—but nothing compelled him to seek the company of such a pest. So Antef watched his chance and slipped through the kitchens and gained the sanctuary of the office.

This was a cubicle off the main room of the first floor and denied, by Senmut's order, to all but himself and his steward. Here at night when the King's Architect returned from his labors, he sat on his stool behind a table and heard his steward's report of the household. Sometimes there were personal accounts to be figured, letters to be written concerning matters on the master's far-flung estates; then Antef doffed the aura of steward and became again a simple scribe, seating himself on the floor and writing to the other's dictation. This parsimony in one who could afford a hundred scribes was an annoyance to Antef—one of many small annoyances, he thought this morning as he sat on the master's stool and ate a leisurely breakfast.

There was the "old croaker"—and Senmut's mother was nearly as bad; she still saved fragments of cloth, however frayed or mended, she still hunted dirt and would scrub it, on her knees like the commonest housemaid, unless watched. But Senmut himself was source of Antef's blackest censure, for his eccentricities lowered his steward's standing in a community critical of deviations. Lord Senmut was one of the great names in the land, a favorite of the king; some whispered that he probably could be Pharaoh if he wished. Why, then, should one possessed of such wealth and power allow himself to be outshone by lesser princes? Antef's standing suffered.

Also, Senmut was secretive. He confined conversation with his steward to the business of reports and instructions, and Antef, if he would learn of the master's private affairs, must resort to intuition or deliberate prying. A large clay jar in a corner of the office held such of the master's private papers as he chose to bring home, and Antef went through these periodically in the other's absence. Soon after his appointment as Steward of the Household, Antef had supplied himself with a copy of the master's seal, thus allowing perusal of any document without detection.

His breakfast finished, he eyed the jar speculatively; Senmut, on arrival the previous evening, had added a new roll to the jar's contents and the steward's curiosity burned briskly. Reluctantly, he decided against investigation at the moment; the women of the household were astir by now, and there were duties on this important morning. In the afternoon there would be leisure.

His first visit was to the apartment of Hat-nefer, Senmut's mother. As House Mistress she had direct authority over many of the activities of the household, and, though a gentle person, she had single-minded ideas of her responsibilities; someone else did any adjusting that might be necessary. Antef had learned never to argue with the good woman, but to ascertain her plans and then rearrange his own.

Her first words, as usual, were, "Senmut was late again last night."

"After the midnight hour, mistress; accounts of Her Majesty's estates, he said."

She was short and plump and nearly bald, the latter a condition that brought her distress. A maid was interbraiding a hank of false hair with the mother's own thin locks, and Hat-nefer watched critically with the help of a beautiful polished-silver hand mirror.

"A gift from Lord Senmut, mistress?" said Antef, indicating the mirror.

She nodded. "Much too nice for me. He is a good son, good to me."

The house was crowded with gifts to the mother—his frugality did not extend to her—fine furniture and linen and dishes and pieces of silver, necklaces and scarab rings, ceremonial wigs, even a great painted coffin which was her proudest possession and which she kept standing in the main room downstairs for guests to admire.

The maid finished and Hat-nefer examined the effect—with the intermixture of gray and black, like an old and balding rat, Antef thought.

"He works too hard," Hat-nefer said.

"He always has, mistress, yet he seems in health."

"Does he wear the blue beads I gave him? The priest said they have strong magical powers of protection. I worry about him."

"He wears the beads."

She shifted nervously on her stool. "Tell me, Antef—honestly—should I wear the new gown tonight? It's the newest mode,

230

designed especially for Her Majesty, and Senmut sketched it for my needlewomen. But—I haven't the figure Her Majesty has; I am an old woman and fat. Still, with the transparent overskirt..."

"Wear it, mistress. It will please Lord Senmut, and the ladies will envy you." ("Though," he added under his breath, "you will look like a hippopotamus in a tent.")

"I will wear it, then. Come, there is much to do this day; the great hall must be cleaned..."

"The maids cleaned it yesterday, mistress," Antef reminded her.

"And the maids will clean it again today. No one shall tell of finding dirt in my house. Also, the lamps must be polished, and..."

Antef bowed himself out of the chamber, shaking his head and thinking, She is still the wife of a farmer, not mother of the High Steward of King Ma-ka-Re.

If Senmut's mother represented commonness, his wife, for Antef's taste, leaned too heavily to the other extreme. She was too patrician. Granted that a member of the noble house of Nekheb was superior, did that license him—or her—to equality with the gods? Lady Min-Hor seemed to think so. She lived in isolation comparable to that of a sanctuary, all communication was through an intermediary, and her orders had the quality of issuing from the holy of holies. At rare intervals—like a god on special days of festival—she allowed herself to be presented to the public eye, as if for worship.

Antef presented himself in her anteroom, a chamber fitted luxuriously and reeking of heavy scent, bowed to the austere waiting woman—another product of Nekheb—and awaited orders. These were soon coming; the lady returned and said, "The singer Harmose; his presence is required."

Antef bowed again and explained that the singer Harmose was occupied at the moment with rehearsals for the evening's entertainment. Perhaps, in another hour or two...

The lady withdrew, and when she returned, said firmly, "At once."

Antef spread his hands. "The master's orders."

The lady was obviously annoyed. She frowned and tapped a painted toe on the rug, shrugged, and disappeared—to return

231

precipitously and announce, "The presence of the singer Harmose is demanded. Immediately!"

Outside the room Antef muttered a curse which, if the right gods were listening, would have dealt adequately with all women—particularly those from southern districts.

He could never understand the attraction that the music of old Harmose held for Min-Hor, or for Senmut and Hat-nefer. Even the old croaker sat blinking and nodding when the blind man stroked his harp, teasing whispers of melody from the strings, a breath of delicate harmonies that, said Senmut, led the spirit wandering among the stars. It put Antef to sleep. He liked bounce in his music, and if a pretty dancer stepped briskly to the rhythm, he could forget the accompaniment and find harmonies enough in the flash of rounded limbs.

Music poured from the room where the musicians and entertainers rehearsed, a lilting, rollicking swing, music that Antef appreciated. He watched from the doorway; four girls danced to an orchestra of lutes and pipes and tambourines, the harp, and a chorus that clapped its hands and established the beat. "Wait," said Harmose suddenly. "TA-ta-ta-ta, TA-ta-ta-ta . . . so, emphasis on the first note. And the pipes a little stronger. And the attack—it must not be ragged . . ."

A girl whispered, and he raised sightless eyes. "Eh? Antef? Come in, come in, Antef. Do we disturb the House Mistress? We forget when we . . . Oh. Of course, the ladies here will not need me. My stick . . . Now, Antef."

He followed with his harp, a hand resting lightly on the younger man's shoulder for guidance.

"I tried to explain that you were busy," said Antef.

"No, no, the Lady Min-Hor does me honor. Poor child, she has few pleasures."

"Child! She has seen forty high Niles."

"One does not always reckon age in years."

The steward swallowed comment; he knew the old man's peculiarities of thought. "Well, there are worse things than luxury and comfort," he said at last. "The master denies her nothing."

"Except, perhaps, his mind. I know, Antef; she talks to me, and that will show her desperate loneliness. She talks of Nekheb, of her life there, and so I say 'poor child,' for she remembers the past with such longing. I admit that sometimes she is bitter; the master has advanced independently of her, and she thinks ... Ah yes, poor child. Once perhaps, she might have helped his career ... Is someone calling your name?"

"The under-steward from Per-haa—the flowers, you know. I've been expecting him."

"Go, go, my friend. I know the way."

Antef watched him stepping confidently, touching the wall occasionally with his stick. A strange man, whose affliction allowed a detached acquaintance with reality, living perhaps in a private world devoid of ugliness, a world of secret vision. But to defend Min-Hor ...

Stewards of Senmut's various estates, or their underlings, were always calling at the house in Thebes, and Antef managed with them a nice balance between superiority and friendliness. An air of calm efficiency, if there was confusion, usually impressed; this morning there was uproar in the courtyard, for the young under-steward herded a swarm of servants carrying baskets of flowers and pots of honey, and a score of struggling and shrieking wild fowl. Antef moved through the tumult with the dignity of a priest conducting temple service, counting the items presented, accepting receipts from those members of the household involved, the chief gardener, chief baker, and chief butcher. Then, in Senmut's office and seated on Senmut's stool, he checked the count against a list offered by the under-steward, confessed his pleasure, signed and returned the roll to the younger man.

Now had come the time for limited cordiality. He inquired into conditions at Per-haa, hinting with an expressive wave of the hand that only press of other duties kept himself and the master from the enjoyment of rusticity.

"By the way," he added, "we shall need more honey on the third Paori—another twenty pots; and a small beef; and papyrus—two large rolls; and perhaps five hekets of barley. . . . Do you want to write this down?"

"I will remember," said the under-steward.

"Indeed!" Antef opened his eyes wide in admiration. "You make a practice of this?"

"Well . . ."

"This is unusual, and commendable. This will please the master. . . . Before you go, a cup of wine, perhaps?"

"Well . . ."

Antef poured a few careful drops from an earthen jar; a more generous portion slopped by accident into his own cup, and he murmured apology for his clumsiness.

He sipped, and smacked his lips. "Ah, nothing like that in Per-haa, I think? From the Royal Vineyards. Oh, yes," he added, enjoying the other's surprise, "Her Majesty's gift to the master. Now, I must not keep you from your duties."

He parted from the young man in the kitchens. These were a series of connected rooms at the back of the palace, each with its ovens and spits and tables and under-cooks and water-carriers and fire-tenders, and all of them under the eye of the Superintendent of the Kitchens. As the hour of dining neared, there would develop here a frenzied riot of sound and action; at the moment there was only a comfortable confusion, with tongues doing the heaviest labor. Seven kinds of meat were being readied for roasting—washed and pounded and salted and spiced and skewered, and larded generously with coarse wit.

Antef decided that he had a few moments to himself. On the way back to the office he saw that the House Mistress had put her threat into action: a phalanx of housemaids on their knees scrubbed at the spotless floor, while Hat-nefer herself polished her painted coffin. This, Antef thought secretly, was a master-work of hideous bad taste. It represented a giant mummiform human figure in black and gold, with eyes staring glassily, with arms crossed over the breast and each hand holding a painted flower. The mother tended it as one cares for a holy and precious relic, and it carried for her some deep significance that Antef could not fathom.

Alone in the office he considered with justifiable smugness that even on this busy day his organization of the work allowed him leisure. When the House Mistress was out of the way, he would have the mats and low tables brought in, and the great silver lamps arranged for lighting the room. Until then he could relax. He rummaged in the jar where Senmut kept his private papers, broke the seal of the roll deposited there the previous night and spread it on the table.

It was covered with random notes in Senmut's precise script, with two or three sketchy drawings, and with what appeared to be a map. One of the sketches showed a kneeling figure with hands uplifted in worship, and near it was written:

> "Giving praise to Hathor for the
> sake of the life, prosperity, and
> health of Hat-shep-sut, by the
> Steward Senmut."

Probably designed for use in his tomb, though inclusion of Her Majesty's name was unusual. For Senmut's tomb one would expect to read ". . . for sake of the life, prosperity, and health of Senmut, Royal Steward." And why Hathor? Why not Thoth, patron of scribes? Or Amon, Senmut's benefactor? Why Hathor, "the Golden One," goddess of wine and music, of beauty, love, joy? Love? He reread the sentence. An appeal to the goddess of love to intervene in his behalf with Her Majesty? Antef rubbed his hands gleefully; had he stumbled on something here? Why, the fool—the crazy, ambitious fool!

Another drawing was a typical tomb decoration: a large center figure, with a smaller figure embracing the first and another, a woman, offering flowers.

The map puzzled Antef until he remembered a teacher in the college mentioning astronomical ceilings in some of the temples. That was it—a map showing positions of the stars and the rulers of the circuits of the night heavens. Another tomb decoration. Even here, though, he found evidence of Senmut's infatuation: Hat-shep-sut's name had been inserted as one of the celestial rulers of the sky!

There were other notations, fragments out of context that carried no meaning for him. He was about to reroll the papyrus when he saw writing on the back. He read it—then a second, and a third time, carefully:

> "Long live the Horus, Mighty of Souls; the Favo-
> rite of the Two Goddesses, Fresh in Years; the
> Golden Horus, Divine of Diadems; the King of Upper
> and Lower Egypt, Ma-ke-Re, beloved of Amon, who
> lives, and the Chancellor, the Steward of Amon,
> Senmut, begotten by Ramose and born of Hat-nefer."

He could think of no excuse for this linking of the names of Pharaoh and a commoner. Unless ... Why, was the man completely mad? Or was there collusion between Senmut and the queen? Were they secretly married—or had he just crept into Her Majesty's bed without the formality of priestly sanction?

He tapped thoughtfully on his chin and gradually his scowl twisted to an ugly grin; perhaps he *could* make something out of this sometime. There were those who were not too fond of the farmer prince, those who might pay well for proof of frailties in the divine Pharaoh of Egypt. ... The sly, impious dog; small wonder that he never reached home until midnight or later.

He'll kill me if he finds I have stolen his secret, Antef thought as he rerolled the papyrus and picked off the broken sealing.

Minutes later he still was staring at the bit of clay in his hand.

He heard himself muttering angrily. "But he can't know. He can't know. I've been careful. I've made no mistakes. I've always put everything back. He can't suspect."

He fumbled in his girdle, and his hands shook so that it was with difficulty that he extracted a bit of folded linen and laid the copy that he had made of Senmut's seal beside the broken piece, and studied them. Next he emptied the jar of all its rolls and compared the seals of each with the broken bit. He sank heavily to the stool and stared at the wall.

Somehow, Senmut had guessed that his private papers were being tampered with, and had altered the seal. The change was minute and would escape casual examination, but Antef was ready to swear that the last roll he had opened, a deed to new property and dropped into the jar a week ago, had carried the impress of the original design. He, Antef, would be the only one suspected; no one else in the household could read. This was a deliberate trap, set to catch him.

His body twitched in a paroxysm of fury and panic. Senmut was normally a quiet man, but he could be roused. The previous month a kitchen-worker had been caught stealing a golden spoon; the master had the man flogged and shipped to the mines—all over a wretched spoon. What would be his reaction to planned, deliberate theft of personal secrets, to betrayal of trust?

Antef paced the narrow room. What could he do now? What could he say to Senmut? Well, then, where could he go? Where

236

in Egypt would he be safe from the reach of Senmut's anger? His legs were trembling. He leaned against the table, pressed hard on the top with his fists. "Come," he said to himself, "you got yourself into this, now get yourself out."

First, to return the scattered rolls to their jar before someone saw them. While he cleared the table, his mind probed a future in which he could find no hint of light. Even if he got out of Egypt, where would he go and how could he live? At one time the courts of foreign kings had swarmed with Egyptian envoys and their scribes and attendants; King Ma-ka-Re, however, preached non-interference in foreign affairs, and he had heard that Lord Hapu-seneb, within the month, complained that she even forbade spies in the countries of Egypt's enemies.

Hapu-seneb? It was known that he had no love for Senmut. It was whispered that he was not in full sympathy with Hat-shep-sut's treatment of young Thothmes, and would this mean that he had little liking for the queen? Would, then, the significant notes in Senmut's handwriting interest him? Would Hapu-seneb hide him?

Antef reached a decision. He found a clean bit of papyrus and copied from Senmut's notes the two entries beginning "Giving praise to Hathor" and "Long live the Horus, Mighty of Souls." Then he composed a letter:

> "Excellency: The enclosure is copied from a
> private document in the handwriting of the
> Steward of Amon. If of interest, the author
> of this letter prays secret audience at your
> house after this night's midnight service."

He rolled the two, inscribed on the outside, "To the hand of Lord Hapu-seneb," and sealed the roll. On a third bit of papyrus he scribbled a note to his son: "Deliver the enclosed *at once* to the hand of Lord Hapu-seneb. At once—and to his hand only." This he wrapped about the roll, addressed the outermost wrapper, "To Seseb—house of Antef," and sealed it. Last, he resealed Senmut's roll, the one that had caused all this trouble, and dropped it into the jar. The master would know at a glance that the paper had been opened, but by then Antef would be out of reach—perhaps. In the courtyard he entrusted his message to a slave and watched the man speed through the gateway.

A part of his mind, functioning automatically, saw that preparations for the banquet were on schedule. In the great hall, cleared of scrubbing women, he directed the placing of mats and tables, but he was thinking, Fifteen years—and now disgrace. Friendless and homeless, too. Perhaps Hapu-seneb can arrange for my wife to be with me. If not, she must wait alone until I can return—or until Senmut dies.

He became aware that the slaves were watching him askance and realized that he had been staring, motionless, into space. He dismissed them and climbed slowly to his room. He moved his bed and from under a loose stone in the flooring withdrew a small sealed packet. He weighed it in his hand, his mind a confusion of hatred and terrors. The packet contained death.

He knew its power; he had seen it work. The ape had died, screaming, in less than an hour. And the girl, too. It had been inspiration, the impulse that caused him to sprinkle the magic powder on the girl's food as well as on the ape's; everyone hunted the girl's enemy, and forgot the ape.

He had hated the ape from the first and when, one day, it reached a filthy hand from the cage and tried to touch him, he went to the Foreign Quarter where, he knew, love or quick death could be purchased. The cost appalled him, but the man stubbornly wagged his greasy beard: "I have done the work; you but sprinkle a pinch of this powder on the food and recite the magic spell."

He still remembered the spell. Soundlessly, his lips practiced the foreign words, recalling the exact intonation and emphasis; repeated them again and again. Outwardly calm, he made his plans; he restored the room to order, bathed and shaved and dressed in his finest linen, secured the packet in his girdle, and went to Senmut's chamber.

He had little to show for his years of faithful labor. His house, and a small farm of well-watered land north of Abdu, these could be taken from him by the king; the only assets of which he could be sure were those he could carry on his person. Senmut, if the plans matured, soon would be beyond the reach or need of earthly possessions. Senmut would not miss a few lengths of gold wire.

The room was filled with treasures, gifts from the king, from

238

admirers, from those who hoped the powerful Steward of Amon would notice them—rings, amulets, bracelets, costly urns and dishes, sticks with gold or silver tops, ivory, silver-and-ebony kohl jars, inlaid game boards with jeweled draughtsmen.... Antef's fingers itched, but these were bulky, too easily identifiable. He helped the master's personal servant lay out the festive linen and ornaments needed for the evening, then, complaining of chill in the room, sent the man to the distant kitchens for a pan of live coals. Alone, he emptied Senmut's secret cache of its store of gold and silver wire. It formed a considerable bundle. Antef's temperature rose a fraction as he translated the value into terms of wine and slaves and concubines; he wrapped it in a soiled apron, hurried to his own room and concealed it. He would pick it up later.

It was time now for the final preparations. In the courtyard he posted stable-boys and slaves near the gate to receive the horses and chariots and the carrying-chairs of guests. The Superintendent of the Storerooms was readying the jars of wine: "Wine of the North," "Wine of the Delta," "Wine, very, very good"—the last with sealings painted blue and the inscription, in yellow, surrounded by the royal cartouche. His men wrapped the jars with vines and flowers, ready to be set about the walls of the banquet room. The Superintendent of the Storerooms also had charge of the many breads and cakes and of the plates of gold and silver and the stone cups of paper-thinness. The cakes were piled in colorful array, a basket for each individual guest; the plates and cups—since the experience with theft—were counted and kept under guard.

The kitchens were an inferno of heat and confusion. All the ovens were roaring, each with its squatting attendant, a purple-faced urchin who fed chips of cow-dung into the insatiable maws; spits were turning, under-cooks salted and seasoned and squabbled and dodged the eye of the Superintendent of the Kitchens who, from his stool in a raised corner, bawled instructions into the din. Somehow, Antef knew, all this would result in refinements of gastronomic perfection which few kitchens in Thebes could match—a circumstance that helped make Senmut's parties popular.

In the banquet room the tables were ready, decorated with the largest of the lotus blooms. Slaves began bringing in the flower-wreathed wine jars and Antef saw to the lighting of the tall five-wicked silver lamps; their radiance lent a softened intimacy to the large room. On the dais at one end of the chamber he placed chairs for the family, those for the mother and father being gifts from Senmut, of light and dark woods and with a carving on the backs of the household god. Inside the entrance, servants were placed with ewers and basins; outside, in the garden before the house, the prettiest girls of the household were stationed behind tables that held fruit and wine. Antef was directing the placing of the serving maidens when a boy darted in to announce the arrival of the master. The steward's heart gave a sickening leap; he dreaded facing Senmut.

The master of the household, however, had other troubles. Antef saw a bruise on his head, and the front of his dress was fouled by bloody stains. Antef's exclamation was a good imitation of concern, but Senmut ignored it. "Where is my mother?"

"Dressing, My Lord; no one is down yet."

"Hot water," said Senmut, and led the way swiftly to his chamber. There, in his bath, he told his adventure. It had happened before—discontent among the workers at the temple over shortages of onions and oil.

"I can't blame them," said Senmut; "they are promised weekly payment, and when something delays it ... Thuti swears the allotment left his storehouses, but ... Anyway, today they were especially abusive; when they began throwing stones, Nebiri drove into the mob with his club and scattered it, but not before someone hit him on the nose. That is his blood on my dress; burn it before the mother sees it—and no word of this to anyone, of course. Does the mark on my head show? See if you can hide it with ointment and powder."

While he was being dressed, he rested his head on his hand; once he moaned and closed his eyes. "This would happen today," he sighed. "It was a large stone, and if I hadn't seen it coming it might have crushed my skull. You know, Antef, if this continues I may consider Her Majesty's proposal to surround myself with a guard. . . ."

Antef was thinking, Amon protected you once today, but perhaps tonight he will be busy elsewhere.

In the kitchens Senmut made a hurried inspection, choosing the meats to be set aside for the family table, goose for the mother, pigeons for Lady Min-Hor, boiled beef for Ramose, kidneys for himself. They heard the harp, and found blind Harmose squatted in his place and entertaining the mother and father while they waited.

Hat-nefer was nervous in her new dress, and Antef thought with a sigh that the effect was more than usually like a badly tied sack surmounted by a mop of tapering braids that ended in untidy spiraling disks. Ramose, of course, was fretful in his apron of fashionable cut, and unhappy about the waste of oil for the many lamps and of the expense in general. But Min-Hor, when she entered the hall, brought with her the dignity that one associates with palaces, the subtle perfuming by which titles, nobly worn, dominate an atmosphere. Her wig, unlike Hat-nefer's, was modeled to a careful perfection of tight ringlets that framed and accented the sulky eyes; the dress was green and planned to reveal her natural slimness.

She was barely seated when the chatter of arriving guests was heard and Antef sped to greet them. The names that he spoke before the dais were not, perhaps, from the highest families in the kingdom; Senmut himself was a worker and preferred as friends those with whom he had intimate contact. The names that Antef called represented the backbone of government rather than the gloss and decoration: Men-kheper, Overseer of the Granaries of Amon, for instance; Baki, who worked with Senmut on Amon's estates; the Head of the Weavers of Amon; Puy-em-Re, the architect; May, the Harbor Master of Thebes, and his wife Tui; a Sculptor of Amon; old Neb-taui, kher-heb and reader of the ritual and friend of Senmut's youth. . . .

When the guests were seated and the ceremonial washing of hands completed, maids placed garlands of flowers about their necks, offered lotus blooms, and anointed each head with fragrant oils. The wine was passed, Harmose and his musicians swept into a gay melody, and the feasting began.

Antef, responsible for smoothness of operation and happiness of the event, found a thousand immediate tasks to occupy his attention. The family, as hosts, were served first; there was no time for thought of private matters until a steady flow of meats and breads and dainties was established and all the guests were served. When at last he could breathe for a moment, Antef

241

collected a plateful of kidneys and sought the Superintendent of Kitchens, who seemed ready to expire on his stool.

"Have you sampled these, friend?" Antef said.

"Food!" groaned the superintendent. "I want to see no food for a month."

"Delicious," said Antef, nibbling a smoking tidbit. "You have outdone yourself again."

The superintendent sniffed at the plate. "H-m," he said, and tasted a morsel critically. "Not bad. The master will like them?"

"This is his second dish."

Antef carried the plate to a far table where, under pretext of decorating it with flowers, he sprinkled the magic powder with a steady hand and murmured the foreign spell.

"For the master," he said to a serving maid. "These are hot; bring the cold dish to the kitchen."

A moment later he was much in evidence in the hall, directing the moving of a table to accommodate a guest, supervising the trimming of a smoking wick—the trusted servant solicitous of his master's prestige.

The party started well. Toasts were offered and accepted, friend called to friend across the tables; there was gaiety and some wit, praise for the host's bounty, admiration of the grace and charm of his handmaidens, determined calls for Harmose and his song. The harpist always was ready; he smiled, struck a ringing chord, and sang:

> Make a joyful day!
> Let unguent and fragrant oil fill thy nostrils;
> Place garlands on the arms and bosom of thy sister
> Sitting beside thee and living in thy heart.
> Put before thee song and music,
> And put behind all cares and evil.
> Be joyful and give thyself to pleasure,
> Against that day when all must come
> To the land that loveth silence."

Harmose was a favorite among them, and once started they would not let him rest.

" 'The Song of Pastime.' "

" 'The Trees in the Garden.' "

242

" 'The Song of Thy Sister.' "

He sang them all; and then there was dancing, solo and group, with accompanist, with orchestra and singers. One of the dancers was an artist greatly fancied by the company, and her dance was one of unparalleled grace and precision. It was restrained, of slight movement and depending for effect on controlled and measured action—the sliding of a foot, lifting of a shoulder, turn of a wrist, motion fluid and harmonious.

Quite different, the dance called "The Wind" that ended the evening, a dance of breathless and furious abandon. It was a daring innovation at a private party, for "The Wind" usually was performed only in religious and funeral processions, and only Senmut, the audience agreed enthusiastically, would have thought of it. Wine had not been spared, and those not already befuddled were excited by the frenzied gyrations of the temple girls. Six acrobatic dancers of the temple, girls trained for this dance since childhood, stepped to a rhythm set by lutes and tambourines. Their only covering a fragment of apron and waist-long hair, they held their arms curved back as far as possible behind the ears and swayed their slim bodies in unison. As the beat quickened, so did the step; the movements became faster, wilder, the music louder, sharply accented, more insistent, then—an explosion. As one, twelve arms flung sharply forward, six slim bodies somersaulted in the air and landed on their toes—to repeat the original slow step and rhythm.

Antef ignored the performance, watching Senmut from the shadows of the room except when occupied by duties. If the master moved suddenly in his chair, Antef's nails bit deep into his palms; if Senmut sighed or loosened his girdle tie or leaned his head for a moment on his hand, drops of sweat appeared on Antef's head. The waiting was agony. The master drank cup after cup, but whether or not he ate of the kidneys . . . Antef found an errand that took him to the dais; the plate of kidneys had been disturbed—the flower decorations were strewn on the table and some of the meat was missing.

A few minor incidents were hardly noticed in the excitement of watching the exotic dance. The father Ramose lay back in his chair, staring glassily, perspiration streaming from his face. Tui, wife of Harbor Master May, overcome by wine, slumped across a table and smashed two of the priceless stone cups. The dance built in frenzy to its climax; the six girls, whirling as one, somersaulted again and again and again, round and round, to the crashing rhythm of the tambourines and the cries of the delighted audience. Their applause, however, was suddenly hushed; Hat-nefer struggled to her feet and stood swaying giddily, panting for breath. She collapsed in Senmut's arms and was carried from the room by servants.

The guests were subdued and they left soon after. As the last torch disappeared, Senmut leaned heavily against the gatepost. When he stumbled over a pebble in the pathway to the house, Antef inquired nervously, "Are you all right, Master?"

"There are a thousand devils stamping about inside my skull."

"The wine?"

"The wine. I drank enough to float Amon's barge—and so, apparently, did the old ones. . . . Come into the office, Antef."

"You mean now, tonight?" The steward felt his throat contract with sudden terror.

"Tonight. There is a matter I want to discuss with you."

"But surely, Master . . ."

He was saved by the first of the screams. It filled the silent rooms, full-throated, torn from a soul in mortal torment. They bumped into figures on the stairs, in the corridors. The terrible sounds came from Hat-nefer's room. The mother was on her couch and surrounded by terrified maids, and her hooked fingers tore at her belly while the awful cries built to a brain-piercing crescendo.

Senmut thrust his steward to the door. "The physician—Her Majesty's own physician! Run, man!"

Antef was halfway to Hapu-seneb's house before he remembered the fat packet of gold wire still hidden in his room.

For five weary days Antef chewed his nails in mingled boredom and dread, watching from the frontier fortress the road that wandered from the west out of Egypt. On the sixth a dust cloud appeared on the horizon and he hid until it was determined that this was not a detachment of police but the under-officer and six bowmen expected by the commander of the fortress.

He waited impatiently while they bathed and then, over food, the commander introduced him. "This is the scribe, Antef. Now, what is new in Thebes?"

The same question was uppermost in Antef's thought, so he listened. The young officer swallowed his meat and drank deeply of beer; a deliberate man and not to be hurried. When he had wiped his chin and belched—behind his hand, politely—he said, "Well, Lord Onen died. An heir has been born to the house of Thinis. Old Bibi who runs The Crocodile's Nest has two new girls, lively and not bad-looking. A new sacred bull has been located in a herd at Abdu. . . ."

The commander cursed. "You know what I mean, Hebet."

The under-officer grinned and shrugged. "Nothing, Excellency; nothing is new in Thebes."

The commander beat a heavy fist on the table. "When will they wake up? Do they read the reports we send them? Upper and Lower Rutenu arming—coalitions, alliances between city states—even the road to Gaza unsafe for travel. . . ."

The officer Hebet signed imperceptibly toward Antef and the commander growled, "He's all right; he has a letter from Hapu-seneb."

Hebet nodded and stretched his legs. "Well, Excellency, all that you say, and more, is known to Lord Thuti and to His Majesty. But—who is Pharaoh of Egypt?"

The commander cursed again and Hebet continued. "Exactly. A woman. Who listens only to the voice of a farmer. Whose hobby is the building of temples, and . . . Do you know what is being whispered in Thebes, Excellency?"

"How can I know anything in this pest hole?"

"It is being whispered that this farmer has ambitions. To Her Majesty's bed and—brace yourself, Excellency—to her throne."

An explosion followed this confidence, of a violence that proved the depth to which the old soldier had been shocked. When his rumblings lessened, Antef's voice was heard: "He is right, Excellency. It was my privilege to submit evidence to the noble Hapu-seneb that Lord Senmut enjoys unusual favors from Her Majesty."

The group stared at him open-mouthed, and he added, "Secret and unprecedented favors."

"Humph. Someone should let a little of the ambition out of him. With a knife."

245

"That has been tried," said Antef; "the day I left Thebes he had been assaulted. I suppose"—he kept his voice level—"you heard nothing of that?"

"Nothing."

One of the soldiers spoke. "There were deaths in his house."

"That was a year, two years ago," said Hebet.

"No, last week. My brother knows one of the kitchen-maidens. Lord Senmut's mother and father and six others."

"Six others?" Antef exclaimed.

"Eight in all. And Lord Senmut's wife fled south to Nekheb; said the house was accursed."

Hebet grinned. "Someone's really trying. Maybe they'll get Senmut next time."

"But—eight deaths?" said Antef. "And you're sure Senmut..."

"I saw him the day we left," said Hebet. "He looked worried, but he was alive."

Antef's thoughts were boiling. Where had his plan miscarried? Senmut would know "who" if not "how." He was not likely to let the murder of mother and father go unnoticed—and he had the power, under Pharaoh's order, to seal the borders of Egypt and then search at his leisure.

He arose and addressed Hebet. "Well," said Antef, "you are refreshed; shall we start?"

"Tonight?" said the soldier in quick anger. "Are you mad? Do you know how far we've marched today? And when you cross the canal you're no longer in Egypt; you're in a country of lawless and murdering thieves, who..."

"You have bowmen."

"Six," said Hebet, "and the best in the world. We'll not be attacked in daylight, but we stay off the roads after dark."

"But I am under orders from Lord Hapu-seneb..."

"And I am commanded by a fancy for a whole skin. Look, Priest—well, Scribe, then, one's as stupid as the other—I know the Gaza road and its dangers. Start, if you wish. I'm not leaving till tomorrow."

"Well," said Antef, seeing the grins and nods that passed around the room, "well, at dawn, then."

"Perhaps," said Hebet, yawning. "If I am rested."

246

CHAPTER XIX

Year 13 of the Reign of Hat-shep-sut
(also reckoned as the Reign of Thothmes III)

"He is greatest of the great in the whole land."

"He is guardian of the secrets of the King, one upon whose utterances his Lord relies, with whose advice the Mistress of the Two Lands is satisfied."

"He is the noble to whom one hearkens, for he repeats the words of the King to the companions."

"He is the real confidant of the Ruler, entering in love and coming forth in favor."

When Lord Thuti read what Her Majesty allowed to be written of Senmut, he thought that the king's acknowledged good sense should be questioned. When he learned further that Lord Senmut was newly installed as Superintendent of the Bathroom of the King, and as Superintendent of the Bedroom of the King, then he decided that she had forsaken prudence as well as sanity. An immediate shift in his plans was demanded.

Thuti had a single ambition. He convinced himself that he had come close to gaining to it when some trick of fate, some insane prank of the mischievous gods, gave the prize to Senmut. This ambition, this determination, was to be first in power under Pharaoh. And since Hat-shep-sut chose Senmut, then he, Thuti, would choose Thothmes. Her Majesty's downfall would automatically insure His Majesty's ascent. It would require ingenuity and daring, and caution and patience and time. Thuti had all these.

He first wrote several letters with his own hand, preferring at this stage of his dangerous game to trust no one, and these letters he dispatched by messengers. He next made alterations in a report under preparation, requested audience with Her Majesty, gave to his handsome features a doleful twist, and said to her, "Majesty, this is your Treasurer's report on the year's taxes. A poor showing, I regret to say. An inadequate Nile, disease among the cattle in Two Mountains Province, failure of the hemp crop—we must make special offerings to appease the gods. And the gold yield was negligible, though extra men worked night and day."

The queen listened, studying the mask with which he hid his real thought. "A record of calamity, My Lord. Lord Senmut reported no shortages in the districts he studied."

"Some sections every year are more seriously affected than others, Majesty."

"Nothing was salvaged from Two Mountains Province?"

"Burned, Majesty; danger of infecting healthy herds was too great."

Hat-shep-sut nodded slowly, apparently accepting his explanations, and Thuti breathed again.

"Did you bring a report of foreign tribute, My Lord?"

Thuti sighed. "Tribute from foreign countries has dwindled, of course, with each year since your august father's death. The heathen have forgotten to fear Egypt. . . . Nothing, Majesty. Not like the days of your august father, when gold and silver and cattle and grain overflowed the king's storehouses, and slaves beyond counting worked the estates of the gods.

"A pity," he added hurriedly, "for I know Your Majesty's desire to restore the beauty of Egypt, wasted by the heathen Shepherd Kings. But see the report, Majesty; it takes bread and oil, sandals, cloth, beer—laborers demand their pay. . . . By the exercise of rigid economies elsewhere, we should be able to finish your mortuary temple and your tomb; Your Majesty knows that I strain every resource to this end. But as for additional building—patience, Your Majesty; the gods decide these matters. Next year, perhaps."

To young Thothmes, brooding in his wing of the palace over the wrongs done him, Thuti presented a smile of courage and optimism, and a different papyrus. "Your Treasurer's report on taxes, Majesty. Satisfactory, on the whole. A fair Nile brought modest increases, and there was a good tally of hides from Two

248

Mountains Province. May I suggest, Your Majesty, special offerings of thanks to the gods. The gold yield from the deserts east of Nekheb was disappointing, but that from Kush adequate.

"Now, I have written today giving orders— with Your Majesty's approval, of course—that surpluses above minimum requirements shall be held aside secretly for Your Majesty's need. Thus a fund is established on which, in emergency, Your Majesty may draw. And the foreign tribute—not what it was in the days of your august grandfather, not what it will be— but the trickle of foreign tribute can be added: silver and lead and lapis lazuli, turquoise from the Sinai mines, grains and hides and weapons. . . . You approve, Majesty?"

Thuti's approach to his young master was one of flexible detachment. It was not always safe to do his thinking for him; a fierce pride and independence subjected to years of repression had built unpredictable and explosive qualities into a nature not famed for stability.

" 'Caution!' " the young king sneered. " 'Do nothing hastily.' The usual advice of priests. And I rot as in a prison, and Egypt rots with me."

In all his interviews with Thothmes, the Treasurer had the sense of dealing with intellectual immaturity. Here was a man of twenty-six years whose highest ideal was perfection in the art of blood-letting. Short, solidly muscled and weapon-wise, he had not matured beyond the age that picks the legs from insects and laughs at their stumbling. Great warriors—essentially agents of destruction—were formed of such stuff, but not great kings; a good minister would keep such a one occupied with campaigns and slaughter while saner tempers ordered affairs in the homeland. Thuti, the good minister, offered bait guaranteed to lead the discussion out of Egypt.

"I talked with one of your grandfather's old bowmen last week, Majesty. He still fights the campaigns of Nubia and Naharin from his little farm near Abdu. Twice awarded the gold of bravery, and still wears a bracelet given by the old king himself. The chatter of such a one might interest Your Majesty."

The king shrugged. "He can tell little that my spies in Gaza do not know."

"Of course. Though he watched the old king set his monument in Two River Land, and that is far from Gaza. He knows

249

the secret mountain roads, the strengths and weaknesses of distant cities, but these are known also to Your Majesty. He spoke of one such road—I thought as he talked, 'His Majesty knows of this, of course'—a mountain pass by which the enemy at Megiddo could be surprised. . . ."

"Bring the man to me." Thothmes strode back and forth in the room, knotting his fists; stopped before Thuti with a despairing gesture. "I go mad with this waiting and planning— the world asleep just beyond reach of my fingers, ripe for harvest. You have said, yourself, that Egypt shrivels and dies. Well, have you any idea what changes the spoils of a single campaign could bring to it?"

Thuti bowed. "I know well, Your Majesty, and every thought in my day is how quickest to place the sword in your hand. For you, and for Egypt." He lowered his voice to a confidential murmur. "It will not be long. Real opposition to Your Majesty's wishes has been narrowed to one man. . . ."

"Senmut!" Thothmes spat the name from between clenched teeth.

"The same. He is powerful, now, but pressures are building around him."

"A dead man is a poor minister. Kill him. An arrow, a knife in the dark. Are you squeamish, My Lord?"

Thuti chanced ignoring the thrust. "Dangerous, Your Majesty. Your prestige. Queen Hat-shep-sut is of true solar descent, she and her ministers sacrosanct. On the other hand, you have the unvoiced sympathy of the thinking men of Egypt; they know that you have been wronged, displaced from the throne of your fathers by an outworn stratagem. Gain your return by peaceful means and you will be welcomed as saviour of Egypt; by violence, and it will be remembered as defiance of the will of Amon."

"Abduct him, then, if his skin is so precious. Hide him from Her Majesty. Hold him as hostage. Come, My Lord, you are so clever—is it called 'violence' just to deprive a man of his liberty? Pamper him, give him sweets, women—is that violence?"

Thuti felt a stab of chagrin; the young fool might have something worth studying. He bowed deeply. "The king who thinks thus clearly needs no advisers. I predict a prosperous and eventful reign for Your Majesty."

He got away finally, leaving the king planning a new Court of Victory to be added to Amon's temple after his first campaign. Thothmes never would be an easy man to handle; insolent, headstrong, intolerant of the lightest rein, blind to the rights and privileges of others if his royal prerogative was involved, boasting a patriotic zeal that was rather the ruthless manipulation of forces toward personal glorification. His ministers could expect little from the association except high-sounding titles, and criticism when affairs went wrong.

This idea of abducting Senmut appealed to Thuti. Hat-shepsut had come to lean heavily on him; he was present at all councils, his advice sought on all public matters; without him her grip on the throne might be pried loose. It was a precarious grip, sustained by the popular fancy that she had been the old king's favorite, and by memory of a god's voice echoing in the temple at night. Thuti did not underestimate her spirit, however, and so preferred Senmut alive to Senmut dead. He must plan carefully: no confederates, no chance of careless talk—strike once and boldly.

He went directly to Hapu-seneb, Chief of All the Priests. "I want you to attach a scribe to the staff of Senmut's office in the temple. One of your own men, loyal, who will report everything to you."

"That will not be easy, My Lord; since the affair of his steward, Senmut trusts no one."

"Arrange it somehow; His Majesty trusts your discrimination."

"Oh—His Majesty. Senmut is suspected of something?"

"No. A simplification of tax methods is considered, nothing more. Order your man to report fully and save his reports for me."

"If it is just the tax records..."

"His Majesty's orders. Report everything."

Thuti hoped to learn enough of his enemy's movements to suggest a plan of action. Hapu-seneb made a reliable tool; no mental giant, he held Thuti in awe and followed with reasonable complacence where the other led. He had conducted, at Thuti's request, a survey of popular unrest and dissatisfaction

251

through priests in the provinces distant from Thebes—information which would guide Thuti in establishing new pressures by which Hat-shep-sut's administration might be embarrassed. Hapu-seneb now reported active criticism north and south of laxity of supervision and repair of dikes and boundaries, of scarcity of employment, and of low pay. Also, there was evidence of growing concern among the laity that the gods might become impatient if repairs to local temples and shrines were longer delayed.

The recital gave Thuti the exact information he wanted, and he reduced the Chief Priest to flutterings by an easy compliment. "You have developed an efficient and powerful organization by which His Majesty, and you, My Lord, will profit. Now, how does work on Hat-shep-sut's tomb progress?"

"Slowly, slowly," said Hapu-seneb, smiling. "Bad rock, constant change of direction . . ."

"Could you finish it in a month if necessary?"

"A month!"

"In six months? If you pressed the work, doubled the laborers?"

"But, My Lord, our plan was delay. Make the operation costly. Remember, My Lord?"

"Plans can change. I but seek an estimate. Six months?"

Thuti reasoned that Hat-shep-sut and her projects would be nuisances if, by a happy fortune, Thothmes won suddenly to the throne. Hence the reversal so confusing to the plodding mind of the Chief Priest: clear the queen's affairs up quickly. Her temple was another matter, he decided, as he waited outside Hapu-seneb's office for his carrying-chair. Perhaps if the harrying tactics of the past year were stopped, Senmut could be prodded into completing it—enough for dedication, anyway.

Puy-em-Re passed, young Puy-em-Re the draughtsman, Senmut's protégé, hurrying as usual and seeing nothing, wrapped in his customary ecstasy of creation. Night or day, the rise or fall of dynasties, these did not touch the young artist while his vision was fed a constant and satisfying orgy of color and form. Part of Thuti's attraction to the youth was based on the problem of weaning him from Senmut's influence; he was Senmut's discovery, but Thuti saw him as the architect of unborn monuments to Egypt's—and Thothmes'—greater glory. In addition, the Treasurer, himself enmeshed in schemes and intrigues, was baffled by the simplicity and directness of Puy-em-Re's ambitions; nothing intruded; his world lay in his brush.

The young man was startled by Thuti's touch on his shoulder. "My Lord!" he said, and smiled. The older man had made a careful play for respect by listening to his ideas on sculpture and design and by advancing a point or two of intelligent criticism. Also, Thuti, commissioned by Hat-shep-sut to build a sumptuous shrine of ebony to house Amon's barque in the new temple, had accepted Puy-em-Re's drawing and allowed him supervision of construction. The young artist might call Sen-mut "master," but he also looked on the Royal Treasurer as a friend; that was enough for now.

"I thought you were working at the new temple," said Thuti.

"I was there before dawn, My Lord, to study the effect of the first rays of the sun inside the sanctuary. An amazing softening and graying of tone. I made color tests, and the faces of the four Osiride statues there must be pink, not red or yellow like the statues in full light. A rosy pink with overlay of clear varnish."

Thuti nodded solemn appreciation of the value of this research.

"We measured, too, for exact placement of the altar to catch the first rays."

"The temple will be finished soon, then. What a day for Egypt, the day of dedication!"

"Well," said Puy-em-Re, "Tet has most of the statues ready, and they will be placed when the wall designs are finished."

"Three months? Six months?" Thuti persisted.

"Oh—a year, I suppose. The scaffolding and ramps have to come down, and the northern colonnade is still unfinished; the main building, though, should be ready in eight months to a year. It will be magnificent, My Lord."

"Magnificent," Thuti agreed. "Meanwhile, have you had time for the working drawings of furniture that His Majesty requested?"

"They are ready, My Lord."

"Bring them to the palace tonight. You are His Majesty's favorite draughtsman; he trusts his ideas to no other. Bring

253

also your drawings of the proposed holy-of-holies for Amon's temple. Tonight; His Majesty expects you. . . ."

On a morning soon after, Thuti brought another to the palace by appointment—the bowman Bani. The old man, obviously dressed in his best and wearing his honors and decorations, was overwhelmed by the prospect of conversing with royalty.

"What shall I say, Excellency? How should I address him? He is a god; is it permitted to look at him as one looks at ordinary men like yourself, Excellency? The old king was a soldier and we talked with him as with one of our platoon—but respectfully, of course. Should I bow, Excellency? The old king did not like formality among comrades; we were respectful to him—he was king, of course, but he was a soldier first, and . . ."

"Bow to him," said Thuti; "address him as 'Your Majesty,' and answer any questions briefly. Await his questions; the king will do most of the talking."

The king was talking when they found him with General Menti in the garden of the palace. He was talking vehemently, striding back and forth before his unhappy general: ". . . in full fighting regalia, padded cap, leather apron, buckler, weapons—at all times. So it is hot and they sweat a little. These men are being trained to fight. They will have to march through heat and storm, all day and all night; they won't be coddled then and they are not to be coddled now. And the quick step—keep them at the quick step till their eyes drop out. If they harden, they'll be good fighters; if they do not, then I do not want them in my army. . . . Who is this?" he said abruptly to Thuti.

"Bani, Your Majesty, the bowman who fought with your grandfather."

"Hah!" said Thotmes, and the old soldier bowed deeply and stammered, "Y-yes, Your Excellency—Majesty."

"You fought the campaigns in Naharin?"

"Yes, Your Majesty."

"As bowman?"

"Pardon, Your Majesty—as under-officer, Your Majesty, in command of a platoon."

"How many in your platoon?"

254

"Ten, Your Majesty."

"We use six," the king said to Menti; "more maneuverable."
To Bani, "You were in Two River Land with His Majesty?"

"A broad, rolling, fertile plain, Your Majesty. Not like
Egypt, where the two banks only are farmed, as Your Majesty
knows. A rich land—wheat and barley, almonds and figs and
olives and vines; a heathen land, of course, but they raise fine
cattle, small and large . . ."

"There are many cities?"

"Countless, Your Majesty, large and small, fortified and not
fortified. His Majesty passed the fortified cities and laid waste
the smaller, pillaged and burned and destroyed and then
marched on."

"Yes, yes. The river?"

"Ah, the River-that-runs-backward-upon-itself!" Bani, excited,
forgot to fear this young man whose interests were his interests.
"You will not believe this until you see it. Rivers come out of
the south and disappear into the north; our Nile—everyone
knows this. But the river of Naharin—sluggish, brown in color
—it really does flow from north to south. I saw it. The king
himself had to believe when he saw it. . . . And no building
stone; not a stone the size of Your Majesty's fist. An amazing
country—heathen, of course, but . . ."

Thothmes silenced him by an impatient shake of the head.
"His Majesty overran all this with an army of twelve thousand?"

"Nearer fifteen thousand, Your Majesty. And another twenty
thousand as baggage-carriers, cooks, servants, women. And not
just Two River Land, Your Majesty; we destroyed the cities of
the coast, first: Joppa, Megiddo, Arvad, Kadesh . . ."

"Megiddo. Do you remember the roads leading to Megiddo?"

For answer, Bani drew with a twig in the soil of the garden.
"Joppa here, Your Majesty, just above Gaza and on the coast.
Megiddo inland, here. Mountains here between Megiddo and
the sea. There are three roads: one leading straight to Megiddo
from Joppa—one swinging east and circling Megiddo to enter
the city from the north—this the road the old king chose. A
third road—so—along the coast and through the mountains,
to enter Megiddo from the west. This mountain road Your
Majesty can forget; I scouted it."

255

Thothmes studied the plan and pointed it to Menti. "The mountain road might allow surprise of the city."

Bani forgot again. "True, Your Majesty; I scouted it and saw no enemy."

"The road is difficult?"

"Narrow, Your Majesty. Horse must follow horse, the chariots must be packed on the backs of soldiers."

"See, Majesty?" said General Menti. "Such a road would be dangerous, foolhardy."

"Did I ask advice, My Lord?" Thothmes squatted beside the crude map and punched at it with Bani's twig, muttering, "Megiddo first, then the ports of Acre and Byblos and Arvad, and then Kadesh. Then we turn east." To Bani he said, "What system of government did His Majesty set over the conquered territory? How did he hold his gains?"

Bani bowed and shook his head. "Pardon, Your Majesty, I am a soldier. I did overhear argument once while on guard— I was not listening, the voices were loud—you understand, Your Majesty? Well, it was argued that if every other city was occupied—like every second bead on a string, you see . . ."

Thothmes clapped his hands. "I have said the same, and you have heard me, Lord Thuti. And in addition, bring the sons and princes of the conquered houses to Egypt for education; then, when their fathers or uncles die and they return to their home cities to rule, they will remember Egypt as one remembers a cherished sister."

"A sound plan which, knowing Your Majesty, will receive full study," agreed Thuti. "Have I permission to ask the soldier Bani what he knows of Sinai?"

"What enemies do you fancy in Sinai?" Thothmes asked tolerantly. "Flea-ridden beggars?"

"The mines, Majesty; many of your prisoners of war will be sent to work the mines, and I would ask how the old king guarded them."

"Oh, yes. You—Bani—you visited Sinai where the blue stone is mined?"

"Many times, Your Majesty. A desolation, bare rock and heat, a terrible place."

"The roads out of the mines are easily guarded?"

"There is but one road, Your Majesty, narrow and following

an ancient river bed, and closed by a wall of stone with a single guarded gateway. No one goes in or out of the area without permission."

"Does that answer your question, My Lord?"

"Yes, Your Majesty."

CHAPTER XX

Year 14 of the Reign of Hat-shep-sut
(also reckoned as the Reign of Thothmes III)

Word that his father would arrive in Thebes on the day before the dedication of the new temple was received by Puy-em-Re with modified pleasure. He revered the old man, and was burning to show him all the wonders of the master's completed work; on the other hand, Im-hetep, like many provincials—he was Governor of the Northern Oasis—was profoundly suspicious of the motives and abilities of city men, particularly men of Thebes. Also, he could become violent on the subject of women in government. Puy-em-Re foresaw possible embarrassments resulting from the visit.

The old gentleman, however, had mellowed, or perhaps the pleasure of seeing again his favorite son worked unusual restraints; he sipped his wine and nodded benevolent appreciation of the lad's progress in a field so removed from his own inclinations.

"You really enjoy this—this puddling with colors? You say you have had commissions from Pharaoh?"

"Yes, Father; you'll see tomorrow."

"And all this for glory, or do they give you a title? Overseer of the Royal Paint Pots, perhaps?"

Puy-em-Re's young wife exclaimed indignantly, "He is Draughtsman of Amon. And King Thothmes will let no one else redraw his sketches."

"Thothmes? The king is an artist, too? What is Egypt coming to! . . . But I thought Paheri of Nekheb was Draughtsman of Amon."

"His father died and Lord Paheri is now Prince of Esneh and Governor of the Southern Lands."

"I remember. A fine family, the princes of Nekheb. General Aahmes used to visit us—shocked your mother with his roaring and cursing. . . . So you inherit his grandson's office. I suppose it is an important post?"

"It's important to me, but I have not given thought . . ."

"It is time you did," said Im-hetep severely. "What are your aims, ambitions? You do not want to play with brushes all your life, I hope?"

Puy-em-Re squared his shoulders. "Perhaps I do. At least . . ."

The old man opened his mouth to correct such insanity, when the son's wife spoke. "Puy-em-Re will one day be Overseer of Overseers of All the Works of the King."

The artist shook his head sharply, but his wife continued. "Lord Senmut will retire some day, and then . . . Anyway, King Thothmes demands more and more of your time, and—and—well, that means something, I think."

Im-hetep, seeing the flush of annoyance on his son's face, relaxed in his chair. " 'Overseer of Overseers of All the Works of the King.' Well, we must not be greedy; that should be honor sufficient for any family. A toast, my boy: a long lifetime of continued interest in the arts to King Thothmes."

The streets of Thebes seemed empty and silent the next morning as Puy-em-Re and his father approached the old temple in pre-dawn darkness. All night boats had ferried sightseers to the scene of dedication across the river, and the lights of their torches wandered now on the far shore, threading inland.

It was Lord Im-hetep's first visit to Thebes since the days of the old king, and he found much to complain about. Inside the temple of Amon, standing beside the queen's obelisks, he gaped in consternation.

"But where is the roof? What has she done with the roof? Where are Ineni's cedar columns, and the statues? Is this improvement? Your queen has ruined the old temple!"

Watching the morning service, he muttered, "Yes, she has dignity. But see the young Pharaoh—there now, there is a real king. . . . How old is he? Twenty-seven? Who can know what Egypt has lost in the eleven years he has been kept from the throne? From what I hear . . . Eh?— Oh, that is your Senmut? A strong face. Now, why would a minister of his intelligence support the woman and not the man?"

At the end of the ceremony the god, instead of being returned to his sanctuary, was borne in procession in his golden shrine to the river and placed aboard his barque. Puy-em-Re hurried to his ship, explaining to the father, "The princes of Egypt form an escort for the god. King Ma-ka-Re in her barge, then King Thothmes and the lesser nobility. And the priests and dancers, of course."

Im-hetep was shaking his head. "Under the old king the Nile swarmed with shipping. These pleasure barques of the rich make a pretty showing, but where is your commerce? Where are the merchants, the foreign boats? Do you know what is said in the north?" he asked of his son. "It is said that your woman king thinks more of the welfare of the heathen than of the happiness of her subjects." He waved his hand. "Can you call this tranquility anything but stagnation?"

"I know nothing of politics," Puy-em-Re murmured uncomfortably.

"Then you should learn." Im-hetep saw the stubborn set of his son's jaw, and changed his approach. "Your friend Lord Senmut—you admire him? You would be like him?"

"Yes, of course, Father."

"Then follow his example. Senmut was an artist, like yourself, but he did not stop there. He learned early that perfection in a single field makes for unbalance. Complements are needed. He learned what you have not yet seen, that diversity of interests need not complicate life—that anything thoroughly learned is of life-long use. He is artist and architect, and administrator of Amon's wealth. . . . What other duties?"

"Oh, Steward of the Queen's Estates, Governor of the Palace, Chief Prophet of Montu, Overseer of the Granaries of Amon— a dozen besides these."

Im-hetep nodded. "You see? He is learning every day, and using his newly acquired knowledge . . ."

His father's words stirred the boy; the thin beam of logic lit with tantalizing brevity a strange and exciting path into the future, a path he suddenly wanted to explore.

Im-hetep's exclamation broke into his thought. "Ah—ah," said Im-hetep, "that is your new temple, is it? Long horizontal lines against the vertical cliffs, white against red and brown. Very nice. Effective. Good planning."

"See the crowds, Father, on the bank and lining the causeway? We march between the sphinxes; it's a straight line to the sanctuary."

"It will take all the day to get the procession started from the landing stage."

"No, Father; Lord Senmut devised a plan, and the boats arrive in a specified order. See, we follow Neb-taui's ship, he follows Lord May's, and so on. The master gave me permission to march beside you so I can explain features of the temple as we pass them."

"He thinks of everything, this Senmut of yours," Im-hetep admitted. "I wonder if he anticipated the damage the mob is doing to the fields along the bank? Good growing land here; those beans reach higher than a man's head."

The soldiers who were to lead the march already gathered by one of the sphinxes, the Dancers of Amon by another. Thanks to Senmut's planning, there were few delays; ship followed ship, each pausing briefly at the landing stage, then pulling away to assigned waiting positions. Puy-em-Re and his father found their places with other princes; from ahead came the hollow throbbing of hand-drums, and the column moved, with slow and solemn step.

Im-hetep indicated the sphinxes as they passed. "Your work?"

"No, Father. I designed one pair, but not these."

"Hat-shep-sut as a lion! That is as laughable as calling a woman 'king.' '*Her* Majesty the King.' Bah! How many sphinxes and statues of her in the temple? Two hundred? Two hundred lies."

Puy-em-Re glanced about nervously. The old man was as loyal in his hates as in his loves and as fearless in their expression; this practice might be condoned as eccentricity in the country, but it was a dangerous recreation here.

"See," said the son desperately, "on your left under the hills— the ruins of the old temple where Lord Senmut got his inspiration. . . . And you remember Lord Ineni, Father? His tomb is in those hills, and his spirit is thought to watch over the building here. His spirit will be happy today. . . . And there on the right, the ancient quarry where we got chips and stone for grading. The gateway of the first terrace, Father, the real beginning of the temple. . . ."

261

The terrace was spacious, wide and deep, bounded on the far side by two columned porches which, in turn, were divided by a ramp that led upward. The sight-seers, the commoners, had been left outside the gateway, and watched the glittering pageant of dancers and offering-bearers and holy men and dignitaries continue its slow march between painted sandstone sphinxes. Puy-em-Re pointed: "Two papyrus pools filled with Nile mud. A garden for the god."

"I see Nile mud and papyrus at home," Im-hetep grumbled. "Ah—the incense trees? From Punt? We heard of the expedition, and the fat woman, the chief's wife, so big that a special ship was made to carry her alone. Was that true, Puy-em-Re?"

The young man smothered his laughter. "You'll see on the second terrace; I drew a report of the expedition, ships and tribute, scenes from the God's Land, everything. Drawn on the back walls of the porches, you know."

"Yes, I want to see your work. Any of it on this lower terrace?"

"No, Father. Her Majesty fowling, and sacrificing to Amon, and the record of transportation and erection of her obelisks— I did none of these drawings."

The procession climbed the ramp and proceeded across the second terrace, between sphinxes of red granite, now. This terrace, like the first, was broad and deep and with porches and ramp on the west side. The porch on the right, Puy-em-Re told his father, carried drawings of Hat-shep-sut's divine birth; that on the left, Puy-em-Re's record of the Punt expedition.

"I'll show it to you later. Now, Father, see—above you."

A row of imposing giant statues looked down on them from the third terrace, Hat-shep-sut as a mummiform Osiris; twenty-two painted limestone statues, Im-hetep counted, acting as supports of the topmost porch and guarding the secret chambers of the temple.

The young priest saw that his father was impressed, though his only comment was: "All this to immortalize the name of a woman!"

"Wait. You have seen nothing. The detail, the imagination. . . . The third terrace is the real temple, you know—a complex of shrines to various gods, chapels cut in the living rock. Whatever you think of Lord Senmut's politics, you'll admit that he's a great artist. Won't you, Father?"

"Perhaps. He likes the spectacular, anyway."

The row of Osiride statues on the third terrace was pierced by a granite doorway, through which the procession passed to the twilight of an open court surrounded by columns. Here the sound of sistrums and drums echoed and re-echoed while Amon's shrine was being set before the closed door to the sanctuary, and while King Ma-ka-Re and the participants of the dedication ceremony were taking their places.

It was a moment of solemn portent. Puy-em-Re knew the labor that old Neb-taui had put into searching the rolls so details of the ritual would be pleasing to the gods; not every day was a new temple born. King Thothmes stood nearby, sullenly aloof. Senmut seemed to hide the satisfaction with which this crowning of years of sweat and sorrow must fill his heart. Lord Thuti waited impassively; General Menti, ill at ease amidst pomp and finery, fidgeted near the entrance.

Her Majesty made a sign for silence, and the High Priest and his twelve subordinates, selected to administer the affairs of the temple, stepped forward and bowed.

"Divine fathers of this temple," she said, "priests, ritual-priests, dwellers in the place of the god, maintain ye the monuments of my majesty; offer ye in my name; remember ye my titulary, and praise ye the statue of my majesty; set my name in the mouths of your servants, my memory among the people. . . ."

Then a priest masked to impersonate the god Thoth knocked for admittance on the door of the sanctuary, and the ceremony called "Opening the mouth" of the temple began. The officiants moved from chapel to chapel, consecrating each statue separately, sprinkling with holy water, censing, purifying, offering meats and fruits and flowers. It was an involved, repetitious and tiring ceremony for those watching, and Puy-em-Re's legs ached with the standing. But finally Amon in his golden barque was placed for the night on the ebony shrine in the center of the sanctuary; the floor was swept, the doors of the holy place sealed and the god left to meditation in the darkness that he loved. Her Majesty chatted graciously with Senmut for a moment before leaving in her litter, escorted by the dancers and guards and members of her household.

The ceremony was ended. Her Majesty had "given the house" to her master.

Those remaining relaxed, formed into conversational groups, strolled through chapels and terraces to admire—or to criticize. Puy-em-Re dreaded the thought of introducing his father to Senmut: a meeting between political opposites, between country- and city-dweller, between northerner and southerner, between one of noble heritage and one of common. So it was with relief that he watched Lord Thuti draw the master aside and engage him in close discussion.

Im-hetep looked about him and shook his head slowly. He said to his son, "In other temples that I have seen I have always a feeling of foreboding, a sense of the imminence of divine displeasure. You know what I mean. It is different here. Why, Puy-em-Re? This is a happy place, a happy house. What makes this difference?"

"The master's genius. He has accomplished a subtle blending of strength and beauty."

"No. Of the spirit, rather. He is said to be specially favored by Amon? A spiritual harmony, perhaps. But more than that— something in his expression when Her Majesty spoke to him. . . ." Im-hetep shook his head again, impatiently. "Come; show me your work in the temple."

"The best of that is hidden in the sanctuary, Father—the ebony shrine, for instance, and some of the wall paintings. You'll see examples of my work later, but while we are here— these giant statues in niches on either side of the sanctuary door: those on the south with the white crown of Upper Egypt and those on the north with the red crown of Lower Egypt. Now, there are statues in the sanctuary like these, but with pink faces; I made experiments, you see, with the lighting. Details like that are important, too."

"Oh," said Im-hetep, "that is why some statues are painted, and others not. The lighting. Very clever."

"No, no, no. Common limestone and sandstone are painted because they do not take a good polish. But the hard stones— their natural colors and textures are beautiful in themselves. Look here, Father, these kneeling statues in red granite—see the luster, the depth of color? No paint could improve that."

"Well, well."

Im-hetep was teasing him. The realization roused a small indignation in Puy-em-Re's breast, and the inspection was continued without lecturing. The old man showed a sober and intelligent interest, however; nodded approval of the right things, ignored the unimportant. He stood for minutes lost in admiration before the beautiful portrait statue of Hat-shep-sut, gave careful study to the gigantic granite stela—Puy-em-Re's work—that filled a wall of her chapel. Quitting the third terrace, he was quiet and thoughtful, and the son saw what he hoped was a hint of respect in the father's manner.

Lord Senmut and Lord Thuti still were talking. Puy-em-Re also noticed a small group near the front of the second terrace: King Thothmes, General Menti and Hapu-seneb; they were facing the causeway, which was clearing rapidly, and the artist got the impression that they were waiting.

Im-hetep became absorbed in the chronicle of the Punt expedition. The entire colonnade south of the ramp connecting the second and third terraces had been given to recording this event, and the old man kept up a running comment as he stood back to admire the whole effect, and stepped close to examine his son's drawing of pictures and explanatory data.

"People live in houses like that, on stilts over the water? . . . All these animals? How could five ships carry all these, and the logs and incense and . . . Here are the incense trees—thirty-one of them . . . You saw this yourself, Puy-em-Re? . . . Ah—the fat woman—a monster; we heard of her in the north, you know . . . Nice balance; the wall space pleasingly filled, without crowding or waste . . . This is good work, my boy. Pharaoh will be proud of his Overseer of Overseers."

This was heady and unexpected praise; from the father, who disapproved his choice of vocation, equivalent to a blessing. Puy-em-Re felt his heart stammer. Senmut appeared on the ramp at that moment and the boy, forgetting his earlier reluctance, led his father forward and spoke his name in introduction.

The older man bowed, deeply as one of inferior station bows to a superior. "My Lord," he said, "if ever a man has made happy his king and his god, you are the man. All Egypt, when it sees this temple, will, like my son, be proud to name you 'Master.' "

Senmut, surprised and touched, returned the bow. "If rewards are necessary, they will be found in generous and unselfish impulses like yours. Thank you, My Lord Im-hetep."

A moment of friendly chatting, and he was gone. Silently, they watched him bow formally to Pharaoh Thothmes and cross the first terrace. Outside the gateway he was joined by his overseer, Nebiri, and together they strode down the nearly empty causeway. Pharaoh and his companions also watched after them.

Im-hetep answered the question in his son's eyes. "He is a great man. Perhaps a good man; these dreamers—who can know the limits or direction of their dreams? Most men playing such a dangerous game—Her Majesty against His Majesty— would be unprincipled schemers. . . . I do not know Senmut; he may act from the highest of unselfish motives, though it is hard to . . . Anyway, a great artist; this temple bears witness."

He gave the birth colonnade the scantiest of inspections; when Puy-em-Re admitted that this contained none of his drawing, the father confessed disinterest and fatigue.

"If you have seen enough, Father, I just remembered that I should ask the master about an inscription he wants in the morning. Perhaps we can catch him at the landing."

Im-hetep nodded. Their bows to King Thothmes went unnoticed, for Lord Thuti had joined the king's group and a lively whispered conference was in progress.

Son and father hurried between the sphinxes of the causeway, Puy-em-Re scarcely conscious that his feet touched the stone. His father approved his work—had praised it, and praised the master, too. This was more than he had hoped, for the old man could be stubborn when his prejudices were ignored. "A happy place," he had called the temple. Perhaps—the priest smiled at this absurdity—if the father remained long in Thebes, perhaps he would accept Hat-shep-sut as his king.

"A happy place." He regretted, a little, that his work at the temple was ended. There had been problems—interesting, stimulating. He had learned much, just from watching the master, and he could learn more. Perhaps his father was right; he had narrowed his interests too closely. Well, Senmut liked him, and if he said to Senmut . . .

The old man's voice interrupted his thought. "What will your Senmut do now?" asked Im-hetep. "Without the temple, time should be heavy on his hands."

"Not for the master," said Puy-em-Re. "The north colonnade

is unfinished—and he is still Steward of Amon, and Steward of Her Majesty's Estates. And perhaps now he can recondition his tomb. It is in the hills near Lord Ineni's tomb, and was partly wrecked some time ago, and he has never . . ."

"Senmut has enemies, then?"

"Yes, Father. No man carries Lord Senmut's responsibilities without offending someone. He has enemies, powerful and relentless. People die mysteriously in his house. Two years ago, eight died in one night, his mother and his father and six others."

"An attempt on Senmut's life, perhaps?" Im-hetep shook his head. "I am not surprised. He should guard himself."

"That is Her Majesty's order. He goes nowhere unattended."

The old man looked at his son questioningly, and then pointed to the two figures ahead of them, the tall man in priestly linen and his companion. "You call that protection? One man?"

"You do not know Nebiri, Father. With his stone club, he is an army. And as loyal as a brother. More than once he . . ."

Im-hetep had stopped and was peering back into the sun, toward the temple they had quitted.

"What is it, Father?"

"Isn't that Pharaoh and his friends—on the first terrace, now? They're still watching. What do you suppose . . ."

Puy-em-Re laughed easily. "Pharaoh is a god. Are you trying to penetrate the mysteries, surprise what motivates a god's actions? Come, Father."

"Yes, yes," said Im-hetep impatiently, and walked again beside his son. "The landing stage still is crowded. You will lose them."

"Watch for Senmut's white dress; a priest's garb is distinctive. And Senmut is taller than . . . There they are, just passing one of the sphinxes. Suppose I go ahead and speak to the master, and meet you on . . ."

"Wait, wait!" Im-hetep pointed. "There is trouble there— by the sphinx. . . ."

Puy-em-Re was running. There was violence, fighting. He saw Nebiri's club swinging, a struggling knot of men about Senmut. He heard the screams of women, shouts—a group overwhelmed Nebiri, and then came the sickening thud of blows on flesh, groans and curses. The master's arms were fastened—he was dragged, fighting, into the tall bean plants that bordered the causeway.

The young priest pushed through the press of gesticulating men and women.

"Eight men, Excellency . . ."

"They were waiting by this sphinx . . ."

"See, Excellency, the blood . . ."

"Where are the police . . ."

Puy-em-Re plunged blindly into the forest of stalks. What had happened? The master—who would dare—Senmut, favorite of King Ma-ka-Re. He was panting. "Master," he called. "Lord Senmut . . ."

He heard a groan, forced his way through the dense thicket and stumbled over Nebiri, covered with blood, crawling on hands and knees. Nebiri knew him, and pointed; slid forward, a great wound in his head. The priest stared in horror and stumbled away in the direction indicated. "Master . . . Master . . ." He was sobbing, retching. What had they done to the master?

The river showed ahead. A boat was near the shore; into the boat men tumbled a dripping and white-clad and inert figure— scrambled after it over the rail. He heard shouts; oarsmen churned the Nile to froth and the boat pulled away—was lost among the hundreds that milled about the river. . . .

He staggered to the landing stage and pulled himself erect, looked about wildly. What had happened? Why, Senmut was Egypt! What would become of Egypt without Lord Senmut?

The sun was dying in the west and a last beam touched for a moment a figure that stood on the first terrace, bathed the figure in a golden glow. The finger of Re caressed the son of the god, Men-kheper-Re Thothmes.

CHAPTER XXI

Year 17 of the Reign of Thothmes III

The men appeared as a line of phantoms stalking out of clouds of dust, passing silently, each with his basket of sand and rubble. Some wore bits of cloth knotted about their loins, others sweated in the colored robes and head-cloths of their native countries; the latter were new arrivals, still dazed by the enormity of the disaster that had torn them from farm or counting-house. Nebiri felt pity for them all.

On the edge of the gully into which the baskets were dumped, he saw an overseer cut at one of the foreigners with his whip and yell, "You crazy, wild-eyed beggars, move along."

"Easy with that whip," Nebiri called sharply.

"Yah, the beggars don't understand Egyptian, but they know the whip's language."

"It's not necessary to cut a man up just because he's a slave. No whip."

"Yes, Master," said the overseer meekly; then with mincing sarcasm, "Now, boys, a little faster, please, a little faster."

Nebiri let it pass. There had been changes in Egypt in the last three years; the influx of prisoners of war was one change of which he did not approve. Slaves there always had been, but mostly in the household and on the estates of the rich where they were identified with a family, accepted as responsible members of that family. Now, with the wars of young Thothmes, prisoners by the tens of thousands must be absorbed into the nation's economy; a native Egyptian now would rather starve than labor on public works and be mistaken for a slave.

Some prosperity had come to Egypt, of course; from where he stood Nebiri could see across the plowed lands to the river swarming with ships, and across the river to the busy quays of

269

Thebes. The gods seemed to smile on Thothmes: victories attended his campaigns, wealth again poured into the temples, there was building in every province, there were good Niles and bountiful harvests, the people shouted his praises in the streets. Nebiri grunted. Thothmes was like a boy released from school, eager and tireless; if his strength held out he might in the years ahead lift Egypt to the eminence of world domination. This was his goal, and the gods seemed to love him.

Bright points on the Nile's edge returned rays of the late sun in a series of flashes. Peering, Nebiri decided that it could be the royal barque moored there—then he saw a funnel of dust speeding inland.

"His Majesty!" he shouted to the overseers; and when the chariot drew abreast, the workers were prostrate with beards in the sand, overseers were on their knees and Nebiri bowed from the waist.

Pharaoh Thothmes drove, while his companion, a Captain of Archers, held with desperate grip to the handrails. The king, short and thick-muscled, handled the restive horses easily; his battle helmet accented the taut sternness of his features.

"Puy-em-Re not returned from the south yet?"

"Not yet, Your Majesty."

"The first stone arrived from Penati in the north this morning. Will your gangs be trained by the time it is ready?"

"They will be trained, Your Majesty."

"They look in condition," the king admitted. "I saw them practicing their pulling in unison. Any trouble finding suitable material?"

Nebiri bowed. "They are hand-picked, Your Majesty, the youngest and healthiest. They will haul anything Penati digs out of the desert."

Pharaoh's sternness relaxed for an instant, then he whirled the horses and sped back toward the Nile.

The overseers cracked their whips and the prisoners picked up their baskets. Nebiri was turning away when a voice sounded close to his ear.

"He has grown, Nebiri. A man, now."

A bearded foreign slave stood nearby, brushing sand from his robe, his face half hidden in a head-cloth—a tall, gaunt man, burned nearly black.

"Where did you learn Egyptian?" snapped Nebiri.

The prisoner turned so his back was toward the others, covered his beard with a hand, and smiled.

Nebiri staggered and his mouth opened to shout a name when the stranger signed caution. "Take me to your house tonight," he murmured. "Can you arrange it?"

Nebiri nodded dumbly, eyes starting from his head. The other retrieved his basket and joined the workers, while the foreman wandered from sight of the rest and sat himself on a rock. His knees were shaking.

Senmut—or a spirit from the Underworld? A spirit would hardly wear a beard, nor would the spirit of a priest grow hair. A prisoner of war, then. If he were recognized, if Thothmes found him, his death would be certain. He must be helped out of Thebes; a ship was sailing north in the morning, and perhaps Penati could hide him, or get him out of Egypt.

When he had regained a part of his composure, he sought the overseer of Senmut's gang and said, "I am taking five men to the East Bank—these three and yes, these will do. No baskets."

Three years out of Egypt. Senmut had aged more than three years—the thinness, the deep-scored lines in his face. . . . In Palestine, probably, from the dress and beard. There had been a thousand rumors after his disappearance: he had been murdered; he had been driven from Egypt; some swore to proof that it was a trick of Senmut's own making, to get himself out of the country. What a grotesque whim of the gods, then, that he should fall into Thothmes' hands, be returned to Egypt, to Thebes. . . . How long had he been here? Had he seen Hatshep-sut's temple yet? His thinness was alarming; he must have suffered. . . .

On the boat Nebiri ignored his passengers and made nervous jokes with the boat-steerer: Be careful, he had a precious cargo and must not lose it to the Nile; land north of the city, else would Pharaoh be angered that they did not visit the palace.

It was night when they reached Nebiri's house, and he called his servant and bade him take torches and put the foreigners to work at repairing the wall of the garden where it had tumbled. The bricks were ready, and when they were done, he was to bed them in the storehouse and bar the door securely. He went then to his wife and ordered her to take the children for the night

271

to her father's house nearby; when she demurred, he shouted and beat his fist on the table until she gathered the children and fled in terror. The lamp was alight; he stirred the fire and placed a vessel of water to heat, and went and stood beside the servant in the garden. His heart was jumping, but he controlled his voice. "I have work for one of the foreigners in the house. This one," he said, touching Senmut's arm, and led him inside and barred the door.

He whirled and caught Senmut by the elbows. "Master! It *is* you and not a spirit, then!"

"Flesh and blood, my friend—what is left of both."

"Puy-em-Re saw you dumped into the ship," Nebiri rattled, "limp, apparently lifeless. So when you spoke my name . . ."

"Can I have a bath?" Senmut interrupted.

"Water is heating, and here is a deep pan, and cloths to dry yourself. Throw that filthy robe away; I'll get one of my aprons."

Senmut stripped off the robe, and the foreman started. "You've been flogged!"

"Many times, friend. Is this the water for the bath? Help me pour it."

Nebiri elbowed him aside and poured the water, helped his one-time master relax comfortably in the pan, fussed over him until Senmut could not hide his amusement. "You are a fraud, do you know it, Nebiri? I have watched you drive a gang hauling stone, but you really have the gentleness of a woman." Then he sobered; his hand closed about the other's wrist. "Friend, I want the truth. Where is Her Majesty? Is she dead?"

"Alive, surely, Master. Thothmes dares much, but Hat-shep-sut is a god and he would think long before harming her."

Some of the strain eased from Senmut's face. "Ah-h-h," he whispered. "Where, friend?"

"Some say in Menefe. I do not know; in health, they say, with her maids and remnants of her court."

Senmut was nodding, eyes closed, a smile on his lips. "You give me life, Nebiri. Alive, in comfort . . . Now," he said briskly, "you have been hauling stones these last three years?"

"Well," said Nebiri uncomfortably, "yes."

Senmut nodded. "I saw evidences of it. At the temple. Tell me, friend . . ."

"You've seen the temple?"

"Yes."

"It was like killing something beautiful and good," Nebiri raged. "Sometimes Thothmes is a fiend; he did to her temple what he dared not do to Her Majesty's body—tore it apart, smashed it, burned it—every statue, her name wherever written. Your name, too, Senmut; he hates you as he hates her."

"I know," said Senmut.

"The labor and love of fifteen years—all gone, destroyed. The smaller statues smashed to powder. The larger statues of hard stone—we had to beat them with hammers—he watched and I'm glad you did not see his face—all Tet's beautiful work. . . . We knocked off the noses, and the emblems of sovereignty, built fires and burned the faces. Then we hauled the fragments down the causeway . . ."

"And threw them into the old quarry."

"Ah, you found them there?"

"I found them. Tell me, Nebiri—before the broken statues were dumped in the quarry, did anyone go down into it?"

"I don't remember. Penati, maybe. It was Penati who suggested using the quarry as dumping place."

"He would. Penati, the friend."

Nebiri sat in silence; he could guess the master's sorrow, the pain over so tragic an ending of a dream. While he lived Nebiri would remember the crash of falling monoliths, the destruction wrought by a single hammer's blow on some product of an artist's loving skill. Fortunately Senmut and Her Majesty had been spared view of these acts of childish spite.

Senmut spoke at last. "Was there violence when Thothmes assumed the throne?"

"No. The voice of the god sounded in the temple as when Her Majesty was proclaimed Ma-ka-Re."

"Hapu-seneb's doing; if it worked once, try it again. Her Majesty was—resigned?"

Nebiri hesitated. "She did not fight the edict. Puy-em-Re says that she was never the same after you disappeared—as if she had lost the will to fight longer."

"At least"—Senmut smiled gently—"she did not see her temple ravaged; that would have been a crowning unhappiness to an unhappy life."

He stepped from the tub and accepted the cloth his friend

offered. "One thing more—has my tomb been disturbed? In th[e] hills near Ineni's tomb?"

"Some of the inscriptions have been destroyed, and the sa[r]cophagus is smashed . . ."

"The burials under the tomb? My mother and father, yo[u] know, and the singer Harmose, and—others."

"No, the burials were not touched. . . . Here is an apron Master. Now you are an Egyptian except for the beard. Thoth[-]mes has a sharp eye; it's lucky he did not see you on th[e] march."

"I saw Thothmes today for the first time in three years."

"But I thought all prisoners passed under Pharaoh's eye."

Senmut drew a stool beside the table. "When I've told m[y] story, will you tell me the happenings here?"

"Of course." Nebiri brought the lamp to the table, sat oppo[-] site his master and waited expectantly. Then he leaped to hi[s] feet. "Wine. You are starved and I offer nothing. Here—cakes fruit. There is no meat but cold goose—and this wine is no[t] from the Royal Vineyards. Is it enough?"

"A banquet." Senmut allowed his cup to be filled, and rose. "To Her Majesty. Life and health."

"Treason, treason, My Lord." Nebiri grinned. "But—to Her Majesty. She is still your king, I guess."

"Always," said Senmut. "Well," he began when they were again seated and the cups refilled, "I was taken directly to the turquoise mines in Sinai . . ."

"Sinai!"

"A planned abduction, obviously, and I suspect Thuti and perhaps Hapu-seneb, though I may be wrong. I suppose they are high in favor with Thothmes?"

Nebiri spat over his shoulder. "Besides his other titles, Lord Thuti is now 'Administrator of the Lands of the Northerners,' governor of the conquered territories, that means. And Hapu-seneb—he's so swollen with importance that you must turn sideways to get past him on the street."

"I had warnings enough—my scribe, Antef, fled directly to Hapu-seneb. . . ."

Senmut shrugged and continued his story. Sinai, he said, was an outpost of hell, a desolation of heat and thirst where jailers and condemned were equally prisoners of the merciless environent. Fights and beatings were daily occurrences, men were illed over a handful of putrid meat, a cup of water. There was o hope, no escape; the only road led through a deep and narrow canyon closed by a fortified gate.

News from the world outside was completely unreliable. One ay it was reported that Hat-shep-sut had been murdered; the ext, Thothmes was slain in battle and Hat-shep-sut had reained the throne. Again, the Egyptian army was destroyed, then he Egyptian army was overrunning Two River Land.

"Water was of greater concern to us," said Senmut, "than the eath of Pharaoh or destruction of his armies. Rainfall was the only source of supply, rain collected and stored in cisterns cut in he rock; if that failed, everyone died. Constant prayers and offerings were made to Horus and to Hathor, companion deities riendly to the district—and then, three months ago, all the prayers were answered in one night."

He shook his head as if memory of that night was still too close. "We in Upper Egypt," he continued, "do not know rain; once in ten or twenty years there may be a brief flooding from the hills bordering the Nile, but—well, imagine if you can, Nebiri, the Nile itself tipped on edge. It was like that, a mass of water tearing at the mountains, the canyon a roaring torrent, boulders the size of this house tossed like chips, huts demolished, men crushed, the fortified gate dissolved as if it were papyrus. I had thought," he confessed soberly, "that Amon had forgotten, but someone supported me that night. I was swept helplessly down the mountain, left bruised and dazed, but uninjured, on a sandy shelf."

"Free? Away from the mines?"

"Miles away. The rest was simple. An old Aamu shepherd fed me and gave shelter. Later I worked my way northward and eventually slipped across the border into Egypt, walked nights and hid by day, stealing food when hungry, and . . ."

"Wait, wait. Do you mean you are not a prisoner of war? You mean you *chose* to return to Egypt, knowing what Pharaoh will do if he finds you?"

"Of course. You see, my king might need my help."

"Now, that . . ." Nebiri found it difficult to believe what he heard. "Are you sure a rock didn't hit you that night? She is imprisoned in a palace in Menefe—how can you help?"

"I did not know it then, my friend."

"Well," roughly, "you know now, and we must get you away from Thebes and out of Egypt. Tonight. Now, there is . . ."

"First, what of the campaigns? Were they successful?"

"Of course. Now, a boat leaves . . ."

Senmut moved his stool and leaned against the wall. "Some more of that excellent goose, Nebiri, while you tell me of the campaigns."

Pleas and threats gained the other nothing. "I should beat you on the head," he muttered, "and dump you in the ship as was done three years ago." But at last he gave in.

"Apparently Thothmes is a natural warrior," he began. "General Aahmes said he was—remember?—as great as the old king or greater. Besides, he has had years to study the problem, he knew how and where to strike, and Amon was beside him every step of the march.

"In the very first campaign he overran all Palestine to southern Lebanon, captured Megiddo and with it the lords of neighbor states who had taken refuge there. He reaped their grain and sent it to Egypt, and in six months was home celebrating his Feasts of Victory. The festivals, Senmut, the parades of tribute: gold and silver, cattle by the thousand, slaves by the ten thousand. He gave to Amon three captured towns, also herds and slaves, and then he began building temples all over Egypt."

He hesitated and glanced sideways at the master. "All this territory had been lost under Queen Hat-shep-sut. Of course, some say her inactivity but made Thothmes' victories easier, that Egypt's enemies became soft and careless during her reign."

"And thereby defeated the reasons for her inactivity? Perhaps. Perhaps, Nebiri." Senmut toyed absently with a crumb of bread. "Few people have troubled to understand the high purpose behind Her Majesty's motives, a desire to protect all humanity—not Egyptians alone—from insecurity and fear. I agreed with her in principle, but the world is not yet ready to grant amnesty to those too weak to fight. Thothmes, of course, represents popular thought: Keep what you are bold enough to steal. So, for the moment, Thothmes is a hero." He snapped the crumb across the table. "What of the rest of His Majesty's glorious achievements?"

"Well, there were no battles in the second campaign," Nebiri resumed, "just an armed tour of the conquered areas, and tribute poured in from all the states—from Assyria, even. This year will be like the second, Penati thinks, and then he says Pharaoh will invade the coastal cities and Kadesh, when he will be free to turn east to Two River Land."

Senmut was long silent, sitting motionless, deep in study. Then he nodded. "Thank you, friend. As you say, Amon must be supporting Thothmes each step of the way. That means that at some earlier date he withdrew his favor from Hat-shep-sut— and from Hat-shep-sut's ministers. . . . We would be gods ourselves, wouldn't we, if we could exactly interpret the god's will, guess at what moment his path might turn?"

"No one can outwit the gods, Master."

"Not outwit—anticipate. If you have ambitions, you must keep the god's favor; you must walk straight in paths always pleasing to him. One misstep, and the god finds his instrument elsewhere. . . . I think I know my misstep," he continued thoughtfully. "For years I built only for the glory of Amon. Then in a woman's eyes I saw promises which even Amon could not fulfill, and from that moment the god went his way and I went the woman's. In time, Amon tired of the divided attention."

Nebiri nodded in irritated agreement. Talk, talk. The master had had three years in which to think; must he waste precious time now? If the ship left without him, where could he be hidden until the next ship? Not in Thebes, not on the West Bank. Perhaps it showed disrespect to speed a guest, but . . .

"Master . . ." he began desperately.

Senmut rose and drew his robe about him. "Does your boat sail to north or south?"

"North, to Hatnub. Here is your head-cloth, Master. Penati is in the desert east of Hatnub, and . . ."

"Will they take me in this dress without question?"

"I have thought of that. You will be a foreigner, an authority on building, and you travel on Puy-em-Re's business. Take this stick; there are dogs about at night. Put out the lamp. Now— the way is clear. . . ."

They hurried through dead alleys, leaving the city behind for a world of open fields and stars, silently, until the broad dike that bordered the river was reached.

"If we meet anyone, hide in the ditch. The police, yo‐
know."

Nebiri led at a swift step. The open countryside was not th‐
safest place in Egypt at night; more to be feared than dogs an‐
police were the spirits of the unburied dead that prowled th‐
lonely watches seeking revenge upon the living for negle‐
visited upon them. In his left hand Nebiri clutched a powerf‐
charm said to be efficacious in softening their tempers; howeve‐
he put as much trust in the strength of his right arm and th‐
stoutness of his stick. But nothing hindered them; the few mea‐
houses they saw were shuttered against the noxious night ai‐
the few dogs were satisfied with token howls of displeasure.

"Around the next bend and by those trees." Nebiri slowe‐
his pace.

"I forgot to ask," said Senmut. "Is my wife still in Nekheb?"

"Puy-em-Re saw Lady Min-Hor there, well and happy. Tha‐
is—she seemed content. . . ."

" 'Happy' is the word, Nebiri; Min-Hor would be happy i‐
her cousin's court. More gaiety and life."

Nebiri cleared his throat nervously. "Now while you are i‐
the ship, Master, avoid the captain's eye. He ferried some ston‐
for Her Majesty's temple—not much, but he might remembe‐
you. Be careful. And when you meet Penati, surprise him as yo‐
did me. Speak his name. He will not expect Egyptian from ‐
foreigner; he will think it is the spirit of a dead Senmut, as ‐
thought. If I could watch his face . . ."

"I shall not see Penati, my friend."

Nebiri stopped in the roadway. *Now* what craziness do you‐
plan?"

"Hatnub is halfway to Menefe. Thanks to you, I ride hal‐
the way in comfort and walk the rest."

"To Menefe? Thothmes' agents swarm over the country. You‐
cannot avoid them. Look, be reasonable, get out of Egypt.‐
Penati will see you safe. In a few years Pharaoh will forget; you‐
know the memory of kings, and his wars and his building‐
will . . ."

"No."

"But what can you do in Menefe? She is a prisoner. You can‐
not help her."

Senmut put an arm about his friend's shoulders. "I have had

three years in which to think, Nebiri, to reassess values, to determine what, in the life that is left me on earth, is important—not to the prince, you see, but to the man. And I find it a sobering exercise, this reviewing of a life—the compromises, expedients, dodgings . . .

"In retrospect, one becomes conscious of habits of thought begun in youth when barriers to ambition seemed insurmountable. Then I was an opportunist who often twisted circumstances and friendships to personal gain. My wife, for instance—even Neni and Aahmes, perhaps, though I loved and respected them.

"I assumed many debts, and debts must be paid, if not in this life, then in the next. And this is one reason why I must remain in Egypt. If I am to hope for any after-life, any chance to repay, I must be buried on Egyptian soil."

"And your tomb is lost to you, of course."

"Yes. My name, however, is hidden in a dozen secret places and Thothmes will not destroy them all. The gods will know my name, and if my soul is permitted trial before Osiris, perhaps some will speak in my behalf.

"This is why I cannot leave Egypt. And I must go to Menefe because Hat-shep-sut is there. She is a prisoner, but Amon may yet allow some small service to—well, I will say it—to the woman whose memory has become dearer to me than breath."

"Loyalty is good," Nebiri agreed, "but she is no longer your king."

"In the days when we were together in Thebes," Senmut replied gently, "for me she forgot that she was king. Well, Amon may not have deserted us; his favor once was strong and constant, and I hope, in Menefe . . ."

This was crazy, insane thinking. "No!" Nebiri exclaimed in desperation. "I will not let you. . . ."

"Sh-h-h, they will hear." Senmut's arm on the overseer's shoulder tightened. "Thanks. Thanks, Nebiri. For the past, and for today."

His arm fell away. "Now," he said lightly, "where is your ship?"

The captain answered Nebiri's call and Senmut waded to his hips and climbed aboard. The foreman squatted on the bank; from this position he saw the ship silhouetted against the night sky. He drew from his girdle an egg-shaped lump of clay, mut-

279

tering, repeating the spell a second and third time for emphas
and clarity. This was a strong magic that insured the safety o
those who traveled by water, and this much he could do to giv
the master safe passage to Hatnub. Presently a robed figure ap
peared in the stern. The captain shouted, sailors pulled th
mooring stakes from the mud, the steersman leaned on his oar
and Nebiri tossed his lump of clay into the Nile.

He watched the ship dissolve into the night, listened lon
after the creak of the oars had been swallowed in the sound o
water lapping against the dike. Then he arose and searched th
shore for a stone, and kicked the stone with violence. The actio
served him doubly: it was his offering to fools and obstinat
lovers, and the pain in his toe gave him a man's excuse for th
tears that burned his eyes.